Praise for the novels of Brenda Novak

"*Summer on the Island* is a big, tantalizing read!"
—Susan Elizabeth Phillips, *New York Times* bestselling author

"*Summer on the Island* will resonate with many readers who, in the midst of a global pandemic, may be rethinking what is truly important in life."
—*Booklist*

"*The Bookstore on the Beach* is a page-turner with a deep heart."
—Nancy Thayer, *New York Times* bestselling author of *Girls of Summer*

"The prose is fast-paced and exciting, making this a breathless page-turner."
—*New York Journal of Books* on *The Bookstore on the Beach*

"An abundance of heart and humor. *The Bookstore on the Beach* is an escapist treat with emotional heft."
—*Apple Books*, Best Book of the Month selection

"This heartwarming story of sisters who bond as adults is sure to please the many fans of Novak as well as those who enjoy books by Susan Mallery and Debbie Macomber."
—*Library Journal* on *One Perfect Summer*

"I adore everything Brenda Novak writes. Her books are compelling, emotional, tender stories about people I would love to know in real life."
—RaeAnne Thayne, *New York Times* bestselling author

"Brenda Novak is always a joy to read."
—Debbie Macomber, #1 *New York Times* bestselling author

"Brenda Novak doesn't just write fabulous stories, she writes keepers."
—Susan Mallery, #1 *New York Times* bestselling author

Also by Brenda Novak

SUMMER ON THE ISLAND
KEEP ME WARM AT CHRISTMAS
WHEN I FOUND YOU
THE BOOKSTORE ON THE BEACH
A CALIFORNIA CHRISTMAS
ONE PERFECT SUMMER
CHRISTMAS IN SILVER SPRINGS
UNFORGETTABLE YOU
BEFORE WE WERE STRANGERS
RIGHT WHERE WE BELONG
UNTIL YOU LOVED ME
NO ONE BUT YOU
FINDING OUR FOREVER
THE SECRETS SHE KEPT
A WINTER WEDDING
THE SECRET SISTER
THIS HEART OF MINE
THE HEART OF CHRISTMAS
COME HOME TO ME
TAKE ME HOME FOR CHRISTMAS
HOME TO WHISKEY CREEK
WHEN SUMMER COMES
WHEN SNOW FALLS
WHEN LIGHTNING STRIKES
IN CLOSE
IN SECONDS
INSIDE
KILLER HEAT
BODY HEAT
WHITE HEAT
THE PERFECT MURDER
THE PERFECT LIAR
THE PERFECT COUPLE
WATCH ME
STOP ME
TRUST ME
DEAD RIGHT
DEAD GIVEAWAY
DEAD SILENCE
COLD FEET
TAKING THE HEAT
EVERY WAKING MOMENT

For a full list of Brenda's books,
visit www.brendanovak.com.

Look for Brenda Novak's next novel
Talulah's Back In Town
available soon from MIRA.

Brenda Novak

the Seaside Library

ISBN-13: 978-0-7783-3351-7

The Seaside Library

For questions and comments about the quality of this book, please contact us at CustomerService@Harlequin.com.

Mira
22 Adelaide St. West, 41st Floor
Toronto, Ontario M5H 4E3, Canada
BookClubbish.com

Printed in U.S.A.

To Kathy Allbritton Bennett, a reader and friend who has done so much to support me and others. Not only has Kathy traveled to meet me in person, but she's very active in the book group I started several years ago on Facebook, attends the monthly meetings, posts to uplift and befriend other members of the group, subscribes to the Brenda Novak Book Boxes (which we put so much hard work into!) and fulfills the annual Brenda Novak Reading Challenge each year. And she doesn't stop there! She goes above and beyond by offering—completely her idea—fun giveaways to the many other readers in the group. Kathy, thank you for making everyone's day just a little brighter!

the Seaside Library

one

Mariners Island seemed like an empty movie set—cheerful and pristine but merely a facade—until the season hit. Then it was as if a director had screamed "Action!" and a flood of tourists rushed in with the tide.

After a long, dreary winter, Ivy Hawthorne couldn't wait for the warm days of summer. She loved the sun and the sand and the happy vacationers who flocked to the island's expensive summer houses, pristine beaches and exclusive shops and restaurants. The influx made for a nice change of pace, especially this year, when fog and bad weather had cut off the island from the mainland more often than usual, curtailing the activity of the supply boats and planes that would otherwise have come in and out on a more regular basis.

After such a hard winter, summer was literally a breath of fresh air. But this year it promised even more than the usual excitement. Ivy was looking forward to seeing Ariana Prince, a lifelong friend who'd grown up with her on Mariners. Ariana lived in New York City these days, and although there were plenty of direct flights, only an hour long, she'd stopped visiting the island regularly a decade ago—about the time she'd graduated from Yale.

She didn't stay in touch very often anymore, either. Until a few weeks ago, she'd worked as an editor for one of the bigger publishers in the city and insisted she couldn't get away. But Ivy ran the only library on the island. She understood how the book industry worked. August was slow because it fell between the big sales periods, so it was the month most editors took vacation. Ariana could've come back for a few days or a week every August—if she'd wanted to.

At least she was coming now. And not only for a week. She'd be on Mariners all summer. Ivy hoped it would seem like old times. But she couldn't avoid a certain amount of trepidation. Ariana had quit her job, but she'd been elusive as to the reason, what she planned to do next and if she'd be going back to New York when the summer was over. Why? And why was she returning *this* summer when she'd missed so many others?

Given the recent headlines, Ivy had a sinking feeling she knew what was drawing her friend. But she was loath to even think of the decision they'd made so many years ago. What was done was done. She didn't want to second-guess herself. She and Ariana had acted according to what they felt was right at the time.

Shoving the memory she'd suppressed for two decades back into the farthest recesses of her brain, she tried to shake off the attendant anxiety. Hopefully, they wouldn't even have to talk about the past.

But when her phone went off as she glanced at the clock hanging on the wall over the popular fiction section—because she was expecting Ariana to walk in any second—it seemed rather portentous that it was the only other person who'd been involved in what'd happened their junior year.

"Hello?"

"There you are."

Cam Stafford sounded as casual as he always did. But the timing of his call made the anxiety she'd been fighting worse. "What's up?" she asked.

"Melanie said she ran into Ariana's grandmother at Anchors Away when she went to pick up my lunch. Did you know that Ariana's coming to the island?"

Ivy froze. Melanie was Cam's wife of four years. He was the only one out of the three of them who was married, and it was seeing Melanie with their child around the island so often that had convinced Ivy to leave everything as it was, despite what was being reported on the news. "Um…yeah. I've been meaning to tell you. Ariana called me a few days ago and said she'd be here for the summer."

"Why didn't she call *me*?"

Deep down, he had to at least *suspect* the reason, didn't he? They'd tried to move on after what'd happened, and for a while everything had seemed fine. As teenagers, the secret the three of them shared might even have brought them closer. They'd both admired Cam and were so certain, so defiant of any doubt.

But after graduation everything began to change, and with change came an increase in tension. It was almost as if that night had put an invisible rubber band around the three of them. As they moved on with their lives and grew apart, it stretched and stretched until…what? Would it finally snap, allowing them to live their lives unencumbered by the friendship and loyalty that'd bound them so far? Or would that rubber band suddenly contract and pull the three of them back together?

Was that what Ariana's return meant? Was it the past that'd finally brought her back to Mariners?

"She probably expected me to tell you," Ivy said, implying it was an oversight. "I've just been so darn busy that... you know...I kept putting it off, thinking I'd talk to you soon and..."

She let her words dwindle away because she couldn't come up with a strong finish. She could've texted him, at least. And yet...something had stopped her. Lately, even before the news broke, she'd found herself avoiding him in general.

"How can she stay all summer?" he asked as if she hadn't given him the most unbelievable and stilted response ever. "What about her job?"

"Apparently, she no longer has one. She told me she quit."

"Why? I thought she loved her work."

"She loves books. Maybe she'd rather write one."

"She's coming here to write?"

"Who knows? But if anyone could come up with the next Great American Novel, she could." Ariana was both talented and clever. But she was also a sensitive person and tended to worry more about morally gray areas than most people. That was what had Ivy on edge. Maybe that night twenty years ago had been weighing on Ariana the whole time, or she'd changed her mind about the morality of what they'd done.

That wouldn't be good news for Cam. Especially now.

After maintaining the lie they'd told for so long, it wouldn't be good news for Ivy, either.

"Her grandmother's getting pretty frail," Ivy continued. "Ariana could be coming to spend time with her."

"Or she could be looking for a place to regroup while she decides what to do with the rest of her life," he said.

"True. She didn't tell me. She'd barely said she was coming to the island when she got another call and had to hang up."

"When will she be here?"

Ivy hesitated but ultimately didn't feel she had any reason to act like she didn't know. Ostensibly, nothing had changed among the three of them. She could simply be creating problems. "Today."

"Today?" he echoed in surprise.

"Yeah. She should be stopping by the library any minute."

"Are you two going out tonight? If so, can I join you?"

"Of course," Ivy heard herself say. She couldn't hurt him. He'd been their best friend since his family moved to the island during middle school. The three of them had done almost everything together. There weren't a lot of kids who remained on the island year-round, especially kids who hit it off as well as they did. They'd always been thankful to have each other.

"Great. Perfect. Call me as soon as she gets in."

He sounded relieved that they'd still include him—or, possibly, that was her imagination. "I will. What about Melanie and little Camilla? Will they be joining us, too?"

This time *he* was the one who paused before answering. "No. Melanie left for Boston after bringing me lunch. She went to see her family and took Camilla with her."

"How long will she be gone?"

"I don't know," he said.

That seemed like a strange answer. Shouldn't he be able to say when his wife and daughter would be back?

Ivy resisted the urge to press him. They'd drifted far enough apart since he got married that such a personal question might seem invasive. "Okay. It'll be just the three of us, then."

"Yeah, like old times."

"Sounds good. I'll text you when we've decided on a restaurant," she said and disconnected as the library door swung open and Ariana walked in.

The library hadn't changed. Established by the oldest son of Richard Taylor, the whale oil merchant who'd founded Mariners in the early nineteenth century and Ivy's great-great-grandfather on her mother's side, it maintained its old-world charm, with original mahogany bookshelves and a circular staircase leading to the second floor. Brass lamps, replicas of a bygone era, and leather wingback chairs were arranged around various tables to give it a warm, homey feel.

Ariana had always loved coming here. Not only did the library offer peace and tranquility during the frenetic tourist season, it also helped satisfy her thirst for knowledge—and it figured prominently in how she'd met Ivy. Before Ivy's grandmother Hazel had passed away, she'd been determined that the efforts of her ancestors would not be wasted, that the collections they'd started would be available and properly maintained. So whenever Hazel babysat Ivy, she'd bring her here. And since Ariana's grandmother Alice had raised Ariana during her preschool years and lived just around the corner from Hazel, Hazel would invite Alice and Ariana to come along. The two grandmothers would take their granddaughters to Story Time before having a picnic lunch at the beach, if the weather was warm enough, or getting hot cocoa and one of Joy Denizen's delicious breakfast rolls at Baked With Love—the most famous of the island's bakeries—if it was rainy or cold.

Those excursions had created some of Ariana's earliest memories. Just walking in and smelling the familiar scent of the printed paper and the furniture polish took her back to those idyllic days. The nostalgia was almost enough to make her forget the reason she'd returned to the island.

Almost. But not quite. As tormented as she'd been, especially lately, she wasn't sure *anything* would have the power to do that.

"Oh my gosh! It's been so long!" Ivy exclaimed as she came around the circulation desk and pulled Ariana in for a hug.

Ariana allowed the embrace but stepped away as soon as possible. While eager to see her old friend, she was reluctant to be thrust back into the net of love, obligation and loyalty that'd captured her when she was only sixteen. "How are you?"

"Good."

"The library looks amazing," she said, turning in a circle as she took it all in.

"The goal has always been to keep it as close to the original as possible. And I'm definitely doing that," Ivy said with a laugh.

Thanks to the money and property she'd inherited from her grandmother—a portion equal to her mother's since Ivy had been so close to Hazel—she didn't need a high-paying job. Instead of leaving the island for the sake of a career somewhere else, she'd made the library her life's work, protecting it from the devastating budget cuts and other funding challenges that'd closed public facilities across the country. She felt it was her duty not only to protect the library but also to preserve what she could of the history of Mariners, since her family was such a big part of it.

"Are you sure it hasn't become a millstone?" Ariana asked skeptically.

"Sometimes I wonder if I should've finished college instead of coming back when my grandmother died. But when I imagine letting this place go and leaving the island for any length of time, I realize I don't want to do that. I belong here." She gestured at the building around them. "This is my family's legacy."

A picture of Ivy's great-great-grandfather hung over the circulation desk in a thick, ornate frame. "Your family's legacy extends to far more than the library," Ariana pointed out. The tourists who came to Mariners learned about Ivy's progenitors while visiting the whaling museum, which wasn't nearly as elaborate as the one on Nantucket but was a popular tourist spot all the same. And during the summer, there were people who took pictures of the house where she lived. Part of the historic district on Elm Street, it was a beautiful example of the Greek Revival architecture that'd been so popular during the island's whaling heyday.

"I'm happy here," she added simply.

Ivy's older brother, Tim, and her parents had left the island. Tim was a dentist who lived in Philadelphia with his wife and three kids. From what Ivy said, he came back almost every summer. Ivy's parents owned a summer home on Mariners that he used when he stayed, but none of the rest of her family seemed to feel the same connection and obligation to the library. Maybe it was because Ivy had spent so much time with her grandmother. She seemed to identify more with Hazel than her mother, who claimed she *couldn't* stay on Mariners year-round. She said it gave her island fever, especially once the fog rolled in.

"I'm glad," Ariana told her. "Are you ready to eat? I haven't had anything since breakfast. I'm starving."

Ivy grabbed her purse and dug out her keys, presumably to lock up. Since most of the restaurants were on this side of the island, near the wharf, the airport and the central shopping district, there was no need to drive. "I'm ready, but..."

Ariana felt her eyebrows go up when Ivy didn't finish that statement. "But...what?"

"Cam called just before you came in. His wife ran into your grandmother earlier today, and Alice mentioned that you were coming for the summer."

Ariana suppressed a groan. "She did?"

"Yeah." Ivy peered at her more closely. "Is that okay?"

Ariana tried to put her friend at ease by shrugging it off. She didn't want the angst and doubt that'd plagued her for the past twenty years to bleed into Ivy's life. Ariana still wasn't convinced there was anything she should or could do to change the way things were. "Of course. Why wouldn't it be okay?"

"You didn't let him know you were coming. I thought—"

"I was just…busy," she broke in.

Ariana's behavior toward Cam was so uncharacteristic, given how close the three of them had been, that Ivy had to know there was more to her reaction than she was letting on. Fortunately, however, she didn't question Ariana's response. "Right," she said. "Well, that's good because he asked when you were getting in."

A knot began to grow in Ariana's stomach, but she tried to keep the sudden tension she was feeling out of her voice. "And? What'd you tell him?"

"The truth. I didn't have any reason not to…did I?" she asked uncertainly.

Ariana curved her lips into a reassuring smile. "No. Of course not. What'd he say?"

"He asked if he could join us for dinner tonight."

Shit. Ariana wasn't ready to see Cam. There was a reason she'd avoided him more and more as time went by. But she'd known when she decided to return to Mariners that seeing him would be part of it. He was the main reason she'd quit her job to come back and, hopefully, make right anything she'd done wrong. She'd just hoped she'd have a day or two to acclimate and prepare herself before facing him. "What about Melanie and Camilla? Are they coming, too?"

"They left a few hours ago for the mainland—to visit her family."

"Then he'll be coming alone?"

"Yeah. Is that better or worse?"

Ariana upped the wattage of her smile. "It's no problem either way. I haven't seen him in years."

"You two still talk, though, right?"

"Not as often as you and I do, but…occasionally. I haven't wanted to intrude now that he's married. The guy-girl friend thing doesn't go over well with every spouse, you know?"

"I do know. At the wedding I got the distinct feeling that Melanie would not appreciate my involvement in his life, so I've been careful about that, too." Although Ivy also smiled, the doubt never left her eyes. "Where should we eat?"

"How about The Jumbo Gumbo? I'm in the mood for fresh fish."

"I'd be happy with that," Ivy said. "Do you want to text Cam? Or should I?"

Ariana cleared her throat. "I'll do it," she said and pulled out her phone.

two

Cam was as handsome as ever. With big blue eyes and long golden eyelashes, he looked like a blond Jake Gyllenhaal, especially because the chiseled contours of his face had only grown more dramatic as he matured. Ariana believed he could easily have modeled had he chosen that profession. He'd become an architect instead and was quite famous for his work. But with his spare, six-foot-five-inch frame, he could make a dirty old T-shirt look appealing.

Tonight he was wearing a salmon-colored Ralph Lauren golf shirt with a pair of chinos and loafers, perfectly matching the stereotype of a gorgeous, wealthy frat boy—similar to so many of the privileged young college students who visited the island.

The toothy smile he flashed the second he laid eyes on her sent a sizzle of awareness down Ariana's spine. Although she'd been careful to hide it, he'd always had that effect on her. She couldn't help but believe her attraction to him was part of the reason she'd made the decision she'd made when they were in high school.

She'd often wondered if he'd used the way she felt about him to his advantage. He had to be able to sense, on some level, that her feelings weren't quite as platonic as she'd always pretended, didn't he?

Regardless, he held a certain power over her she wished he didn't.

"Hey," she said as he unfolded from the chair where he'd been waiting at the entrance.

"There you are, stranger." He embraced her, and she briefly closed her eyes as she breathed in the clean scent of him. She could already tell that her stay on Mariners this summer was going to be even harder than she'd thought. After all the time they'd had to grow apart—after countless hours of self-talk and years of avoidance—she'd expected to have more emotional distance when she saw him again.

But that *distance* melted instantly away, putting her right back where she'd been twenty years ago. She'd always loved Cam, and that hadn't changed.

"You could've come to the city," she said to combat the accusation in his voice.

"You were too busy climbing the corporate ladder to be bothered with a visit from me," he joked, sobering as he added, "And then I met Melanie, she got pregnant and you know the rest of the story." Although he shrugged to mitigate some of the heft of those words, there was a hollowness in his eyes that had never been there before. "Life happens, I guess." He turned to embrace Ivy. "You've made yourself a stranger lately, too, and we live on an island that's only ten miles long and five miles wide. Where've you been?"

"I haven't wanted to intrude. It's important for us to be respectful of Melanie."

"I can see why you'd feel that way," he said as he released her. "She's been none too friendly to you. But I don't think you're going to have to worry about her for much longer."

The hostess interrupted. "Are you Cam? I have your table ready."

Cam gestured for Ariana and Ivy to precede him into the main dining area.

It wasn't until they were comfortably seated in a corner booth that Ivy circled back to the statement he'd made at the entrance. "What did you mean when you said we won't have to worry about Melanie for much longer?" she asked.

He sighed as he raked his fingers through his thick hair, which was cropped close on the sides but remained longer on top. He didn't seem to care that he was causing it to stand up in front, but Ariana supposed there wasn't any reason for him to care. The unruliness only made him sexier. "I don't think we're going to make it," he said.

Ariana felt her eyes go wide. "You're talking about your marriage?"

He carefully rearranged his silverware. "What's left of it, yeah."

Too shocked to speak, Ariana gaped at him. It was Ivy who filled the sudden silence. "I'm sorry," she said. "What's going on?"

"She's so damn paranoid and possessive," he complained. "I've never strayed. Not once. And yet she constantly goes through my phone, searching for illicit calls or texts. She gets mad if I talk to either of you, refuses to even let me have friends. She appears at my office at random times, using one excuse or another to check up on me. And when I get home at night, she accuses me of preferring to be with the girl I hired at the office just because I have to spend so much time there."

"There's no truth to it..." Ariana said, leaving the ending open.

"No!" he cried. "Courtney's only in her twenties! It's insulting and upsetting and exhausting trying to reassure Melanie all the time. And now that the remains of Emily Hutchins have been found..."

Ariana felt herself tense. The possibility that Cam might've had something to do with the twelve-year-old who'd gone missing when they were in high school still gave her nightmares. She was surprised he'd be the one to bring her up, especially so casually. Was that a good sign? Or the sign of a complete psychopath? "Melanie thinks you might be responsible for what happened? Even though Ivy and I..." She couldn't bring herself to finish that sentence, but he jumped in at that point, saving her from trying to force the recalcitrant words from her throat.

"Yes."

"Why?" Ariana asked.

"Because of the rumors. Because I was a person of interest in the past. She'll bludgeon me with any weapon she can."

"But you're not a person of interest now..." Ivy said.

"Not that I know of."

Ariana shifted in her seat. "You haven't heard from the police?"

"They've stopped by once or twice," he replied. "But I think they're just poking around, asking questions. They're under pressure to solve the case. I get that. But seeing them at the house freaks Melanie out." He sighed. "I don't like it, either. Believe me, the last thing I want is for the investigation to focus on me again. It was bad enough the first time. But she's only making it worse by saying weird shit."

"Like..." Ariana prompted.

"Like I'm so aloof she doesn't really know me. Or I only married her because of Camilla and would leave her if we didn't have a child together." He waved a hand. "It goes on and on. I'm dealing with enough doubt and suspicion. I'd like to be able to rely on my *wife* to trust me."

"It must be hard to feel she doesn't," Ariana agreed.

"Exactly," he said. "There are other people on the island, people I've known most of my life, who are watching me closely, too—like I'm a wolf in sheep's clothing."

Being one of his doubters made Ariana feel slightly guilty. How could she? He'd been a good friend to her.

She'd allowed the "what-ifs" that'd cropped up since leaving the island to overshadow all her reasons for believing in him. But maybe that would change now that she'd returned. To feel absolutely secure in standing by him would lift a huge weight from her shoulders. He sounded sincere—truly tortured over what'd happened to Emily Hutchins—and she felt terrible for what he was going through as a result.

What if they'd been correct when they were in high school? What if he was completely innocent of any wrongdoing, and they'd stopped circumstances from making him a victim, too?

Instinctively, Ariana reached out and felt the old longing and admiration return when he took her hand. Ivy did the same thing, and a moment later they were clasping hands in a circle. "We're here for you," Ariana said. "Just like we've always been."

"It would be terrible if this cost you your marriage," Ivy added, wearing a pained expression. "Especially since little Camilla would be the one to suffer most."

"She's the reason I've hung on as long as I have," he said. "If we split up, Melanie would take her and leave the island, and it would be difficult for me to spend time with her. But if

I were to become a suspect in this investigation… That would be the death of our marriage. I can't continue to placate her the way I have if I'm fighting for my own safety, reputation and future. I'm struggling too much as it is."

"She doesn't offer you any of the love and support you need?" Ariana asked.

He gave her a wan smile as the waitress approached to take their drink order and they let go of each other. "Our marriage started out difficult and has only gotten harder," he admitted.

What Cam was going through was taking a toll on him. Ivy could tell. His words were one thing. But it went beyond that. He'd lost weight. His skin wasn't the same robust golden color it normally was. And his smile seemed forced and unnatural. Her good friend had been struggling, and yet she'd been keeping her distance from him, telling herself he had his wife to support him while she tried to figure out how to react to the news that Emily Hutchins's remains had been found.

Maybe if the body had been discovered elsewhere, she would've reacted differently. That a girl had been killed upset her, but it especially freaked her out that the body had been found so close to the lighthouse. That made her rethink everything she'd believed before.

In the bathroom she stared at herself in the mirror above the sink, taking advantage of a moment alone to collect her thoughts before returning to her friends at the table. She was enjoying dinner, enjoying seeing Cam and Ariana again. But the past hung over them like a dark cloud. Was the location of Emily's remains merely a coincidence?

It could be. The island wasn't that big, and the lighthouse was the most remote place on it. If someone wanted to hide a body, that would be a great spot to do it, what with the sand and grasses to obscure any digging or footprints.

Whoever had buried Emily had dug a deep grave, or the body would've surfaced long before now. Without the terrible erosion problem the island was suffering, Emily might *never* have been uncovered.

So much digging in one night would require a strong man.

Cam had always been strong.

But he wasn't the only person capable of digging such a deep hole. She had to remember that.

"You okay?"

When Ariana poked her head into the bathroom, Ivy quickly turned on the tap to wash her hands. "Yeah. I'm fine."

Instead of leaving, Ariana came inside. "It's good to see you again, Ivy. I—I didn't realize how much I've missed you."

"I'm *so* glad you're back," Ivy told her. She felt that way for many reasons. She missed the closeness and the camaraderie they'd shared. But it was also true that Ariana was the only other person who knew what happened that night. She was as caught up in the nightmare as Ivy was, which meant Ivy wouldn't be alone this summer as she wrestled with the terrible conflict recent developments had once again dropped in her lap.

That provided some relief. But it also created greater worry. What if the two of them came to different conclusions on whether what they'd done was right and how to proceed from here?

Ariana met her gaze in the mirror. "I'm sorry that..." She seemed to have difficulty finishing her sentence. She ended by simply repeating the apology. "I'm sorry."

Was she contrite for trying to escape the memory that haunted them both by avoiding everyone and everything related to it? That was how Ivy interpreted her words. "Did you come back because of what the police found?" she asked, her voice barely audible.

A pained expression registered on Ariana's face. "That has to be part of it, because if I could have, I would've turned my back on you, Cam, the island, everything, so I could embrace a future with no more guilt or uncertainty."

Being included on the list of people she was willing to sacrifice stung. "I hope you don't really mean that," Ivy said.

Ariana dropped her head in her hand and began to rub her temples. "I need a respite, the chance to forget the past—and what we did."

"Do you think you're the only one who's been struggling because of it?"

"I don't know. You make it look easier than it's been for me."

"From a distance, maybe. You've been careful to stay away. But I still live here. I can't avoid Cam, or the gossip about Emily Hutchins, even if I want to."

Ariana dropped her hand. "Point taken. Again, I'm sorry. I'm at such a loss, Ivy. I really don't know what to do. When I think about the way we took matters into our own hands—at sixteen!—and how easily we could've been wrong, I worry that we're denying Emily's loved ones the justice and closure they deserve."

Ivy shut off the water. "Then why haven't you come forward?"

"I almost have—a thousand times. But as soon as I decide it *has* to be done, I think about Cam and how easy it would be for what I say to send him to prison for the rest of his life, whether he's guilty or not. The police don't always get it right. Do you know how many innocent men DNA evidence has been responsible for exonerating in the past ten years?"

"No," she replied, using a paper towel. "But I would guess too many."

"And you'd be right. I've looked it up. According to the internet, there have been almost four hundred people released from prison thanks to DNA evidence. Twenty-one were on death row! And the police here… I don't think there's ever been another homicide on the island, not one that wasn't related to a domestic dispute or drunken brawl that made the answers clear, quick and easy."

"But if we don't trust the justice system, what do we do? Do we keep our mouths shut and hope we got it right? Or tell the police everything we know and hope they'll do their jobs?"

"That's the question, isn't it?"

Ivy tossed the paper towel into the wastebasket. So much for not talking about the past. It was only Ariana's first night back and already they'd addressed the problem they'd both rather avoid. "Do *you* think he did it, Ariana?"

Suddenly, inexplicably, tears welled up. "No. If I thought that, I would've come forward already." She started to go, but Ivy reached out to catch her arm.

"Even though they found her body at the lighthouse?" Where the three of them had been partying earlier that night? That was quite a coincidence. When Cam had walked them both to Alice's house, where they'd stayed the night, he'd claimed he would make his way home from there. But he could've gone back. It seemed his parents were off the island more than they were on it. Or they were fighting and out trying to get revenge by hooking up with someone else for the night. They'd left him with minimal supervision for long periods of time. As a matter of fact, he'd needed security and love so badly he used to crawl through Ivy's window and spend the night on her bedroom floor just so he wouldn't have to be alone.

"The lighthouse is where almost anyone hoping to hide a body would go," Ariana replied. "This is an island, Ivy. There aren't any national parks with acres upon acres of wilderness."

"Yeah, that's what I keep telling myself, too."

They continued to stare at each other in the mirror, as if

looking long enough might peel back the layers of false hope and denial and finally lay naked their true thoughts and intents.

A second later Ariana shook her head. “I was hoping, now that I’m older, I’d be able to figure this out. I believed that looking at it with fresh eyes and a less partial heart would make all the difference. But…”

“But?” Ivy echoed.

“Nothing’s changed,” she said, and Ivy followed her out of the bathroom and back to their table.

three

The moment Ariana woke up the following morning, she regretted saying what she did last night about wishing she could be rid of Ivy, Cam and the island. Ivy was the last person she wanted to hurt. She was just so desperate to escape the torture of her own conscience that she was willing to cut anyone out of her life.

But Ivy hadn't done anything wrong—at least nothing Ariana hadn't agreed with and done herself.

The sound of pots and pans clanging downstairs in the kitchen signaled that Alice was up. She'd always been an early riser. Ariana used to be one, too, when she was working. But she hadn't been able to sleep last night. Images of Cam, both from when she'd known him in high school and last night, had swirled in her head, causing strange and unsettling dreams. Ariana had thought with the maturity afforded by two decades of learning and growing, she'd finally be capable of handling what was waiting for her here. Everything had seemed different, more clear-cut when she was in the city.

But now that she was back home and felt so close to it all, she couldn't seem to maintain the same perspective. The lines began to blur until, once again, she couldn't decide where they should be drawn.

With a sigh, she grabbed her phone from the nightstand beside her and checked the time. Sure enough. It was barely seven o'clock. She needed another hour of sleep. But instead, she went on the internet and searched for articles related to Emily Hutchins.

Body Found at Lighthouse.

Remains of Girl Discovered in Twenty-Year-Old Cold Case.

Mariners Island has its First Great Mystery.

Is There a Killer on Mariners?

What Happened to Twelve-Year-Old Emily Hutchins?

Those headlines popped up, but Ariana had already seen the attached articles. Excruciating as it was to feel the pain of Emily's family, she didn't care to read them again. She was looking for new information, a piece that would shed some light on the truth—instead of raising more questions than it answered.

But there was nothing like that.

She was about to set her phone down when a text came in from Bruce Derringer. Did you arrive safely?

This time of the morning, he was probably riding the subway to work. She'd broken off their relationship when she left the company, where he held a position in upper management, and hadn't expected to hear from him.

Should she answer?

She was reluctant to start communicating with him again. It would only make things harder. She'd told him from the very beginning that she wasn't open to a relationship, but he'd been so unfailingly consistent in pursuing her that over time one thing had led to another until she'd found herself sleeping with him.

But his question was completely innocuous. How could she not answer?

"Why can't anything be easy?" she muttered and sent him a reply. Safe and sound. Thanks.

Miss you, he wrote back.

That message she decided to ignore. Not because she was hard-hearted. She felt terrible for hurting him. But saying something distant or merely polite, like "thank you," wouldn't satisfy him. And telling him she missed him, too, would only raise his hopes. She'd tried to break up with him one other time, but because they worked at the same place and saw each other every day, and he kept trying to get back with her by saying sweet things like what he'd just sent in his text, she'd given in. It was too hard to continue to disappoint him.

How ironic that she'd gotten into a relationship with someone she'd only ever considered a friend and yet maintained such a long friendship with the only man she'd ever really loved. Maybe it wouldn't have gone that way if Cam had ever shown any romantic interest in her. Instead, for as long as she'd known him, he'd talked about the girls he was attracted to and hoped to date and how things were going in his love life as if she wasn't a consideration. And she'd never expressed her feelings to him or anyone else—even Ivy, for fear Ivy would tell him or, worse, was hiding the same secret. Why would she risk changing the chemistry of the friendship they'd all shared?

At the very least, she was determined to keep the small part of Cam's heart he willingly gave her. So it was another irony that she'd tried so hard to distance herself from him as the years went by. No doubt it wasn't only the angst and turmoil she'd suffered as a result of the night Emily Hutchins went missing. It was also the disappointment that came when he married someone else, knowing after that there'd be no chance of their friendship turning into more.

But now he and Melanie might be splitting up. Ariana wished he hadn't revealed that little nugget of information. Knowing he might be single again soon only made her hate herself for the flicker of interest that'd suddenly sprung to life.

Stop it, she told herself. Regardless of what happened between Cam and Melanie, she was here to make sure she'd done the right thing twenty years ago—not to fall more deeply in love with a man she didn't know if she could entirely trust.

After setting her phone aside at last, she rolled over and pulled the covers up. She wanted to go back to sleep so she'd have the fortitude to get through the day. Part of her—the part that could compartmentalize that night when they were juniors—was excited to be home. She hadn't realized just how much she'd missed Mariners. Other than possibly Nantucket and Martha's Vineyard, there was no place like it, and yet she'd been lucky enough to grow up here.

But she knew what everyone would be talking about. That the body of a twelve-year-old girl had been found after she'd gone missing so long ago was a huge deal, especially for the locals. Most had insisted it had to be a tourist who'd taken Emily. They didn't want to believe one of their own could do something so atrocious.

They could be right—it'd been the fifth of July, when the tourist season was in full swing. Although there were only about twelve thousand year-round residents, summer saw that number swell to eighty thousand or more.

Sleep. She closed her eyes and struggled to block the noise her grandmother was making. But a few seconds later she could smell bacon. Alice was busy cooking a big breakfast for her. Ariana figured the least she could do, since she'd gotten in after Alice went to bed and hadn't yet had the chance to see her, was drag her butt out of bed and go down to say hello.

With a yawn, Ariana kicked off the covers, got up and yanked on a pair of yoga pants and a sweatshirt. It was early June, and they'd had a gorgeous day yesterday, but the weather could be so changeable on Mariners, which was why she pulled her slippers out of her suitcase and shoved her feet inside them before plodding down the creaky old staircase. Her grandmother still lived only a block away from where Hazel had lived when she was alive—where Ivy lived now. But Alice's home had never been updated the way Hazel's had been. Except for the basics, like replacing some of the knob and tube wiring and sections of the old plumbing, it looked just as it had when it was built in the early 1900s.

"Hi, Grandma," Ariana said, but her grandmother was getting hard of hearing, so she had to raise her voice before Alice realized she was in the room.

"Oh! There you are," she said, putting down the tongs she'd been using to turn the bacon so she could give Ariana a warm hug. "How have you been, honey? Did you have fun with Ivy and Cam last night?"

"I did. Sorry we stayed out so late. I meant to get here before you went to bed, but—"

"I understand," she broke in, waving Ariana's apology away. "It's been so long since you've seen them. And Cam probably needed the time. I can't imagine what he's going through these days."

Ariana leaned against the counter as her grandmother went back to frying the bacon. "What do you mean?"

"You've heard they found that poor girl's remains..."

Ariana had purposely not mentioned it when she spoke to her grandmother on the phone. "Yes, but...everyone knows Cam couldn't have had anything to do with what happened to

Emily Hutchins. He was with Ivy and me that night." What she said was *technically* true. She, Cam and Ivy had been together that Friday. But only until ten. According to what the police had put together so far, Emily hadn't gone missing from the vacation rental near Cam's house until ten-thirty.

Did Alice know they'd said he was with them until eleven to protect him?

That was possible. Ariana and Ivy had been staying with Alice that weekend. She'd raised Ariana when she was a preschooler, because her mother wasn't reliable at that time and her father had been a tourist who'd visited the island for only one month before returning to Scotland. Once her mother met and married Kevin, her stepfather, and she took on his two boys, who were only toddlers at the time, she became more reliable. Then, Ariana had been adopted by her stepfather and lived with them for several years. But she was only a sophomore when her mother and Kevin decided to take the family and leave the island to get a fresh start. Rather than force Ariana to go with them and abandon all her friends and graduate from somewhere else, Bridget had allowed her to move in with Alice again.

Ariana had often wondered…was it possible that Alice remembered what time it was when she and Ivy came in that night? She'd still been awake, watching TV.

If so, she'd never spoken up.

Maybe she'd acted to protect Cam, too.

Or she'd remained silent to protect Ariana…

"There's still talk," Alice said. "People are saying that maybe she went missing later than they first thought. That sort of thing."

No wonder Cam had looked so shell-shocked. If the timeline changed by a mere thirty minutes, he'd no longer have an alibi. "Hopefully, now that they have her remains, they'll find hard evidence that leads them to the culprit."

"That's what I'm hoping, too. But the chances of finding DNA evidence after so long..."

"I know." Ariana started to set the table. "Should I make toast?"

"No, I've got fresh biscuits in the oven," Alice replied. "And some delicious raspberry jam I put up last summer."

"Sounds wonderful," Ariana said.

Soon they were seated at the small breakfast table that looked out on the postage-stamp of a backyard where her grandmother used to grow a garden, their plates filled with eggs over easy, thickly sliced bacon, hash browns and homemade biscuits and jelly. But Ariana could hardly taste the food. Something about the way Alice had brought up the missing girl and the case surrounding her made Ariana believe Alice knew she'd been lying about that night.

Melanie wouldn't pick up.

Cam frowned as he hit the end button after leaving another message. He'd been trying to reach her ever since he got home from dinner with Ariana and Ivy last night. She had to have seen the missed calls and texts. But she did this sometimes—purposely made him worry—to punish him for his many failings as a husband. She loved to get him worked up. In her mind, it was the best way to prove he still cared.

He understood that she had needs he was unable to meet—although he'd tried, especially at first. Now he simply turned a blind eye to the games she played. If he *didn't* do that, they'd be bickering all the time, and he didn't want Camilla to grow up in a toxic environment.

But the constant manipulation made him feel like a puppet on a string. Melanie's mother would've called if she and Camilla hadn't gotten in safely. He was confident they were fine. If he assumed that, however, and quit trying to get hold of his wife, she'd accuse him of not loving their daughter. She'd say the plane could've flown into the ocean for all he cared—or that once again he'd put his work first and forgotten about the two of them.

What man wouldn't want to escape a wife like Melanie, he thought. He adored his daughter, but Melanie's involvement made even that relationship difficult. She used their daughter to manipulate him whenever she wanted something yet treated him as though he couldn't do anything right with Camilla, hovered over them constantly and had to direct every action and every word.

In all honesty, his business *had* become an escape. The more he achieved, the more he threw himself into his career. It was the only way he could feel successful at anything.

"Is something wrong?"

He glanced up to see Courtney hovering at the entrance of the room and quickly altered his expression so that it wouldn't reveal the despair roiling in his gut. He and Melanie had had their problems, but this was the first time he'd wished he could see his daughter without ever having to see her again. Apparently, the stress of Emily's body being found had used up the emotional reserves he typically relied on when dealing with his wife. "No, nothing," he said. "I was just…thinking. What's up?"

She gestured over her shoulder. "I hate to interrupt. But… there's a man here to see you. He says he's a—" she lowered her voice "—private detective."

Cam sat up straighter. Having a private detective come to his office was something new. He had a terrible feeling the investigation wasn't going to fizzle out this time, leaving him to go on his way, which meant, as bad as he felt right now, his life could get a lot worse. "Did he give you his card?"

"No. He told me who he was, though—Warner Williams. He said he's been hired by the Hutchins family."

He hadn't discussed the case with Courtney, but she obviously knew what was going on. Everyone did. He cringed to imagine what people were saying, what she'd probably heard.

But he couldn't focus on that right now. A private investigator was waiting in the lobby.

Warner Williams. Cam had never heard of him. But he was willing to bet the guy was good. Cam had seen the GoFundMe page Emily's family had put up to raise money to help solve the case. Last time he'd checked, they'd received nearly a hundred and twenty thousand dollars in donations—thanks, in part, to all the media attention they were receiving.

They were doing a fantastic job of keeping pressure on the police.

That was smart—*for them.*

It could easily prove to be a disaster for him.

He didn't want to talk to this guy, didn't want to risk saying something wrong. But he couldn't refuse. That would only make him look guilty, and he was afraid, if he wasn't careful, he'd become the sole focus of the investigation. He wasn't convinced, if it came right down to it, that he could still count on Ariana and Ivy to protect him. After all, lying to the police was illegal and put them at risk, too. "Send him in."

"Okay." She sounded as reluctant as he felt, but she disappeared, and a moment later a mountain of a man, around fifty years old, well over six feet and at least three hundred pounds, filled the doorway.

"Mr. Stafford?" Williams wore snakeskin boots, which added a couple inches to his height, a pair of stiff jeans, a button-up shirt and a cowboy hat.

"Yes?" Cam said.

He came farther into the room. "I'm Warner Williams from Abilene."

"Abilene..."

"Texas," he clarified.

"I realize Abilene's in Texas." Even if he hadn't, Cam would've been able to guess where Williams was from by the twang in his voice. "I'm just…taken aback that you'd come so far." Surely, there had to be top-notch PIs closer to the east coast…

"I admit I'm a little out of place on an island as ritzy as this one," he said with a "good old boy" grin. "But I go where the job leads me."

Cam gestured at the seats across from his desk. "What can I do for you?"

Instead of sitting down, Mr. Williams circled the room, still carrying his briefcase with one meaty paw as he examined the awards and framed magazine clippings hanging on the walls—accolades for some of the buildings Cam had designed. "I hear there's no one better when it comes to drawing up plans for a home."

As a child, Cam had never dreamed he'd become an architect. He'd had a talent for drawing—used to fill notebooks with video game and Marvel characters he'd sketched when he was in school—but his father, who now lived with his mother in Italy, had pressed him hard to major in computer science and go into business with him. Like Elon Musk, Jack had made millions during the early days of the internet. He'd seen plenty of opportunity still ahead so he hadn't been happy when Cam told him he had no interest. He was happy partying and hanging out with friends while skating through his undergrad years at New York University, majoring in communications. It wasn't until his roommate, Eddie Schultz—someone he'd met his freshman year at the university—was diagnosed with cancer, and he took a semester off to help him through his treatments and take care of him, that Cam taught himself 2D AutoCAD with the intention of creating his own dream home one day.

Once he realized he was good at the program—that spatial concepts were rather intuitive for him and he could make a good living, if not as much as his father, by drawing on a computer—he was hooked. He finally had some direction in his life, got back in school and changed his major.

By the time he met Melanie and she wound up pregnant, Eddie was cancer-free and living in Virginia with a wife and two kids of his own, and Cam had already passed the Architecture Registration Exam, received his license and started a one-man firm on the island.

"I grew up here," he told Williams. "I'm intimately familiar with Mariners, Martha's Vineyard and Nantucket and the building styles that work best on each, both functionally and aesthetically."

"That's a mouthful of words, son," Williams said. "But what I think it all boils down to is this—as well-known as you've become, you make a lot of money."

Mr. Williams didn't come off particularly clever or astute. Rather, his manner made him seem slightly slow or, at the least, prosaic. Cam got the distinct impression that was partly intentional. But even if Williams wasn't making a conscious effort to appear harmless, Cam knew better than to underestimate him. Someone had to be paying him. Cam guessed it was Emily's family, and that they'd chosen someone from halfway across the country for a reason. "I'm sorry," he said. "Why is that relevant?"

"Just sayin' you've made good since Emily went missin'."

Williams's response bothered Cam even more than the reference to his income. "But…those are two completely unrelated things." Or was Williams intimating that he was surprised a murderer could come back from something like that and live a good life? Cam was fairly certain that was exactly what Williams was thinking, which was why it upset him.

"Oh, I know that," the PI said. "It's nice to see your success, is all. The hotel clerk where I'm stayin' told me you're so busy it takes a year or more to get any plans from ya."

Why was he talking to a hotel clerk about Cam? This was a small island, where word traveled fast. Just insinuating that Cam might be responsible for what happened to Emily could damage his reputation and his business. But those investigating the case didn't seem to care if they destroyed—deservingly or undeservingly—his life in the pursuit of justice. "I'm lucky there's sufficient demand for my work," he said simply.

Williams lifted his scruffy eyebrows, giving Cam the impression he hadn't expected such a modest response. Then he took off his hat, revealing a ring of matted gray hair, while finally putting his briefcase on the floor and sitting down. "I'll quit beating around the bush, Mr. Stafford," he said. "I've been hired by Emily Hutchins's family, so you may not consider me much of a friend."

This hardly came as a surprise. "I don't consider you an enemy, either," Cam said. "I'd like the truth to come out, too—since I didn't do anything wrong."

Williams studied him for a moment, obviously trying to decide if that was true. "From what I've read in the police file, you were at the lighthouse the night that little girl went missing," he said. "Ain't that right?"

At twelve, Emily had been a young girl, not a *little* girl, but Cam didn't bother to correct him. "I was there for a short time—with two friends."

"Did you happen to see Emily?"

"Not at the lighthouse."

"Where *did* you see her—if you don't mind my askin'?"

Cam did mind. He'd been interrogated so many times it was getting to the point where he was just repeating what he'd said before. But he had to pretend he didn't mind, or he'd only invite more scrutiny. "At my house, earlier the same night."

Williams withdrew a small pad and pen from his shirt pocket and began taking notes. "What time was that?"

Tamping down the helplessness and frustration that threatened to overcome him, Cam drew a deep breath. "Around five-thirty. Her family was staying in the vacation home two doors down from where I lived with my parents," he explained. "She knocked on the door because she was locked out and needed my help."

"How'd she get locked out?"

"She told me her parents had gone to Boston for the day, to some special meeting with a branch of her father's church, and she'd left her older sister, Jewel, at the beach and come back alone, not realizing Jewel had locked up when they left."

He glanced up from his pad. "Were you able to help her?"

"Yes. We walked down the street and checked around the front door, hoping to locate a spare key. When we didn't find one, we circled the house together, looking for a way to get in."

Williams pursed his lips in obvious consternation. "Why didn't she come on inside your place and call her mom?"

"I don't know. She didn't ask to do that, and I didn't offer. I just followed her down the street and tried the doors and windows until I found that the bathroom window wasn't latched."

After shoving his notepad back into his shirt pocket, Williams put the battered old briefcase on his lap, opened it and withdrew a picture, which he handed across the desk. "Was this the window?"

Cam tried to block out the memories that suddenly assailed him, to show no sign of distress, as he peered at the photograph. "That's the window," he said calmly, giving it back.

"You look like a good-size man to me. I doubt you could fit through a window—" pronounced *winda* "—that size."

"I couldn't," he said. "Not even at sixteen. But I lifted her up, and she managed to crawl through."

"Is that the last you saw of her?"

"No. As I was starting home, she came after me to show me that she'd found a spare key on the kitchen counter. She wanted me to come back and help her find a good place to hide it, so she couldn't get locked out again."

"And? Did you do that?"

"I knew it would only take a minute, so I did. We were putting the key under a rock in the front planter area when Jewel returned from the beach."

"Jewel witnessed you hiding the key?"

"She did." That was the reason he'd been implicated. He was one of the last people to see Emily. He'd also known how to get inside the house without forcing open a door or breaking a window. "We told her what happened and what we were doing."

"What'd she say?"

"Not much," Cam said with a shrug. "Banal stuff, really. Nothing I particularly remember."

"*Banal* stuff?"

"Conversation of no consequence."

"Right. Then you left?"

"I did." He didn't add that he'd been eager to get away. Jewel, who was also sixteen at the time, had invited him into the house for a brownie, ostensibly to thank him for going to the trouble of helping Emily. But she'd made it clear she found him attractive, and while he would've been interested in the brownie, he hadn't been interested in her. Instead of agreeing, he'd avoided what could become an awkward situation by telling her he had to go.

"You never saw Emily again?" Williams pressed.

Cam forced himself to maintain eye contact, but it wasn't easy. "I never saw her again," he lied.

four

"Have you ever been tempted to tell anyone?"

Ariana knew what Ivy was referring to without even having to ask. It'd been twenty years since The Incident, and they'd rarely spoken of it. For good reason. It was like a hand grenade, better off buried and forgotten so that no one could pull the pin.

But if she was having second thoughts now, Ivy could be, too. And if that was the case, Ivy might do something Ariana didn't agree with. So far she'd been unable to decide on the best path forward—but at the same time she didn't want anyone else making that choice for her. "I have," she admitted.

They'd met at Buy the Book, a popular bookstore in the heart of the quaint downtown shopping district, almost two hours ago, and were now sitting on the beach, gazing out at the Atlantic Ocean. Ivy typically worked during the week, but when she'd called to say she could ask one of the volunteers who staffed the library on weekends to step in for her today, even though it was only Friday, Ariana had agreed to get together. As much as she'd avoided Ivy and Cam and anything to do with Mariners in recent years, she was back now, and it was the same old island and the same old people she'd loved before.

Besides, although she'd spent the morning helping Alice reorganize the attic, Ariana had been eager to slip away ever since she'd gotten the unsettling impression that her grandmother knew what she and Ivy had done for Cam. The longer she was with Alice, the more she was tempted to break down in tears and confess everything. And she could be wrong about what her grandmother knew. Maybe she was merely projecting, thanks to her own guilty conscience.

Ivy had visibly tensed at her answer, but she didn't respond right away. When she did speak, she said, "You've been tempted, or you've actually told someone?"

The fear in her voice reminded Ariana that they were in this together. Whatever she did would affect Ivy—and vice versa. That was another aspect of the problem that made it especially thorny. "I've been tempted," she clarified, sending her friend a sideways glance. "What about you?"

"I've been tempted, too, I guess. It would be nice to off-load such a terrible secret—to have someone, especially someone in authority, reassure me and tell me we did the right thing. Not to worry. But I'm not confident it would go that way." She wrapped the shawl she'd brought tighter around her shoulders. It wasn't quite warm enough to get in the water, or even to strip down to their suits so they could sunbathe. A chill wind rushed in from the sea, ripping at their clothes and rustling the tall grass behind them. "Besides, who would I tell? I didn't leave the island the way you did. Everyone here knows everyone else, and as famous as Cam has become, thanks to his work, he's better known than almost anyone else."

Other than the influx of wealthy families who came during the summer, they had a couple of local authors who wrote popular fiction and an aging actress who called Mariners home. But Ivy was right. Cam was probably as famous as any of them—with the possible exception of the actress. "Anything scandalous, especially about him, would travel around the island like wildfire," she agreed.

That wasn't true about New York, however. There, no one knew Cam. No one even knew *of* him, except maybe a select few in architectural circles. Once Ariana had reached what she termed "escape velocity"—meaning she no longer missed the island quite so badly and had adjusted to her new life—she'd wanted to confide in someone. She'd thought discussing it with the right person might help her cope with the guilt, so she'd contemplated going to a therapist. She probably would've seen someone, if she hadn't been afraid a professional would be legally obligated to notify the authorities. Whoever she told might find it a moral obligation, even if it wasn't a legal one.

Just in case, she'd decided not to trust anyone, even someone with a psych degree. But once she'd started seeing Bruce on a regular basis, she'd thought she might tell him. Not only was he one of the most intelligent people she'd ever known, he was well-read, measured, kind. Even when she'd broken up with him, he'd accepted it graciously. If anyone could offer sound advice on such a difficult dilemma, she felt he could.

It was the risk of having him look at her like he never really knew her, like she was reprehensible for doing something so unethical, that kept her from breathing a word of it. She believed he'd be understanding of her choice at sixteen. She'd been only a kid when she lied for Cam. But she'd kept her silence for so long, well after becoming an adult. That was where she thought Bruce would find fault with her.

And maybe she deserved it. So she'd come home. To figure out how to make what she'd done right.

But then she'd seen Cam, and all the doubt and turmoil she'd waded through over the years had come rushing back in one big tidal wave. How could she betray him when it mattered most? Like her, he'd been no more than a kid when Emily went missing. She didn't truly believe he could harm someone—*murder* someone—least of all a young girl, did she?

"I thought sharing what I knew might give me a better perspective," she confessed to Ivy. "There was this guy at work. Twelve years older than me. Divorced. Quiet. Thoughtful. I believed he'd be a good sounding board. But…"

"You never told him?"

They had the beach almost to themselves. There was only one small cluster of people who sat, burrowing deep into their sweatshirts, about fifty yards away. But those people weren't paying any attention to Ariana and Ivy. They were too caught up in their own conversation, and for that, Ariana was glad. Having some private time with her old friend felt good.

Maybe she should never have pushed Ivy away.

"No. Because then I'd be putting him exactly where we are now—trying to decide how to navigate this nightmare. What's right. What's wrong. What we should do."

"Who was the guy?"

"Someone at my publisher—Bruce Derringer."

"You mentioned him to me once on the phone. He's the man you've been seeing for the last couple of years, right?"

Ariana didn't remember that conversation. She'd mostly dodged Ivy's calls, and when they did talk, she got off the phone as soon as possible. Just hearing her friend's voice dredged up the doubt and confusion she'd been trying so hard to avoid. "Yes."

"You're no longer with him?"

"I broke it off when I quit my job."

"Why?"

Ariana watched a seagull striding confidently down the beach, scavenging for insects, mollusks, carrion or whatever else it could find. "He was nice. And we got on quite well. But I never loved him the way I should."

Ivy adjusted her ponytail. Her hair was as long as Ariana's these days, but it was a sleek, gorgeous black instead of a mix of blonds and light browns, like Ariana's. "How'd he take the news?"

"He was disappointed. He would've liked the relationship to continue. But…I doubt it came as a huge surprise that I didn't feel as strongly as I should."

"You don't think you'll ever go back to him…"

"Not now that we're no longer working at the same place."

Scooping up a handful of sand, Ivy let it sift through her fingers. "What are you going to do after summer ends? You're not considering staying here, are you?"

"I'm thinking about it. Maybe for a year or two. Alice is getting old. I don't like the idea of her being alone, especially during the winter."

"What about your apartment? You'll just continue to pay?"

"I gave it up and put my stuff in storage, which doesn't cost nearly as much."

"That was smart. I'd love to have you stay. I bet she would, too. But what will you do for work? Or are you now independently wealthy?" she joked.

Ariana pulled her knees in to her chest. "Definitely not wealthy. But I have some money saved up, enough to carry me until I find something. I know it could be a while. There aren't a lot of jobs on the island."

"You could always freelance as an editor," Ivy said. "Or write a book yourself. You've talked about that now and then."

"I'm considering it."

"Even if you're not quite ready for that there're plenty of job openings for the summer," Ivy said. "But I admit I'm surprised you quit with your publisher. I thought you really liked it."

"I did." Ariana tucked her hair behind her ears to keep it from flying across her face. "I just…needed a change."

"Did Bruce have anything to do with your decision to come back?"

"To a point. I knew if I didn't leave the company, maybe even the city, I'd continue seeing him. There's nothing wrong with him, nothing I don't like. It's just…I wasn't in love, and I didn't want to wake up married and staring down the rest of my life with the feeling that I hadn't really chosen my own future."

"You could've gone to Chicago or somewhere else if you were merely trying to get away from Bruce."

"I had to come here. Learning that Emily's body had been found was the catalyst that finally opened my eyes and made me realize I was just…drifting along with the current, trying to avoid the past without really moving toward a future I could fully embrace."

"It'll be interesting to see what develops while you're here," Ivy said.

"Interesting?" Ariana echoed.

Ivy offered her a sheepish grin. "An understatement. It'll be terrifying."

"It could be," Ariana concurred.

She sobered. "No matter what happens…will you make me a promise?"

Ariana was leery of committing to anything. It was the promises she'd made two decades ago that'd caused her so much grief. "What's that?"

"If you decide to come forward, you'll tell me before you do it? I feel…I feel it's only fair we make such an important and impactful decision together."

Ariana had given her word way back when. She owed Ivy as much, didn't she? Probably. But she also knew how much harder it would be to do whatever she ultimately decided if it required someone else, even Ivy, to agree.

"Please?" Ivy said when she hesitated. "What happened has been hard on me, too, you know."

It'd been hard on all of them. Ariana could only imagine what Cam had to be going through. And on top of everything, his marriage was falling apart. "Of course," she said, slinging an arm around Ivy. "We'll figure this out together."

"Thanks." Ivy sagged against her in apparent relief. "It's too cold out here. Do you have any interest in seeing Cam's office? I bet he'd be excited if we stopped by."

Getting to know Cam again was the only way Ariana could determine if he was the man they thought he was—or not. And everything hinged on that. "Sure," she said and cast a final, troubled glance at the ocean before following Ivy back to where they'd parked.

Ever since the private investigator left, Cam had been too distracted to get anything done. He'd texted Melanie one more time to tell her he couldn't understand why she wouldn't answer him, and she finally responded with a brief line, admitting she was fine—as he'd already guessed.

"When are you going to grow up and quit playing games?" he grumbled. He was finally off the hook with her, at least for the time being. But Warner Williams was a different story.

Although the Texan had come off friendly and nonthreatening, Cam could easily imagine why a PI might affect such a "don't mind me" manner.

Had he played his hand as well as Williams had played his? Been likable? Believable? What was Williams thinking now?

Courtney came to the door, drawing him out of his thoughts by clearing her throat. "I don't know if you remember with…with everything that's been going on," she said, "but I have a dentist appointment this afternoon."

She'd mentioned that? If so, he hadn't logged it in his brain. But losing her help for a couple of hours was the least of his concerns. "What time?"

"It's in thirty minutes. I'm taking off now, okay?"

"That's fine." He tossed her a cordial smile. "Here's hoping you don't have any cavities."

"Thanks. I hate the dentist," she said with a grimace and left.

Normally, Cam would've been thrilled to have the rest of the day to himself. He didn't have to hurry home at five, wouldn't have Melanie on his back, accusing him of being interested in Courtney if he was a few minutes late. And he wouldn't have to agree to go over to the neighbors' house for dinner or drinks. He understood that after being home all day with a four-year-old, Melanie craved adult conversation—more stimulation in general. He'd encouraged her to take some online classes, finish her degree and do something with it. But she wasn't interested in that. She wanted him to be with her all the time—something he couldn't do and still maintain his business—and she must've told the neighbors that he wasn't treating her right, because their attitude toward him had cooled considerably. She'd complained about him to her family, too, which made his relationship with her parents tenuous.

Fortunately, her sister and brother weren't as easily fooled.

They seemed to understand how difficult Melanie could be and were reserving judgment.

Rather than blasting his favorite playlist on iTunes and throwing himself into his work, as he normally would've done given such an opportunity, Cam rocked back in his seat and stared at his phone. He was tempted to call Ariana. He'd been thinking about her all day—when he wasn't speaking to a client, scrambling to meet a pressing deadline, trying to prove his concern to Melanie or worrying about whether he'd wind up spending the rest of his life behind bars. Seeing Ariana and Ivy last night had been an oasis in the middle of the vast desert that'd become his life, because it'd allowed him to feel something positive for a change.

He craved more of that. But in recent years, he hadn't been good about keeping up his relationship with Ariana. And considering what was going on with the Hutchins case, reaching out so soon could come across as an attempt to charm her into sticking by his side.

He should've moved away from the island when Ariana did, he decided. That would've been wiser, safer. But he'd never dreamed Emily Hutchins's body would be found. He also doubted he would've fallen into the design niche that'd made him so successful. Had he relocated to New York or LA, he'd probably still be scrabbling along, trying to make a name for himself working on skyscrapers or something else.

Every decision had a cost…

If he'd learned anything, he'd learned that.

His phone went off and he watched it rattle on the desk. It was turned over so he couldn't see the screen, but now that his wife had finally responded, he assumed it was her, calling with instructions on what she expected him to get done around the house while she was gone, and he was loath to hear her voice. He couldn't tolerate her fake excuses for why she hadn't picked up when he'd called so many times before.

But when it stopped ringing, and he finally turned it over, he saw that it hadn't been Melanie—it'd been Ariana.

Instantly regretting that he'd let it go, he touched the screen to call her back, and felt a surge of anticipation and relief when she answered.

"What's up?" he said.

"Not much. Sorry if I interrupted something at work."

"You didn't. I was just…taking care of a few things. And I didn't know if I'd be lucky enough to hear from you today, so I wasn't paying much attention to my phone."

"I wasn't sure you'd *want* to hear from me," she said. "You're such a big shot these days. You have a lot of people vying for your attention."

He smiled at her teasing, wishing they could go back to simpler times, when the three of them would lie around on the beach, go body surfing, throw a party at his place (since his folks were rarely home), or help Ivy in the library that meant so darn much to her. He couldn't believe how far they'd drifted from the foundation of their relationship, which now seemed more solid than anything else he'd ever known. At the time, he hadn't even realized he should be grateful, that life would never get better than it was right then. He'd always been looking for the next best thing, the one thing that would *finally* satisfy the hunger inside him.

But everything he'd grasped since high school had turned into fool's gold. He'd grabbed hold of Melanie and let go of Ivy and Ariana, and now he was doing his best just to keep his life together.

The last thing he needed was to pine for what he'd lost and couldn't get back, however. He also didn't want to feel the lack of real emotion in his current life by comparing it to the warmth and acceptance he'd felt when he was closer to them. They were the sisters he'd never had.

And yet…they didn't share any of the same DNA. Ariana and Ivy could abandon him if they wanted to—and because of his own choices and mistakes, in many ways it felt as if they had.

"I'll always make time for you," he said. "And with Melanie out of town, I won't even have to worry about catching hell for it." He laughed, but the silence that met those words indicated Ariana didn't find the joke funny. "Just kidding," he added.

"I wish you were," she said flatly. "I'm sorry you're not happier in your marriage, Cam."

She sounded sincere, which only made him regret his marriage even more. "Well, let's face it. I've never really been in love with Melanie. We would never have gotten together, if not for the pregnancy. I guess you can't expect too much from a marriage like that."

"Then why'd you settle for it?" Ariana asked emphatically. "When you got engaged, I tried talking you out of it. Making yourself miserable doesn't do Camilla any favors."

"I didn't see how I could *not* marry Melanie," he explained. "What was I going to do, wave as we passed each other here on the island while she was pushing my kid in a stroller down the street? That didn't seem right. I thought Camilla deserved more. I wanted to do right by her."

"So you sacrificed your own happiness, since your parents were never willing to give up anything they wanted for you?"

"Different problem entirely," he insisted.

"Not really."

"They were so busy trying to find a way to make themselves happy that I was just an afterthought, the ball and chain that stopped them from traveling and doing all the other wonderful things they thought would finally make the difference—until I got old enough that they could pawn me off onto other people, or have me stay by myself, and learned that they didn't get along any better even when they could do those things. They were still responsible for whatever trouble I got into, though. And we both know…I found plenty of trouble." That he'd been well-known to the police—for petty stuff—even before Emily Hutchins went missing certainly hadn't helped.

"You wanted to give Camilla the love you never had."

It wasn't *all* Camilla. Melanie had been so determined to have him, so obsessed with him, he hadn't been able to shake her. While that had been cloying and irritating on the one hand, it'd also been comforting and reassuring on the other. It'd made him confident, for the first time, that he'd never be able to destroy the love he was being offered, that Melanie would always be there for him, and finding *durable* love had been important to a boy who'd felt his own parents didn't really care about him.

But that wasn't something he would ever voice.

"I definitely wanted Camilla to have a complete family," he said, since that part of it was much easier to talk about.

"You've done everything you could, Cam."

"Obviously, that's not true," he argued. "Or I'd have a better relationship with my daughter, and my wife wouldn't be so damn angry and resentful all the time." The love he'd thought he could depend on was still there. He'd been right in that he couldn't get rid of it. She'd never leave him, never divorce him, as he now wished she would. But there was a thin line between love and hate, and Melanie's love had morphed into something dark and ugly—a razor-sharp sword that sliced him daily.

"She's angry and resentful because you can't love her back—not the way she wants you to, anyway," Ariana said.

"She demands too much, not only my complete and utter devotion but my admiration, as well. That's something I just can't fake. And instead of supporting me in having a close relationship with Camilla, she sabotages every effort I make."

"Why?"

"She's jealous of her own daughter. She wants us both all to herself. It's weird."

"If that's true, it's grossly unfair to you *and* Camilla."

"Trust me. It's true. She won't even let me feed Camilla, take her off the island to go to the zoo or put her to bed. She's got to insert herself between us at all times."

"The more I hear about Melanie, the more upset I get. There's something wrong with her, Cam."

His wife was trying to destroy him, and he felt she was accomplishing it. He was bleeding out, but no one could tell because he was doing it one drop at a time. "If she can't have me, no one can—even Camilla. She makes being a father so much more difficult than I'd thought it would be," he admitted, lifting a picture of his wife and daughter from his desk. "Or maybe it's me, and I just suck as a father. We both know I didn't have the best example."

"I don't believe it's you," Ariana stated flatly.

"I appreciate the vote of confidence," he said, but he couldn't fully accept her response as the truth. Their friendship could be blinding her to his shortcomings. Or maybe she needed to be around longer before they became apparent. "Enough about me. What are you doing tonight?"

"I promised my grandmother I'd play bridge with her."

"She still goes to that same group every week?"

"Without fail. So I'm out for tonight. But Ivy and I were thinking about driving over to your office right now. I could see it, if you have the time and wouldn't mind another interruption."

"I'd love to show you around," he said. Lord knew he wasn't getting any work done, anyway.

"Great. We'll be there in a few."

"Sounds good." He started to pull the phone away from his ear but put it right back. "Ariana?"

"What?"

He winced as he rubbed his forehead. Should he say something—or not? He didn't want her to be blindsided… "I need to warn you about something."

"What's that?"

He could hear the apprehension in her voice. "There's a private investigator on the island. He was here at my office not too long ago."

"What did he want?"

"Answers, of course."

"What did you tell him?"

"The same thing I told the police before."

"And? How'd it go? Do you think he believed you?"

"He didn't let on. But I'm guessing he'll want to talk to you and Ivy to…to corroborate my story."

There was a long silence. Then she said, "What's his name?"

"Warner Williams. He's from Texas."

"He came all the way from Texas?"

"Must be good, right?"

"Or he has some connection to the family."

"Unfortunately, I didn't get that impression."

"Are you nervous, Cam?" she asked. "Does having him around scare you?"

She was probably wondering how nervous *she* should be, but he didn't want to alarm her. He couldn't afford to have her act skittish or uncertain when she met Williams, which was partly why he wanted to prepare her.

"No." He tried to sound convincing, but he had a knot in his stomach that wouldn't go away. So much depended on what Ariana and Ivy had to say about that night. Even if they tried to stand by what they'd said to the police before, after so many years it would be far too easy to get it wrong.

five

The lobby of Cam's office was impressive. The building codes on Mariners stipulated that almost any new construction had to have unpainted shingles, which turned gray with weathering. The buildings Cam designed were no different in that regard, but he used more open spaces and clean lines on the inside. Just like farmhouse chic mixed two opposing styles and somehow came up with something new and appealing, he combined the steep roofs, dormer windows and cedar shingles of the traditional Cape Cod home with a touch of contemporary, connecting indoors with outdoors and using more glass and natural light. According to Ivy, he didn't work cheap, but his plans were in such high demand, he was backlogged for months.

"Look at this place!" Ariana exclaimed as Cam showed them around.

"Isn't it great?" Ivy said.

"You like it?" he asked, sounding pleased.

"I *love* it." Ariana had seen pictures of various structures he'd designed in the past, but once he got married, she'd quit following him. She'd been trying to let him go, to forget her feelings for him along with what'd happened their junior year and focus on building her own life. So she hadn't seen his office, although he'd probably posted pictures on social media and/or his website.

"Of course, this building was already here, and I had to work with the existing exterior. The city planners wouldn't let me change that, not in downtown. But I completely gutted it and did what I could with the inside. I figured if I was going to pay for office space, I should at least use the opportunity to showcase my work."

"I'd say you've done that quite well," Ariana said.

Ivy nodded. "So would I."

When he smiled, seemingly flattered by the compliment, his gaze caught Ariana's and held, and the attraction she'd always felt flared up again. He had to be the handsomest man she'd ever met. But it wasn't just that. He was her crush, the boy she'd secretly loved since forever. Back in high school, whenever he snuck through the window to join her for a slumber party at Ivy's, she'd snuggle as close to him as possible while pretending to be asleep.

Embarrassed by that behavior now, she was shocked the truth had never occurred to him.

Or maybe it had. Did he know? As she'd grown less and less confident of the decision she'd made twenty years ago, she'd begun to suspect he'd used her childhood crush to his advantage. Ivy didn't seem to want him that way—or she hid it even better—but she followed Ariana's lead, so if he could convince Ariana to lie for him, he had Ivy, too. And that was exactly what'd happened.

Ariana pulled her gaze from his while steering her mind away from the unwanted feelings he aroused. He was a married man. And even if he wasn't, he'd never offered her anything more than friendship. The last thing either one of them needed was another wrinkle in an already complicated situation.

"This is where I do my thing," he said, leading them into a large corner office on the second floor.

More expansive than the rooms they'd visited so far, Cam's office had brick walls, painted eggshell white, with eight large windows, framed in black, overlooking the cobblestone streets and elm trees lining the central district below.

"What made you decide to work in town instead of on the other side of the island?" Ariana asked as she moved from one set of windows, where she gazed down on Mariner Street, to the other set, where she could see an art gallery that was new since she'd lived on the island and Buy the Book bookstore, which had been around forever. "You could've been on top of the promontory with a view of the sea."

"Then he wouldn't be able to walk to work," Ivy volunteered.

Ariana felt her eyebrows slide up. "I thought you lived in your parents' house." The last thing she knew, he was purchasing the home he'd grown up in from his folks, who were living in Italy where his mother was born.

"No," he said. "Melanie didn't like my parents' house, so once we got married, I sold it—"

"And bought a home in the *captain's* neighborhood," Ivy broke in to inform her in a supercilious voice.

Stunned that he could afford the captain's neighborhood, Ariana gaped at him. "That's swanky. You must be doing even better than I thought." Everything on the island was insanely expensive, but that was especially true of certain neighborhoods. The Greek Revival homes that'd once belonged to the richest whale oil merchants of the day—like the one Ivy had inherited—were worth millions. But the homes the captains had built in the nineteenth century had become outrageously expensive, too.

That neighborhood was also very trendy these days, so Ariana could see why Melanie might've chosen to live there. Judging from the extravagance of the wedding, Cam's wife enjoyed making others envious.

"It was a risk at the time," he admitted. "I was just getting rolling. But fortunately, it all worked out."

Because of him. Because he'd worked so hard and was damn good at what he did.

Ariana studied him as he shoved his hands into the pockets of faded jeans that had holes in both knees. He was wearing a RVCA T-shirt that fit nicely across his broad shoulders with a pair of Vans and looked far too young to be as successful as he was, especially because his parents, though wealthy, had made him earn everything. "You've done a lot to try to please Melanie," she said.

"Too bad none of it's worked," he joked with a lopsided grin.

Ariana exchanged a look with Ivy. The woman they'd met only days before Cam tied the knot had done little to impress them. But Ariana had chalked that up to the stress Melanie was under because of the wedding. Melanie was also ten years younger than they were, only twenty-two then, and expecting a baby. It wasn't entirely unreasonable that she'd be prickly and territorial and feel threatened by Cam's closest friends, both of whom were female *and* single—especially because Ariana's feelings for Cam weren't quite as platonic as she pretended. Maybe Melanie's intuition had alerted her even though Cam seemed oblivious.

Ivy had had no problem complaining about Cam's wife, however. After Melanie had made it clear they weren't to stand in his line, since they weren't male and having traditional pictures for her wedding album was vastly important to her—and she'd refused to include them on her side—she'd made even more of a statement by seating them at the periphery of the party during the reception, well away from Cam, as if they were fifth cousins or new acquaintances or something. Ivy had been so angry, she'd leaned over and whispered, "What a little bitch."

Ariana had purposely said nothing. She had no right to complain. She didn't like Melanie any better than Ivy did, but she figured that was because she wanted Cam for herself. The only thing she'd done was try to make sure he loved Melanie enough to enter the marriage and wasn't doing it only for the sake of the baby—although that talk a few days before the ceremony had fallen on deaf ears. The die had already been cast. "It doesn't seem fair," she said as she turned away from the window to survey the rest of his office.

Distracted by a message or something that'd come up on his computer, he'd sat down at his desk. "What doesn't seem fair?" he asked as he started to type.

"You had to deal with such selfish parents," Ariana said. "And now you're saddled with a spoiled, petty, dysfunctional wife."

He stopped typing long enough to slant her a quizzical glance. "And here I thought you liked her," he said with a chuckle.

He always tried to turn everything into a joke. That was how he handled emotionally sticky subjects—with a pithy comment—or by avoiding them altogether. But he was obviously struggling in his marriage, and that caused Ariana to second-guess everything she'd thought she believed before landing on Mariners—that he'd manipulated her into covering for him on the night Emily Hutchins went missing, that she should've told the truth regardless of the consequences, that she was coming back to right a wrong. "Other than when I tried to talk to you before the wedding, I've just been keeping my mouth shut because I wanted you to be happy," she admitted with a slight shrug.

"I bet you're glad she's gone for a few days." Ivy was studying a huge painting of a whaleboat that hung on the wall behind his desk, but her comment proved she was listening.

Finished with whatever small task he'd taken care of, he stood up and opened his mouth to respond. He was smiling as though he'd joke it off again. But he must've thought better of that, because he sobered as he closed his mouth and simply nodded.

Ariana frowned. The breakdown of Cam's marriage didn't bode well for little Camilla. That made her sad. But the way he dealt with his wife—how hard he'd tried to make his marriage work—brought Ariana a small amount of comfort and reassurance. The type of guy who would harm a twelve-year-old girl would not put up with someone like Melanie.

Would he?

Ivy sat at the granite-topped island in the middle of the kitchen she'd had remodeled, with a little design help from Cam, shortly after her grandmother died, eating an egg-and-bacon burrito with homemade guacamole and salsa. She loved to cook. And her salsa had turned out pretty darn good tonight—so good that she wished she had someone to share it with.

Even though she'd grown up on Mariners and knew almost everyone who lived on the island, year-round, anyway, she found herself getting lonelier and lonelier as she grew older, especially during the winter months when a thick fog blanketed the island or a strong nor'easter began to blow, keeping everyone huddled inside their homes. During those stretches of bad weather, she rattled around her Greek Revival mansion, cleaning, knitting, cooking, canning and reading—each of which was enjoyable, except for the fact that she often felt cut off and forgotten. Since Cam had married, and they'd had so little contact, and Ariana had moved to New York, Ivy could go days without any real social interaction, besides what she got from working at the library. Even then, there were weeks at a time when the library had to close because of power outages caused by the bigger storms that ripped through.

Last year she'd thought she might go stir-crazy. She'd considered getting a roommate—anything to break the silence and the monotony—but who would she invite? The people she knew best, those she'd be willing to live with, had homes, husbands and families of their own. In so many ways, she was the luckiest person in the world—someone who didn't have to worry about money, someone who lived in a beautiful, exclusive area others paid a fortune to visit, someone who cared about the library and felt a great sense of purpose—and yet…something was missing. Her life wasn't nearly as idyllic as others probably saw it.

Maybe things would be different if she had a partner, kids. She wanted both. But if the pool of potential friends was small on the island, the pool of potential mates was even smaller. And it was just as hard to meet someone on the internet, since getting together in person required so much effort, and moving to the island wasn't an option for many people her age.

Ariana's question, asking if the library had become a bit of a millstone, rose to the forefront of Ivy's mind. She'd denied it at the time. She didn't want to face reality. But she did feel stuck—in the same way people who had a prestigious job that paid too handsomely to leave could feel stuck. People in that position might want to get out and experience other things, but how did they justify leaving something that was so good?

Maybe Ariana would stay after the summer was over. That would make a big difference in Ivy's life. She didn't enjoy any of her other friends quite as much as her girlhood bestie. Despite all the time they'd spent apart, and as stilted as their relationship had become in recent years, it felt as though they were falling right back into step.

The doorbell rang.

Assuming it would be Ariana, that the card playing must've ended early, she was taken aback when she opened the door to find a behemoth of a man standing on her stoop, holding a cowboy hat in one hand.

"Can I help you?" she asked, involuntarily taking a small step back.

"Yes, ma'am." He smiled and lifted his free hand, as if to put her at ease. "My name is Warner Williams, and I was hopin' to have a word with you."

Ivy's stomach dropped to her knees. As they were walking to Cam's office, Ariana had warned her about Williams—and why he'd come to Mariners. "I'm…um…in the middle of dinner," she said. "Can I ask what this is about?"

He handed her his card. *Warner Williams, Bucking Bronco Investigations.* Since she'd already known he was a private detective, the name of his company wasn't what caught her eye. It was the line below his name that made her catch her breath: "We get the job done."

"I'm sorry I've come at a bad time," he said when she looked up again. "If it's okay with you, I'll just wait out here. This is a gorgeous street, and the weather's beautiful, so I won't mind one bit. You take all the time you need."

He was going to wait outside?

She was tempted to tell him she had plans after dinner, that he'd have to come back another time. But it wasn't true, and she was afraid he'd be able to tell. She didn't want to sound as though she wasn't open to talking to him or had something to hide. And yet she *didn't* want to talk to him because she *did* have something to hide. "You—you haven't said what this is about."

She knew what he wanted, and she was worried he knew that she knew, but she was afraid he'd find it odd if she didn't at least ask—kind of like all the crime shows she'd watched over the years where the police questioned a husband about the suspicious death of his wife, and while feigning grief he didn't even think to ask how she died.

"It's about Emily Hutchins."

"Right. I…I thought so," she said to cover for herself either way. "Okay. Let me finish eating and…I'll be right back."

He nodded as he settled his hat on his head. "Thank you for bein' willin' to take the time."

"Of course. I feel so bad for her family. I want whoever did this to have to answer for what they've done." She struggled to bear up beneath an onslaught of guilt. Was she babbling? Saying too much?

"We all do, ma'am. That poor little girl deserves justice, and I'm goin' to make sure she gets it."

Why did hearing the conviction in his voice terrify her? Ivy had been telling the truth; she did want poor Emily to receive justice. Why wouldn't she? It wasn't Cam who'd killed her. He'd had nothing to do with what happened to Emily Hutchins. Ivy firmly believed that, or she wouldn't have lied for him when Emily went missing.

Swallowing against a dry throat, she nodded before closing the door. But instead of going back to the kitchen to finish eating, she leaned against the panel and squeezed her eyes shut. She had to think, prepare herself, so that she didn't contradict anything she'd said before.

That wouldn't be easy. She had no idea how much the police had written down when they'd talked to her. Warner probably had access to the police file, which included her statement, but she didn't.

She had only her memory to go by, and it'd been twenty years.

six

It was Debbie Tyler's turn to host the "Mariners Island Bridge Club." Ariana had accompanied Alice to bridge night many times as a child, so she'd been to Debbie's house before. She'd sit and watch a movie, munching on popcorn in the living room while the adults played cards somewhere nearby.

Occasionally, another member of the club brought a grandchild, too. Having a playmate made it extra fun. But Ariana had loved coming, regardless. Even before she was old enough to play cards with them, which she started doing her freshman year, she'd felt like part of the group and enjoyed the friendship they offered each other, the banter, the laughter—and the gossip.

Except she wasn't enjoying the gossip tonight. They were discussing Emily Hutchins. Ariana couldn't remember ever being so uncomfortable. She tried to concentrate on the game instead of the conversation, but almost every time she looked up, she found her grandmother watching her closely.

She doesn't know, she told herself, even though it felt like Alice could see right through her. *She would've said something.*

That was probably true—unless Alice had been okay with the way things had gone, at least until Emily's body was found. Was she second-guessing herself, too? Sometimes, like when she was standing in Cam's office a few hours ago, Ariana was certain she'd done the right thing. And other times she was equally convinced she'd made the gravest of errors.

"I feel *awful* for that girl's family," Diana Fahrenbruck said.

Tena Burns, who was sitting to Ariana's right, straightened the giant solitaire on her finger while waiting for Diana, her partner in the game, to take a turn. "I saw her poor sister coming down the street as I was stepping out of the White Sand Gallery the other day."

Alice had been studying her cards. At this, she lowered them. Since she was Ariana's partner, they were facing each other across one of the small square tables Debbie had put up. "Jewel's back on the island?"

"Apparently," Tena said as Diana took the trick with a ten of hearts.

Jen Miller was seated at the other table. "What about her parents?" she asked. "Are they here on Mariners, too?"

Usually, each foursome had a separate conversation going. But every once in a while a subject came up that grabbed the attention of everyone.

Since there'd never been another murder like Emily's on Mariners, this subject was one of them.

Brenda DeJesus, also from the other table, answered Jen. "I think they're still in Iowa. When they were on the news last night, they appeared to be standing in front of an office building in their area. Wherever it was, it wasn't here."

"I bet they can't bear the thought of coming back to Mariners," Diana commented. "I wonder if they even know Jewel's on the island."

"If they do, I can't see how they could be happy about it," Shirley Reagan chimed in from the other table. "I'd be afraid whoever murdered my youngest daughter would kill my oldest. It could be that someone on the island has it out for the family."

"Sounds morbid, but I'd be afraid of that, too," Brenda's partner, Linda Phillips, said.

Looking past her grandmother, Ariana saw Brenda nod. "There's no way I'd come to Mariners alone," Brenda said. "Not if I was her."

"How do you know she's alone?" Jen Miller piped up. "She's got to be in her thirties. She could have a boyfriend or a husband by now."

"I don't get the impression she's married," Brenda said. "She's done a lot of media interviews lately, and I've never seen her with a man. Besides her father, she's never referenced one, either."

"What a brave girl," Diana said.

"She's determined to find her sister's killer," Linda added in agreement. "That's got to be why she's here. She's putting pressure on the police."

Alice had taken her turn at bridge, quietly and quickly, but Tena was so caught up in the discussion she wasn't paying enough attention and the game stalled. "How do you know?" she asked Linda.

"I follow her on Facebook. Don't you?"

"I didn't think to look her up," Tena replied.

Brenda shook her head. "Her posts are absolutely heart-wrenching. I donated to help the investigation, but I'm considering giving more."

Tena, after a nudge from Alice to remind her to play, finally put down a five of spades. "I didn't realize they were raising money."

As Ariana considered her next move in the game, Linda said, "I can send you the link. I donated, too."

After Ariana played, Diana took another trick—her fourth in the round. "Last I heard, they'd collected quite a bit of money."

"These things *take* a lot of money," Shirley commented.

Until Emily came up, Ariana had been chatting right along with the rest of them. To avoid being conspicuously silent, she spoke up as Alice put down a four of diamonds. "Cam said the Hutchins family has hired a private investigator."

This comment seemed to interrupt both games. "*Cam* told you that?" Tena asked.

Ariana drew a deep breath. Everyone was looking at her. No doubt they all remembered that there'd been some suspicion swirling around Cam. If *anything* remarkable happened on Mariners, news of it traveled through the local community almost immediately. "Yeah," she said, trying to play it off as nothing. "He stopped by Cam's office today."

"Don't tell me the police think Cam was involved, after all," Brenda said. "There's no way he'd ever harm anyone."

Ariana studied her cards even though she already knew which one she was planning to play next. "He's not officially a suspect," she said. "The investigator is just following up on every possible lead, trying to see if anyone's story has changed, I guess."

"Whoever hurt that girl couldn't be a local," Diana said.

"Exactly," Linda agreed. "No one else has gone missing since, and it's been twenty years. That says something."

"But he was one of the last people to see her that night," Jen pointed out.

"Doesn't mean anything," Shirley argued. "Would he have stayed on the island, married, started a family and built a business on Mariners if he was guilty of such a terrible crime?"

"Of course not," Brenda replied. "It can't be Cam. It has to have been a tourist, someone who felt safe doing what he did because he could get on a plane and fly away."

"That's what I think, too," Tena said.

Diana popped a potato chip into her mouth. "From what I've heard, they don't have anything on him except circumstantial evidence."

"None of that matters, anyway. He has an alibi." Tena turned to Ariana. "You were with him at the time Emily went missing, weren't you?"

Ariana's chest constricted, making it hard to breathe. The lie she'd told seemed to be growing bigger by the moment. She'd never been more aware of the fact that she could be standing in the way of justice. Was she right for doing what she'd done? Wrong? A fool?

Trying to ignore the penetrating stares of those around her, she cleared her throat. "Yeah. Ivy and I were both with him when Emily went missing. It couldn't be Cam." She spoke with conviction, because she had to. The questions would only continue and grow more and more pointed if she didn't.

The conversation finally moved on to other topics. But all Ariana could think about as they continued to play was hanging out with Cam near the lighthouse, where Emily's body had been found, for most of that long-ago evening.

Ivy paced back and forth in her 1820s drawing room, watching for Ariana to come through the front gate. She'd been agitated ever since the private investigator had appeared at her door, and her anxiety certainly hadn't eased since she'd admitted him into the house and allowed him to grill her about the night Emily Hutchins went missing.

It was *so* hard to speak with any authority when you were lying. She felt certain he knew she wasn't being entirely truthful, too. Why else would he ask the same questions over and over, altering his phrasing only slightly each time as if that might elicit a different answer?

Had she messed up? Forgotten some small detail she'd mentioned to the police two decades ago that someone in her situation would definitely not forget? The voiceover in almost every true crime show she watched talked about some suspect, or one or more witnesses, "changing their story" as though that was the pivotal moment when the police knew they'd found the thread that would unravel the whole mystery.

She desperately hoped she hadn't inadvertently changed *her* story.

At last, she spotted Ariana on the sidewalk outside and hurried to open the front door.

"Bridge run late tonight?" she asked as her friend came up the walkway.

Ariana checked her watch. "Not really. It usually goes until ten. Once I got your text, my grandmother and I left earlier than everyone else."

Maybe it only seemed as though it had taken forever because Ivy had been counting the minutes until they could talk. "Was it any fun?"

"I like my grandmother's friends. I don't mind going with her now and then."

In other words, it probably wasn't something she'd attend if not for Alice. Ivy understood how that went. She used to quilt with her own grandmother, even though she never had any real interest in picking up a needle and thread. "Who was there?"

"The same people who always go," she replied.

Ivy peered up and down the street, halfway expecting Mr. Williams to jump out from the shadows and demand to speak with Ariana before Ivy could go over what they'd already discussed.

"What's wrong?" Ariana asked. "Your text said you needed to talk to me right away."

Ivy held the door for her friend. "I do," she said but wasn't about to explain until she could speak without even the remote possibility of being overheard.

Once her friend was inside, she locked the door and waved Ariana into the kitchen. "Would you like something to drink?"

"No, thanks." She sat on a stool at the island where Ivy had eaten dinner. "Now, can you tell me what's going on? You're acting strange."

Circling the room so she could pull down the blinds, Ivy kept her voice low out of an abundance of caution. "That private detective—Warner Williams—came to see me."

"Wow," Ariana murmured, slumping over slightly as Ivy climbed onto the stool across from her. "He didn't waste any time, did he?"

"No. And I bet you would've heard from him tonight, too, if you hadn't gone to bridge."

"Thank God I wasn't home."

"I wish *I* hadn't been home. I was caught flat-footed, trying to remember what we said before," she complained.

"Maybe I *could* use a glass of wine," Ariana said.

Ivy got up to open a bottle. "Cab okay?"

"Right now I'd take rubbing alcohol," she said. "I just need a drink. Besides, I might as well hang out for a bit. I can't go back to my grandmother's yet. I'm afraid he'll be there waiting for me."

"You think he'd show up this late?"

Obviously agitated, Ariana nibbled on her bottom lip. "Who's to say what he'll do? He only cares about getting the information he came here to get. I doubt he's worried about being polite."

Ivy put two glasses filled with a J brand dry cabernet on the granite countertop and slid back onto her seat. "What will Alice tell him if he shows up at the door?"

If anything, Ariana looked even more worried. "Hopefully, she's in bed and won't answer."

"And if she does?"

"I have no idea." Ariana shook her head. "The way she looks at me since I've been home..."

"You don't have to worry about her," Ivy insisted. "She'd take a bullet for you."

"I believe that, too. But this is way out of the ordinary. If she believes we covered for Cam, she could pressure me to come forward."

The conflict once again threatened to tear Ivy in two. "Maybe we *should* come forward."

"I've decided we should a thousand times," Ariana said. "The secret is eating me up inside. But then I think about Cam."

Ivy turned her glass as she stared at the liquid inside it. "He'll be okay, won't he?"

"That's just it. I don't know that he will. I'm afraid the police, this investigator, Emily's family—they'll all focus on him instead of continuing to search for the real culprit. That sort of thing has happened with plenty of other crimes."

Ivy didn't say it, but there were a few rare moments when she wondered if he *was* the real culprit. He'd been so troubled back then, so reckless. Maybe something strange had happened, some sort of accident, and he'd been too afraid to admit it. "What's going to happen?"

Ariana shook her head. "I have no idea."

"Can we go to prison for lying?" Ivy asked quietly.

"Probably."

The sick feeling Ivy had been battling since speaking with Warner Williams grew worse. "Even if we did it with the best of intentions?"

"If you were a district attorney, would you take that into consideration?" Ariana asked.

Ivy shrugged. "Maybe. If we came forward on our own."

"But we don't plan to do that."

"I know. I don't see how we can, not in the middle of this media frenzy," Ivy said. "The mere fact that we lied will make Cam look guilty."

"And if he's convicted in the press…"

"Things could go very badly for him."

"Yes." Ariana drained her glass. "So…what did Williams ask you?"

Ivy closed her eyes as she went over the conversation in her mind. "He was most interested in the timeline."

Ariana began to rub her forehead. "Because everything hinges on that."

"You don't think he'd ever try to play us against each other, do you?" Ivy asked.

"What do you mean by that?"

"If he thinks something isn't adding up, he could change what I told him and present it to you as if it came from me. If you deviate from what you said before—if only to agree with me—he'll have created a discrepancy between what we said in the past and what we're saying in the present."

Ariana straightened. "Could he do something like that?"

"If the police don't have to tell the truth—and I've learned from watching various true crime shows that they're under no legal obligation to be truthful in their interrogations—

Williams could certainly play the same game. Since he's not a cop, he can probably take it even further."

Ariana pressed a hand to her chest. "That's terrifying!"

"It is. Maybe I should've refused to talk to him."

"What reason could you have given for that?"

"I don't know." Ivy frowned. "I couldn't come up with one at the time—not one that didn't sound hinky."

"Shit," Ariana cursed. "We have no good options."

Ivy finished her wine. "That's been the problem from the beginning."

"All we can do is hope they find the real killer soon. The longer it goes, the harder this is going to get."

"I wonder if Cam is worried that we might crack under the pressure."

"He has to be," Ariana said. "I'd be scared. Wouldn't you? It feels as though we hold his fate in our hands."

Ivy blew out her cheeks as she sighed. Emily's parents had pointed an accusing finger at him almost from the beginning. Ivy knew if she and Ariana gave them even more reason to believe he'd hurt their beloved daughter, they'd move heaven and earth to get what they believe was justice. Jewel was on that same bandwagon now, too. And the police, to be able to solve the case and escape the tight spot they were in, could easily decide to make sure Cam was punished… "I think we do."

Barring the months directly following Emily Hutchins's disappearance, until enough time had passed that all seemed normal again, Ariana had never felt unsafe on Mariners. The island could grow slightly foreboding in the winter, when so many houses sat empty, the weather turned cold, the wind wailed through the eaves or ghostly fingers of fog curled through the cobblestone streets. But most visitors didn't imagine the island in the off-season. They came to enjoy the quaint shops, the great art galleries, the delicious food, the mild sun and the white sand Mariners was known for during the summer. So it was odd that her hometown would feel somewhat inhospitable and threatening as she let herself out via the wrought iron gate that enclosed Ivy's yard.

Was Williams waiting for her at her grandmother's on the next block?

Staying where she was, she squinted in that direction, trying to cut through the darkness with her eyes. But the trees that lined the sidewalk, with their big, leafy canopies, blocked much of the light from the streetlamps, making it hard to see anyone on the sidewalk leading to her grandmother's, and there were no cars in the street.

Was he already there?

Eleven o'clock was too late for visitors. He wouldn't bother them now, she told herself. But since he'd spoken to Ivy, she knew he'd be eager to speak to her—and preferably before Ivy had the chance to warn her of his presence. That meant she couldn't really predict how aggressive he might be.

Bracing herself in case she encountered him, she walked beyond Ivy's line of sight and stopped. She felt too uneasy to go home, too wound up. She wouldn't be able to sleep even if she didn't bump into the investigator. She knew she'd have to talk to him soon, probably tomorrow, if not tonight.

After pulling her phone from her clutch, she texted Cam.

You still awake?

Yeah. Just catching up on some things for work. Why?

He'd allowed his career to become his whole life—that seemed to be the only place he could find joy. On top of all her other conflicted emotions, Ariana felt sad for him. She also felt a renewed desire to protect him and make his life better, which definitely wasn't what she'd initially come home to do.

She was about to let him know that the investigator had quizzed Ivy, but she was afraid to do that via text. If the police ever had reason to get a search warrant that included access to her phone, it would be possible for them to read their exchange, and anything that wasn't completely private made her skittish.

Can I stop by and see your place?

Of course. Is Ivy coming, too?

No, it's just me.

Come on over.

He sent his address, and she cast a final glance at Ivy's. There was no reason not to invite Ivy except she was eager to be with Cam on her own, and that wasn't something she was willing to examine too closely.

Although she didn't recognize Cam's exact street, she was familiar with the general area. It would take fifteen or twenty minutes to walk there, perhaps longer, because she kept turning around to make sure she wasn't being followed.

"Hey, come on in," he said, stepping to one side as soon as he answered her knock.

She stood back instead and gestured at the house. "Pretty cool place you got here."

"These are historic homes, so, again, I was limited as to what I could do with the outside. But I hope you'll be impressed with the interior."

"If it's anything like your office, I'm sure I will be."

She could smell a hint of his soap or cologne when she stepped past him and wondered if she'd made a mistake coming here when his family was gone, especially so late. It was hard enough to hide her attraction to him under regular circumstances.

"It's chilly out for June," he commented as he closed the door.

"Whoever said they'd never spent a colder winter than a summer in San Francisco has never been on Mariners in June."

"Agreed. Dude was a lightweight," he added with a lopsided smile.

She knew he was referring to Mark Twain, but it was a little-known secret that Twain didn't actually say that. She didn't bother to correct him, though.

Cam led her into a large living room with gleaming hardwood floors, Turkish rugs and large, modern chandeliers hanging from the ceiling. Leather couches, coffee tables and various side chairs were arranged throughout the room, and a large picture TV hung on one wall. "You've really opened it up in here," she said.

"The older homes in this area are typically cut into so many rooms. I prefer fewer rooms and more space—almost loftlike. And Melanie grew up on the mainland. She hadn't even visited Mariners until a friend talked her into coming for the summer and waiting tables after her first year of college. So she was used to having a much bigger kitchen than the one that was here before. I swear it was the size of a small bathroom. Anyway, I had to come up with ways to modernize—to make the place less functionally obsolete and more comfortable without everything warring with the historical context."

Again, the walls were brick, only this time they weren't painted, and it didn't look as though the building department had given Cam as much leeway with the windows as he probably would've liked. Still, he'd made the most out of the bones of the building, and it appeared that Melanie—or whoever had done the decorating—had done an admirable job. His house could be featured in an architectural magazine or a decorating magazine or both. Maybe that had been the goal—another shining example of his work.

"Would you like me to take your jacket?"

She stripped off the leather coat she'd worn to bridge, and he hung it on an elaborate yet unique coat tree next to some built-in bookshelves that were so extensive his living room almost resembled a library—at least on that side. Ariana guessed he'd put them where the staircase used to be. The new staircase was made of wrought iron and was no longer against the wall.

"I love your shelves," she said.

"Thanks. I built them myself."

She gaped at him. "You're into carpentry, too?"

"Not really. I don't have the time to devote to it. But I was eager to try my hand at a few things right after we bought the place."

Ariana ran her finger along the gleaming wood. "It's too bad you don't have more time."

"Maybe I'll be able to get back into it one day." He gestured at a chair. "Have a seat. I'll grab a bottle of wine."

"None for me," she said. "I've had a few glasses already."

"What's one more?"

She hesitated, then shrugged. It wasn't as if she planned to drive. "Okay. If you're having one, I will, too. Then you can show me the house."

"Rosé okay?"

"Whatever you've got is fine."

A cork popped in the other room. Then he returned with two stemmed glasses—overfilled in her opinion, considering she'd at first tried to refuse—and handed one to her. "Ready for the grand tour?"

"I don't know. Since I quit my job, I'm already feeling like an underachiever." She waved her glass around her. "I'm afraid seeing all of this—everything you've accomplished—will only make it worse."

His eyebrows came together. "Don't say that. You wouldn't want this if it came with the same problems I've got."

The pain that accompanied his words made her reach out to touch his arm. He reacted by taking her hand and brushing a kiss across her knuckles before letting go. "It's great to have you back," he said softly.

For no good reason, her heart began to beat out of her chest. She wanted to throw her arms around him and feel his body against hers, reassuringly warm and solid.

He'd be safe. She and Ivy could keep him safe—as long as neither of them talked.

seven

As he showed Ariana around and viewed what he'd created through her eyes, Cam realized that somewhere along the line he'd stopped seeing his own house. He returned to it each day and slept in it every night, but it wasn't the haven he'd expected it to become when he'd been working his ass off to design a better living space than he'd ever designed before.

Once the house was finished, Melanie had hired a professional decorator from New York City to furnish it. The woman she found had cost a fortune and been almost as difficult to deal with as Melanie was. But he'd been pleased with the results—pleased enough that he'd included pictures of various rooms, and the enclosed patio that looked out onto the backyard, in a brochure he sent to prospective clients.

After all the time, effort and money he'd put into it, he should feel more attached to this house, he thought. But he and Melanie hadn't formed many fond memories here. The construction process had created more stress than their fragile relationship could handle, and the more they bickered, the more he stayed at the office to avoid her, and the more he stayed at the office to avoid her, the more Melanie punished him when he *did* come home.

They'd been caught in a downward spiral for so long. These days all he could think about was when they'd hit bottom. He was looking forward to the relief he'd feel when it was finally over—so long as he could maintain a relationship with his daughter.

As he stood next to the dresser, drinking his wine and watching Ariana wander through the master suite, he told himself not to even think about his wife. Melanie was gone for the time being, and while he missed his daughter, at long last he was able to spend time with a friend he rarely got to see.

But he couldn't help the direction of his thoughts. Ariana reminded him of how much his life had changed since they were young and had hung out day after day—and made him wonder how the genuineness of those relationships had come down to the house of cards that was his marriage.

While she stepped out onto the balcony, he picked up the family photograph Melanie had insisted they take last Christmas. Something had changed recently, if only inside him.

"You really outdid yourself."

At the sound of Ariana's voice, he put down the picture and reclaimed his glass. "You like it?"

"Of course I like it." She gestured around her. "It's clean, spare, tasteful. You have a gift, my friend. I'm sure you've had a thousand people tell you the same thing, but I'm happy to be number one thousand and one."

Her face lit up when she spoke. Although she'd been a tall, gangly teenager—and his mother frequently commented on how unattractive she was—somewhere in her twenties, Ariana's features had matured and created what almost anyone would call a beautiful face. And the pride in her voice reminded him of what it was like to feel good about himself, for a change. "The other thousand people don't matter to me like you do," he said.

Although he meant every word, she gave him a dubious look. "If that was true, I would've heard from you a little more often in recent years."

"The night I got Melanie pregnant changed everything, Ariana. Since I married her, I've just been trying to make things work."

"Most people don't have to give up their friends," she pointed out.

He lifted his glass. "Most people aren't married to someone like Melanie. She's never been able to understand why I'd want to talk to another woman, let alone care about one."

"She's determined to control every move you make."

He heard the accusation in that statement, and he supposed he deserved it. He'd had to choose, and, because of his daughter, he hadn't chosen his friends. "She claims she doesn't care if I hang out with my guy friends…"

"Is that true?" Ariana challenged.

There hadn't been many boys his age who stayed on the island year-round, and he'd always preferred Ariana and Ivy to the ones who did. But as an adult, he'd been able to find more male friends. Eddie from college was one of them, but Eddie lived in Virginia, and if he were ever to go to Virginia to see him, Melanie would throw a fit. "No. She gives me trouble every time I want to be with anyone else. She thinks she should have all my time and attention."

"And you've done what you can for Camilla's sake."

He took another sip of wine. "Camilla's a big part of it. But

I think I'm also trying to compensate for the fact that Melanie's right—I've never really been in love with her." He'd never come right out and admitted that before. He'd known that acknowledging it would only undermine his efforts to stay with Melanie. But now with Ariana back in town, knowing him as well as she did, he couldn't hold the truth inside any longer.

Maybe that was the change he'd noticed—the change he felt marked the beginning of the end.

"Then your marriage isn't going to survive, regardless," she said.

"Probably not. We fight too much as it is."

Lines formed on Ariana's normally smooth forehead. "You're obviously unhappy, Cam. Why don't you just divorce her and get it over with?"

"You already know the answer to that question."

"Because of Camilla."

He breathed out a heavy sigh. "Yes. Because of Camilla. I know how hard Melanie will make it for me to see her if I leave."

"So…where will it all end?" she asked.

"I don't know. But I wish it would end now. I wish she'd just…give Camilla to me and stay in Boston."

"Would she ever do that?"

"Give Camilla up?"

"No, I know she wouldn't allow you to have your daughter. I mean stay in Boston."

He groaned. "I doubt it. Now that she's trapped me, she's not going to let me go that easily."

Ariana hugged herself. "Do you hear yourself? Every time you talk about Melanie, I feel this terrible sense of claustrophobia."

"I'm sorry." He drained his glass. "Let's forget about her for the night, okay?"

Ariana's chest lifted as she drew a deep breath. "Okay, but…I don't think you're going to like what I came to tell you, either."

Anxiety began to sour the wine in his stomach. "Is it about that investigator? Has he contacted you already?" He'd told her about Warner Williams to prepare her, so that she'd be ready. What she had to say about the case and that night was so important.

"Not yet. He's spoken to Ivy, though."

Cam felt his grip tighten on the glass. "When?"

"Tonight."

"Why didn't she call me?"

"She's a little…rattled by the encounter."

Of course she would be. As good-natured and nonthreatening as Williams pretended to be, there was a shrewdness in his eyes that revealed the clever mind at work behind them. "What did she tell him?"

"She tried to stick to the story she gave the police in the beginning."

He cringed. *"Tried?"*

"She told me he kept rephrasing his questions, forcing her to give the same answers over and over. It was awkward and uncomfortable, and she was afraid Williams could tell she wasn't being completely truthful with him."

"He doesn't know she wasn't being completely truthful. That's an interrogation technique."

"Which interrogators use because it's effective."

The walls around him seemed to be closing in as he put his glass back on the dresser. "Was it effective with her?"

"She doesn't *think* she said anything wrong. But it would be nice to get hold of the police file, so we could read our previous statements. It's been a long time, Cam. We're afraid we're going to screw up."

He was afraid of that, too. But there was nothing he could

do. Maybe if he became a suspect and not just a person of interest, he'd have to hire an attorney, and then the attorney could do something. But… "I doubt they're just going to hand that over," he said wryly.

She bowed her head.

"Ariana?"

"What?" she said dully.

"Look at me."

She lifted her gaze.

"I know I've pulled you and Ivy into a terrible situation by claiming I was with you that night. But I *didn't* hurt Emily Hutchins. I swear it. You believe me, don't you?"

She reached out to take his hand. "Of course."

She might only have meant to give him a reassuring squeeze, but he felt such a strong need for contact and reassurance, he threaded his fingers through hers. "You've always been there for me. Thank you."

Something about what he said seemed to strike her oddly. "You know why, don't you?" she said.

The frank tone of her voice and the full weight of her stare suggested she was about to make a big revelation. "Because we're friends?" he guessed.

"You honestly don't know," she said, pulling away.

He felt his eyebrows go up. "What is it?"

"I've been in love with you since the day I met you, Cam," she replied.

Cam felt his jaw drop. He'd always cared a great deal about Ariana—enjoyed her, relied on her, admired her even. But he'd never dreamed her feelings went any further than his own. "You can't be serious."

When tears suddenly filled her eyes, she didn't even have to answer that question. She was *definitely* serious. "You've hidden it well," he said softly. "I—I had no idea."

"*Really?* Because I thought it had to be obvious, not only to you but to everyone."

He'd always thought she was pretty, in spite of what his mother said. His mother didn't know how sensitive, kind, loyal and sweet she could be. But he'd grown up with Ariana; they'd been friends since forever. And he'd been satisfied with their relationship. She'd never acted as though she was let down or disappointed. Even now he could tell she didn't expect anything to change. "I'm sorry I missed it. Maybe it would've stopped me from taking the path I took. Or—" he sighed "—maybe it wouldn't have. You and Ivy were my family. I needed you too badly to risk losing you by trying to turn our friendship into something more."

"There were too many girls who were willing to fulfill your other needs. You definitely didn't need me in that way." She finished her wine and handed him the glass. "I'd better go."

He followed her down the stairs to the entry hall, where she grabbed her coat. He tried to help her put it on, but she resisted his efforts. "I'm sorry, Ariana."

"I know. It's not your fault. I don't expect you to feel something you don't."

"I love you," he said. "I just…I've never looked at you in that way."

She lifted a hand. "You don't have to explain."

He felt terrible, wanted her to stay. He'd been looking forward to spending some time with her—taking a break from his regular life—and didn't think he could survive this loss, too.

She had her hand on the knob when he gently pulled her away from the door. "Why did you finally tell me?" he asked. "Why now? We haven't seen each other for so long. And I'm married."

"Because…"

As he waited for her to formulate her thoughts into words, he tried to read her face. He'd known her for so long he felt he should be able to guess what was coming next. But she shocked him all the same. "I just…I wanted to know if…if you used my feelings to get me to lie for you the night Emily Hutchins went missing."

Straightening, he let go of her and stepped back. He knew she could tell her words had come as even more of a blow than she'd expected when her expression immediately filled with regret.

"I—I didn't mean that."

Except she *had* meant it. What she regretted was letting him know she wasn't as confident of his innocence as she'd always pretended. "Go to the police and tell them the truth," he said softly. "There's no need for you to lie for me anymore. Ivy will back you up. Then you'll both be in the clear."

"No. I won't do that. I'd be too afraid of what would happen to you."

"I'll be fine," he insisted. "I've got this." Suddenly eager for her to leave, he opened the door. "Good night."

She stepped out because he'd moved forward, giving her nowhere else to go, but she immediately turned to face him. "Cam, I'm sorry."

"Don't be," he said and shut the door.

What had she done?

Ariana stood on the steps of Cam's house, feeling sick to her stomach. The doubts and emotions that'd torn her apart, especially since he'd married and she'd lost so much of him to Melanie, had confused her and upset her enough that she'd made a terrible mistake. Not only had she revealed how she'd always felt about him—something she'd hidden for good reason—

she'd hurt him and made what he was going through that much worse.

"Oh, God..." She tried knocking on his door again. But he wouldn't answer, even when she called his name. Had she blown up their entire friendship?

Tears rolled down her cheeks as she began to walk home, and it wasn't long before she was crying hard enough that she was taking big, shuddering breaths. She'd been only sixteen when the boy she loved had been accused of kidnapping a twelve-year-old girl. It was understandable that she'd come to his rescue. It was also understandable that she'd stand by him all these years. She'd never known Cam to be violent.

But that was an excuse. It didn't change the fact that she was lying to the police. Any good citizen understood why that was wrong. She could be obstructing justice, denying critical answers to a grieving family!

Part of her *did* want to go to the authorities and unburden herself, then move on and try to forget. That was one of the main reasons she'd come back to Mariners, wasn't it? To cut free of the guilt and find a way out of the mental anguish?

She should go to the station now, get it over with...

But how? What would her grandmother think? Would Alice applaud such a move or be disappointed in her lack of loyalty? And how would it affect Ivy? She'd at least have to consult with her first. She'd promised she would.

In the end, it wasn't Ivy or Alice that kept her from telling the truth. It was the memory of the look on Cam's face when she'd said what she had about her fear that he might've been using her feelings for his own benefit. Someone who was guilty of murder would not have reacted that way.

The wind was picking up, causing the temperature to drop even further, and because it was June, she wasn't wearing a heavy coat. Her nose and fingers felt like ice cubes as she stopped outside her grandmother's house.

The light was still on inside. She hadn't expected that. If Alice was waiting up for her—perhaps to talk about the conversation at bridge tonight—she couldn't walk in with her eyes red and puffy and her nose running.

Go to the police and tell them the truth… That was what Cam had said.

After pulling her phone out of her purse, she opened her text messages, wishing she'd hear from someone. Anyone. She needed a diversion from the soul-crushing pain of thinking Cam would never speak to her again.

After she managed to pull herself together, at least a little, she wiped her nose with the back of her hand and texted him.

Please forgive me.

No response.

He'd probably never speak to her again. She'd let him down when he needed her most.

Fresh tears welled up. Should she go over to Ivy's and tell her what'd happened?

No. She didn't want Ivy to know what she'd said. She hoped Cam wouldn't tell her, either. But why wouldn't he? What was there to hold him back?

Okay. You can hate me if you want. I understand. I just have to say that…you don't have to worry. I'll never say or do anything that could hurt you ever again.

Coming back to the island was making everything worse instead of better, she thought, and was opening the gate when she heard her phone buzz with an incoming text.

She braced herself as she once again drew her phone out of her purse.

But it wasn't Cam. It was Bruce.

I can't quit thinking about you.

Ariana closed her eyes. She wished she could tell him what she was going through. She'd wished she could confide in him all along. But if she explained her dilemma, he could decide to come forward himself. Knowing him, there was a chance he'd consider it his moral obligation. Then she'd no longer be able to protect Cam.

Although her fingers were numb, she managed to text a response.

I'm sorry. I never meant to hurt you.

Of course you didn't. I just wish things could be different.

She knew the feeling. So do I, she wrote, but she wasn't talking about him.

eight

Fortunately, Alice was asleep when Ariana went in. Her grandmother had obviously been waiting up, but it was well past her bedtime, and she'd dozed off in the recliner in front of the TV.

Ariana removed her glasses, which had fallen low on her nose, before jiggling her arm. "Grandma?"

Alice opened her eyes. "Oh! There you are."

"Don't wake up too much," Ariana whispered. "It's late. I'm just going to help you upstairs to bed."

Without her glasses, Alice couldn't see very well. Relieved that her grandmother probably wouldn't be able to tell she'd been crying, Ariana kept her face averted as much as possible, just in case, and brought Alice to her feet.

"How was Ivy tonight?" Alice mumbled.

"She was fine." Ariana kept her voice low as they climbed the stairs. "We had a great time catching up."

"That's good. You've been away from the island for far too long."

Her grandmother was so groggy that she didn't attempt to say anything else, and Ariana breathed a sigh of relief once Alice was in bed. If Alice had been waiting up to talk to her, Ariana had managed to stay out late enough to avoid whatever conversation they would've had.

As she stepped out of the room, she closed her grandmother's door before going through the rest of the house, turning off all the lights until she reached the living room. There, she paused to check her phone again. She'd received another text from Bruce. She wasn't going to respond to this one. Seeing Cam since she'd returned to Mariners had shown her that she really didn't care for Bruce the way she should, and her feelings weren't likely to change. As hard as it was to know that her desire to exit their relationship hurt him, she believed it would be kinder to force him to move on. He was a good man. She hoped he'd find someone who *could* give him the love he deserved.

Unfortunately, she'd received no message or missed calls from Cam.

Dropping her head into her hand, she pinched the bridge of her nose while trying to ward off more tears. When she couldn't quite hold back, she decided it didn't matter, anyway. There wasn't anyone to see her.

After turning off the last of the lights, she sniffed and wiped her cheeks as she started toward the stairs. She was planning to take a shower. After the way things had ended with Cam, she'd be looking at a sleepless night; the hot water should help her warm up, at least.

But at the last second, she turned to grab a tissue from the box her grandmother kept on the coffee table—and noticed movement in the dim moonlight outside the front window.

Quickly stepping to one side, she watched what looked like a large man wearing a cowboy hat walk from the cover of the trees at the edge of the property to a car parked down the street.

Someone was calling.

Ivy opened her eyes to find sunlight pouring through her bedroom window. She didn't have to work on weekends, so she hadn't set an alarm. Rolling over, she fumbled around on the nightstand until she managed to lift her phone from the charger. She'd been up half the night worrying about what she'd said to Warner Williams—replaying it in her mind and studying what she could remember of his facial expressions as he listened to her responses. She was terrified she'd gotten tripped up on some small detail, that this would be the police, asking her to come to the station to talk to Mariners' only detective. She knew that was coming. But fortunately, it wasn't coming now. Her mother's picture showed on the screen.

She closed her eyes for a split second in relief before pressing the answer button. "Hey, Mom."

"You sound half-asleep. Did I wake you?"

In an attempt to speak more clearly, Ivy propped the pillows behind her so she could sit up. "That surprises you?" She covered a yawn. "It's only eight o'clock, and it's Saturday, my day to sleep in."

"Would you rather call me back later?"

"No. It's fine. I'm happy to hear from you. I was just up late."

"Doing what?"

She adjusted the pillows to make herself more comfortable. "Ariana's back on the island. She came over for a while, and then… I don't know why, but after she left, I couldn't sleep."

Her mother hadn't been a fan of Cam's since the night she caught him climbing through Ivy's bedroom window, so she wasn't going to mention him, or the case, if she could help it. She didn't want this problem to get any worse than it was. She preferred to minimize it whenever possible and hope it would finally blow over.

"What brings Ariana back?"

"Alice is getting older and needs help, so she quit her job and came home for the summer."

"It's nice of her to look after her grandmother. But what's she going to do in the fall?"

"She'll figure that out, I guess. What have you been up to? Did you make it to your hot yoga class this morning?"

"I did. I just got back."

Her mother was an exercise fanatic; never missed a day. Ivy felt like a slug next to Priscilla, who also never skipped a fingernail or Botox appointment. "I don't know how you manage to drag yourself out of bed at five o'clock every morning when you could easily attend a later class." It wasn't as if her mother had to work. Ivy had inherited Hazel's house, but Priscilla had gotten as much or more in the form of other assets.

"I like getting it over with," Priscilla told her. "I try to be home and showered by eight, but I'm running a little behind today. I got caught in the garage talking to Kitty on the phone."

Her mother's best friend still lived on the island and owned The Human Bean, a coffee shop that was part of the darling collection of shops in the downtown area. "You called Kitty even earlier than you called me?" Ivy asked in surprise. "And she didn't mind?"

"She was up," her mother said. "Why would she mind?"

"Because she was probably trying to get ready to open."

"She has plenty of help, at least during the summer," her

mother insisted. "Besides, it's her birthday. I wanted to be the first to acknowledge it."

"It is? I'll take over a cupcake before she closes for the day."

"That would be nice. She adores you."

"I adore her, too." Her mother's best friend had been a lot easier to deal with than her mother—and had often helped restore peace between them.

"Have you heard from your brother recently?"

"He called a few days ago. He's planning to bring the family here in July, so that should be fun." She missed her brother. He was the only sibling she had, and they'd always been close.

There was a slight pause before Priscilla said, "I talked to him yesterday. I wonder why he didn't mention that he was going to the island this summer."

Immediately regretting having volunteered that information, Ivy winced. Tim hadn't said she should keep it secret, but… "I'm sure he thought you expected it. He comes almost every summer."

"If he's going to be there, maybe your father and I should come, too."

This was probably exactly what her brother had been trying to avoid. He and their mother butted heads too often; he couldn't cope with her intensity. Priscilla's high-strung nature had always been a challenge for Ivy, too, especially while growing up. That was why she'd spent so much time with Hazel. Hazel was more similar to her father—steady, even, calm.

Still, Ivy was somehow able to let her mother's behavior go more easily than Tim could. "It's always so crowded in July. If I were you, I'd visit Tim at his place in August for a few days, then come here afterward and stay as long as you'd like."

"You don't think it'd be nice to have us all together again?"

In an effort not to ruin her brother's vacation, she'd apparently been too transparent. "It's always nice to have more family on the island. I know you don't like it at the height of the tourist season."

"I hate waiting for a table or feeling as if I can't get a parking spot or a place on the beach. That's all."

"And that's what it's like in July," Ivy pointed out.

"There's no guarantee August will be slower..."

"It's never quite as crazy in August as it is in July," Ivy told her confidently. "Especially with school starting earlier and earlier as the years go by."

There was another pause. "I'll talk to Tim," her mother said at length. "See what he says."

Ivy silently let her breath go. If Tim hadn't wanted their mother to know he was coming, he should've warned her to keep her mouth shut. "That's a good idea."

"What's been going on with the Emily Hutchins case?" her mother asked, changing the subject. "Anything interesting that's not being reported on the news?"

Ivy couldn't help but tense. This was all anyone could talk about. "You probably know they found her body out by the lighthouse."

"Yeah. That's been reported a thousand times. Have the police contacted you yet?"

"No, and I'm hoping they won't," Ivy replied. "I don't have any more to tell them."

"You should expect a call," she said matter-of-factly. "Now that they've found the body, there'll be a lot of pressure to make an arrest, which means they'll dig back into their investigation, and the only logical place to start is to go over everything that's been done already, searching for some detail they may have missed."

"Cam didn't hurt Emily Hutchins," she stated flatly.

"Are you sure?"

Ivy jumped out of bed. Her mother had never doubted her

before. "Of course I'm sure, Mom," she said. "He was with me and Ariana that night, remember?"

"I'm just wondering if… Is it possible you could've gotten the time wrong, honey?"

The private investigator had drilled her on that aspect of her story. So far she'd stuck to what she'd said before. She had to hold strong, because the second she wavered… "No. I—I distinctly remember the time." Aware that she sounded rather frantic and eager to be believed, she held her breath as she awaited her mother's reaction.

"Okay, for Cam's sake, I'm happy to hear you're confident," Priscilla said. "Because Kitty just told me that someone else has come forward to say they saw him at the beach during the time he was supposed to be with the both of you."

Ivy's heart seemed to come to a sudden, shuddering stop. "*Who* said that?"

"Kitty didn't feel at liberty to tell me."

But her husband was a cop, so Ivy could easily guess where she'd gotten the information—and that it was reliable.

Ariana shifted nervously at the small table inside The Human Bean, and it seemed to her that Ivy did the same. They both had the jitters. Ivy had called almost as soon as she woke up this morning to report what she'd learned from her mother regarding the Hutchins case. Now they were hoping to find out who'd spoken up—and why that person hadn't said anything twenty years ago.

Was it a credible witness? If so, what was Cam doing out again when he'd told them he'd gone straight home?

If only his parents hadn't been in Europe at the time. They could've corroborated his claim that he was at home when Emily went missing. Then she and Ivy wouldn't have had to lie for him. But saying he went home to an empty house would've left him without an alibi. Even at that age, they were all smart enough to understand the risk they'd be taking with that.

Ariana eyed the many small parties, people wearing shorts and tanks and bikini tops, with ponytails and various large and small tattoos, expensive sunglasses and gleaming lip gloss, crowding into the basement coffee shop. "What are you going to say to her?"

"I'm just going to wish her a happy birthday and give her the opportunity to mention what she said to my mom."

"And what if she doesn't?" The Human Bean was probably the most popular coffee shop on the island; today it was an absolute madhouse. Ariana wasn't convinced Kitty would be able to take the time to see them. When they bought their coffees, they'd told the girl at the register that they'd come to say hello to Kitty, and they'd been told she'd be right out, but it had been ten minutes.

"I might try a few leading statements," Ivy whispered, glancing at the next table, which was filled with teens talking about how much fun they had at Coachella a couple of months ago. "We'll see how it goes."

"Don't be too obvious," Ariana warned. She was about to say why when she saw Kitty come out of the back and lift a portion of the front counter so she could venture into the main section of the coffee shop.

"Hey, there." Kitty had ultra-curly blond hair and was wearing a brown The Human Bean apron like everyone else who worked in the shop. She smiled as she reached their table. "Sorry for the wait. We always get busy during the summer, but tourist season seems to be off to a bigger start than usual, and I'm a bit understaffed."

Ivy slid the greeting card and cupcake they'd brought toward her mother's friend. "We don't want to take you away from your work. We just thought we'd drop by and wish you a happy birthday."

"How sweet! Thank you." She read the card before giving Ivy a hug. "Your mom called me this morning. It was good to talk to her."

"She's thinking about visiting this summer," Ivy told her.

"I hope she does. It's been too long." Kitty turned a smile on Ariana. "It's good to have you back. How long are you going to be here?"

"Through the summer."

"Well, let me know if you'd like to work while you're here. I could definitely use the help."

Ariana hadn't expected such an offer, but she was somewhat interested. The Human Bean was only open until two each day. The hours were ideal and having a job would mean she could stretch out her savings. It would also give her something to do—besides obsessing about the Emily Hutchins case—that wouldn't take a lot of thought or concentration, which she didn't feel entirely capable of at this juncture in her life. "I might take you up on that."

Kitty rocked back. "Really?"

"Why not? I prefer to be busy, and this place looks like it's always hopping."

"That's wonderful. If you decide you'd like to talk about it, come by tomorrow or the next day anytime. We can go over your salary and provided I can pay you enough to make you happy, I'll train you, and you can start as soon as you'd like."

"Thank you. That's a nice offer. I'll think about it and get back to you." Ariana wanted Ivy to ask Kitty about the witness who'd contradicted their claims. She almost kicked Ivy under the table to get her to voice one of those "leading questions" she'd mentioned. But she knew it would come out of nowhere and sound odd. This had to be information Kitty volunteered.

Otherwise, it would look as though they'd used Kitty's birthday as an excuse to come by and ferret out the details.

"I hope to hear from you." Kitty glanced at the ever-lengthening line, which was going out the door, before adding, "I'd better get back. Thanks for remembering my birthday, Ivy. You've always been such a great kid."

They hugged and Ariana told Kitty goodbye before she and Ivy took their to-go coffees and nudged their way through the crowd to escape the building.

"I'm bummed she didn't say anything about what she told your mother," Ariana said as they climbed the stairs to the cobblestone sidewalk.

"So am I," Ivy said. "It's scary, not knowing what—or who—we're up against."

Ariana thought about her visit to Cam's last night, what she'd said and done and how he'd reacted. She'd chosen not to tell Ivy, but that didn't mean Ivy wouldn't learn about it from him—or even her—in the future.

"Should we text Cam to see if he's working today?" Ivy asked as they started down the street.

A spike of alarm nearly caused Ariana to trip on an uneven brick in the sidewalk. She couldn't face Cam, not after last night. But if she said no, Ivy would guess something was up. "With his wife and daughter gone, he's probably using the time to catch up on his work," she said as casually as possible.

"Maybe we can offer to bring him lunch," Ivy said, undeterred. "He's got to eat, doesn't he?" She took a sip of her coffee as they passed through the dappled sunshine of a much warmer day. "It's sad that we've drifted apart. I feel like we should take advantage of the time Melanie is gone to reconnect. She can't interfere right now, and the way he's acting—I think he needs us. Don't you?"

"I just...don't want to bother him," Ariana replied. "I'm guessing he'd rather work."

Ivy stopped and handed over her cup for Ariana to hold while she pulled out her phone. "Then he can tell us that. Let's at least ask him."

Ariana's mind floundered for a better excuse. She almost said she forgot she had to do something for Alice so she could abandon Ivy to whatever she was going to do with Cam. But she'd already agreed to spend the day at the beach. Such an abrupt reversal wouldn't seem credible.

Besides, she was going to see Cam at some point. Given their past relationship, what was happening now, the small size of the island and Ivy pushing to do things together, there'd be no avoiding it. She figured she might as well get it over with. "Okay," she said and held her breath as Ivy sent the text.

Would he refuse? she wondered while they awaited his response.

She wouldn't blame him if he did. First, she'd revealed that she'd been in love with him since the first day she'd met him, even though he'd never shown any romantic interest in her—and was now married. Then she'd asked if he'd used her emotions to manipulate her into lying for him.

Just remembering the exchange caused her to cringe. She was positive he'd either refuse outright or give Ivy some excuse. So she was shocked a few minutes later when he not only answered the text but also agreed to let them come back to his office.

Cam hadn't even bothered to shower this morning. He hadn't slept well. After tossing and turning all night—and having terrible dreams about being dragged off to jail when he did go to sleep—he'd crawled out of bed at the crack of dawn feeling like roadkill. He'd brushed his teeth before yanking on an old T-shirt and a pair of sweats, but that was about it. He'd left immediately to go running, hoping it would clear his head, and he'd driven himself long and hard enough that it'd required all his focus just to keep going. But instead of returning to the house after, he'd stopped by the office to take care of a few things, gotten caught up in various projects and never left.

He probably should've used an excuse to keep Ivy and Ariana from bringing him lunch. But he was torn and confused about almost everything in his life, and they were the two people he'd been able to count on most through the years. They'd been there even when his parents weren't, which had happened a lot during his formative years, because Jack and Giselle had always been so goddamn caught up in their own lives. He needed his friends, saw now that allowing Melanie to pressure him into giving them up was a mistake. What was going on with the Hutchins case upset him. What was going on with his marriage upset him. What was going on with Ariana upset him, too.

Or was *upset* even the right word? He couldn't believe Ariana would accuse him of *using* her. She was the one person, beyond Ivy, who knew him best. He'd believed she'd always be there for him—even if they didn't talk for years at a time—because real friendship endured almost anything. That she could think he'd be capable of harming a young girl made him sick.

At the same time, however, there'd been a far more flattering side to their conversation—the connection of two opposites, which elicited completely different emotions. It was almost like getting punched in the face by the same person who'd just gently stroked his hair. Knowing how difficult it was to catch Ariana's attention, at least in a romantic sense, he couldn't help feeling a strange sort of—excitement? Was that the word?

He turned over the hourglass on his desk, something he'd bought simply because it looked cool, as he recalled teasing her, on several occasions, about being hard to get. Over the years, he'd watched guy after guy make a play for her. His own cousin, a dude most women liked, had expressed interest in her at Cam's wedding. And yet Travis had struck out like every other guy. Before Travis had flown back to the mainland, he'd called her "Teflon." Cam had chuckled at that, because he had to agree with the metaphor. She was never rude or mean, stuck up or bitchy. She was nice but unresponsive—emotionally inaccessible.

So how could it be that she had a thing for *him*? Especially one that'd lasted so long?

He was even more surprised she'd admit it out of a clear blue sky *after* he was married. Why hadn't she said something before?

Would it have changed anything?

Remembering where he'd been back then when he got Melanie pregnant, probably not. He'd still been immature, reckless, angry—and, in many ways, stupid.

He'd learned a lot in the past four years. Felt like he'd aged forty. Why it had taken him so long to grow up, he had no idea.

"Fuck," he muttered for probably the hundredth time as he raked his fingers through his hair.

A knock at the door outside his inner office brought him to his feet. He wasn't sure what he was going to feel when he saw Ariana, could hardly believe she'd come over, especially so soon. Had she told Ivy about last night? If not, would she?

He didn't feel it was *his* place. Unless there was a good reason to do otherwise, he was going to keep his mouth shut.

That might be the only way to salvage the relationship he and Ariana had built over the years. After what he'd experienced since she left, he knew he didn't want to lose her friendship.

The offices were quiet on weekends. He rarely worked himself. He usually spent Saturdays and Sundays on projects around the house, hanging out with Melanie's favorite couple friends or taking her to hair or nail appointments and watching Camilla while she was inside.

As he passed the receptionist's desk, he could see his friends through the glass door, holding a bag from one of his favorite restaurants—The Charles W. Morgan, named after the last wooden whaling ship in the world, according to a placard at the entrance. The ship had sailed from somewhere along the coast of Massachusetts, not Mariners Island, but the owners apparently didn't care about getting that specific.

As he unlocked and opened the door, it was easy to guess by the way Ivy was smiling that she didn't know what'd happened between him and Ariana and experienced a rush of relief. If they kept it contained enough, maybe they could just forget about it. He could tell Ariana felt bad that she'd done what she'd done, that she was extremely uncomfortable seeing him again. She'd look anywhere except right at him.

"Hey, you," Ivy said as he let them in. "Hungry?"

"Starving," he admitted as she handed over the sack. "I went running this morning without bothering to eat and haven't been able to make it home."

"There're half a dozen or more restaurants a stone's throw away from here—you realize that," she said with a roll of her eyes.

He gave her a sheepish look. "Yeah. But it takes pulling away from what I'm doing long enough to figure out where to go. And then I'd have to wait for the order."

"If you can't even do that, you're entirely too busy," she said with a laugh.

"I *am* too busy," he admitted. "I'll give you that."

They followed him back to his office, where he slid a couple of chairs closer to his desk before circling around to take his own. "Smells good," he said as he delved into the bag.

"Fish and chips. Can't go wrong with that," she said. "Unless you're trying to avoid a heart attack."

"I'll worry about heart disease when I get older," he said with a grin and looked over at Ariana.

She acted startled when their eyes met, and her face turned beet red.

"Who do I pay for this?" he asked.

"Ariana got her debit card out faster than I could."

He reached for his phone. "How much do I owe you?"

"It's my treat," she said.

Part of an apology? He got that impression. Why else would she have come with Ivy, who didn't even know what'd happened, if she didn't want to make up? "What are you two doing today?"

"We're going to the beach," Ivy replied. "Any chance we can drag you away from work? It's been ages and ages since the three of us were at the beach together."

He had tons to do, but it would all be waiting for him when he got back. Or he could do it on Monday. He would've had to take the weekend off, anyway, if Melanie were home. Why not let himself enjoy his old friends? He hadn't realized how much he'd missed them. Although last night's encounter with Ariana had been odd, he was willing to chalk it up to the stress they were all under since Emily Hutchins's body had been found. Surely, she didn't really believe he would use her. "Sounds good to me," he said.

nine

It'd been a long time since Ariana had been in the ocean. After she left Mariners, she'd been all about the big city, especially once Melanie came on the scene and refused to accept them. But as soon as they arrived at Right Beach, she was feeling a strong desire to recapture even a small piece of the fun she, Cam and Ivy had enjoyed in their youth. She couldn't escape, at least not for very long, the serious issues she was facing knowing Warner Williams would probably be waiting for her when she got back. But they had a few hours in which she could refuse to think of poor Emily, the police or the PI.

"Looks like this *is* the 'right' beach," she joked as they found the beach far less crowded than she and Ivy had expected.

Cam had insisted on driving them in his Land Rover. The ocean was rougher on this side of the island, but still swimmable, and he'd insisted there'd be fewer tourists.

That had turned out to be true.

"You know why they named this Right Beach, don't you?" Ivy asked as they carried their stuff to the same spot they'd frequented in high school.

Ariana shaded her eyes. They had a beautiful blue sky overhead, only a slight breeze and mild waves lapping at the shoreline. "I don't. Why is it called Right Beach?"

"Isn't it named after a whale?" Cam asked, shifting the big blanket he was carrying onto his other shoulder.

"Yep." Ivy kicked off her flip-flops and bent to pick them up. "The right whale was one of the species that was most hunted back in the day, which is why there are so few of them now."

"I've never even considered where the name came from," Ariana said.

Cam nudged her with his elbow. "Didn't you pay attention in history class?"

The fact that he'd engaged her instead of interacting only with Ivy made Ariana feel instantly better. "I probably wasn't *in* history class," she told him. "If I remember right, I was ditching with *you*."

Ivy hitched her beach bag higher. "If I wasn't the town librarian, I probably wouldn't have thought about it, either."

"Wait… Didn't they also hunt sperm whales?" Ariana asked, and Cam started to laugh.

"They did," he replied. "Can you imagine a bunch of drunken sailors bandying *that* name about for the beach?"

Ariana laughed with him. She hadn't meant to offend him last night. She'd just been riddled with guilt for committing a crime on his behalf and had started to imagine crazy things.

It wasn't until she left Ivy swimming in the ocean, and he followed her back up the beach, that they had a moment to talk privately. "I'm sorry for last night," she murmured.

He sat beside her. "It's okay."

"Just so you know, I didn't tell the police anything, and I won't."

The smile he'd been wearing disappeared, and she almost regretted bringing up last night. She'd just yanked them both back into an unpleasant reality when they'd been laughing and body surfing and dunking each other like they used to when they were kids. "I didn't do it," he said.

"I know." Once again she was tempted to take his hand. She felt the need to touch him. But she held back. Now that he knew how she felt about him, she couldn't touch him as freely as before, or he might assume she was trying to get some sort of sexual thrill or satisfaction from it. "Will you forgive me?" she asked.

"I already have," he replied.

She assumed that was the end of the conversation and was glad to have it behind her. But after he slid his sunglasses back on, he looked over at her. "Did you mean the rest of it?"

He was asking if she was really in love with him. She understood that.

Her heart began to pound as a denial rose immediately to her lips. With a little effort and a lot of fast talking, she could probably convince him that she'd exaggerated what she felt, because she was so freaked out by what was happening with the Emily Hutchins case.

But she'd loved him for almost twenty-five years. There was a measure of relief that came from admitting how she felt at last. "I probably shouldn't have told you," she said. "I hope we can just…continue on as we have in the past. That it won't make our relationship weird."

"That's a yes?" She couldn't see his eyes behind those dark shades, but she could hear the surprise in his voice. He was shocked all over again—because she felt the way she felt, or she'd had the guts to own up to it, she couldn't tell.

She waved to Ivy, who was motioning for them to come see a sand dollar, as she gathered the nerve to answer. "That's a yes," she confirmed and got up to run back to the water.

Cam didn't bother taking off his sunglasses as he returned to the ocean. He wasn't planning on swimming, just looking at what Ivy had found.

"Isn't it cool?" Ivy said as they stood ankle deep in the foamy surf, and she allowed Ariana to take the soft brown creature.

Ariana seemed more carefree than Cam had seen her since she'd been back. "Look at its fine hairlike feet!"

"Most people think sand dollars are seashells, but they're not," Ivy told them. "They're animals—part of the sea urchin family. Their endoskeleton doesn't turn white and hard until after they die. There's a children's book about them in the library."

The animal was only about two inches wide. Cam had seen bigger sand dollars around the island. But it was a perfect specimen.

Ariana handed it off to him, and he examined it closely before putting it back in the ocean.

"Do you find much sea glass around here anymore?" Ariana asked.

Ivy frowned as she shook her head. "Not nearly as much as when we were kids."

Obviously hoping to uncover a piece, Ariana pushed the nearby sand around with her bare feet. "I wish I'd kept more of it. I've seen it turned into beautiful jewelry—on Etsy and other places—and it always reminds me of Mariners."

"Why not make it our goal to find as much as we can this summer?" Ivy asked enthusiastically. "It'll give us something fun to hunt for, and we could have it made into some sort of jewelry to commemorate what could be our last summer together."

Ariana turned her face up to the sun, and Cam saw her chest lift as she drew a deep breath. "I'd like that," she said on a long exhalation, but he was more focused on the second part of Ivy's statement—about this being their last summer together.

"Why would it be our last summer?" he asked. "What terrible thing do you think's going to happen?"

Fortunately, she didn't point to the possibility that he might go to trial—and prison from there—for the murder of Emily Hutchins. No one had specifically banned that subject. It was more of an unspoken rule that they wouldn't ruin the afternoon by dragging their problems to the beach.

"Ariana could go back to the mainland, get caught up in a new job and not return," Ivy said. "Or she could marry and start a family, which would also radically change the dynamics of our friendship." Instead of saying she could marry, too, if not get a new job, Ivy elbowed him playfully. "Look what happened with you. We only have you with us today because Melanie's not around to get mad about it."

His wife had never felt so far away nor so easily forgotten. He hadn't even talked to her this morning. He knew he'd pay a price for not calling, but he hadn't been able to bring himself to do it; couldn't deal with her complaints about how hard it was to care for Camilla while traveling, even though their daughter was well-behaved for a four-year-old, and how much her parents bothered her by what they said or did, or that everyone was asking her about Emily Hutchins. When he'd first met Melanie, Emily had been a moot point. He'd had to answer some questions about her once upon a time. That was all. But now she made it sound as though having something like that come up was more than she'd bargained for—as if he owed her for the embarrassment she felt and the negative attention she was receiving. He fully believed that was why she'd chosen this particular time to leave the island. She usually went home during the winter, when Mariners wasn't nearly as much fun.

Before she'd made her travel plans, she'd admitted that she felt besieged. She said people were giving her suspicious and sidelong looks, and she was convinced they believed she knew the truth about what'd happened to Emily just because she was married to him.

"Even if she and I stay together, I can tell you right now, I'm no longer going to let her dictate who my friends are or when I see them," he told Ariana and Ivy.

Ivy seemed concerned instead of relieved or gratified. "Are you sure you want to take on the grief it'll cause to hang on to us a little tighter?"

"I should never have let her have her way in that regard," he said. "I can't allow her to continue to use Camilla to control me. It isn't right. So I'm down with finding as much sea glass as we can this summer—not because it might be our last summer together but as a promise to each other that it won't be."

"I like the sound of that!" Ivy said enthusiastically, but Ariana didn't seem to be paying attention. She still had her eyes closed and her face tilted skyward.

Cam examined the few freckles on her nose, the delicate bone structure of her face and the thick locks of blond hair she'd pulled into a ponytail. He'd known her for so long as a friend that he'd quit looking at her as he would almost any other woman. Ariana was just Ariana. But learning that she was in love with him had somehow jarred him awake, made him aware of her in a different way—like noticing how sexy she looked in her white bikini—and he wasn't convinced that was a good thing. It probably wasn't, given his situation and the fact that it put their friendship at risk.

"Ariana, are you in?" he asked.

When she opened her eyes, he found himself admiring the light green of her irises—almost like pieces of sea glass themselves—and noticing how long and thick her eyelashes were. "With being friends forever?" she said. "Of course."

Except…if she was truly in love with him, she'd prefer to be more, wouldn't she?

That was such a novel thought. It blew his mind. But he was also surprised to find the idea wasn't unappealing to him. That was strange, wasn't it?

Or was he just *that* unhappy in his marriage? So unhappy that even being with a good friend seemed a better alternative?

When he didn't look away, neither did she. She smiled up at him and he smiled back—and the exchange felt oddly new, almost as if they'd just met.

Something was different. Ivy couldn't put her finger on exactly what it was, but Cam and Ariana were acting strange. For one, Ariana was quieter than usual. Once the wind had come up, she'd sat on the beach, wrapped in a striped beach blanket while digging her toes into the sand and staring out to sea, and Cam had been happier and more talkative—more like his old self—than he'd been in years. After he'd met Melanie, he'd not only withdrawn from her, he'd been withdrawn generally, except possibly when it came to his work.

Now that she understood more clearly what he was dealing with inside his marriage, she guessed he'd simply been focused on the battle he was waging to hold his family together. That explained a lot, made her feel less pain and resentment at the loss of their friendship and her time with him. But with Melanie in Boston, and the decision he'd made to draw some lines where his wife was concerned, Ivy could see why he'd feel as though a huge weight had been lifted off his shoulders.

He was looking forward to some positive change at last, or at least a decision—an end to the situation he was in—if things didn't get better.

Was that all of it, though?

"What's going on with you and Cam?" she asked Ariana after Cam dropped them off at her house and went home to shower. He'd offered to take Ariana around the block to her grandmother's place, but she'd insisted on getting out with Ivy. She'd said if Williams was waiting for her, she preferred he not see her in Cam's truck. Mr. Williams knew they were friends. Everyone did. But she felt it would make the detective less likely to believe what she had to say if he saw them together.

Ariana's head had jerked up at Ivy's question. "Nothing, why?"

"The way you both acted today was…unusual."

"I think Cam's feeling he's tried hard enough with Melanie—that he can finally give up if things don't improve. Knowing you're at the end of something difficult, one way or another, sometimes creates a sense of…euphoria."

"That's what I was thinking, too. I just… Never mind." Ivy managed a shrug. What Ariana had said was true. But none of that should've left *her* feeling upset. While she'd been careful to stay away from Cam, not to get in the way of his marriage, it hadn't been easy. She'd had feelings for him for most of her life—feelings that could easily have turned into more if only he'd shown some interest. She'd tried to take care of him, too, as far back as when she'd risked her parents' wrath to let him sleep in her room so he wouldn't have to go home to an empty house or parents who treated him as though he was a big bother. To think he was getting closer to Ariana than he was to her now that his marriage was imploding made her feel overlooked, like she was going to get left out in the cold again.

But maybe she was imagining things. "Do you think Williams will be waiting for you?" she asked, changing the subject.

Ariana gazed down the street. "Even if he's not, he'll come tonight."

"We don't know how long he's staying on Mariners. You might not see him until tomorrow or the next day."

She nibbled worriedly on her bottom lip. "He thinks we're the key to solving the case. I can tell."

"How?" Ivy challenged.

"He's been watching my house, for one."

Ivy froze with her hand on the wrought iron gate at the end of her walkway. "What did you say?"

"I saw him last night. It was late, too late to be standing in someone's yard. And yet…he was there. I watched him leave."

Ivy's heart sank. "You didn't tell me."

"I didn't tell Cam, either. I didn't want to ruin the day. But now…we need to be careful, Ive. He's determined to get to the truth of where we were that night—and when."

Ivy could hear the trepidation in her voice, since the truth wasn't what they were telling. "It'll be okay," she insisted. "Some sort of forensic evidence will lead the police in the right direction."

Ariana said nothing, but she didn't seem encouraged, so Ivy added, "You'll see."

With a nod, she started to move away. "I'll call you when I'm ready to head to the restaurant." They were getting together with Cam for another dinner. They weren't willing to let the celebration of their reunion end too soon now that they'd finally found each other again amidst the concerns and cares of life as adults.

"Sounds good." Ivy watched her walk down the street and around the corner. She hoped whatever Ariana told Williams, it wouldn't contradict anything she'd said. It was hard enough to maintain a lie in the face of so much pressure, publicity and suspicion, especially over twenty years. She understood all too well that depending on someone else to tell the exact same lie significantly raised the chances of getting caught.

They both loved Cam. But were they willing to go to the same lengths to protect him?

Ariana breathed easier once she reached her grandmother's back door and let herself inside the tiny mudroom. She'd used the alley to avoid approaching the house from the front, but as far as she could tell from craning her neck to see, Williams didn't seem to be lurking about. If she could get showered and slip back out of the house right away, she might be able to avoid him.

As soon as she walked inside, however, she heard her grandmother call out for her. "Ariana? Is that you?"

Ariana passed through the kitchen and separate dining area to find Alice in the drawing room, gathering up dirty plates, crumpled napkins and empty cups. "Hey."

"How was the beach?" she asked, pleasantly enough, but her voice was somewhat subdued.

"Nice. We went to North Shore." Ariana took a dirty plate off the old phonograph her grandmother had owned since she could remember. "Looks like you had company while I was gone."

"It was a meeting. I'm still active in the historical association. Tena Burns from Bridge Club is president. She wanted to get together with the people who've volunteered to help with the fundraiser for The Wedding House. We needed to start making plans for what we're going to do to save it, so I offered my place."

The Wedding House was the oldest house on the island. Built in the late seventeenth century, when the Indigenous people dramatically outnumbered the English, it was a wedding gift from one of Mariners' earliest settlers to his second wife. There were tales of Jeremiah McCauley hurrying the death of his first wife to be able to embrace his second, the beautiful and much younger Mrs. McCauley, which gave the historic landmark a more colorful past than it would've had otherwise. But colonial history was taken very seriously on Mariners. A great deal of effort was made to preserve every aspect they could, and Ariana had already heard her grandmother say it needed to be moved or it would fall into the ocean, thanks to erosion. "When is the fundraiser?"

"Not for several weeks. But big events take a lot of time to pull off, especially when you're using volunteer labor."

"I'd be happy to help, too—when I can. I might be working this summer. Kitty at The Human Bean has offered me a job. But even if I take it, I'll still be available in the afternoon and evenings."

"I'll let you know when we're having our next planning session, in case you'd like to attend. But that isn't why I called you in here. While we were having our meeting, a Mr. Williams came to the door."

"What did *he* want?" she asked flatly.

Alice seemed as discomfited as Ariana was. "He left his card. Asked me to have you call him." She navigated the furniture, moving much slower than she used to, thanks to her age, to reach the mantel of the fireplace, where she got his card.

"When's he expecting me to call?" Ariana asked as she accepted it.

"I told him you'd do it as soon as you came in."

"It can't wait until morning? I need to get showered." Taking the card with her, Ariana started to go, but Alice stopped her by calling her back.

"It should only take a few minutes," her grandmother said.

Although Alice was always polite, Ariana could tell she was determined this would happen, no matter how unpleasant it might be. "You want me to do it now?"

"I think that would be a good idea, yes. Otherwise, it might look as though you have something to hide."

"I *don't* have anything to hide," Ariana insisted, but she loved and respected her grandmother so much she couldn't look her in the eye while saying it. "It's just—"

"You've already told the truth to the police," Alice broke in, her voice velvet over steel. "All you have to do is repeat what you said to them, and it would probably be best if you did it while I'm in the room."

Ariana felt her eyebrows snap together. She didn't want to talk to Williams at all. She certainly didn't want an audience. "Because…"

"Because he asked if he could speak with me, too, when I have a minute."

Ariana blinked in surprise. "Why?"

"For the same reason he's talking to you, of course. He's establishing details, timelines, making sure nothing's changed since the last time we were asked." She spoke slowly, choosing her words carefully as if she was trying to say enough but not too much. Ariana knew her grandmother all too well; there was a deeper reservoir of meaning behind her words than what she communicated on the surface. This was Alice's way of trying to tell Ariana that they needed to get their story straight.

Damn it. Alice knew exactly what was at stake. Ariana hadn't been wrong about that. Now *she* was complicit, too.

What had she done? She'd dragged her grandmother into this…

Sinking onto the couch, Ariana rubbed her forehead while anticipating the conversation to come.

Alice gave her a few seconds. But then she sat down next to her and patted her knee. "Let's get it over with, honey."

"Okay," she said, resigned, and took out her phone.

ten

Once she heard ringing, Ariana was too agitated to remain on the couch. She jumped up and began to pace, then froze in the middle of the room, with her grandmother looking on, when Mr. Williams picked up.

"This is Warner Williams."

When he pronounced his name as Warn-a, she couldn't help conjuring up an image of the large man with the cowboy hat she'd seen leaving the property so late last night. "Mr. Williams, this is Ariana Prince. My grandmother gave me your card and said you'd like to speak with me."

"Yes, thank ya for callin', Ms. Prince."

Ariana bit her lip, waiting for whatever came next.

"I'm workin' with the Hutchins family. You're probably aware of who they are."

"Yes, sir, I am." She wasn't usually that formal, but the way he was talking set a precedent. "They've been in the news quite a bit."

"They have. They've been through a terrible ordeal, somethin' no family should ever have to go through, and I'm here to help them figure out what happened to their little girl. Would you mind if I came over and sat down with ya for a bit?"

She had to give him points for feeling passionately about what he was doing. "Right now?"

"It shouldn't take long."

Ariana had never been a good liar. She felt much safer speaking to him over the phone, where he couldn't read her body language. "I would, except I'm meeting friends for dinner and need to get ready. Is there any chance we could handle this over the phone?"

"What if I came first thing tomorrow mornin'?" he suggested.

"I have to get up early and go speak to someone about a job." She hadn't fully decided to accept Kitty's offer to work at the coffee shop, at least not right away, but she was leaning that direction. She figured she might as well move on the opportunity if it meant she could avoid Williams.

"I see." He sounded disappointed but continued, "I just want to ask you a few questions about the night Emily Hutchins went missin'."

"I already told the police everything I know," Ariana said. "Isn't it all there in the file?"

"Yes, ma'am. But it's been twenty years, and I've found that checkin' back with people can very often provide new insights. You were with Ivy Hawthorne and Cam Stafford that night, correct?"

Now that she was on the phone with Williams, Ariana was even less convinced that speaking to him was a good idea. He wasn't the police. She didn't *have* to talk to him. Could she be making a mistake?

She worried about that, but Alice seemed convinced that she should answer his questions. *Just keep it simple. The less you say, the better.* "I was."

"Can you tell me what you remember from that night?"

"It was July fifth, a Friday. We'd gone to see the fireworks the night before, but it was the start of a weekend, so we were at the beach again, this time for a bonfire. A strong wind was coming off the ocean, so it was chilly. That's why we didn't stay out as late as we could have. Ivy and I didn't have sweatshirts and wanted to go home."

"I've spoken to a few of the other kids who were at the bonfire."

Ariana had no idea how he'd tracked down those people. They'd only been visiting the island for a week or so. She, Cam and Ivy had met three guys and one girl—a sister to one of the boys—at a restaurant where they'd been eating before going to the beach. She didn't even remember their names, except one. Their quick and easy friendship with Ben Something, his sister and two other dudes had lasted only as long as the group was on Mariners. As locals, she, Cam and Ivy were used to having tourists filter through their lives. "Then you already know all of this," she said, acting as confident as possible.

"They confirmed you were there. But they say the three of you left together shortly after ten."

That was true. Ariana had been hoping to fudge the timeline from the bonfire by acting—as she had when the police first questioned her—like she hadn't been keeping close track of time. "It may have been," she said. "I wasn't aware of the exact time."

"But you know when you got home."

"I do. Ivy was staying the night with me, and I glanced at the clock when we came in to check it against my curfew, which was midnight. I also realized my grandmother would be asleep at eleven and asked Ivy to be quiet so we wouldn't wake her."

"Was she asleep?"

"Actually, she wasn't. She'd stayed up later than usual to watch a show."

"I see. How long did it take you to walk home that night?"

"I have no idea. We weren't in a hurry, so it probably took longer than usual."

"Accordin' to your earlier statement, you'd been drinkin'."

Knowing it would make her more credible to tell the truth about something they'd done wrong, something she'd rather they not know, she'd admitted to drinking from the beginning. "Yes. Another reason it took longer than normal."

"You're sayin' Cam had been drinkin', too."

"We all had."

"Was he with you when you got home?"

"He didn't come into the house. But he walked us to the edge of the yard to make sure we got in safely and went to his house from there."

"He left at eleven."

She curled her fingernails into her palms as she pumped more conviction to her voice. "Almost on the dot. So you see? Cam couldn't be responsible for hurting Emily Hutchins. From what the police told me before, Emily's sister heard a strange thump at ten-thirty. She didn't get up to check on her sister because she was tired and thought Emily was just going to the bathroom, but she believes Emily was taken at that time. And Cam was with us." She held her breath after she finished, wishing she hadn't gone quite so far. She didn't want to come off overly defensive, but she was desperate for Williams to believe her—wanted him to leave them alone—which made it difficult not to be emphatic.

"What would you say if I told you I have a witness, one of the kids who was with y'all earlier at the bonfire, who saw Cam again after you left? Who said he returned to the beach with a smallish female around eleven?"

Ariana's stomach dropped to her knees. This must've been what Kitty was referring to when she was talking to Ivy's mother. But Priscilla hadn't said Kitty had told her there was a *smallish female* with him. Was that new? And could it be true? Ariana could see him running into someone he knew and deciding to return to the beach. Back then he'd been listless and bored and lonely so much of the time. He never wanted to go home.

But that would mean he'd lied to her, and she refused to even consider the possibility, not after how guilty she'd felt for doubting him last night. She had to decide, one way or the other, and stick to it, or she'd get them all in trouble. "I'd say whoever told you that would have to be wrong." What else could she say? "Did he or she *speak* to Cam?" she pressed. "Can he say who Cam was with?"

"No. *She* told me Cam didn't approach their group again. She said she just happened to look up and recognize him. She claims Cam was arguing with the girl."

Ariana noted the pronoun change. Was it Ben's sister? "Can she say for sure it was Cam she saw? Because I doubt it. Those kids were just tourists we hung out with for a few hours. None of them really knew us, and it was getting late, so it was pretty dark."

Williams didn't respond right away. Ariana got the impression he wasn't just thinking, though. He was hoping she'd fill the silence—babble nervously and reveal some nugget of information she hadn't meant to.

She kept her mouth shut and waited for him.

"Well, that's something to consider," he said at length.

She hoped he'd end the conversation right there, but he simply moved in a new direction.

"Did you know Emily Hutchins?"

"No, sir."

"Did Cam ever mention her?"

"He was late meeting us that night. When he arrived, he said he had to help a girl get into her house because she got locked out. I'm assuming that was Emily."

"Yes. He knew where she was stayin', that her parents were gone for the day and how to get into the house."

"That doesn't mean he's the one who kidnapped her!"

"You believe he's innocent."

"I *know* he is," she said, but was it truly possible to *know*? Cam had been conflicted about so many things back then. He really was what she'd consider a "lost boy." Could he have done something stupid? Something that resulted in an accident that harmed Emily and then panicked?

His parents were difficult, hard on him. And how well could anyone ever really know someone else? There'd been wives who'd been astonished to find their own husbands were serial killers. Was she a better judge of character than they were? Or, like them, was she simply blinded by love?

"He seems like a nice man," Williams said.

She stiffened. "But you think he did it."

The investigator paused for a moment. Then he said, "The logical story is usually the right one, Ms. Prince."

She gripped her phone tighter. "What does that mean?"

"It means chances are better that he did it than someone else."

As she walked to Ivy's, Ariana couldn't get Williams's parting words out of her head.

Fortunately, she had a few minutes to gather herself before she had to see Cam. He was meeting them at the restaurant.

"So? Was he there?" Ivy asked as soon as she opened the door.

Knowing she was talking about Williams, Ariana looked behind her. As they were hanging up, he'd asked if he could call her grandmother. He was probably talking to Alice now, so it was unlikely he was watching her, and yet she was afraid she'd find him sitting in his car across the street. Sometimes the island could feel small and confining—like now, when she desperately wanted to avoid someone. "He wasn't there when I got home, but he'd been there earlier. He gave my grandma his card and she had me call him."

Ivy's expression grew pinched with worry. "How'd it go?"

"Okay, I guess."

She lowered her voice even though there wasn't anyone to overhear them. "Are you going to tell Cam that Williams got hold of you?"

"Not tonight. It won't change anything, and we've been having fun. I don't see any reason to ruin dinner."

"I agree." Seeming relieved, Ivy was digging around in her purse, presumably for her keys, when Ariana nudged her back into the house and closed the door behind them so they could talk for a moment. She'd been planning to wait until the end of the evening, so that she didn't ruin Ivy's dinner, either, but she just couldn't. She was too freaked out by what she'd learned. "Before we go, did Williams tell you there's someone who claims Cam returned to the beach after walking us home?"

Ivy looked startled. "No. He said that to you?"

"He did."

"He must've just learned what Kitty told my mom. Otherwise, he would've mentioned it to me, too, if only to get my reaction."

"I agree. Except it's a little different than what Kitty said.

Not only is Williams claiming Cam went back to the beach, he's saying Cam was with a *smallish female* when he did."

"You've got to be kidding me. That's a terrible description, given Emily's age and size. Could someone be making it all up just to lead the police back to Cam?"

"I have no idea. The fact that this has never come up before makes it suspect, in my opinion. But the same person also claims it was before eleven."

The blood drained from Ivy's face. "That calls into question everything we've told the police."

"Exactly why Williams mentioned it to me. He wanted me to account for the discrepancy."

Her shoulders slumped. "This just keeps getting worse."

"I know." Ariana wasn't sure what she'd expected before she returned to the island. She'd stupidly thought it would all become clear to her, she supposed. Instead, it was murkier than ever. "I think he's asking Alice—right now—what time we got in. But I'm almost positive she'll back us up."

"Does she even know the time we got in?"

Ariana remembered the subtle clues that led her to believe Alice was more aware than she'd ever imagined. "I think so."

"Shit. Now she's coming under the microscope, too. That's three people who have to stick together and remain consistent."

"We can count on her."

"For now. But with all the media attention and sympathy for the Hutchins family, that could change."

"Nothing's for certain," Ariana agreed.

Ivy frowned. "How credible is the person who's saying she saw Cam come back to the beach?"

"Remember the girl who was with us that night?"

"Ben's sister?"

"She was related to one of the guys who was there. I seem to think it was Ben, too. Tourists passed in and out of our lives so fast back then I didn't make a mental note, just had fun in the moment. But I'm guessing that must be her." They didn't even know Ben's last name, but Williams must've come up with it.

The Hutchinses' PI seemed more and more formidable as time went on. Would they be able to hold up in the face of everything he was doing—and everything he would do in the future? Would Alice?

Ivy peered out the window, suddenly acting spooked herself. "Her name was Delilah, I think."

"It must've been her," Ariana said. "Williams used 'she' when he was referring to the person who'd given him the information, and Delilah was the only other girl with us that night."

"But...why didn't she come forward before now?"

Ariana sighed. "That's what I'd like to know. Maybe she wasn't keeping up with current events. We were in high school. It's not like we were paying much attention to the news."

"True. If it hadn't happened here, we probably wouldn't have paid any attention. Sadly, girls go missing all the time."

"Right. There's that, and we couldn't miss it because we were involved in the questioning. But Delilah's not from around here. Even if she heard of a girl who went missing on Mariners, why would she connect Cam to the story? That he might be involved was local gossip, not national news."

"The police have never really had the evidence to put him forward as a true suspect, so that makes sense. But—" Ivy grabbed Ariana's wrists with both hands "—do you think it's true?"

Ariana wished she could say no. But something about Cam saying he was going home while finding a way to avoid it rang true. He'd hated being at home. He was either alone or with parents who were drinking and fighting and holding him accountable for all the misery in their lives. "Who knows?"

Ivy sank onto the seat of the hall tree in the entryway. "What are we going to do?" she asked, her eyes wide with uncertainty.

Ariana had no idea, but she had to keep Ivy calm. The worst thing they could do was panic. "Even if Cam went back to the beach, it doesn't mean he hurt anyone," she said practically.

"That may be true, but it would prove him a liar. He told us he went straight home!"

"It would definitely cost him some credibility." He'd lose credibility with them, too, which was arguably the bigger problem. Even if only one of them began to lose faith, the whole thing could unravel.

"Is that all she said?" Ivy asked. "She saw him at the beach with a smallish female? What were they doing?"

"She told Williams they were arguing."

"Did she recognize the girl?"

"Williams didn't tell me that, either. But I can't believe Delilah *could* recognize Emily. Emily was here on vacation, too. What're the chances they'd ever met?"

"Delilah barely knew *us*," Ivy agreed. "But it won't really matter if she knew her back then or not as long as she can look at a photo lineup now and say, 'That's the girl who was with him.'"

The mere possibility was alarming. If Delilah said Cam returned with Emily instead of some other girl, it would be her word against theirs. "I doubt her memory could be that clear about a face she saw briefly in the moonlight twenty years ago. She was drinking, too, remember?"

"If she thought it was Emily, she probably would've said so," Ivy allowed at the same time her phone went off.

"Don't tell me that's Williams," Ariana said as her friend looked down at it.

"No, it's Cam, wondering where we are," Ivy replied in relief.

Ariana checked the time on her own phone. They were late. "We'd better talk about this later."

Ivy caught hold of Ariana before she could reach for the door. "We're doing the right thing, Ari. And we *will* get through this."

"Of course we will," Ariana said, but that seemed less and less certain by the day.

Cam was relieved to be with his best friends again, to be talking and laughing so freely. It was a gift just to be able to forget his current situation for a while, both with his wife and the investigation into Emily's disappearance. He'd always had to fill his time with something. Ever since he was a young boy, he couldn't bear to be alone *and* idle. When Melanie and Camilla were gone, visiting her parents, he devoted every moment of the day to work, because if he gave himself the chance to think too deeply, all the issues he tried so hard to ignore would take center stage again.

He preferred to focus on problems he could solve—like how to maintain the historical integrity of an old house while making it more functional and appealing to a modern sensibility. He loved that challenge in particular, because if he got creative, there was always an answer.

Which simply wasn't the case in so many other areas of his life. His relationship with his parents was a prime example. The resentment he felt toward them was probably why he'd fought so hard to save his marriage—that and his daughter, of course. He knew if he failed, his mother would point to that as evidence he couldn't navigate his own life any better than they'd navigated theirs.

But he was beginning to think there were times when couples *should* give up on a marriage. He believed it would've been preferable—for them and for him—if his parents had split, putting a stop to the constant emotional upheaval in the house. Jack would never allow that to happen, though. Even now.

Then he'd have to give up half his net worth. Besides, he probably couldn't get along with anyone, regardless of who it was.

"Should we have another drink?" Ivy asked when the waiter came around to check on them.

Cam thought they'd had enough. But they weren't driving, and while they couldn't hold reality at bay forever, they could stave it off a *little* longer. "I'll have an old-fashioned," he said.

Ariana and Ivy ordered another drink, too, and they lingered over a shared piece of Key lime pie for another thirty minutes, reminiscing about the time they'd had to dissect fetal pigs in biology class.

"I had to do both of yours," Cam complained, rolling his eyes.

Ariana grimaced. "I couldn't even look at the poor thing, let alone touch it."

Ivy was chuckling as she shook her head. "I realized then that I wasn't cut out for anything in the medical field."

"I realized the same!" Cam said. "I just didn't have anyone to pawn it off on—like you did."

"That's when we knew what a good friend you really were," Ivy said.

Cam grinned. Of course he would do it. They were the sisters he'd never had, the "family" who listened and cared and was there for him when his parents weren't. "I can't believe how often you'd let me sneak in to spend the night with you," he said.

"Or we'd sneak over to your place," Ariana piped up.

They'd risked getting grounded so he wouldn't have to be alone. He still hated being alone—it was just that now he knew it was better than being with Melanie. "I couldn't have made it through those years without you," he admitted. "My folks were out of control."

"Speaking of Jack and Giselle, what have they been up to lately?" Ariana asked.

He could tell she was feeling the effects of the alcohol. She sounded relaxed and happy—and yet she wouldn't hold his gaze. Whenever their eyes met, she'd flush and look away, and he could guess why. "Still fighting like cats and dogs," he said. "Still using prescription drugs and alcohol to get through the day. Still spending money as if the more they spend the happier they'll be."

"They have money after all they've squandered over the years?" Ivy asked.

Jack had made millions in technology. More recently, he'd become interested in the crypto craze and had helped lay the groundwork for a new exchange that was also paying well. "He seems to have the Midas touch when it comes to business."

"I'm surprised his alcoholism and toxic marriage haven't gotten in the way of his professional success," Ariana said. "Do you speak to your folks very often these days?"

"Every couple of months," he said with a shrug. He didn't mention that his mother tried to contact him more than that—she used every excuse she could think of to reach out—and seemed to be making the attempt, for the first time in his life, to build a real relationship. More often than not he chose to ignore those calls. In his view, it was too little too late.

"What about visits?" Ivy asked.

"I see them about once a year. I think I told you they live in Florence. My mother says it's the only place she's truly *fulfilled*, and it's far enough away that I like it, too."

The ice in Ariana's glass clinked as she took a drink. "Your dad works from there?"

"No doubt he does *some* work from there, over the internet. He also flies to the States quite often."

"Yet, you don't see him?" Ivy asked.

"Now that I'm married and have a child of my own, and he's so busy trying to build this new crypto platform, he doesn't contact me very often. He mostly works in California, anyway, which feels almost as far away as Italy."

Ariana finished the last bite of pie and put down her fork. "It's hard to believe they aren't more interested in Camilla."

"If they could get along with Melanie, they probably would show a little more interest in Camilla." If he had to guess, he'd say his daughter was part of the reason his mother had been trying harder. But Melanie hadn't been very friendly to his folks from the start—she'd cared only about her own family—and his mother wasn't one to ever let go of a slight.

"You wouldn't want her spending a lot of time with them, anyway," Ivy said.

"True."

"I'm sorry." Ariana gave him such an honest, pretty smile, he got lost in it for a second.

Fortunately, the waitress caught his attention by sliding the check onto their table. "That's okay," he said, looking away. "I've learned not to expect too much from them. Makes things easier. Besides, I've got the two of you." He'd said similar things in the past. They'd all said similar things. But tonight he didn't feel quite the same as he had before—at least when it came to Ariana. And that had him a little spooked. The more time he spent with her, the more he became aware of her in a whole new way.

Was he just looking for a sexual outlet? Because after losing any real interest in his wife, and years of refusing to let himself look at anyone else, it'd been a long time since he'd found any joy in making love. But seeing Ariana in a bikini today—and in the white sleeveless dress she was wearing now—made a visceral impact that reminded him a little too much of what he was missing.

He was going to have to be careful this summer, he realized as he insisted on paying the bill, or his life could get even messier and more complicated than it already was.

eleven

Many of the restaurants had street seating and were full of people, most of whom were in their twenties and thirties, looking rich and successful in casual wear with designer labels while drinking expensive wine and talking animatedly to friends. Ariana couldn't help but think the scene would make for a nice painting, with the cobblestone streets, Cape Cod architecture and strings of round white lights adorning eaves and trees and short fences. Paintings like this already hung in the many art galleries on the island.

As she walked home with Ivy, listening to the laughter emanating from the restaurants and the small clusters of people they passed, she was reminded how wonderful the summers really were on Mariners and was sort of jealous that Ivy had been able to stay.

But she knew being on the island wasn't *always* this wonderful. Christmas was special, what with the beautiful decorations and Santa coming out from the mainland on a boat for picture taking and to give away books and little trinkets to kids in the town square. But the winters could drag on forever and get cold and lonely.

Besides, Ariana *could* stay if she really wanted to. She just had no desire to work in tourism. She'd done so much of that as a teen she'd been anxious to go in a different direction after college.

"You're quiet," Ivy said as they rounded the corner.

"I'm just enjoying the good weather."

"You're not thinking about Cam?"

Ariana stiffened. Every time Ivy said something like that she had to wonder if the secret she'd guarded for so long wasn't much of a secret, after all. But a quick glance at her face indicated the question had no hidden hook. "Considering what's going on with Cam, I'm always thinking about him," she admitted. At least she had a good excuse for her obsession.

"I wonder what will happen next."

"I'm hoping the police will be able to find the clues and the evidence they need to figure out who really murdered Emily." Ariana looked behind them to be sure Cam had walked the other way, as she'd expected. "It's so weird that Melanie would leave right when he needs her most."

"I wouldn't leave my husband at a time like this, but maybe there was something going on with her family. He seems relieved to have her gone, so it could be for the best."

"Maybe," Ariana agreed, but it bothered her to think that Melanie could be so selfish.

"And Melanie's young and immature."

Ariana had just opened her mouth to respond when she looked up and saw a woman crossing the street, coming toward them with a determined gait. She didn't recognize her at first.

She'd only ever seen her on TV, on various talk shows and news programs. But there was a striking resemblance to Emily.

This was Jewel Hutchins. It had to be.

Jewel stopped in front of them, essentially barring their progress. "Warner Williams just called me and told me what you said."

Discomfited by the sharp edge in her voice and the fire in her hazel eyes, Ariana stepped back even though she was at least a head taller. "Are you talking to me?"

Jewel's jaw remained determined as she tucked her curly red hair behind her ears. "I'm talking to both of you."

Ivy must've realized who she was, too, because she grabbed Ariana's arm.

"I don't know what exactly you're referring to," Ariana said.

"You're both lying, and I know it."

"About..." Ivy said this, but the word hadn't come out as strongly as she'd probably intended.

"Cam didn't walk you home the night Emily was killed. He was at the beach when you said he was at your house."

"Says who?" Ariana demanded.

Jewel folded her arms. "A witness has come forward."

Ivy seemed as flustered as Ariana was. "To say he was at the beach? She must be mistaken. I'm sorry about what happened to your sister—" she started, but Jewel cut her off before she could finish.

"Then do the right thing and tell the truth."

Those words hit Ariana like a punch to the gut. She felt so guilty. She opened her mouth to say something—she was at such a loss she had no idea what—when Ivy jerked her to one side so they could circumvent Jewel. "Come on," she muttered. "Let's go."

"We hope you find out who really killed your sister, because it wasn't Cam," Ariana said over her shoulder as she gratefully accepted the escape.

"How do *you* know?" Jewel called after them. "You're as blinded by his success and his handsome face as everyone else is."

Jewel felt like she was having a panic attack. As soon as Ivy tugged Ariana away, she ducked behind a vine-covered pillar, hoping she wouldn't be seen as she squatted down and put her head between her knees to help the blood reach her brain. As she gulped down big breaths of air, she squeezed her eyes closed, too, and tried to quell the fierce anger that'd compelled her to approach Ariana and Ivy the second she saw them.

Damn them. She knew they were lying.

What could she do to make them admit the truth?

Her phone went off. Bringing her head up, she checked the screen. Her mother was calling. Her parents were depending on her to bring them the closure they craved, and she felt a strong responsibility to come through for them—as soon as possible. This nightmare had dragged on long enough, had almost destroyed their lives.

If only she could see to it that Cam Stafford was arrested, then the mystery would be solved. Maybe then they'd be able to heal.

Pressing a hand to her chest in an attempt to slow her racing heart, she came to her feet and took a final breath before hitting the answer button. "Hey, Mom."

"Hi, honey. How are you?"

"Fine," she lied, even though she hadn't been fine since she'd left this godforsaken island the last time.

"I've been worried about you."

She turned the phone away from her mouth so that her mother wouldn't be able to hear her labored breathing before she managed to suppress her anxiety again enough that she could answer normally. "I've got this. There's no reason to worry."

"I don't like that you're back on Mariners. The most traumatic and terrible experience of our lives is tied to that place."

This was the last place she wanted to be. But she had no choice. "I *need* to be here. At some point we have to do more than pray."

"What does that mean?"

"That taking action might be the only way we'll ever put the past to rest."

"Prayer works, honey. It's because of prayer that her remains were found. Now at least we have her back."

As far as Jewel was concerned, nothing failed like prayer. But her minister father and his equally devout wife would be horrified to hear her say something like that. So she attended church regularly and held hands with her parents and other members of her father's congregation and routinely pretended to beseech a supreme being, even though it was something she considered a complete waste of time. If there was a God, her life would not have taken the path it had.

"We're praying for you now," her mother added.

Jewel had to grit her teeth to stop herself from revealing her true feelings on that subject. "Thank you."

"Have you learned anything yet?"

"Not a lot. It'll take some time."

"I don't—" her mother's voice cracked "—I don't know how much longer I can hope. It's been two decades."

"God will answer your prayers." Jewel would say anything to comfort her mother. She was *so* tired of watching her parents suffer. Now that Emily's remains had been found, and she had the media on her side, she needed to answer their prayers herself so they could move on. "He'll help me while I stay here, and eventually we'll get the justice Emily deserves."

That it'd taken twenty years for God to answer even part of their prayers did not receive an acknowledgment. "How could they let a boy do what Cam Stafford did to Emily and get away with it?" her mother asked.

"The police here are inept. Tourists come and go every year. They only care about the locals."

"He's married, has a child. We'll never get to see Emily fall in love or start a family, because *he* stole her future. It's so unfair." The discovery of Emily's remains had ripped the Band-Aid off the wound they'd sustained when she went missing, and it was bleeding again. Although her father had restarted all the prayer vigils, and her parents claimed those vigils helped so much, her father had become withdrawn and depressed, and her mother had started drinking again.

"We'll get him," Jewel promised. "Warner Williams is doing a great job. I'm so glad I stumbled into that online chat forum where that woman who almost went to prison for killing her husband told me about him." She'd gone looking for emotional support, others who had suffered similar things to what her family had been through but learned through the experiences of those people, as well.

"I'm glad, too. But he certainly charges enough. If we're not careful, he'll burn through all the money we've raised."

"Then we'll raise more."

"If people will still give. There are other parents who've lost a child. I'm sure they, too, would like the help we're receiving. But there aren't enough resources to go around, which is why so many of these cases go unsolved."

"We'll be the exception," Jewel insisted. "I'll see to it."

"But I don't want this to undo all the progress you've made on…on an emotional level," her mother said.

Jewel had struggled so much since Emily's death. The therapist her parents had sent her to right after they got home from that fateful trip to Mariners said she was suffering from "survivor's guilt"—in addition to regular guilt, of course, for being the person who was supposed to watch over Emily that day. If only she and Emily hadn't argued, Emily wouldn't have left the beach by herself and asked Cam for help getting into the house. Then nothing else would've happened, either. "Emily was my baby sister."

"I know how much you've missed her. How much you need answers. We need them, too. But I hate that you're there alone. Wouldn't you rather your father handled this?"

"You and I both know he's not feeling up to it." Her father had myasthenia gravis, which caused weakness in his ocular and respiratory muscles, as well as the muscles of his arms and legs. Before he'd been diagnosed, he'd been having trouble chewing, swallowing and holding up his head. Now he was managing his symptoms with drugs that boosted the signal between the nerves and muscles, but too much stress could cause a setback. Jewel didn't want him on Mariners. She couldn't believe her mother would even suggest it, except that Emily had been her favorite, so she expected Blaine to do whatever was necessary where Emily was concerned. Jewel had always been closer to her dad.

"He could be there to help you," her mother said.

"He's busy with his ministry. I'd rather you both stayed away from this place and the memories it holds, anyway. You're better off where you're at. Just take care of Dad. Try to keep him from getting too upset and trust me to handle the rest."

Her mother sniffed, evidence that she was crying. "Okay. Just…be careful. After losing Emily, it would kill us to lose you, too."

How many times had Jewel heard that? Her parents had been so paranoid about the dangers a young girl faced they wouldn't even allow her to date when she was a teenager. "I know. I'll survive."

"How long will you be there?"

She thought of Ariana and Ivy. If she could just figure out a way to come between them, maybe one of them would crack.

Or, as Williams had pointed out, if he could find some discrepancy in their versions of events, he could use that like a crowbar to break open the whole case.

Even if they didn't crack, maybe Alice would. Williams had talked to Ariana's grandmother today. She told him that she'd been watching a movie when Ariana and Ivy came in, that she had no idea what time it was. But he'd gotten the feeling she knew more than she was saying—and a sweet, old church-going lady like Alice might be struggling enough with her conscience that she'd tell the truth before Ivy or Ariana would, if only to make sure she didn't wind up taking such a terrible secret with her to the grave.

Cam wanted to invite Ariana over, but for the first time in his life, he was worried about being alone with her. The more he thought about her, the more he liked thinking about her. That right there told him he was in trouble—which was why, after he got home, he left his phone in the kitchen and went into the living room, where he turned on the TV and began surfing through channels, trying to find something interesting enough to distract him.

Unfortunately, nothing worked. All he could do was obsess over calling Ariana before she went to bed. He didn't know when Melanie would be home and make it more difficult for him to see her. And it was hard to believe it would be a big deal to have her over. They'd spent many chaste nights together through the years.

But the shift in his feelings since she'd told him she was in love with him was as significant as it was subtle. He was starting to experience a new kind of interest in her. So as much as he wished he could pretend nothing had changed, he couldn't. He was too afraid of what he might do. Despite Melanie's many accusations, he'd never cheated on her. Even if they weren't going to make it as a couple, he preferred to reach the end of their relationship before getting involved with someone else, especially someone he had a previous relationship with that he wanted to protect.

But his head was so screwed up, he still wanted Ariana to come over.

Shit.

He'd gotten up to pace—he had too much energy flowing through him to remain on the couch—when the phone rang, drawing him back to the kitchen. If it was Ariana, he knew he wouldn't be able to resist answering.

Fortunately, it wasn't. It was his mother. He didn't necessarily want to talk to Giselle but taking her call would keep him from doing anything stupid, at least for as long as they were on the phone. And by then Ariana would probably be in bed.

Or maybe not. It was only eight-thirty. He had at least a couple of hours to kill.

"Hello?"

"There you are. I tried to reach you a week ago and couldn't get an answer."

He remembered seeing her call come in. "My voice mail didn't pick up?"

"I didn't bother to leave a message."

Because she knew he wouldn't return it. He never did. "Sorry I missed your call. Is there something I can do for you?"

This question met with such a pronounced pause he thought she'd say never mind and hang up. A lot of their conversations ended badly. She hated that she "couldn't get through to him" as she put it, but she was the one who'd taught him that caring about her only caused pain, disappointment and anger. He wasn't going to make the mistake of getting his heart caught in that blender again. "I was just…worried about you," she said at last.

It was a bit late to start acting more motherly. But he didn't say that. The past was the past. She couldn't change it, and neither could he. "What for?" he asked. If she didn't know what was going on, he wasn't going to be the one to tell her.

"Carol Strobel called. She said the whole island's in an uproar over the discovery at the lighthouse."

So she did know about Emily's remains being found. A former neighbor had told her. "That's true. And with the tourist season just cranking up, it's crazy here right now." He could've added that the Hutchins family had hired a private investigator, who was trying to stir things up even more, but he held back. Typically, the less she knew the better.

"I'm surprised *you* didn't call to tell us," she said. "We're your parents. Didn't you think we'd want to know?"

"It's been all over the news, Mom."

"We live in Italy, remember?"

But they'd only lived there the past few years. Yes, she'd been born there, but to American parents who were both in the service. And her family had moved away when she was only two. He found it odd that she'd be so insistent on calling it "home."

"You stay in touch with a lot of people here."

"I do. Some of them contact us more than our own son," she said drily. "You're acting like this has no effect on us."

"It doesn't. It has an effect on *me*," he clarified.

"What affects you affects us."

"Not anymore. I've been taking care of myself for a long time, Mother. You're off the hook."

"We're your family!"

"Yeah, well..." He almost said, *I guess that's true, if you use the term loosely enough*, but he swallowed the rest.

"Well what?" she snapped.

"Nothing," he bit out, but he could tell by the pique in her voice that she understood whatever he'd been about to say hadn't been flattering to her.

After a moment of stilted silence, she cleared her throat before attempting to speak to him again. Now that she didn't hold any power over him, she typically behaved better, but that was part of the reason he had such a difficult time forgiving her. He believed if she still held any power—even if it was just a small amount of emotional leverage—she'd abuse it again. "Have the police been over?"

"Of course."

She gasped. "What'd they say?"

"What they said before," he replied. "That they're investigating the kidnapping of Emily Hutchins—only this time they said the murder of Emily Hutchins—and needed to ask me some questions."

"Should we hire an attorney, son? Someone who…who would know how to navigate this?"

Did she think he might be guilty? He'd always wondered. She hadn't said much at the time, just glared at him for causing yet another problem—this one far more serious than any of the others. His father had said even less. Determined not to let anything interfere with his work, Jack had ignored the whole thing and carried on with his rigorous schedule as if nothing of any import was going on at home.

Fortunately, it hadn't turned out to be anything more than a dark cloud that'd hung over him for a few months. Cam had believed the whole thing was behind him. But now that everyone knew Emily was dead, he could wind up in prison—unless DNA or some other evidence finally led to someone else.

"I'm hoping it won't come down to that," Cam said. "If it does, I'll hire my own attorney."

"You're saying you don't need our help."

"Not anymore. Which is good, right? At least I'm not a pain

in the ass any longer. That should make you happy. And you can't let me down anymore, which makes *me* happy."

When she hung up rather than respond, he closed his eyes and tilted his head back to stare up at the ceiling. He always went too far with her. It was the resentment. It'd formed an impenetrable wall—solidified like concrete—and he couldn't seem to find his way over or around it, especially when he needed her most. Somehow, it was much easier to be generous with her when he didn't.

A ding, signaling a text, made him look at his phone again. It was Ariana.

I need to talk to you. Do you mind if I come over?

He stared at those words for probably sixty seconds, trying to decide how to respond. He could tell her he was already in bed and set a time to talk to her tomorrow morning. But he wasn't convinced it would be believable. Not this early.

Sure, he wrote. Do you want me to pick you up?

Ariana had refused to allow Cam to come get her. She was afraid Williams was watching her grandmother's house, which was why she let herself out the back and hurried down the alley.

As she cut through town, she passed small groups of college students who were laughing and talking as they searched for a restaurant or bar to their liking, and several vehicles slid past her even after she got beyond the majority of the businesses and restaurants and the streets grew quiet. She didn't see anything to suggest Williams was aware that she was out and about. But a Mariners Police car rolled by, which made her nervous. If she had her guess, someone from the force would be contacting her soon. This must've been a regular patrol, however, since they didn't pull over or try to engage her.

When she reached Cam's house, she was breathing hard from having walked so fast. She was eager to get behind closed doors before she could bump into Jewel again, or someone else she knew—like Williams, or even Ivy, since she hadn't invited Ivy to come with her. She was drawing so much attention on Mariners. Maybe she should've anticipated that, but she hadn't even considered what coming home would be like in that regard. Instead, she'd let the case draw her back in spite of any and all risks. She'd felt it was her responsibility to return and make a more informed decision.

Not that it had changed anything. Here she was defending Cam again. But she couldn't decide if she was wrong to do what she was doing. In a case like this—a political hot potato where the police felt they had to solve a crime for which they had no other viable suspect—she knew how easy it would be for him to be convicted solely on circumstantial evidence.

Now that she was an adult, however, she was much more aware of the risks involved in lying to protect him.

What if the truth ever came out?

She thought of her mother, stepfather and stepsiblings. Her mother cared so much about what other people thought, especially the wealthy people she knew on the island. If Ariana were to be exposed as a liar, especially so publicly, it would absolutely humiliate Bridget—not to mention what might happen to her.

Cam opened the door as soon as she knocked. "Hey. What's going on? You okay?"

"I'm fine."

"You look rattled."

She stepped inside and felt an immediate rush of relief when he closed the door. "I guess I *am* a little rattled."

"Why? What's going on?"

She could tell he was now feeling *her* anxiety on top of his own and felt bad for making things harder for him. But she needed to talk to him—to make him fully aware of all the forces that were gathering against him. Was he prepared for what could happen?

Was *she*? How long could she and Ivy hold up if the district attorney decided to try Cam? Would they go so far as to perjure themselves? "Ivy and I ran into Jewel on our way home from the restaurant," she told him.

His eyes widened. "Jewel Hutchins?"

"Yes. She's in town, and she's absolutely convinced you're the one who killed her sister."

"Because I'm the only person who's ever been named in the investigation. But there were a lot of people on the island that night. It was right after the Fourth of July."

That was part of the reason Ariana had covered for him. The evidence pointing at him just wasn't that convincing—not to her. "She called me a liar to my face, Cam. She did the same to Ivy."

He dropped onto the leather sofa.

"And you should've seen her when she said it," Ariana continued. "She looked positively unhinged."

"I heard she had some kind of breakdown after."

"How'd you hear that?"

"The police told me. They were trying to appeal to my conscience, get me to confess."

"You've never said that before. How long did they keep bothering you?"

"Most of the rest of that summer."

"Well, as sorry as I feel for Jewel, I'm scared of her, too. She's determined to see you behind bars."

"Putting me in prison won't give her family any justice."

"It won't bring Emily back, either, but she's on a mission."

He shook his head in a way that suggested he had no idea how he should react. "It's been three weeks since Emily's remains were found and no revelation as to the cause of death."

"You've been waiting for that?"

"Hoping for it."

"How will they be able to determine the cause of death after so long?" she asked. "They have little more than teeth, bones and hair."

"According to the internet, a coroner can determine quite a few things from those remains."

"Like…"

"If Emily was bludgeoned, her skull would show it. If she was stabbed, there's a chance they'd find a nick or cut mark on her ribs or other bones. If she was poisoned, they can sometimes find evidence of it in the hair shaft."

"You and I both know it's unlikely she was poisoned."

"You asked for examples."

But none of those examples covered Ariana's worst fear. What if Emily was strangled? Then there'd be no point in even looking for a murder weapon, which took away one more piece of potential evidence that could lead the police to the real culprit.

When she didn't respond, he shot her a look that suggested he knew what she was thinking. "There has to be *something*, Ariana—something that leads to the person who murdered Emily. Or Jewel may get her wish."

Ariana sat down next to him. They were both wearing shorts, so she could feel the warmth of his leg against her own and wanted to put a reassuring hand on his thigh—something she wouldn't have thought twice about in all the years of their long history. But she didn't dare touch him anymore, not after what she'd revealed. "There's something else."

He wore a beleaguered expression. "What is it?"

"There's a witness."

"To what?" he cried. "I didn't do anything!"

"She claims she saw you come back to the beach after you left with us that night."

She was waiting for him to jump in and tell her he *hadn't* gone back to the beach that night. But he didn't. He just sat there, staring off into space, which caused a feeling of foreboding to build inside her.

She leaned closer. "Do you know who the witness might be?"

"I have no clue."

That wasn't a denial. "Ivy thinks it must be Delilah—Ben's sister. They were tourists that summer, remember?"

"Of course I remember. But if it *is* Delilah, why didn't she come forward earlier?" he asked.

"Maybe no one asked her, Cam. Maybe it took this long to track her down to see what she had to say. But…there's more."

"What do you mean?"

"She's not only claiming you returned to the beach—she says you were there with a smallish female."

He froze. *"With Emily?"*

Ariana winced. "Not with Emily necessarily."

He jumped to his feet. "But you know what *smallish female* will be taken to mean."

Ariana got up, too. "Cam, I hate to ask you this after…after what I did before. I'm sorry about that. I truly am. But I have to know. *Did* you go back to the beach after you walked us home?"

When he didn't answer, Ariana's heart sank. "Cam?"

"You don't really want to know," he said. "It'll only make what's happening harder for you and Ivy."

Harder to trust him and stand by him?

Shaking her head in disbelief, she muttered a curse.

He *had* gone back, just as she'd suspected.

twelve

It felt like his life was completely unraveling. Cam watched Ariana dig at her cuticles, something she'd always done when she was nervous or upset, as she began to pace in his living room. "Why didn't you tell us before?" she asked, her voice low but angry.

"Because I knew it would only make things worse," he said. "And it doesn't matter."

"How can you say that?" she asked, her voice rising.

He scowled. "The only thing that matters about that night is this—I didn't hurt Emily."

"Then who were you with at the beach? Why'd you even go back there?"

The tension in his body made him feel hamstrung—so tight he could barely move. He stretched his neck, trying to relieve some of the pressure.

"You're not going to tell me?" she demanded when he didn't reply.

He didn't want to tell her. He tried not to think of that night; didn't want to remember it even now. But he had to explain what really happened, or she was going to lose faith in him. He could already see the suspicion building in her eyes. "After I walked you and Ivy home, I went home myself. But Jewel knocked on the door only seconds later. I got the impression she'd been waiting and watching for me."

"What'd she want? You'd only seen her for a few minutes when you helped Emily get into the house, right?"

He went over and pulled the wand that would electronically lower the blinds. His house sat up high enough that no one except the neighbors directly across the street could see in—if they happened to look—but he craved privacy, didn't want anyone to catch sight of him and Ariana storming around. "That's right. She offered me a brownie for helping her sister, but I didn't take it because I didn't want to go back inside the house."

"Then...why'd she come over?"

Feeling sticky and clammy—overheated, even though it wasn't that hot—he pushed the hair off his forehead. He wasn't proud of his behavior that night. It wasn't anything he cared to talk about, especially now that he knew Ariana had felt more for him all along than he'd ever realized. He hadn't even been attracted to Jewel. But Emily's sister had made it clear what she was offering him, and he'd been young, stupid and drunk enough—not to mention just coming into his sexual prime—to figure he might as well take a free piece of ass. It would certainly beat spending the next couple of hours alone, listening for the sound of the door and wondering if his parents were going to show up. They'd called to tell him they were flying into Boston, but they hadn't been sure whether they'd be able to make the last ferry. "She had a bottle of Jack Daniel's."

"That's why you let her in?"

"I didn't let her in. I was afraid my parents would come home, and I couldn't risk them catching me with a girl."

"So you suggested going back to the beach."

"Yes. I said I'd show her the lighthouse. I knew there probably wouldn't be anyone there. It was deserted when you, Ivy and I were there earlier."

She frowned at him. "Emily wasn't with her?"

"No, of course not. Just as we were walking away, she came out of the house and started shouting for her sister to come home, but Jewel told her to shut up and go back inside."

"And? Did she?"

"From what I could tell, yeah."

"Did you speak to Delilah and Ben and the others we met that night when you went back?"

"No. I didn't speak to anyone."

"You didn't even see them?"

He came around the couch. "From a distance. I didn't realize they noticed me, but I wouldn't have cared. It wasn't as if I was hiding, Ari. I had no idea Emily would go missing, and I'd get blamed if I happened to be seen back at the beach."

Growing even more agitated, she strode to the fireplace, where she turned and walked back toward him. "What happened then?"

He stared down at his flip-flops, noticing the tan lines they were making on his feet. "I'd rather not tell you."

"I'm part of this, too," she said. "I've stood by you throughout it all. I think you owe me the truth."

His lie had compromised her and Ivy, which wasn't fair. But telling them the truth wouldn't make things any easier. They'd still face the same tough decision—whether to believe him or go to the police. And the more people he told, the more it put him at risk.

But he didn't want to be the kind of prick who'd only think of himself. This was Ariana. If he couldn't be honest with her, who could he be honest with?

"Fine." He scratched his head as he tried to decide how to say what he needed to say. He knew it would sound tawdry and opportunistic, but he'd been a directionless boy of sixteen, and he'd never shied away from a good time. Being reckless and, occasionally, self-destructive, was the way he got back at his parents for not providing the kind of security and support he needed. "We got drunk and had sex at the lighthouse." He stated it bluntly because he couldn't come up with anything better. "That's it. Then I went home, assuming she'd leave the island when her family's vacation was over, and I'd never see her again."

Ariana didn't comment on the first part, which came as a relief. She'd been a virgin through high school; hadn't slept with anyone until college. He'd never forget the year she came to spend Christmas with Alice and to see him and Ivy. It was the first time he'd ever felt strange about anything she confided in him. Although Ivy had been eager to hear all the details, it'd upset him somehow. He'd attributed his reaction to the fact that it hadn't been a good experience for her. She'd gotten drunk and gone home with some guy she didn't even care about, and she hadn't been willing to accept the dude's calls after. But now he couldn't help wondering if it was a possessiveness he'd refused to acknowledge that had made her revelation so hard for him to hear.

"So...where was Emily?" she asked.

"At the house where we left her. Or...somewhere else, I guess," he replied. "I can promise you she wasn't with us."

When Ariana didn't comment further, just kept chewing on her bottom lip, he said, "Hey, what's going through that head of yours?"

"I'm thinking...if Jewel was with you at the beach, why

hasn't she said so? She's trying to get me and Ivy to tell the truth—to take away your alibi—when she can do that herself. She can even do us one better by placing you directly at the lighthouse!"

Jewel was odd. He'd known it even then, which was part of the reason he'd first tried to steer clear of her. "I've thought about that a lot over the years. I don't have a good answer, except… Her father's a minister," he said with a shrug.

"What difference does that make?" she asked, obviously bewildered that he'd even bring it up.

"My guess is she doesn't want him to know what she was doing that night instead of watching her sister."

"Oh." Ariana's eyebrows slid up speculatively. "That's a thought. If I'd slipped out to have sex with a total stranger while on vacation, especially at sixteen, I wouldn't want my stepfather to know, and he's not even religious. But why don't you just tell everyone she was with you at the lighthouse? That you weren't with Emily, you were with Jewel?"

He'd often wondered if he should've done that from the start. But he'd been a teenager trying to stay out of trouble. Of course he'd say he wasn't there. And once he'd established that lie, he'd had to stick with it, or things would only get worse. "I can't ruin my credibility like that. Especially when she could just deny it—claim I'm now starting a smear campaign against her to save myself. It's not like I have any proof. It'd be my word against hers, and changing my story would not only compromise you and Ivy, it would place me right at the scene of the crime."

She frowned. "That's true. How late were you two out?"

Fortunately, Ariana didn't seem to be as mad as he'd thought she might be. "About an hour and a half. It was almost one when I got home. I know because I was afraid I'd find my parents waiting for me. But they weren't there." More often than not, Jack and Giselle had left him to his own devices.

But occasionally, if he wasn't home at a decent hour, or he did something else wrong, they'd flip out and ground him for an unreasonable length of time, or worse. There were instances when his father really lost his temper and came after him with a belt. Cam still had a scar on his lower back from a buckle.

"We have to figure out what Emily did that night," Ariana said.

He threw up his hands. "As far as I know, she went back inside and stayed there."

"She could've been wandering around the beach, looking for her sister."

"That's possible."

Ariana flopped onto the couch and propped her legs on the coffee table. "That means anyone there could've gotten hold of her."

A sense of futility rolled over him. Now that Emily's remains had been found, he had no idea how he was going to get out of the mess he was in. "Exactly. It could've been one of a hundred or more people who were on the beach that night. The police made a big deal about me knowing where Emily was staying and how to get inside the house, but I don't believe whoever killed her took her from the house. She was probably out running around like Jewel was. She certainly hadn't been hesitant to make her own way home from the beach earlier, when she and Jewel got into an argument."

Ariana let her head fall back so that she was looking up at the ceiling. "Then why haven't there been any witnesses coming forward to say they saw a young girl by herself at the beach?"

"I have no answer for that, either. But it doesn't mean she wasn't there."

"True." She lifted her head. "Okay, what about this? Why didn't their parents sound the alarm when they finally got home and found Emily gone? Why'd they wait?"

"Because, like my folks, they didn't get home until morning. That's when they found Jewel asleep in her bed and Emily's bed empty."

Sitting up, Ariana tucked her legs beneath her. "They left their two daughters home alone all night? Why haven't I heard this before?"

"Probably because no one thought it was a big deal. Jewel was sixteen, and Emily was twelve, and the island is considered safer than most places. We don't have a lot of crime here. Anyway, the way I heard it they were planning to make it back, but the last ferry got canceled because the captain and some of the crew weren't feeling well. That's why my folks didn't make it, either."

Shock registered on her face. "Then how do they know when Emily was taken?"

"They don't. They only think she was taken at ten-thirty because Jewel claims that's when she was awakened by a strange noise—a thump of some kind."

Ariana gaped at him. "She had to have made that up."

"Of course she did. She said it so her parents wouldn't know she went out."

"Which means Emily could've been taken from her bed anytime before her parents arrived!"

"Or she was taken from the beach, as we said earlier."

"Jewel wouldn't have noticed Emily wasn't at home once you guys got back?"

"Maybe she was so drunk she never thought to check. Or she didn't want to risk waking Emily up by going into her room. Then that would've started another argument since Jewel left her alone."

"Wow." Ariana rubbed her forehead. "You know what this means, don't you? Jewel has been hampering the investigation herself. Why would she give that bogus timing on the *thump*?"

"To make her parents think she was in bed as they expected her to be and taking good care of her little sister. She was babysitting. She had to have some answer."

Ariana got back to her feet. "She might even have said that before she realized all the implications."

"True," he said. "Then, like me, she couldn't take back what she'd already told them."

"The way she confronted me and Ivy earlier makes a lot more sense now. She probably blames herself for what happened to Emily because she was busy with you instead of watching her little sister. And if Ivy and I admit that you weren't with us when we said you were, it places you at the beach without her having to admit what *she* did wrong that night."

"She gets off the hook, but I get caught."

"That's what she's trying to do. It's sort of clever, if you look at it that way. But what's going on inside her head? I couldn't live with myself if my little sister was kidnapped while I was supposed to be watching her. Feeling as though you had some part in it... God, that'd be terrible."

"No doubt it has been."

"But...what's her play? Why is she so intent on going after you? She doesn't truly believe you kidnapped Emily after you had sex with her, does she?"

"She could. After all, Emily's body was found at the lighthouse I'd just shown her. Jewel knew I was drunk and out and about when I was supposed to be home. And I'm sure she's heard I was in trouble for various things before, and that I was the only one who knew how to get into the house without breaking a window." He shoved his hands into the pockets of his shorts. "Besides all that, she might be a little bitter. I never followed up on our encounter."

"How could she expect you to contact her again when all hell broke loose the next morning?"

"I don't know, but she came by before she and her parents left and told me she knew I'd never do anything to harm her little sister and gave me her number."

"You didn't call her?"

"No. I should never have touched her in the first place. I knew I wasn't interested in her."

Ariana twisted a lock of her hair between two fingers as she began to pace again. "I'm still stunned that she'd change her mind and start to believe you snuck in and kidnapped Emily after she went to sleep."

"*I'm* not surprised," he said. "It's probably what her parents and the police have been saying for years. After all, no other viable suspects have surfaced. And finding Emily's remains has dredged up all their pain and loss, making them more determined than ever to get justice. Sometimes an answer is an answer even if it's not the right one."

Cam had been watching Ariana for a sign that she accepted what he was saying. He'd never been more desperate to prove his innocence. He had so much more to lose now than when he was sixteen. But he had no proof to offer her. He had only his word, and he'd already tainted that. "Do you believe me?" he asked.

A sulky expression came over Ariana's face. "I shouldn't. You've been hiding the truth for the past twenty years."

"My future was on the line, Ari," he said. "It still is."

"I know," she responded, obviously softening. "I *do* believe you. But this witness who's cropped up—Delilah or whoever it is—is a real problem, Cam. Now it's my word—and Ivy's—against hers."

He gave her a sheepish yet hopeful smile. "That's two against one."

She smiled back at him, although a bit reluctantly. "True, but we happen to be your best friends, which means we have incentive to protect you, and everyone knows it. I'm not sure we can get enough people—or the right people—to believe us. Warner Williams doesn't. I swear that man can sniff out a lie like a dog can sniff out a bone."

"I'm sorry I held out on you," he said. "But I couldn't tell anyone, even you and Ivy. I was afraid it would make you both wonder if it *could've* been me."

"Any other frightened sixteen-year-old boy would've done the same thing," she said. "You were in a panic. We all were. But…what do we do now?"

"What *can* we do except stick to our stories and hope Jewel won't suddenly decide to come forward and tell the police that she and I were at the lighthouse together that night?"

"If she was going to come forward, she would've done it by now," she said. "Don't you think? She'd look too bad admitting the truth after twenty years of grieving and pretending to be doing everything possible to find her sister's killer."

"You never know," he said. "Guilt can make people do some weird things."

Ariana stayed at Cam's to watch a movie. They decided they wouldn't talk about Emily and the case anymore, wouldn't let it ruin this brief time they had together before Melanie returned to Mariners. Instead, they made popcorn and got comfortable—Cam on one side of the L-shaped sofa and her on the other—with cold beers and lap blankets. Relaxing together while watching the latest James Bond movie offered a brief respite from all the worry and allowed them to simply be friends again.

After the movie was over, Ariana knew she should probably leave. It was getting late. But Cam started asking about her life in New York, and she couldn't help staying to enjoy the conversation, probably because they were firmly on the same team again.

"Why would you ever get with someone you don't love?" he said when she told him about Bruce.

They were still sitting in the same places from which they'd watched the movie, and they were being careful not to acknowledge what she'd said about who she *did* love. Acting as though nothing had changed between them enabled her to pretend her true feelings weren't all that different from what they should be, and she assumed it was the same for him.

"That's hard to explain," she replied. "I admired Bruce. I liked him. I still do. And he was so eager to be with me. It can be hard to say no—over and over again—to someone who would rather hear a yes, especially if you care about them." She gestured at the large black-and-white photograph of Melanie, flexing and wearing a revealing gym outfit, that hung on the wall over the bar. "Besides, didn't you do something similar?"

He glanced over at the photograph and rolled his eyes. "She insisted on putting that out here."

"Instead of…"

"In the bedroom or the study or somewhere else where it wouldn't be seen by everyone who comes over."

Ariana looked at it again. "You don't like it?"

"It's just so obviously vain, right? To put up a picture of yourself like that in the living room?"

Ariana couldn't help feeling a little inadequate. "I guess she has reason to be proud. Is she still weightlifting?"

"Not so much anymore. That was during her bodybuilding phase."

"I never would've expected an interest in bodybuilding from the woman I met at your wedding."

"I didn't expect it, either. But after Camilla was born, she started going to the gym to 'get her body back.' One of the trainers ended up befriending her and got her to enter some contests." He tipped up his beer. "She loved the attention. And it kept her busy, making it possible for me to work without the pressure she puts on me, so I was hugely supportive."

They both laughed.

"But I didn't do what you did with Bruce," he continued. "I didn't get with Melanie just because she wanted me to. There was a baby involved."

Ariana took the twisty she'd put on her wrist before coming over and used it to tie her hair on top of her head. "You let yourself get cornered. That's sort of the same thing."

He finished the beer. "When you put it that way..."

"Remember when I came for the wedding, and you said—" She stopped midsentence, suddenly second-guessing whether she should ask such a question.

"Said what?" he prompted as he sat forward to put his empty bottle on the coffee table.

"Never mind. You and Melanie are already struggling. I shouldn't ask. It's just...I've always wondered."

His expression took on a sardonic edge. "Why I didn't use a rubber?"

"You told me why at the wedding. She claimed she was on the pill. But do you really believe the pill failed? I mean, if you use it correctly, it's like ninety-nine percent effective."

"She claims she was on some antibiotic that made it less effective."

Ariana had heard that some medications could interfere, but she was still too skeptical to believe Melanie. "Have you ever Googled that?" she asked doubtfully.

He shot her a wry glance. "Of course."

"And? Is it true?"

"There's only one antibiotic that's known to make the pill

less effective. I can't remember the name of it, but it's used to treat tuberculosis."

"Meaning she was probably never on it..."

"Exactly," he said. "From what I read online, there are other drugs out there she could've named. But she insists she was taking an antibiotic for a urinary tract infection and all the research must be wrong. Or she was an outlier, an exception to the rule."

Ariana said nothing.

"You don't believe her..." he said.

"No."

"Well, I have to—or at least I can't dwell on it—or my marriage gets even harder," he explained.

Ariana shook her head. "I'd be so angry."

"Trust me. I've been angry. Why do you think we've had more than our fair share of trouble?" He shot her a speculative look. "But...there's something I've been meaning to ask you, too."

A twinge of foreboding made Ariana shift uncomfortably. Hopefully, he wasn't going to bring up what she'd said the last time she was at his house. "What is it?"

"Do you ever wonder about your dad? Your *real* dad?"

This was a much easier subject than she'd anticipated. They used to speculate about her real father all the time. Scooping up the last of the popcorn, she set the bowl aside. "My Scottish sperm donor?"

"Yeah. You have to be curious."

"I am."

"Do you think you'll ever try to learn more about him? Maybe try to meet him one day?"

"I had my DNA done at one of those sites," she said. At the time, she'd told herself she was doing it to receive general health information. Did cancer run in her family? Diabetes?

Bipolar disorder? That would be good information to have. But deep down she knew there was more to it. She'd liked her stepfather, even if he'd shown blatant partiality toward his own offspring, but she'd craved more love and attention than he'd ever offered her. Besides that, there were times—a lot of them—when she'd felt more like a sister to her mother than a daughter. It was almost as if she'd never really had parents. And the obvious differences between her and her siblings in looks and character traits created questions she would love to have answered. If she could have a picture of her real father, it'd be *something.*

Given the way her mother got pregnant, however, she couldn't imagine her father would be pleased to hear from her. He probably had a wife and other children and hadn't thought twice about the one-night stand he'd had while visiting America. Her mother claimed she wrote him to let him know about the pregnancy, but he never responded. Maybe he never even got the letter.

"You checked your DNA?" Cam said. "And? Were there any matches?"

"So far only a distant cousin."

"More and more people are doing it."

She could tell he meant that by way of encouragement. She told herself that all the time, too. But… "If he's afraid it'll lead me to him, he might not be eager to take the test."

Cam cast her an empathetic look. "If he feels that way, it's because he doesn't understand what he's missing, Ari."

A lump swelled in her throat. "That's nice of you to say."

"I mean it. You know I do."

Maybe that was one of the reasons she'd always loved Cam. He understood her and her vulnerabilities and buoyed her with his kindness and support. She supposed that was why she'd done what she'd done for him—because he'd do the same for her if their roles were reversed. "You've always shown up for me." She smiled. "Remember that time we ran away together?"

When he chuckled, she knew he did remember. "Right after your parents said you'd be moving?"

"Yes. It was *so* cold that night. I was sitting in the pouring rain, waiting for the ferry, and you showed up with a backpack full of clothes and food. You said if I was running away, you were going with me, even though you were already in trouble for ditching school and your parents said if you did anything else they'd send you to a reform facility in California." She'd never forget him putting his arms around her and holding her against him to protect her from the worst of the weather on the bumpy ride to Boston, where they'd spent three days living by their wits and sleeping in alleyways and door fronts with the rest of the homeless population.

She wouldn't have lasted a day without him, but she was able to hold out long enough that her mother finally relented and allowed her to live with Alice until she could graduate from high school. "Do you remember hanging out behind that pizza place and grabbing the leftover pizza they threw in the Dumpster at closing?" She grimaced. "It was so gross in that alley. I never would've had the nerve to reach in there. But you didn't think anything of it. You knew we had to eat."

"Best pizza I ever had," he joked.

She sobered as she looked at him. "You took that risk for me. You lived like that for three days when you didn't have to. And you looked after me."

"You've risked a lot for me, too." He gestured at the portrait of Melanie that was so flattering she wanted everyone to see it. "And I know I've let you down since I married. I would've still been there for you, if not for Camilla."

"I understand why you pulled away." She'd pulled away, too, for other reasons. Fortunately, he didn't call her on that.

They continued to stare at each other, this time without speaking. When they were their closest, during high school, she'd never had sex, hadn't known what she was missing.

But now… She couldn't help thinking about what it might be like to be held naked in Cam's arms.

When her gaze fell to his lips, she knew her mind was drifting into dangerous territory and kicked off the lap blanket she'd been using. "It's getting late. I'd better go."

"No." He stopped her while she gathered up the empty beer cans and popcorn bowls. "Don't go."

"It's almost one o'clock."

"So?" He took the cans from her. "Stay the night. You can have the master. I'll take the pullout in my studio."

"My grandmother will wonder where I'm at in the morning."

"You're in your thirties," he teased. "I don't think we have to worry about that anymore. She'll just assume you stayed with Ivy."

When she hesitated, he added, as an enticement, "I'll make you breakfast in the morning…"

She'd been planning to speak to Kitty at the coffee shop first thing. She'd told Williams she had an appointment. She'd even mentioned it to Alice, so that was probably where Alice would assume she'd gone. But Williams wouldn't know any different. And there was no rush. She could go later in the day. She got the impression Cam still hated being alone.

And if he needed the company…

"Okay," she said.

thirteen

Once he finally nodded off, Cam slept better than he had in ages. Just knowing Ariana was in the house made him happy. He was glad he'd finally told her the truth. He'd been afraid that if she ever found out he'd returned to the beach the night Emily went missing, she'd never trust him again. But she seemed to understand why he'd lied, and for that he was grateful. So much of his sense of well-being depended on her.

That had been true even before Emily went missing. Ivy and Ariana were like sisters to him. Or…maybe not Ariana. He hadn't been feeling very brotherly toward her recently. Last night it'd been tough to stop thinking about the fact that she was in his bed.

Covering a yawn, he reached over to check his phone. Yes, it was morning, but it was still early. He was too accustomed to waking up at six, regardless of when he went to bed, to be able to sleep longer. Even on weekends he got up with Camilla so that Melanie could lie in. It was the only time she ever really allowed him to be alone with their daughter, and he looked forward to those few precious hours. Otherwise, if Melanie was up, she demanded all of his attention and seemed jealous of the love he gave Camilla.

Steering his mind away from Melanie, he climbed out of bed, put the couch back together and the bedding away and showered and brushed his teeth in the guest bath before going upstairs to see if Ariana might be stirring. He enjoyed spending time with her and Ivy when they were a threesome, but it was a nice change to have Ariana all to himself.

After a soft knock to which he got no response, he poked his head through the double doors of his own bedroom and found her buried beneath the covers of his bed. She wasn't moving, so he decided to go down and put on some coffee and start breakfast. As soon as he began to retreat, however, a voice issued from the lump in the bed. "Don't tell me you're already awake," she said.

"You heard my knock?"

"I heard you stomping up the stairs first."

He could tell she was teasing him. "I was trying to be quiet," he protested, laughing, as he strode into the room and pounced on the bed to make it jiggle. "But I'm excited you're here. Let's get up and get going."

"Where?" she asked, the word a tired syllable as she tried to kick him off.

"We'll eat and then… I don't know. We'll call Ivy and head back to the beach or something. Maybe do a little more body surfing and then look for some sea glass."

"You don't have to work?"

"It's Sunday."

She shoved her hair out of her face as she lifted her head.

"Fine. I'll get up and we'll have breakfast. Then you can go over to The Human Bean with me. I need to talk to Kitty about a job."

He was trying not to notice how pretty she'd become, but seeing her so rumpled and wearing the T-shirt he'd given her before bed was more appealing than it should've been to him. "You plan to work this summer?"

"Not all of us are as rich as you," she said, throwing one of the pillows at him.

"You shouldn't have done that," he said and started an all-out pillow fight, one she apparently didn't want to lose, because she fought as hard as he did. They were both exhausted by the time he managed to pin her down on the bed, using his body weight to help subdue her.

"I win," he said, grinning in triumph. "At last."

The laughter fled her face as she gazed up at him, and he realized he had an erection. No doubt she could tell. Normally, he would've rolled off her immediately. But after what she'd said about being in love with him, he found himself imagining things that were better off not being imagined.

"Ariana?" There was a breathless quality to his voice that even he could hear; he couldn't remember the last time he'd experienced such strong desire.

He guessed she was feeling the same thing, because he saw her throat work as she swallowed and, like last night, her gaze lowered to his mouth as if all she wanted to do was kiss him. "What?"

"I think we'd better get off the bed," he said and was just about to let go of her when the door flung open and hit the inside wall with a resounding bang.

Shocked by the intrusion, he twisted his head to see what was going on and found his wife standing there, her face red as she glared at them. "I knew it!" she yelled. "I knew the moment I heard she was back. You cheating son of a bitch!"

"It—it's not what you think," Ariana stammered as Cam rolled off her.

Melanie was shaking with rage. "It's *exactly* what I think," she said, focusing her anger on Ariana. "You've been after him for years, and now you've come back, hoping if you run to his rescue again you'll finally get what you've always wanted."

Cam lifted a hand as one might when trying to soothe a dog or a horse. "Melanie, you need to calm down and listen," he said. "Nothing happened. I mean it. *Nothing.*"

"Nothing?" she echoed. "You slept with her *in my bed*!"

"No, I didn't," he argued. "I slept downstairs. She just… stayed over. As a friend."

His wife marched closer, shouting while pointing at Ariana. "Her grandmother lives on the island! She doesn't have to sleep over!"

What had sounded like so much fun last night seemed like a stupid mistake now. Ariana wished she could get dressed and get out of there. But Cam was standing between her and her clothes, which were piled on a chair under the window.

Melanie was blocking the door, anyway.

Obviously afraid that his daughter would come up the stairs and hear her mother's screaming and accusations, Cam leaned to the left to be able to see around Melanie. "Where's Camilla?"

"I left her in Boston with my mother," Melanie snapped. "I knew when you didn't call me that you were up to something. And then Liz from down the street texted me last night to say she saw Ariana come to the door and…and—"

"You rushed home, thinking you'd finally caught me," he said drily.

The fire in her eyes suggested jealousy had blocked her ability to reason. "You're saying I haven't?"

"That's what I'm saying, yes," Cam said. "You're not listening."

Ariana scrambled out of bed. She was afraid of Melanie seeing her wearing one of Cam's T-shirts. But at least she had something on. "Cam's right, Melanie. We didn't even touch each other. He's always been true to you. We're just friends."

Melanie's long fake nails flashed as she gestured with her hands. "If you think I'm stupid enough to believe that, you're crazy. I've seen the way you look at him."

Ariana felt her face heat. It was difficult to launch much of a defense when Melanie's assumption was accurate—and even Cam knew it. "I'll go and leave you two to work this out," she mumbled.

"Yes, get out of my house!" Melanie cried.

Steeling herself against the most baleful glare she'd ever encountered, Ariana slipped around Cam to grab her clothes. She was just crossing the room to reach the bathroom so she could change when Melanie lunged and caught her by the arm, spinning her around.

"Look at you! You're even wearing his clothes. You make me sick. You know that? I *hate* you. I've always hated you! You…you whore!"

Cam reacted immediately, pulling Melanie away. "Let her go."

"She won't get away with this," Melanie promised, clawing at his fingers until he released her. "I'm going to tell everyone on the island that the two of you have been fucking each other."

A muscle moved in his cheek. "No, you won't, because it's not true," he said calmly.

Tears began to streak down Melanie's face, causing her thick mascara to run, which made her look even more unhinged. "I saw it with my own eyes—found you both *in my bed*!"

Cam's eyebrows knitted. "We were…we were having a pillow fight," he tried to explain. "Just…messing around."

"You're lying!" she insisted. "Just like you've been lying about Emily!"

Cam's voice dropped an octave. "What are you talking about?"

"I can't trust you. I've never been able to trust you. That's what I'm talking about!" she said and slapped him across the face so hard it sounded like the crack of a whip.

Ariana screamed and froze right where she stood. She didn't know whether to try to come between them or get out, as she'd been trying to do a moment earlier. "Please don't! He's telling the truth. I swear it!"

Cam had reared back when she struck him. Now he fingered his cheek where her hand had left a palm print. He looked stunned, but he didn't move out of reach. He stood there, his expression so stony Ariana almost didn't recognize him. "That's it," he said softly. "I'm done. I can't live with you anymore."

Melanie began to sob. "*You're* done? No! *I'm* the one who's done! I married a fucking murderer. No woman could live with that."

Ariana nearly fell trying to yank her shorts on right there in the middle of the room. "Melanie, please," she began to plead. "Don't be rash. Think of what's best for your daughter."

"I *am* thinking of my daughter," she said, turning on Ariana. "She doesn't need a psychopath for a father!"

Cam said nothing. He was staring at her, looking horrified, as if she'd turned into a hydra right before his eyes—as if she'd finally revealed herself as a true monster.

"Cam's not a psychopath!" Ariana said. "He's a wonderful

person. You need to settle down before you say or do anything else you'll regret."

Cam touched Ariana's arm. "Don't try to stop her. It won't do any good. She won't quit, and even if she did, there's no putting our marriage back together."

Ariana could tell he meant every word. Melanie must've heard the resolution in his voice, too, because the blood suddenly drained from her face. Her jaw fell slack as if he'd struck her, even though he hadn't moved. "You'll be sorry for what you did to me. Now you'll *never* see your daughter again."

For the first time Ariana saw anger leap into Cam's eyes, replacing the revulsion and disgust that'd been there so far. "You'd better not try to keep her from me," he said.

"Then don't fight me—on anything," she snapped in response.

"That isn't fair—" Ariana started, but Cam cut her off.

"She's *never* been fair. That's the problem. This goes way back to when she got pregnant. We all know she did it on purpose."

Melanie gasped at the accusation. "I didn't trap you. It—it was an accident. I was on antibiotics!"

"Sure you were," he said. "I think I've pretended to believe that long enough."

"You think *I'm* the one who wronged you?" she cried. "You just wait! We'll see how many people believe you're innocent of Emily's murder when I tell them you've been fucking the person who's providing your alibi!"

Ariana covered her mouth. She couldn't bear to see this happening. Cam had already been through enough. "You can't mean that," she said.

"I mean every word," Melanie spat. "Now, get out of my house."

"*Your* house?" Cam challenged.

Lifting her chin, Melanie glared down her nose at him. "We'll see who ends up with it."

Although Ariana wasn't properly dressed, she was essentially covered. She had on Cam's T-shirt and her shorts. She wasn't wearing a bra or shoes and her shirt had fallen to the carpet, but as soon as she bent to grab it, Cam took her by the hand and pulled her toward the door.

"We'll go out through the garage," he told her, moving quickly since Melanie was following them down the stairs, cursing and screaming like a banshee.

Cam felt strangely disconnected from his emotions as he started the Land Rover and pushed the button for the garage door to rise.

"Are you okay?" Ariana asked, sounding unnerved.

Oddly, he was better than he should've been. The scene in the bedroom had been ugly. But he and Melanie had had many fights like that throughout their marriage. Melanie never held her tongue. If she was disappointed or felt cheated or slighted in any way, she went after him, then expected the damage she caused to disappear as soon as she was happy again.

He was tired of trying to accommodate her—tired of feeling as though he was the only adult in the room. And for the most part he was relieved, as he'd expected to be, knowing his marriage, and all the struggle that went with it, was finally over.

There were other considerations, though. No doubt they'd hit him sooner or later. He might even decide that divorce was more difficult than marriage. That was why he'd stayed with Melanie so far, wasn't it? He couldn't think of Camilla without being heartsick. He was letting their daughter down. But he didn't see how continuing to live with Melanie would be any better for Camilla. Their marriage was too toxic.

"I think so," he said and shifted into Drive.

Ariana reached out to stop him when he started to give the SUV some gas. "Wait! Let me get the rest of my clothes on first."

Melanie hadn't followed them into the garage, but he knew she was just on the other side of the door, probably calling her parents to tell them how deeply she'd been wronged. She was always the victim, always the martyr, and he wanted nothing more than to put some distance between them.

Truth be told, he wished he'd never have to see her again. Their relationship had gotten *that* bad.

But he could understand why Ariana might not feel comfortable leaving the garage dressed as she was, and he couldn't expect her to change while they were moving.

With a nod, he shifted back into Park.

"You're not going to turn away?" she asked in surprise when he looked at her expectantly.

"Not unless you want me to," he said. "I may as well get *something.* She's going to tell everyone I slept with you, regardless."

He was mostly joking, and he knew she understood that. He expected her to tell him to turn around, anyway. But she cast a glance behind them, through the back window, and smiled devilishly, as if it was nothing more than what Melanie deserved, before pulling off the T-shirt she was wearing.

Cam hadn't expected to have much of a reaction. He was too numb. And yet…seeing Ariana for the first time since they went skinny-dipping when they were only thirteen somehow cut through the fog in his brain.

She moved quickly, perfunctorily, as she put on her bra and her own shirt. She acted as though a brief flash of her breasts wasn't any big deal. But Cam already knew it was a sight he wouldn't soon forget.

She wasn't thirteen anymore. And she had a beautiful body...

"Okay. Let's go," she said, tossing his shirt into the back and looking straight ahead as she buckled up.

When he didn't make any move to comply, she glanced over. "Cam?"

He closed his mouth, which he suddenly realized was hanging open, and blinked. "Sorry. That was... That might very well be worth the price I'm going to pay for it," he said.

Despite everything, they started to laugh. And why not? He probably couldn't have saved his relationship with Melanie even if she hadn't surprised them this morning. His marriage had become an apple that'd rotted on the tree and would eventually fall to the earth no matter what anyone did. He just would've wasted more time trying to save it. Then, when it was over in two or three years or however long it took, he'd still have all the same problems he was dealing with now.

Or...most of them. Having Melanie turn against him when Jewel and Warner Williams were floating around the island, trying to hold him accountable for Emily's death, could prove catastrophic—and he knew it.

They drove to the beach. Ariana expected Cam to ask if she wanted to invite Ivy to come along. The three of them typically did everything together. But he didn't mention Ivy and neither did she. She assumed he needed time to process what'd just happened.

"That was nuts," she remarked as they sat on the sand, facing the ocean. They didn't have a blanket or anything to sit on, except the T-shirt she'd slept in, so she was using that, and he wasn't using anything. It was nice that the beach was mostly deserted, though, except for a lone runner and his dog who were closer to the water.

The sea was where they'd always gone when they needed peace, Ariana realized. She thought of the saying by e.e. cummings she used to have on a plaque that hung on her bedroom wall: *For whatever we lose (like a you or a me), it's always ourselves we find in the sea.*

She believed that. As hard as it was to be home, it felt right, almost inevitable, as if this was the only place where she could be truly whole.

"It could've been worse," he said, staring out over the water.

Ariana sent him a sidelong glance. "How?"

"Camilla wasn't around to see it. And Melanie didn't throw anything."

"She *throws* things?"

He leaned over to be able to reach a twig and began digging in the sand. "Sometimes."

"In front of your daughter?"

"It's usually when Camilla's at preschool. Or sleeping. Then when Camilla sees the mess, Melanie pretends whatever got broken was by accident."

Ariana rolled her eyes. "Melanie acts like a child herself. You realize that."

He kicked off his flip-flops as he settled in to dig deeper. "I realized it within the first few months of our marriage."

Ariana started to dig with him, making a deeper and ever-widening hole. Something about the texture and movement of the sand was as comforting as the roar of the waves not far away. "Will Camilla be safe with her?"

"I can't imagine Melanie would ever harm her. Her anger has always been directed at me."

"But if you're not there…"

"Maybe when Camilla gets old enough to resist whatever it is Melanie wants her to do… Who knows? I hate to even imagine that."

"I can't believe she'd threaten to make it hard for you and Camilla to see each other. That's unconscionable."

"She doesn't care about what's fair—only that she gets what she wants."

"What if you gave her the house?" Ariana asked. "At least then Camilla will remain on the island."

They shoved the piles of sand they were creating farther from them to make more room. "If I give her the house, Melanie will just sell it, take the money and buy something near her folks," he said.

Ariana couldn't stand the thought of him feeling so boxed in and powerless. "Then sue her for custody."

He looked up. "You think I'd have a shot?"

"Times have changed, Cam. Fathers have more rights. You're stable. You're a good provider. And—"

"I'm suspected of murdering a child," he broke in with a scowl. "Melanie will make all she can out of that. And what judge would take the chance of being wrong about such a serious matter?"

Ariana could tell the immediate euphoria of thinking he was done with Melanie was wearing off and certain other realities—like the situation with his daughter—were beginning to weigh on him. "They'll find whoever *really* murdered Emily. Then you'll be in the clear, and you can sue for custody without having that hanging over your head."

"The police haven't been able to come up with one other suspect in twenty years. What makes you so confident in them now?"

It was wishful thinking. But they *had* to maintain hope. It was all they had. "Even if they don't find who did it, they need hard evidence to convict you of such a horrific act."

Laughing humorlessly, he shook his head. "That's not true.

A lot of people have been convicted of murder on circumstantial evidence alone."

How could she have doubted him? It was the lack of contact between them during the past five or six years. The silence had allowed doubt to get the best of her, to bore holes like weevils in her brain.

Leaning forward, she caught his troubled gaze. "You'll fight what's happening, and we'll fight with you, and…and if there's any justice in the world, we'll win."

He didn't answer right away. He seemed to be contemplating her words as he continued to dig. He could've said that Emily's family didn't seem to be getting any justice—that justice wasn't a given for everyone—but he grew distracted by something he'd found.

Wearing a vague smile, he wiped off the sand and handed it to her.

It was the first piece of sea glass she'd seen on the beach in a long while.

fourteen

The sound of the doorbell woke Ivy from a deep sleep. Yawning, she opened her eyes to see the sun spilling into the room and forced herself to roll out of bed. She was just reaching for her robe when what had kept her up worrying until the early-morning hours hit her again. Was Williams outside, wanting to check back with her now that he'd spoken to Ariana? Was there some discrepancy in their stories?

Or was it the police? After encountering Jewel, Ivy was almost certain she'd be hearing from the island's only detective. The Emily Hutchins case was heating up so much there was no way she could avoid it.

But it wasn't Williams or the police. The peephole showed Cam's wife, Melanie. And although it was difficult to tell with such a distorted view, she didn't look happy.

Ivy hurried back upstairs to check her phone. With any

luck, she'd heard from Cam. Before she spoke with Melanie, she wanted some idea of what this might be about.

But she'd missed no calls or texts. It was ten-thirty, later than she usually slept, and with a good portion of the day gone, she felt behind, out of the loop.

Damn… She glanced over her shoulder, back toward the hallway that led to the stairs, wondering what could've brought Melanie to her house. Melanie had never visited her before…

When the doorbell sounded again, she decided she didn't have time to call Cam.

After tossing her phone on the bed, she hurried back down and cracked open the door.

"Hello?" Stepping into the gap, she saw what she couldn't see clearly through the peephole. Melanie *was* upset. Normally, her hair and makeup were perfect, she was dressed in expensive clothes and wearing what smelled like half a bottle of perfume. Today sunglasses hid her eyes, and Ivy suspected that was intentional. She'd been crying. Her face was puffy, she wasn't wearing any lip gloss, her hair didn't look combed and she was wearing a wrinkled blouse, some loose-fitting shorts and flip-flops.

"Is Cam here?" she asked, her voice cold, stilted.

Ivy cleared her throat. "No. Is he supposed to be?"

"He has to be somewhere. I need to talk to him."

Ivy squinted against the sunlight bombarding her eyes. Melanie spoke imperiously, as if Ivy should be able to snap her fingers and conjure Cam up on the spot. But Melanie had always acted entitled. "Have you tried calling him?"

"He's not answering."

Another stiff, angry response… Ivy could only guess they'd had an argument, and it appeared as though it had been a bad one. "I have no idea why. What makes you think he'd be here?"

"He's not at Ariana's grandmother's. I've checked."

"You should try his office."

"Why would they go there?" she asked.

"They?" Ivy repeated.

"Ariana's with him," she said, somewhere between rage and tears. "Have you heard from either one of them?"

What had she missed? Ivy had only gone to sleep for a few hours, but it felt like there'd been a much greater jump in time. "Not this morning."

Melanie stood back and gazed up at the windows of the second story as if she wasn't convinced Ivy was being honest with her.

"Do you see how I'm dressed?" Ivy said, gesturing at herself. "I'm not lying to you. I just got out of bed. What's going on?"

"You don't know?" she asked suspiciously.

Ivy shook her head. "How would I?"

"Ariana and Cam are having an affair."

Ivy pressed a hand to her chest. "No..."

"Yes," Melanie insisted. "Ariana slept over last night. I caught them in *my* bed when I got home this morning."

"I—I find that hard to believe," Ivy stuttered, but that wasn't entirely true. She'd sensed a change in her friends, could tell something was different. The air had been charged with a certain kind of attraction she'd never noticed before. She'd assumed it was just Ariana trying to reconnect with Cam after being gone for so long—to reestablish trust. But were their feelings for each other changing? And if so, where did that leave her?

She remembered her grandmother saying, "It's hard for three people to be best friends. But somehow you girls and Cam make it work. I've never seen anything like it."

Had they come to a point when that was no longer the case? Just the thought of Ariana with Cam made Ivy feel cheated.

It didn't seem fair to change the rules of their friendship so late. "Where's Camilla?" she asked dully.

"That's none of your business," Melanie snapped. "*I'll* worry about my daughter. You just tell Cam that he'd better call me right away, or I'm going to tell everyone he confessed to me."

Bemused, Ivy stepped outside. "Confessed to what? You just told me you caught him with Ariana yourself."

"I'm talking about *Emily*," she clarified. "He killed her. He admitted as much to me."

The strength nearly left Ivy's knees. She only managed to remain standing because she grabbed hold of the door frame for support. "What are you saying? That can't be true!"

"Maybe it is and maybe it isn't," she said with a bitter smile. "It doesn't really matter. If I say it, the case against him only grows stronger." With a sniff, she straightened her shoulders. "So he'd better be careful."

Ivy felt her jaw drop in astonishment. How could anyone be so vindictive? "I don't think I've ever met anyone else like you, Melanie. What exactly are you after?"

"I need money. My parents are traveling to Europe in a month, and now I'm going to take Camilla and go with them. That'll cost at least twenty thousand dollars, which I'll need right away. So tell him he'd better make a transfer from his business account by tomorrow morning, or he'll be sorry," she said and stomped down the walkway.

Ivy sank onto her front steps as she watched Melanie climb into a Mercedes sedan and pull away from the curb. That car had always looked too big for her. The way she had to lean forward to peer over the steering wheel reminded Ivy of Cruella de Vil, flying down the street in that big car with the long "bonnet," as the British would say, searching for puppies she could turn into a new coat.

Except that Melanie was after Cam's head.

"This can't be happening," she mumbled and slowly managed to pull herself up, go inside and climb the stairs to reach her phone.

Jewel sat in Mariners' tiny police station, a block outside the main shopping district, tapping her foot impatiently. She'd hardly slept since she arrived on the island. Being here was already like stepping into an old, reoccurring nightmare. She couldn't let down her guard, couldn't relax, or the memories would overwhelm her: meeting Cam Stafford at the rental where she and her family were staying twenty years ago. Thinking he was the most beautiful boy she'd ever seen. Wanting him to notice her and seek her out. Knowing she wouldn't be around long enough for that and feeling the need to make something happen herself, before it was too late. Stealing a bottle of her parents' whiskey and taking it over to his place. Feeling his hands on her breasts and his hard body against hers at the lighthouse. She'd slept with other boys by then. But none who were even half as cute as Cam.

Then there was Emily that day: the fight they'd had on the beach because she was bored and wanted to go home, and Jewel was too busy looking for new friends and fun to head back where there was nothing to do. The resentment that consumed her at always having to babysit her little sister. The second, bigger argument she'd had with Emily because, when she left for Cam's with the Jack Daniel's, she told her sister to go to bed and not get up until morning.

What had she been thinking when she was doing and saying those things? What the hell had been wrong with her? She could still hear Emily screaming at her as she held the bedroom door closed until Emily fell silent for fifteen minutes or more, and she thought her sister had finally gone to sleep…

"Ms. Hutchins? *Ms. Hutchins?*"

Dimly, Jewel realized someone had called her name—louder the second time—and pulled her gaze from the spot on the blank wall that'd held her transfixed. She shouldn't have drunk any coffee this morning, let alone two cups. She was too agitated. It felt like she was coming apart at the seams. And yet, the world kept turning, as if no one cared that she was begging it to stop long enough to give her the chance to get her life figured out again. "What?" she said to the uniformed policewoman standing before her.

"Detective Livingston can see you now." She gestured at a door across the open work area that led to an inner office.

After jumping to her feet, Jewel weaved through a mosh pit of desks and people to reach what turned out to be a small, messy cubicle-like room with files stacked on every flat surface. Detective Livingston had a picture of himself sailing a boat on the wall, but there were no other pictures, no photographs of him with a wife or kids, which made Jewel decide he'd either never married—or he was divorced.

"Ms. Hutchins. Welcome back to Mariners. It's nice to see you."

The forced politeness in his voice told her he was irritated she was bothering him again. For the past couple of weeks he'd been ducking her calls, which was part of the reason she'd come to Mariners. It'd be much harder for him to ignore her if she showed up at the station whenever he let her call transfer to voice mail.

"What can I do for you today?" he asked as he rounded the desk to reclaim his seat after moving a stack of files so she could sit down, too.

She glanced at the stained upholstery of the chair he'd provided and chose not to use it. *For such a wealthy island, you'd think the police would have a bigger budget*, she thought. "I came to tell you that I saw Ariana and Ivy in town last night."

He'd aged quite a bit since she'd first met him. Instead of being a young, thirty-something new detective, he was now in his fifties, and he looked it. His hair was sprinkled with gray, he had deep lines at the corners of his eyes and mouth and he'd gained quite a bit of weight. He gave her a wary, sidelong look through eyes that'd become jaded. "Tell me you didn't approach them."

"Of course I approached them," she snapped. "*Someone* has to make them tell the truth, or my sister's murder might never be solved."

He sat up taller. "If you're implying that I'm not doing my job, I assure you that isn't even close to the truth. As I've explained on numerous occasions, I have to gather more information, make sure there are no other suspects. Otherwise, the circumstantial evidence in this case might cause me to get hung up on the wrong person, which definitely wouldn't be fair to Cam Stafford."

"Except you know Cam Stafford is the *right* person."

His left eyebrow slid up speculatively. "Let's not forget Mr. Stafford has an alibi."

Why did she claim to have heard a bump in the night? And, even worse, why did she assign it a specific time? She could've said she heard something but was so sleepy she had no idea when it was. Instead, she'd been desperate to hide what she'd done, so she'd said too much in an attempt to raise her own credibility while putting herself where she was supposed to be at bedtime. Otherwise, Cam might already be behind bars, and this terrible chapter of her life would be closed.

That *she* was to blame for such stupidity, and that she couldn't change her statement to something less specific now, caused acid to churn in her stomach. But she'd been only sixteen. A lot of sixteen-year-olds made poor decisions. "And as

I've said many times, he only has an alibi because his friends are lying for him."

"Both Ariana Prince and Ivy Hawthorne are longtime residents of Mariners—"

"Which doesn't mean anything," she broke in. "They can lie as easily as a visitor."

"What I'm saying is that they are known to be of good character. I can't go around accusing people until I have some sort of proof."

Jewel shifted on her feet. She was dying to tell the detective the truth, but how could she change her story after so long?

She couldn't. She could never explain to her parents how badly she'd let them down, especially because, ever since they'd left the island twenty years ago without Emily, they'd doted on her—done everything they could to help her recover from that night. She couldn't bear the thought that, in the future, she'd get the derision she deserved instead of the sympathy that had become a lifeline for her. If they knew, they'd hold her accountable for their greatest heartache instead of feeling she shared their pain.

It would also be humiliating—for them as well as her. She had no doubt, given how big Emily's story had become, that her part that night would be picked up by the major news networks and broadcast across the nation.

Besides, if Ariana and Ivy just told the truth, she and her family wouldn't have to suffer any more than they'd suffered already.

"They're *best* friends with him," she pointed out. "As I said, they're protecting him."

"Everything has to be documented, and that takes time." Unruffled, he blinked at her. "On another note… A private investigator has come to Mariners. I take it I have you and your family to thank for that."

"Yes," she said. "You're working too slowly. It's been twenty years, for God's sake. How much longer are we supposed to wait?"

Sighing, he pinched the bridge of his nose. "I'm doing everything I can, Ms. Hutchins. I haven't taken a day off since your sister's remains were found."

"But what do you have to show for your efforts? Have you discovered anything—besides the witness Mr. Williams tracked down who's willing to testify that she saw Cam on the beach with a small female not long after ten-thirty?"

"Mr. Williams has notified me of that witness." He fished through the papers on his desk and came up with a notepad, where she could see he'd written the name Delilah French Jones. "But I haven't yet been able to reach her."

"Why do you need to reach her? You think she's lying?"

"Not at all. I'd just like to talk to her myself before making any kind of judgment call."

"She's not a local, so I hope you'll still believe her."

His expression suggested he didn't appreciate the sarcasm. "How did Mr. Williams find her?"

Jewel could no longer meet the detective's eyes. She looked down and swiped at her capris as if she had lint or something on them. "He didn't tell you?"

"He said it was an anonymous tip. But that makes no sense. Why wouldn't whoever it was contact me? I would assume it's more natural to go to the police, wouldn't you? How did Mrs. Jones even know Williams was working the case? She lives in Albany, New York, and he's from Fort Worth, Texas."

"I guess she's been watching the news," Jewel replied. "I've mentioned Mr. Williams several times when asking anyone with information to come forward."

The detective rocked back in his chair and used one finger to press his bottom lip between his teeth.

"What?" she said, growing even more self-conscious. "Why are you looking at me that way?"

"I'm just…thinking."

"About…"

"Who was the anonymous tipster?"

It was Jewel. She'd sent Delilah's name to Williams via a computer-generated letter that said: *If you're looking for information on the Hutchins case, you might ask Delilah French. She was on the beach that night with her brother, Ben.* She'd sent it without a signature from a city she'd purposely driven to that was not her own. Since *she* couldn't place Cam on the beach that night, she'd needed someone else to do it, and she remembered Delilah waving at Cam when they passed by. He was the one who'd told Jewel her name, as well as Ben's. And she'd never forgotten them, like every other detail attached to that night.

But it had been a risk. That was why she hadn't done it before. She'd been afraid Delilah would look at a picture of Emily and say that wasn't the girl she'd seen with Cam at the beach. Depending on what she remembered of that night, there was even a chance she could identify that girl as Jewel. Except she'd been drinking—they all had—so Delilah's memory couldn't be that sharp, not after twenty years…

And the gamble had paid off. The most Delilah said she could remember was Cam with a *smallish female.* Jewel knew he was the one who'd stand out for almost any girl.

"How should I know?" she responded. "Anonymous means they didn't provide their name."

"Surely, you and Williams have discussed who it *could* be."

Williams had tried to guess, to formulate something plausible, but he'd been wrong, of course. "He said if he had to venture a guess, he'd say it was Delilah's husband."

"Why?"

"Maybe she was reluctant to step forward—didn't want to

deal with the media attention—and he felt the information was important enough to force her hand but didn't want her to know he was the one who did it."

"Why couldn't it be Ben, Delilah's brother?"

"It could be," she said. "But Williams talked to him, as well. Ben said he doesn't remember anything about that night. It's been too long."

"And yet Delilah remembers it clearly enough to place Cam at the beach and know the time?"

Jewel shrugged. "I don't find that surprising. You know what he looks like. He makes a strong impression on the opposite sex."

"Has he made that kind of impression on you?" he asked.

The question took her by surprise. But Jewel had always believed a strong offense was the best defense. "You're talking about my sister's killer!" she nearly shouted. "How could I feel any kind of admiration for him?"

He raised his hands to calm her. "I'm sorry. I was just wondering if you ever had any dealings with Cam."

Why was he asking her this? What would make him think she had? Had someone recognized her at the beach with Cam?

Panic began to circulate through her body as if she'd been put on an IV of ice water. But after taking a deep, calming breath, she answered as stridently as possible. "I met him when he helped my sister get into the house and hid the key—right where he'd be able to find it later—in the front planter."

"That's the only time you saw him when you were visiting twenty years ago?"

Shit. Was there another witness who was telling the detective differently?

Either way, she had to stick with her story. Curling her fingernails into her palms, Jewel nodded. "That's it."

"And yet, you're *sure* he's the one who killed your sister."

"It has to be him," she said. "Who else could it be?"

★ ★ ★

Cam stood at the window, looking out. Ivy had just called him, and he'd come to her house only fifteen or twenty minutes later—with Ariana.

"Cam and I have never slept together," Ariana said emphatically. "Last night after I got home, I couldn't relax. I was too worried. So I went over to his place to talk about Williams and the witness he's dug up. I wanted Cam to be aware of everything that's going on behind the scenes."

Her explanation sounded innocent enough. But if it was that innocent, why hadn't Ivy been included? All three of them had been together earlier in the evening. Jewel had accosted Ivy *and* Ariana, and it was Ivy's contact—Kitty—who'd told them about the witness. Why would Ariana head over to Cam's without even calling her? "And then you stayed the night?" she said.

Ariana shifted on her bar stool. She sat across from Ivy at the kitchen island and seemed uncomfortable, which made Ivy uncomfortable, too. Ivy wasn't used to the odd, slightly panicky feeling that'd come over her since Melanie's visit. "Yes. After we talked, we—we watched a movie, and then it got late, and I ended up staying over instead of heading home. That's all."

"I slept in the study," Cam clarified from his spot over by the kitchen sink. "But unfortunately, I'd already put the couch back together and cleaned up the bedding by the time Melanie came home."

Ivy had made them each a cup of coffee. She turned hers around and around, staring down into the dark liquid, as they talked. She was worried for Cam's sake, knew he was in a terrible position—one that'd gotten even worse this morning. However, what roiled in her gut wasn't worry so much as jealousy. Ariana had only been home since Thursday. And even if Cam was unhappy with Melanie, he was still married.

She didn't want to be the odd one out. It was so hard to meet someone on the island. And yet, she couldn't leave. She felt trapped by her responsibility to maintain the legacy her family had established.

If she were to marry and have children, however, that would all change. And Cam belonged on Mariners, too. Ivy couldn't imagine him ever wanting to leave. In that regard and many others, they were perfect for each other—if Cam's marriage was going to break up, anyway. "Melanie said she found you both *in her bed*."

Cam spoke before Ariana could respond. "She also said I confessed to killing Emily."

"You're saying you weren't in the same bed?"

"We didn't share a bed!" Cam insisted.

Ivy took another sip of coffee. Could she believe him? Melanie had been so convinced, so clear, on what she claimed to have seen.

But Melanie was a spoiled, narcissistic, immature bitch. "I thought it sounded…unbelievable." That wasn't necessarily true. But it was an appropriate response. "I probably would've laughed it off if she hadn't seemed so upset by what she claimed she saw."

"What she saw was nothing," Cam said. "I was fully dressed when I walked up to the master to see if Ariana was awake—and the next thing I knew, Melanie barged into the room and started freaking out."

"You know she's been jealous of you and me from the beginning," Ariana added quietly, her focus on Ivy. "She doesn't want Cam to have anything to do with us. Add in the stress of having her husband connected to the Emily Hutchins case, all the scrutiny and publicity, and…she snapped, I guess. Jumped to the wrong conclusion and went into hysterics."

Ivy wanted to believe them. She'd always trusted both of

them in the past. But today they hardly looked at each other, which seemed strange. And right after they first walked in, while Ivy was making coffee, it seemed as if they were careful not to get too close to each other.

Something was going on…

"She wanted me to tell you that she's going to the police to say you did kill Emily—that you confessed to her—unless you transfer twenty thousand dollars into your joint checking account, where she has access to it, so she can go to Europe with her parents next month."

"I can't just transfer twenty thousand dollars," he said. "It's not that easy. What money we have is invested in our house, our cars, my business, our retirement accounts. We have bills, overhead. She has no idea how much money goes out each month. She's never been interested enough to learn."

"So what are you going to do?" Ivy asked.

"I'll text her to let her know Europe isn't an option—not right now." He pulled out his phone, but Ariana told him to wait.

"How long are they planning to be gone?" she asked.

"Almost a month."

"If you could raise the money, it might be smart to let her go. You're not able to see Camilla right now, anyway. At least it would get rid of Melanie, keep her preoccupied these next few weeks while you deal with what's happening here. It might improve Camilla's situation at the same time. Wouldn't you rather she was around loving grandparents as opposed to being stuck, alone, with an angry, bitter mother?"

He leaned against the counter as he considered Ariana's suggestion.

"It would give Melanie less time to try to sabotage your life, too," Ivy said.

"Both good points," he agreed. "I guess… I guess I could

put the trip on one of our credit cards and get her enough cash that she'd have spending money."

Ariana winced. "It's an expensive fix, but..."

"A fix is a fix," he said wearily. "At this point if I have a problem money can solve, I should just pay and get it over with."

"Letting her go to Europe won't solve anything," Ariana pointed out. "But it would buy you some time."

He stared down at his phone. "I don't want to talk to her. I don't want to exchange messages. I don't ever want to see her again. If not for Camilla, I'd be done completely. I guess I didn't realize how close to the edge I was, because this morning pushed me over it."

Was having Ariana around part of the reason? Ivy couldn't help wondering. "If you do your best to remain civil, maybe she will, too," Ivy said.

Cam glanced up at her. "Melanie will only take that as a sign of weakness."

Ariana frowned at him. "But because of Camilla, you have no choice."

"True. Here goes nothing," he said and had just started tapping on his screen when the doorbell rang.

Ivy slid off her stool. She hoped it wasn't Melanie again. With any luck, Cam's wife was already off the island and would soon be on her way to Europe.

But when she opened the door, she wished it *was* Melanie. Anyone would be better than who was standing there.

fifteen

There was a sloppy air about Detective Livingston. He was dressed in slacks, a button-up shirt and a tweed sports jacket. He was even wearing a tie. But none of it was wrinkle free, and none of it quite matched. He slid his wire-rimmed spectacles, which looked like they needed to be replaced, higher on his nose while holding out his card. “Ms. Hawthorne? You might not remember me, but I’m with the police department. I’m the investigator on the Emily Hutchins case, and I’d like to ask you a few questions, if you have a moment.”

“I told you everything I know about the night Emily went missing twenty years ago,” she said. “And I repeated it to a private investigator who came here recently.”

“I realize that. But there’s been a new development I’d like to speak with you about.”

Ivy could only hope it wasn't incontrovertible evidence that they'd been lying. "What new development?"

"I'd be happy to explain if… Could I come inside and visit with you for a few minutes?"

Ivy didn't know whether to put him off or let him in. Would he believe her if she said she didn't have time this morning? Cam's Land Rover was parked at the curb. Surely, Detective Livingston had noticed it and knew who it belonged to.

"I have company," she said. "Cam's here. You know we've been friends since we were kids. Ariana's here, too. She's back on the island for the summer. Would you still like to do this now?"

He didn't even need to think about it. "If you wouldn't mind."

She got the impression he was looking forward to seeing the three of them together, to watching how they interacted and deciding just how close they were.

Ivy wasn't sure whether this would be a good thing or a bad thing, but she wanted to cooperate with the investigation as much as possible. She really did want Emily's murderer to be found, and the sooner Detective Livingston realized Cam wasn't the man they were after, the sooner he could focus on someone else and, with any luck, get the job done. Ivy couldn't wait until she could relax and forget about the whole thing. "Give me a moment to check with them," she said and left the detective on the front stoop.

"It's Detective Livingston," she said when she reached the kitchen.

Cam and Ariana exchanged a concerned look before Cam said, "I wondered how long it would take for him to track me down."

"You think he's here because of you?"

"My Rover's out front."

"I could be wrong, but I get the impression he would've

shown up anyway. He said he wants to talk to me. I have no doubt he would've visited both of you at some point, though. The question is…should I let him in?"

Ariana deferred to Cam. Ivy looked at him, too, since he was the one with the most to lose.

"Yeah, let's get it over with." He lowered his voice. "But let me do most of the talking."

When Ivy returned to the front door, she opened it wide. "Right this way."

Livingston dipped his head in acknowledgment and followed her into the kitchen, where he greeted Cam and Ariana. "I hate to bother you on such a beautiful Sunday when you probably have better things to do. But I'm under a great deal of pressure to find whoever killed Emily Hutchins, so anything you could tell me that would help would be much appreciated."

Ivy hadn't expected this kind of appeal. Part of her was tempted to respond to it with the truth—to tell him that Cam really hadn't been with them when they'd said he was, but he would never hurt anyone. Then she realized that acting as if the detective was supportive of them and simply enlisting their help—instead of putting Cam at risk—would be a smart way to slip beneath their defenses.

"I'd help if I could," Cam said. "But I can only tell you what happened that night—again."

Ivy spoke up, hoping to turn the tables and get more information out of Detective Livingston than they gave him. "You said there's been a new development."

"Yes, there's a witness who claims she saw Cam on the beach with a smallish female about the time he was walking the two of you home."

"You're referring to Delilah, Ben's sister," Ariana said.

Livingston nodded.

"Williams told me about her," Ariana said. "And I told Ivy and Cam, because that's not possible. Cam was with us."

"To be honest, we met Ben and his sister that night for the very first time," Ivy added. "We hung out with them for only a couple of hours, and we were on the beach in the dark around a bonfire, so it wasn't easy to see."

"Besides all that, we were drinking," Ariana chimed in. "The way I remember Delilah… Well, she had much more to drink than the rest of us, so I can't say I'd feel comfortable relying on her word or her memory. You have to admit it would be easy for someone in that situation to mistake him for someone else."

"Anything's possible," Livingston agreed. "What about after that night, though? Did Delilah or her brother ever try to contact you?"

They looked at each other. "No," Ivy said, speaking for all of them. "We didn't even exchange numbers. We knew we'd probably never see them again, so there didn't seem to be any point."

"It was just a spontaneous thing," Ariana explained. "They were sitting at the table next to us at the restaurant where we had dinner that night. We struck up a conversation, and they asked if we could tell them where they could find the best beach. We said we'd take them to one, and we did. They brought the alcohol, we built the bonfire and someone put on some music. We laughed, danced, swam and drank. And then Cam, Ivy and I left because it was so cold, and we didn't have sweatshirts."

"That's when Cam walked us home," Ivy said.

Cam folded his arms. "You know what I've been wondering…"

Livingston looked mildly surprised that he'd preface whatever he had to say in that manner. "What's that?"

"How do you know Emily was taken at ten-thirty?"

"That's when Jewel heard a thump," he replied.

"But that could've been anything. Emily could've dropped something. Or slammed a door. Or gotten up to go to the bathroom. Jewel could even have imagined it—or dreamed it."

"I don't know where you're going with this. Changing the timeline won't do you any favors," Livingston pointed out. "That'll only strip away your alibi."

"I'm just saying that we're relying on the word of a sixteen-year-old girl who says she was asleep. That's not much to build a case around."

"We have to start somewhere," he said, somewhat defensively.

"That might be true, but I'd rather you focus on the facts. If you don't, I could wind up standing trial for murder simply because I helped a girl get into a house when she was locked out, which is something almost anyone would do."

Livingston nodded. "I get your point."

"Isn't the autopsy—or whatever you call it when a coroner goes over remains this old—telling you anything?" Ariana asked.

"I'm afraid I'm not at liberty to reveal what the coroner is saying," he told her.

"You can't even tell us how she died?" Cam pressed.

"Not yet. And even if I could, I don't know if I would. I'm sure you can understand I need to hold back certain pieces of information in hopes it'll give me an advantage at some point."

"No one wants you to find the truth more than I do," Cam said. "I don't expect you to believe me, but I didn't hurt her. After I helped her get inside the house, I didn't ever see her again."

"With all the publicity Jewel's stirring up, I've had a few

calls and tips," the detective said. "With any luck, I'll find the answers sooner or later."

Ivy wondered if he was talking about people who'd stepped forward to corroborate Delilah's claim. The mere possibility that there might be others who'd say the same thing made her nervous. But she and Ariana had already committed themselves; all they could do now was wait—as agonizing as it was. "It must be hard to sift through them all."

"Since most lead nowhere, it can be a huge waste of time," he allowed. "But it's all part of the territory."

"You know that Jewel is on the island…" Ivy said.

"I do. She was just at the station."

He didn't sound any more pleased about her presence on Mariners than they were. Ivy knew it couldn't be easy having a bereaved family on his back when he was trying to solve a crime like this one. "What did she want?"

"To whip me into a case-solving frenzy."

"Is that why you're here?" Ariana asked.

"I would've come anyway. She may not think so, but I'm dedicated to finding the person who killed that girl."

Were his words a warning? Was he putting them on notice?

Ariana shoved her coffee away. "We saw Jewel last night. She's certainly not out to make friends."

"Not with the two of you," he said. "She believes you're lying."

"And she was trying to convince you?"

"You can't blame her, I guess." He got out two more cards and handed them to Cam and Ariana. "If you think of anything you haven't told me already, I hope you'll give me a call."

"And I hope you'll remain open-minded and search for the person who *really* killed Emily Hutchins," Ariana said.

"Of course. But that'll be much easier if I have all the facts." He tilted his head in parting before Ivy showed him out.

When she returned to the kitchen, Cam was leaning against the counter again and Ariana was staring at him, obviously worried, from where she sat at the kitchen island. "How do you think that went?" she asked.

Cam shook his head. "Not good. You could tell he doesn't have any solid leads. And now Jewel's in town, putting pressure on him."

Ariana rubbed her forehead. "And if Melanie decides to get involved..."

"I'm going to give her the money," he said.

A slithering, snakelike unease crawled up Ivy's back, wrapped around her heart and began to squeeze. "But what guarantee do we have that she won't do all she can to hurt you after she gets it? She never knew we were covering for you, did she?"

"No," he said, but Ivy could tell he thought Melanie knew more than she should.

Jewel sat on the bed in her hotel room, which cost a fortune even though it was tiny—at least by Iowa standards—and stared at the screen on her laptop. She'd been recording every piece of information she learned about Emily's case. The timeline. What had been done so far. Who had said what. She needed to make sure she kept it all straight and nothing was missing that could be used to close the case. After twenty years, she knew she couldn't rely on the police to take care of it. Almost nothing had happened, which was why, once her sister's remains had been found, she'd jumped in to make it happen herself.

She'd have to stay on top of Livingston, but she'd done what she could for today. Because she'd been able to remember Delilah's name, and she'd returned to the beach herself that night, she'd also provided them with a witness they would've missed otherwise. And she'd confronted Ariana and Ivy, hoping to make them rethink their lies, which would protect her own.

She supposed that was progress. But it still felt as though the case was moving at a snail's pace—or worse, not moving at all.

What more could she do?

With a sigh, she leaned back and rested her head against the wall. This whole thing *had* to be over soon. She simply couldn't take it any longer. She was desperate to kick free of the past, which had hung on to her ankle for twenty years, threatening to pull her under and drown her in a sea of despair.

Too restless to remain sitting, she got up and went to the window where she could see a portion of the stylish, expensive shops and restaurants in town, and simply watched the people who were on the street one story below her. Some were shopping. Others were visiting the art museums, eating at the restaurants or getting ice cream. But most were just arriving. Car after car, many of them Jeeps, inched through traffic—all coming from the wharf or the airport, which emptied onto the same road, as summer vacationers flocked to the various rental homes around the island.

She couldn't help remembering her excitement the day she first arrived here at sixteen. Her mother had always wanted to see Mariners; it'd been the setting for one of her favorite books. So she'd saved up, arranged the trip and meticulously scheduled what they would do each day. Because they lived in Iowa and had never seen New York City or Boston, Karen had planned to spend some time in those cities, as well, which was why Jewel had been left at the beach with Emily. After their meeting with the pastor who headed up a different branch of her father's church, Karen and Blaine were going to Manhattan to see a show.

At first, Jewel had asked to go with them. She hated being left out, especially if it meant babysitting again. But her mother said the play wasn't something she'd enjoy, and the tickets were too expensive, anyway. According to Karen, she'd have a lot more fun at the beach.

If she hadn't known the church meeting would take up a large portion of the day and would be about as much fun as watching paint dry, Jewel probably would've fought harder to go. She knew her mother regretted leaving them now. Had Karen not gone—or had she taken her children with her—they'd most likely still be a complete family.

So in one sense, what'd happened was her mother's fault, Jewel thought bitterly. Karen was the adult. She was the one who was responsible for their welfare. She should've been around to look after Emily herself. Instead, Jewel had that responsibility, and now she had to live with the consequences.

Jewel doubted anyone else would look at it that way, though. They'd all blame her.

She checked her phone to see if she'd heard from Williams. She'd tried to call him an hour ago, while she was walking back from the bookstore. The bookseller had said something interesting when she purchased a book by a forensic pathologist on how to solve a murder—she never knew where she'd get the idea that would finally bring the case to a satisfactory conclusion—and she was anxious to talk to Williams about what she'd heard.

Unwilling to wait any longer for him to respond, she called him again and, this time, he answered.

"Yes, ma'am, Ms. Hutchins. You got me."

It was hard not to snap at him for ignoring her previous call. She put up with enough of that with Detective Livingston. And Williams was working for her and her family. But she had the feeling he wouldn't take kindly to a rebuke, and she needed him badly enough that she bit her tongue. "I have to tell you something."

"Don't tell me you've got this thing solved, darlin'," he said. "I certainly wouldn't put it past ya. Anyway, I'm all ears."

She didn't find him remotely amusing, so she ignored his teasing. "Before I get started on that, I wanted to let you know that I went over to the police station this morning and tried to rattle Livingston's cage."

"And? How'd he react?"

"With the same assurances we've been getting for twenty years, which doesn't give me a whole a lot of confidence in him."

"That's why you've got me now. I've talked to him, too. This is his one and only open homicide, which means he should have plenty of time to devote to it."

"He's solved other murders?"

"Don't be too impressed. A child could've solved those other cases. A few were obvious suicides—overdoses. One was a wife shooting her husband. Another was a husband beating his wife to death with a statue she purchased for the house—he wasn't happy about how much it'd cost. And the rest resulted in vehicular manslaughter charges for people who killed someone while driving under the influence."

Distracted in spite of herself, Jewel grimaced. "You can't even drive that fast on this island. The top speed limit is… what? Forty? Don't tell me there've been a lot of those."

"Five, which was more than I'd expected. All the money here and the privileged youth… It's not a good mix. You get cocky sixteen-year-olds driving their parents' SUV after a kegger and…it's not good."

Jewel didn't care about that. Shaking her head, she returned her focus to where it should be. "Well, with any luck, we'll learn something from the coroner soon."

"I doubt the coroner will share much with me."

"Why not?"

"The police will keep what little they have to themselves until they can put together a case. You never know when some detail will turn out to be important."

Jewel had seen enough crime shows to know why. After so long, she couldn't imagine there was anything left, anyway. Still, she said, "I hope you'll be able to find out."

"I'll certainly give it a try."

He acted as if he was about to sign off. "Wait. I was actually calling about something else."

"What's that?" he asked.

Jewel remembered what the bookseller had told her. "I was wondering... Have you considered approaching Cam's wife to see what she might have to say?"

"No. I haven't even talked to Cam yet. I wanted to let his friends tell him I've been poking around, get him good and nervous. The more nervous a person is, the more likely they are to confess or make a mistake that reveals a bit too much."

"Maybe you should approach his wife first—sometime when she's not with him. It's possible that during a low moment, when he was drunk or depressed or whatever, he told her what he did to Emily."

"I'll try. But even if she has insider information, chances are good law enforcement won't be able to use it—not for the trial, anyway. The law views a married couple as one entity."

"So?"

"I'm talking about spousal privilege. A wife cannot be compelled to testify against her husband."

"What if she *wants* to?"

"Still might not work. There are circumstances where he could actually keep her from testifying."

Damn it. Jewel turned away from the window and crossed over to the bed. There must be some way to capitalize on what she'd learned... "What if the couple gets divorced?"

He seemed taken aback. "The privilege no longer applies. Why? Do you know anything about them? How harmonious is their marriage?"

"Today I spoke to a woman named Annette who works at the bookstore. She recognized me from the news and struck up a conversation right away. I could tell she wanted to be helpful, so I asked her if she knew Cam. She said she doesn't know him well, that she's seen his wife in the store more often. But she told me she attended the open house when Cam first opened his office and could tell that he and Melanie weren't getting along. She's also heard Melanie make snide remarks about him while she was in the store, shopping with a girlfriend. She admitted she doesn't like his wife much. She said Melanie's spoiled and immature but might be acting out because she's so miserable being stuck in a marriage with a man who could do what Cam did to Emily."

"Why'd the bookseller tell you all this?"

"She feels sorry for me, of course. Most people do, so they try to help."

"She thinks Cam's guilty..."

"Yes."

"What makes her believe he did it? Does she know anything we don't?"

"No, but...where there's smoke, there's fire. That's why we think he did it, right?"

After a long silence, Williams said, "Okay. I'll talk to the wife."

sixteen

As Ariana hurried to The Human Bean, hoping to get there before it closed, she was glad she'd had an excuse to escape Ivy and Cam. The way Ivy kept looking at her, as if she suspected that Ariana and Cam really had slept together, made her feel self-conscious and guilty. The fact that they weren't lying about last night was beside the point. The attraction she'd felt as she wrestled and laughed with him on the bed—the rush of awareness, the smell of his cologne on the sheets, the feel of his soft cotton T-shirt on her bare breasts, having nothing on underneath except a pair of panties and knowing he had to be well aware of that—had made it far more erotic than a simple pillow fight.

And she had removed her shirt while changing in the car. Her face grew hot just remembering it. She didn't want Ivy to see her reaction and realize how deeply all of that had affected her. Knowing he didn't feel the same way—and hoping not to make their friendship weird—Ariana had hidden her attraction to Cam from the beginning. It hardly seemed fair to change the rules after so long, especially because she knew Ivy was beginning to wonder if *she'd* ever find love. Ever marry. Ever start a family.

Seeing her two best friends become a couple would make Ivy feel even more isolated.

Besides, Melanie was still part of the picture. Even if Cam's feelings for her were changing—and he certainly hadn't indicated that was the case—Ariana couldn't believe he'd want to get involved with her or anyone else, not until well after he was safe from the nightmare he was going through now. He couldn't risk introducing a brand-new element into his life; the slightest thing could destabilize the whole situation.

She spotted the chalkboard sidewalk sign outside The Human Bean on the next block and checked her watch. Hopefully, Kitty was still there and hadn't left closing the shop to her employees. It was well after lunch, so business had probably died down. That meant if Kitty *was* there, at least they should be able to grab a few minutes to talk.

She found herself looking over her shoulder as she crossed the street, searching for Williams or Livingston or Jewel Hutchins. She didn't want to run into any of them. Jewel knew she and Ivy were lying and that made Ariana extremely uncomfortable. It was one thing to have someone suspect she wasn't being truthful and quite another to have someone accuse her outright.

As she was about to head down the stairs to the basement café, one of Kitty's employees—a young man with dreadlocks and piercings all over who was wearing a branded apron—came out to carry in the sign.

"Hello," Ariana said. "Is Kitty still here?"

"She's in the kitchen," he said, and followed her into the shop, carrying the sign.

"I'll get her for you," he added after he put the sign near the door so it could be easily hefted back out in the morning and then disappeared into the back.

This time it took only a few seconds for Kitty to appear. "Hey! I hope you've decided you'd like the job."

Ariana smiled in relief. She needed something to keep her busy, and she liked Kitty and the atmosphere of the coffee shop. "I have."

"That's wonderful! I was afraid you'd prefer to take the summer off."

"No. I think it might be wise to have something else to focus on for at least part of the time I'm here."

Kitty looked confused. "Something else?"

"I'm referring to the Emily Hutchins case. Jewel's in town, trying to say Cam murdered her sister. And while I want her to get the closure she needs and deserves, I'm afraid of where her crusade will lead. Things can go so wrong when this much emotion is involved."

"You know my husband works for the Mariners Police Department."

"I do. But he's not assigned to the Hutchins case..."

"No, that's Detective Livingston, but they have briefings every morning and talk about what they have on various cases and where they should go next."

"I hope the coroner can provide more information. It seems everything hinges on that."

"Not everything..."

Ariana felt her eyebrows shoot up. "What's that supposed to mean?"

Kitty waved her over to a corner table, where they could

have some privacy, and lowered her voice as they sat down. "The police have identified another suspect."

"Are you kidding me?" Ariana cried. *"Who?"*

"I can't say. But I'm sure you'll be hearing about it soon enough. I just…wanted to offer you some encouragement that there might be an end to what you, Ivy and especially Cam are going through. Cam comes in here occasionally and… well, he just hasn't seemed very happy the past few years, and I know this can't be making things any easier."

Ariana felt as though a tremendous weight had been lifted off her shoulders. "He's struggling in his marriage." She figured that wasn't a secret. Even if it was, it wouldn't be one for long, not with Cam talking about filing for divorce.

"I got that impression. His wife comes here, too, with her friends. And I hear things."

Ariana was having trouble focusing on the subject of Melanie. That was a problem for later. Emily Hutchins's murder was what they had to think about now. "This other witness… How did the police find him—or her? Did the autopsy reveal something that was previously unknown?"

"Nope. This came a different way."

"That's interesting. Now that the police have identified this other individual, if the autopsy provides additional evidence, and the two could be linked, this would all be over."

"That's what I'm hoping. I know my husband and the rest of the force feel the same. They would rather it's not someone who's lived here his whole life. It's more comfortable—and better for the image of the island—if it was a stranger who did something that horrific, you know?"

"I agree. Does Williams know there's another suspect?"

"Williams?" she echoed in confusion.

"Warner Williams, the private detective who's in town. Emily's family hired him to…to get to the bottom of what happened. But after speaking to him, and running into Jewel in the street last night, I'm getting the impression they both came here just to make sure Cam goes to prison."

"I've seen Jewel on the news. She's never named Cam specifically, but she's not shy about intimating that the police already know who did it."

"That's incredibly unfair," Ariana said. "What evidence does she have?"

A sympathetic expression creased Kitty's forehead. "Grief isn't always rational."

Ariana slumped over in her seat. "You're right. I guess I'm so worried they'll put the wrong person in prison I'm losing my compassion for the Hutchins family."

"The police will get this right," Kitty assured her. "Livingston is a good detective. My husband really likes him."

Was he a good detective or a good person? There was a difference. And liking people didn't mean they were proficient at a particular task. But Kitty was trying to comfort her, and Ariana was grateful. "Thanks for letting me know. I can't tell you how glad I am to hear it."

Compassion filled Kitty's eyes. "You bet. Now, let's talk about the job. Would you be able to work five days a week?"

Since she'd be off at two, Ariana couldn't see why that would be a problem.

They negotiated her salary, and she agreed to come for training on Tuesday and start on Wednesday morning.

"You'll get the hang of it quickly," Kitty assured her as they finished up.

Ariana thanked her and left the shop. Black clouds were beginning to scuttle across the sky—a marked change after such a beautiful morning. But Ariana didn't care about the coming rain. She was too relieved to have learned that the police were looking at someone other than Cam as a possible suspect.

How'd they finally come up with another possibility? How viable a suspect was this? *Who* was it?

Kitty had indicated it wasn't a local. That was nice.

Ariana wondered if Williams knew about this development. He seemed to be on top of things. Perhaps he'd known when he spoke to her and just hadn't said anything.

And what about Jewel? How would she react to learning that she might be wrong about Cam?

Ariana took a deep breath and was finally able to smile freely at the people she passed. This was the first thing that'd gone their way.

As soon as she'd put some distance between her and The Human Bean, she pulled out her phone to call Cam. She couldn't wait to tell him what Kitty had said. He needed the good news even more than she did.

Cam sat in his daughter's bedroom, holding one of the army of stuffed animals she arranged in her bed when she went to sleep. He felt terrible for Camilla. She was too young to realize what was going on with her parents, had no control, and yet their decisions would drastically affect her life. He'd been so worried about how a split with Melanie would affect their daughter that he'd done everything he could to hold his family together. But they were dealing with too much resentment on both sides. Even if he tried to put the marriage back together, Melanie would never believe he hadn't slept with Ariana. She'd hold last night against him and throw it up to him at every opportunity. She'd been jealous of his best friends almost since she met them and was determined to make sure she was the only woman in his life.

Sadly, that same jealousy and possessiveness extended to Camilla. So maybe a divorce *was* the best path forward. He could get an attorney, handle the paperwork, and without

Melanie's interference and demands, build an even stronger relationship with his daughter.

That sounded hopeful, but he wasn't as relieved as he felt he should be, considering he'd just learned that the police had finally found another suspect. He wanted to put the Emily Hutchins case behind him more than anything, but he knew he wasn't in the clear yet. After Emily's remains were found, Melanie had started harassing him with questions about what'd happened, and he might've said a few things that could come back to haunt him. Now that their relationship had deteriorated to such a degree, he was afraid, just when he might have the chance to escape the mess he was in, she'd go to the police and try to drag their attention back to him.

Did she know anything that could get him into more trouble? What, exactly, had he said to her about the case?

Dropping back onto the bed, he stared up at the ceiling as snippets of their various conversations ran through his mind.

Why would they come here, Cam? What could the police possibly want with you? Melanie had asked while they were getting ready for bed the night the police had come by after Emily's remains had been found.

They had a few questions about the Emily Hutchins case. That's all.

That's all? She'd gone into the bathroom, so she'd had to raise her voice. *What'd you have to do with that?*

Nothing.

She'd come back to stand in the doorway, where she could see him lying on the bed. *They wouldn't have come here if you didn't have something to do with it.*

I met Emily earlier that night, before she went missing. That's all.

Melanie had refused to accept such a vague answer, so he'd had to explain exactly what had happened from the moment Emily had knocked on his door until he'd left the beach with Ariana and Ivy. He'd used the version of the story he'd given the police, hadn't mentioned returning to the lighthouse with Jewel. He hadn't even known Melanie when he'd met Jewel, but it would still make her jealous. Or she'd use it in their next argument to prove how easily he could be enticed by a woman offering him sex.

Although that conversation had finally ended with his declaration that he'd walked home after leaving Ariana and Ivy at Ariana's grandmother's house, Melanie had brought up the case a few days later at the grocery store after she began to believe that people were whispering about them and staring at them because of the past.

They all think you killed that girl, she'd said as they passed through the produce aisle.

Camilla, who'd dropped her doll, was with them, sitting in the front of the cart. *Well, I didn't, so it doesn't matter*, he'd responded as he stooped to pick it up.

If your parents were any kind of parents, they would've been home with you more.

I can't argue with that.

What'd your parents say when the police came knocking on their door?

He'd reached over to put a head of lettuce in their cart. *They were none too happy.*

But…

Melanie had been relentless that day—as always. *But there was nothing they could do*, he'd told her.

She'd stopped walking and whirled around to face him. *Why do you always have to be so difficult?*

What are you talking about?

I'm trying to have a conversation with you about a very serious subject. I'm your wife. I'm connected to you now, even though you didn't even think to tell me about Emily Hutchins when we were dating.

Why would he? He'd been trying to forget that ordeal, put it behind him. He wasn't proud of what he'd done with

Jewel. Also, he and Melanie hadn't dated long. She'd gotten pregnant after only three weeks; there hadn't been time to tell her about a lot of things. *What do you want to know?* he'd asked, tamping down his impatience so the tone of his voice wouldn't set her off and start a fight.

I'm asking you to tell me about it. And you won't.

I told you about it at the house after the police came over. And we've been talking about it ever since we arrived at the store.

You're saying as little as possible.

Shocked by her insensitivity, he'd said, *Because it's not exactly a fun subject for me.*

If you didn't do it, why would it bother you to talk about it?

Would it be fun for you *to have people think you're guilty of a heinous crime against a young girl even though you're innocent?* At that point, his irritation *had* leaked into his voice. He'd known she'd heard it because even Camilla looked up at him in surprise.

Are you mad, Daddy? his daughter had asked.

No, honey. Everything's fine, he'd said, but Melanie had completely ignored Camilla's question.

I'm just asking what happened with the police! she'd said to him.

You know what happened with the police! I answered their questions, and that was that.

It couldn't have ended there. Have you heard from them since?

At that point they'd come around an endcap displaying bags and bags of tortilla chips and had nearly run into Alice, Ariana's grandmother. He'd stopped to say hello, but Melanie had dragged him away after only a few seconds, saying they were in a hurry.

He'd hoped, after that interruption, however brief, she'd let the subject drop. But in true Melanie fashion, she'd gone right back to it, repeating her question.

I haven't heard from them since, he'd insisted.

They'll probably be back, she'd predicted. *This thing is far from over.*

He'd sighed in exasperation. *Are we still talking about Emily Hutchins, Mel?*

Yes! People are gossiping about you, saying you killed that girl! Our neighbor across the street told me that their friends saw Emily's sister on a news program, and she claims it had to be you.

We've been over this. I didn't kill anyone, he'd snapped. *According to Jewel's own testimony, Emily was abducted at ten-thirty. I was with Ivy and Ariana at that time. Ask them about it.*

As if they wouldn't say anything *to help you,* she'd grumbled as she dropped a package of Oreo cookies into their cart to stop Camilla from begging for them. *They're* both *in love with you.*

Who, Daddy? Camilla had asked.

A couple of friends of mine, he'd replied. Camilla should've been more familiar with Ivy and Ariana. It was Melanie's fault she wasn't, and he remembered feeling particularly annoyed about it that day. *Do we have to talk about this in front of Camilla?*

She's four. She doesn't know what's going on, Melanie had replied, shrugging off his concern.

At that point he'd brought their cart to a sudden halt. *She picks up more than you realize. I'm done talking about it.*

You always wall me out, Melanie had complained, and since there *were* things he was hiding from her, he'd wondered if it would help them get along if he came clean. If he told her Ariana and Ivy had to stretch the timeline a bit, but that was all, maybe he could convince her that he confided in her as much as he did them.

But—thank God—he hadn't. From what he could remember, he was fairly certain he'd gotten through those early conversations unscathed. It was the one that came later, at Courtney's parents' house, that had him concerned. Vera and Chaz Golding had started out as clients. He'd drawn the plans for their house. Then he'd hired their daughter to work in the office, and they'd become good friends.

Melanie told us the police came by your place the other day, Vera had said while Chaz was in the other room getting drinks and Melanie had gone to the bathroom.

This had taken Cam completely by surprise. If Melanie was upset that there were people gossiping about them, why would she make it worse by initiating that kind of talk herself?

He'd come straight from work and shown up a few minutes after Melanie, so she must've been talking about it before he arrived. He remembered being disgusted that his own wife was making his life harder than it had to be. Melanie shared all kinds of things he would rather she didn't. But that had been true ever since he'd married her. And because she could never let anything go, getting angry about it would only create a problem that would ruin the entire weekend. To avoid that, he'd kept a smile pasted on his face and tried to dispense with the subject before Melanie could return. *It was just routine. I was the last person, besides her sister, to see Emily Hutchins. They wanted to determine what I remember about that night. That's all.*

Didn't they talk to you about it twenty years ago, when it happened? Vera had asked, concerned.

They did, but now that they have her remains and might be able to glean new evidence, they're reopening the investigation. It's customary to go back and reinterview folks.

Vera had reached out to squeeze his arm. *Customary or not, it must be upsetting. I'm sorry. I know they're wasting their time talking to you, because you're not the kind of person who could harm anyone. And if you knew anything that could help, you'd already have told them.*

He'd been so grateful for the vote of confidence, and her kindness, that he'd covered her hand with his and smiled—and, of course, that was when Melanie had walked back into the room. As soon as she saw them touching each other, the paranoia she felt toward other women flared up, and they'd had to leave before they could even have dinner, which had provoked one of the worst arguments they'd ever had.

On the ride home, Melanie had screamed accusations at him—that he thought Vera was smarter than she was, that he wanted Vera more than he did her, that if he and Vera weren't sleeping together yet they soon would be.

He'd told her that while he and Vera liked and respected each other, they hadn't crossed any lines. But that hadn't been good enough. Eventually, Melanie had brought up Emily again and said for all she knew, he was guilty of murder. Then she'd threatened to take Camilla and leave the island for an extended period of time, and he'd told her to go. As much as he wished he could keep Camilla, he knew Melanie would never leave without her, and he couldn't take his wife piling on along with the police and everyone else.

But then, when Melanie had kept after him, asking and asking if he'd been out later than he'd said, exhaustion and the desire he'd always felt to tell the truth had finally gotten the best of him—along with the stubborn belief that he wasn't truly in danger because justice would eventually prevail—and he'd conceded that he *had* gone back to the beach that night. He'd said he'd done it to hang out with the friends he'd met at the bonfire, hoping that would finally satisfy her and she'd back off. But he hadn't mentioned Jewel and he'd said he hadn't even seen Emily.

Fortunately, he hadn't specified the time he'd gone back, hadn't revealed that Ivy and Ariana were lying to provide him with an alibi. But he'd told the police—both then and now—that he *hadn't* gone back. If Melanie came forward to contradict him, it could damage his credibility as well as add more weight to the claim of the witness who said she saw him with a *smallish female*.

And that could be enough to once again shift the scales.

seventeen

Jewel was standing in line for coffee at The Human Bean, only a block from her hotel. She'd spent the past few days trying to learn what the autopsy had revealed—since everything depended on that. She could scarcely think of anything else—but Detective Livingston had quit taking her calls again, and when she'd gone to police headquarters yesterday, he hadn't been in his office.

It was Wednesday already. She'd been on Mariners for five days, and there'd been almost no movement on the case. Something had to give, had to change… Her hotel room alone was costing a fortune. She had to pay for Williams's expenses, too. But what better option did she have than to stay and keep pushing?

Problem was, Williams didn't seem to be making the difference she'd hoped he would.

Or maybe she was just getting impatient. A school counselor had evaluated her when she was in second grade—because her parents couldn't get her to do her homework or obey her teacher—and determined she had a "low frustration tolerance." He'd said she could learn to cope with frustration, and to some degree she must have, since she'd graduated from high school and finished two years of college. But frustration seemed to be getting the best of her again. Just the line at the coffee shop was making her unreasonably angry. How long could it take to get a freaking cup of coffee?

She checked her watch. In thirty minutes, she was supposed to meet Williams at the lighthouse. Should she forget the coffee and go?

She was tempted to shove her way through the people behind her so she could get out the door and up to the street. But returning to the lighthouse was going to be extremely difficult for her emotionally. She needed something as comforting and familiar as her morning coffee to bolster her nerves and her resolve. That wasn't too much to ask—especially if she added a bagel so the coffee wouldn't make her too jittery—was it?

After another fifteen minutes she was finally approaching the register when she got a call from Williams. Halfway hoping he'd say she didn't need to come to the lighthouse, after all, she answered in spite of all the people around her. "Hello?"

"Have ya heard?"

The excitement in his voice caused her to tighten her grip on the phone. Was this potentially good news? "Heard what?"

"The police have themselves a new suspect."

The person ahead of her slid over to wait for his food. It was her turn to order. But she couldn't focus on anything other than her call. So she waved the group of girls behind her to the young man with dreadlocks who was waiting at the counter to help the next customer. "You're kidding."

"No. I finally got a return call from Livingston. He's in Albany."

Albany? Why Albany? she asked herself. And then it occurred to her… "Delilah Jones lives in Albany."

"Exactly."

"He went there to talk to her? She's named someone else?"

"She didn't really *name* him. Livingston's take is that she was tryin' to cover for him."

The girls she'd sent ahead of her were finished and the man at the register was looking at her expectantly. She waved the couple behind her up to him as she said, "Who are you talking about?"

"Her brother, Ben."

"Ben…" she repeated in astonishment.

"Yes. That night Delilah left the beach earlier than he did with a young man. They went to his place. But she said the followin' mornin', her brother told her he'd bumped into a young girl wanderin' 'round the beach after she left."

"What time?"

"He couldn't get specific. He was pretty wasted, so he doesn't remember that night very clearly. It doesn't help that it's been twenty years. But he does recall tryin' to talk to a girl close to Emily's age who seemed upset."

Jewel's throat constricted and she could hardly speak. "Was she hurt?"

A middle-aged woman in line with her sent her a surprised look, and it was all Jewel could do to refrain from snapping at her to mind her own business—even though she was the one talking on the phone in a crowd.

"He said he doesn't think so—not physically," Williams said. "Delilah still claims she saw Cam with a *smallish female* before she left, but Livingston isn't sure if she's just sayin' that to take some of the heat away from her brother."

"Is Livingston going to talk to Ben?"

"Already did."

"What did Ben have to say?"

"Just that the girl he spoke to was lookin' for her sister."

"She wanted me," she echoed, feeling sick. Just imagining Emily at the beach, searching for her, made it difficult to breathe. Jewel hung her head. Why hadn't she stayed home that night? Why had she felt so compelled to be with Cam? The son of a bitch had never even called her afterward. "If she was lost or disoriented, why didn't Ben help her?" she asked, lowering her voice because others were beginning to stare. "Why didn't he guide her home?"

"He claims he tried. She wouldn't let him."

"He could've called the police."

"He was drunk, didn't want to get in trouble himself. He assumed she'd find you eventually and left. At least that's his story."

"So why are we just hearing this now? Why didn't Ben and Delilah come forward years ago?"

"Ben said they didn't even know a girl had gone missing."

"How is that possible? News of it was all over the island."

"It may have felt that way to you. You were caught in the vortex. He and his family left to go back home on Sunday—only a day later. It takes time for word of something like that to spread, especially if you don't know anyone who might tell you."

The island wasn't as small as it sometimes felt. She had to remember there were probably fifty-five or sixty thousand people on Mariners during the summer, and that summer had been no different. "Where does that leave the investigation?"

"It muddies the waters a bit. We were so certain it had to be Cam. But now Ben's probably the last person—that we know of—to have seen your sister alive."

The young man behind the counter was once again waiting for someone to order. Finally stepping out of line completely, Jewel stumbled to a table—an elderly man and woman were just getting up and disposing of their trash—and sank into a chair.

"Jewel?" he said.

A small group of people who'd been waiting for the table shot her a dirty look for cutting in front of them, but she ignored it. "What?"

"Are you comin' to the lighthouse?"

She swallowed against a dry throat. The lighthouse… "Would you still like me to?" she asked tentatively.

"I think so. I need you to show me exactly where you were on the beach earlier that day, so I can retrace Emily's steps—see how visible you were from certain vantage points, maybe figure out, out of all the people there that night, who might've been in a situation to not only see Emily but follow her home when she left. That's another way someone might've come across her. And perhaps they found the key simply by searchin' for a few minutes. It was in the front planter. It wouldn't have been hard to find. Anyway, the beach is typically crowded and the lighthouse has more parkin', so let's meet there."

She glanced over at the long line, which still extended out the door. She wouldn't even get her coffee. "Okay. I'll be there in a few minutes."

"Unless it'll be too hard for you…"

She almost admitted that she'd rather meet him anywhere else. But he continued before she could voice a response.

"I just thought you might like to see where your sister was found. There might be something about that particular spot that jogs a memory."

It would bring *a lot* to mind—all things she'd rather forget. What she'd done with Cam had turned into another terrible regret from that night long ago. But she was pressing Williams so hard to bring this case to a close she needed to be willing to do anything he required. "I… I'll be there in a few minutes," she stammered.

"Okay. See you soon."

She was just getting up when she spotted Ariana Prince carrying a couple of breakfast sandwiches to some dudes at a nearby table. She was wearing a bistro apron, which surprised Jewel. She had no idea Ariana was working at the coffee shop.

Ariana nearly stumbled when their eyes met. Jewel could tell she wasn't happy to see her. After their encounter on the street, Jewel could understand why.

But Ariana didn't have to worry. Jewel wasn't going to speak to her today.

The regret that overwhelmed Jewel the second she stepped out of the rideshare at the lighthouse was so palpable it felt like a crocodile had grabbed hold of her and was dragging her under water for a death roll. She should never have come here that night. Nothing would've happened to Emily if she hadn't. And she'd done it for *Cam*. A boy she didn't even know. A boy who would never have shown the slightest bit of interest in her if not for what she'd offered him. He was a man now, who looked at her with a mix of pity and wariness.

Her stomach churned as she remembered how eager she'd been to get his clothes off. He'd been more interested in the alcohol than he was her.

Williams, who was standing in the shade of the lighthouse about twenty feet away, caught sight of her and trudged over. There were a handful of tourists nearby, taking pictures, so he didn't speak until he was close enough to be heard if he lowered his voice. "Thanks for coming."

She was struggling to remain calm. She didn't want to start trembling again. Once the shaking started, she couldn't control it. And she was so reluctant to approach the spot where she'd had sex with Cam that her feet felt as though they were encased in cement.

"You okay, darlin'?" Williams asked.

She nodded. It was easier than trying to speak.

"Follow me. I'll show you where the dog found Emily."

Tears sprang to her eyes as she imagined a golden retriever named Eddie digging in the sand and uncovering something so revolting his owner, Regina Chism, had vomited at the site. From what Jewel had learned, Regina was a longtime Mariners resident. Because of that, she'd heard about the missing girl, so she'd known almost immediately what her dog had discovered. Once the police and the coroner had been called, Emily's clothing and jewelry had confirmed her identity; dental records later verified it.

Williams looked back at her when he realized she wasn't keeping in step with him and stopped. She hadn't moved. Swallowing hard, she summoned all the energy she could and forced herself to catch up to him and continue walking by his side until they'd nearly reached the promontory.

"It was over here," he said, pointing.

There was a slight depression in the earth but nothing else to mark the former grave of her younger sister. The detective had told her it was a miracle, really, that Emily's remains had ever been discovered.

A miracle, she repeated in her mind. It'd been so long, Jewel had begun to believe Emily would never be found. She'd begun to count on it, and to try to put the past out of her mind.

Now she had to do that a different way—by facing the past and doing what she could to find peace.

"Did Emily express any interest in this place?" he asked. "Would there be any reason she might come here on her own?"

His words seemed distorted as though she had her head underwater. She didn't remember Emily mentioning the lighthouse, but she certainly remembered being eager to come here herself—for the privacy it afforded that night. "No. She never mentioned the lighthouse."

"But she'd seen it, hadn't she?"

"Yes. Our parents brought us here the day we arrived on the island. We have pictures of it." Jewel had subsequently refused to look at those pictures. She would've destroyed them if she could. But her mother hung on to that sort of memorabilia. It was part of the shrine Karen had made in Emily's old room.

"Then she knew where it was," he said as though confirming something he'd been thinking earlier.

"I don't know that she would've known how to get here on her own, though," Jewel volunteered.

He turned to gaze down the coastline. "It isn't far from the beach."

"Not for you or me. But a twelve-year-old?"

"She made it home from the beach earlier in the day, and that's much farther." He stood and waited, expecting what, Jewel didn't know. Confirmation? What could she say? Every moment in this area was agony for her.

She stared up at a pair of birds circling high above them. Their lonely cries sent shivers down her spine. "It's going to rain," she said. She was stating the obvious. The sky was growing dark, and she was hoping he'd suggest they go. She'd come; she'd done her duty. Now she needed to get out of there.

"There's one other thing," he said as though she hadn't spoken.

"What?"

"If Emily was abducted from her bed, why wasn't she wearing pajamas?"

That was a telltale sign, one of the signs that made Jewel fear she'd be caught in her lies. "I don't know."

"Did she have her pajamas on the last time you saw her?"

"Yes. She must've gotten up and changed."

"I guess that's possible. Other children have been abducted from their rooms and been forced to dress first. But Emily was even wearing a sweatshirt, as if she was *planning* to come outside."

"If someone could make her dress, they could make her put on a sweatshirt."

"It's just odd—that's all."

Jewel rubbed her arms, trying to get rid of the chill bumps running up and down them. The cold seemed to be seeping through her clothes, even though she'd dressed warmly enough.

I'll show you mine if you show me yours, she remembered saying to Cam, her head spinning from the whiskey and the biggest instant crush she'd ever had.

Are you sure you want to do this? he'd replied.

Don't you?

I'm afraid we'll get in trouble.

How? My parents are off the island. So are yours. You said so when I first knocked on your door.

"Can we go?" she asked Williams abruptly.

He looked over at her in surprise.

"This isn't easy for me," she admitted. "My sister was murdered—or at least buried here after she was murdered. It…it gives me the creeps."

"Of course," he said. "I'm sorry. But first, can we walk down the beach a ways so you can show me where you were sunbathing earlier in the day?"

"I don't know that I'll remember the exact spot. But…I'll try."

Although he started to go, and she turned with him, she couldn't resist looking over her shoulder at the dip in the sand. A big sister was supposed to protect her younger siblings.

I'm so sorry, Emily, she thought.

eighteen

When Melanie wouldn't answer the phone, Cam texted her.

Please pick up. I want to talk to Camilla. I miss her, and she's got to be missing her daddy by now.

While he awaited her answer, he went back to work. It was easier to get through the days if he kept his mind occupied. But after fifteen minutes he still hadn't received a response, so he sent another text.

Melanie, please act like an adult. Let me talk to my daughter. For once in your life, think of someone besides yourself, okay?

He saw the three dots that indicated she was responding but winced when he read what she'd written.

Fuck you.

This was going to be a battle. He'd known it would be, or he would've left her much earlier. He wished he *had* left her now. Instead, he'd endured four years of hell.

You can't deny me visitation. Why would you even try? I sent you the money you wanted to go to Europe. Don't I deserve something for that?

Don't contact me ever again. You can talk to my lawyer, she replied and sent him a phone number.

She had an attorney already?

"That was fast," he muttered, guessing her parents had jumped in to help her find one. They always tried to make everything right for their little girl. Cam thought they were doing her a disservice, not holding her accountable for her bad behavior, but her parents obviously loved her much more than his had ever loved him.

He clicked over to Google and started to search for a reputable divorce attorney. He'd been so busy worrying about the Emily Hutchins case and trying to keep up with his workload that he hadn't hired anyone yet. He needed to get on that, or it would be a long time before he got to see his daughter.

Damn Melanie. She'd always been so unfair.

He was just picking up his phone to call a lawyer named Simon Bench who lived in Providence, Rhode Island, and had excellent reviews, when Courtney popped her head into his office. "Ariana Prince is here to see you."

He put down his phone. "Send her in."

Ariana looked tanned and healthy in a white sleeveless blouse, a pair of blue shorts that hit her midthigh and white sandals. She took off her sunglasses as she sat down, and he couldn't help admiring the sleek blond hair that fell around her shoulders and the pretty green of her eyes. He'd always known she was attractive, but she seemed to be getting more attractive every day.

"Hey," he said, coming to his feet.

"I know who the other suspect is!" she announced as she slid her sunglasses case into her purse.

He came around the desk. "Who is it?"

"Ben."

Cam took a step back. "Delilah's brother?"

"Yep."

"You've got to be kidding me."

"That's what I thought when I first heard."

"Who told you?"

She put her purse on his desk. "I had my first full day of work today. When I stayed late to help Kitty clean up after we closed, she finally let me in on the secret."

"That was nice of her."

"I think she's grateful I'm there to help out," she said with a laugh. "Everyone else who works for her is a lot younger, so I add a much-needed dose of maturity."

"I'm glad she's married to a cop who tells her a few things. So…what's the connection between Ben and Emily? How'd he even come across her that night?"

"He saw her at the beach, looking for Jewel."

Cam felt a twinge of guilt. If he hadn't allowed Jewel to tempt him out of the house, Emily wouldn't have had to come looking for her sister. His actions were partly what'd put her at risk. "Just because they were both at the beach that night doesn't mean Ben killed her. That's like saying I knew how to get into the house, so it must've been me."

"I get that, but he's now the last one to have seen her alive. And he didn't come forward to let the police know he spoke to her that night. They had to drag it out of his sister. That rings some alarm bells."

Cam shook his head. "I barely remember Ben. But it's hard to believe the dude we met would do anything like that."

Ariana returned to the door to close it and then lowered her voice. "Someone did. And think about it. He didn't have to break into the house, because she wasn't in the house."

"The police only assume she was in the house because of Jewel. They don't know Jewel was out with me." He shoved a hand through his hair. "Should we tell them?" He hated what that would do to Jewel, knew how bad it would make her look. He would not want to be her and feel responsible for a sibling's murder. But he had a daughter himself. He could only imagine what he'd feel if Camilla were to become a victim. He'd do anything to get to the bottom of it, so it was hard to blame Jewel and her family for coming after him, considering what they believed.

"At this late date?" Ariana said. "Why would you even ask that?"

"You know the old quote, 'Oh what a tangled web we weave…' I wish I'd never lied in the first place."

"Well, we can't tell the truth now," Ariana said. "If they eliminate Ben as a witness—"

"They'll just come right back to me," he finished.

She nodded. "Let's allow the investigation to go a little further, see what they find. At least they're finally looking elsewhere."

"That's true. Okay."

She took one of the seats across from his desk. "That's not all that happened today."

He was trying not to notice her long toned legs as he returned to his own seat. "What else happened?"

"Jewel came into the shop this morning."

"The Human Bean?" He grimaced. "Don't tell me she caused a scene on your first day."

"She didn't, thank God. To be honest, she seemed upset—too upset to really focus on me."

"I guess that's understandable," he said. "We're in the middle of an upsetting situation."

"No. This was worse than how she's been lately. It was more like…she'd just heard something she didn't like. Maybe it was that she wasn't going to be able to pin her sister's murder on you," she added with a humorless laugh.

"I have no doubt she believes I *did* murder Emily," he said. "I was there that night. I interacted with her little sister. I knew where the key to the house was."

Ariana tilted her head. "And you never called her after meeting her at the lighthouse."

"True. She probably feels used, which makes her hate me even more. Maybe she believes I distracted her on purpose that night to be able to get to Emily." He took a drink from the water bottle he kept on his desk. "I think she's just searching for a way to stop the pain."

"It's big of you to look at it from her perspective," Ariana said. "I'm so mad at her it's hard for me to be that kind."

"I'm mad at her, too. After all, she's the one who came to my house. I didn't go to hers. But we were just dumb kids. I should never have left with her. I still don't know why I did."

Ariana gave him an "it's not that hard to understand" look. "If a sixteen-year-old boy is that confident he's about to get lucky…"

Except it really hadn't been his sex drive that had led him into that mistake—at least not entirely. It'd been loneliness. He'd needed someone, and she'd shown up in the middle of the night, when each minute seemed interminable and no one else was available. But he'd rather take the rap for being a hormone-fueled fool than the pathetic figure being that needy made him. "Yeah. My testosterone has gotten me into more trouble than that."

Ariana crossed her legs. "How's Melanie treating you?"

"Won't talk to me. Won't let me talk to Camilla. Has already hired an attorney."

"Have you?"

"I was just about to call a guy," he said with a sigh.

"You sure you want to file for divorce—that you're done with Melanie?"

"I was done before we even got started. I think that's the problem. There's no way I can compensate for not truly being in love with her."

"You've had some bad luck in your life," she said.

He smiled back at her. "I had good luck when I met you."

A look of confusion crossed her face. She didn't know how he meant what he'd said—because he was grateful for her friendship or felt something more? The crazy thing was…he wasn't sure how he meant it, either.

"Why don't you take the afternoon off?" she said. "We'll rent bikes and go for a ride. You could use the fresh air."

He was so conditioned to saying no to anything but work, he almost refused. It was only three o'clock. He typically didn't leave the office until much later.

But Melanie was gone. He didn't have to worry about not getting home for Camilla's sake, either. And everything he'd been working so hard for suddenly seemed far less important than it had before. If the Emily Hutchins case turned around again, he could lose everything. Why not enjoy the afternoon with one of the people he cared about most? "We don't have to rent. I have a couple of bikes at the house we could use. But isn't it going to rain?"

"It was sprinkling when I arrived, but it'll be fun, anyway."

"Okay," he said with a shrug.

She reached for her purse. "Should I call Ivy to see if she wants to join us?"

Ivy would be at the library until six. Sometimes she could close early. She wasn't under any hard-and-fast rules, since she wasn't a paid employee. She wasn't even technically a librarian and was always the first to point that out. She worked only for the love of books—and making sure the library survived for the benefit of all.

But today he wasn't interested in hanging out as a threesome. He wanted to be alone with Ariana.

"No need to ask her to leave early," he said. "I doubt she'll want to go out in the rain, anyway. We can always hook up with her later for dinner or something."

He could tell Ariana hadn't expected that response. "Okay. Do you have to finish something first? Some work? Or should you call the attorney before we go?"

"I'll call him tomorrow." He slid away from his desk. "To hell with work. To hell with everything. Let's have some fun."

As always, it was easy to be with Cam. Ariana knew him about as well as she knew anyone. And yet, this afternoon carried an extra energy she'd never felt from him before. The way he looked at her. The way he teased her. The tingly sensation that went through her whenever he got close. For her, there'd never been anyone else. But when she'd lived on Mariners, even since she left, she'd understood that they were just friends and she'd be foolish to hope for anything more.

Now, knowing that he might be single again, she was beginning to worry she was misconstruing his need for security and support through this dark time as something else. It was almost impossible for her not to feel more than she should when they laid their bikes on the ground so they could sit on the promontory and look out to sea, and he put his arm around her and pulled her against him to keep her warm.

"I'm glad you got me out," he said.

She almost said, "I always have a good time when I'm with you" but caught herself before the words came spilling out. "Despite the rain?"

"It's only sprinkled a bit so far. No big deal." He nudged her with his body. "As long as you're not freezing to death."

"I'm fine." Any excuse to be close to him was a good excuse, but she knew how pathetic that really was.

"Are you missing New York?" he asked.

"Not really. I'm happy to be back."

"You came when I needed you most." He looked down at her and smiled. "You've always been there when I needed you most."

"That's what friends are for," she murmured. She'd said it to remind herself of the true nature of their relationship. But she also didn't want him to feel uncomfortable or worry that she was suddenly expecting him to become interested in her in a romantic sense. "How are you feeling about Camilla?"

"It's hard knowing she'll be caught in the tug-of-war between me and Melanie. I feel guilty for giving up on my marriage whenever I consider what it'll put her through. I've been so angry with my own parents for being selfish. Now I'm following in their footsteps."

The wind tugged at her hair, causing several strands to escape the messy bun she'd arranged and whip around her face. "Melanie inserted herself between you and Camilla whenever she could. She tried to isolate you from everyone you care about."

"Except my parents," he said drily.

She gazed up at the sky. The storm was gathering strength; large black clouds obscured the sun. But she didn't mind. As far as she was concerned, it was atmospheric and moody. She was glad there weren't a lot of people out. They'd had the run of the island they loved so much, without any interference or competition from the horde of tourists who visited this time of year. Today she hadn't even had to share Cam with Ivy. She already knew it was an afternoon she'd never forget. "Because you're not close to your folks. Melanie's never been threatened by them. She only went after anyone she felt she had to destroy. She was determined to be the only one you cared about."

"True," he said with a frown. "I was willing to let her have her way on almost everything, as long as Camilla didn't have to suffer. But now... I've lost my ability to fight for my marriage."

Bigger drops of rain than they'd felt so far began to hit her face, blowing in from the ocean. "Because of everything else you're going through. I don't see how you'd put it back together even if you tried. I mean...if you don't love Melanie, isn't it better to let her move on and find someone who can give her the devotion she needs? You both deserve to be more fulfilled than you have been." *He* did, anyway. She felt she was being generous by including Melanie.

"So it's a kindness that I'm letting her go?" he said with a chuckle.

"In a way," she said, refusing to let him make a joke of it. "Except for Camilla."

He nodded, then shifted to hold the hair that was whipping across her face, keeping it out of her eyes. "You're beautiful, Ariana. You know that, right? And your heart is even prettier."

She'd never known *he* thought so. Embarrassed, she lifted her hand to hold her own hair. "You wouldn't know it by the number of boyfriends I've had."

"I'm sure there's been plenty of interest." He cocked one eyebrow. "You probably don't realize it, but you don't make it easy on a guy. You come off as unapproachable."

Because her heart wasn't available. There was only one man she'd ever wanted.

"I feel sorry for the dude who tried to get with you at your publishing house," he added.

She winced as she snuggled closer to him. Being damp and as exposed as they were on the cliff chilled her to the bone, but Cam was warm. "So do I. Bruce is a good man."

Sobering, he looked out to sea again. "Unfortunately, we don't get to tell our hearts what to feel."

That was the problem, wasn't it? She'd probably be married by now if she could've gotten over Cam. Instead, she was in her thirties and wondering if she'd ever meet someone who could take his place. "I have to agree with you there."

"Would you change anything if you could?" he asked, point-blank.

"Of course," she said without hesitation and got up and dusted off her hands.

He followed as she returned to her bike. "What does that mean?"

Grabbing the handlebars, she pulled the bike upright. "Why would I want to love someone who doesn't love me back?"

"Ariana..."

He looked pensive when she glanced over at him.

"Never mind," he said.

She studied the sky, trying to gauge how much time they had before the weather grew significantly worse. "We'd better go," she said. "Before we get caught in a downpour."

Jewel had known it was only a matter of time before Detective Livingston contacted her, so she wasn't surprised when she got a call from him. The weather had been threatening rain since noon, but it was coming down hard now. The wind was crashing the trees against the hotel, and every few minutes the sky flashed with lightning.

Pulling herself away from the window where she'd been

watching the storm, she stared at his name as her phone rang. He was going to ask her if she was really at home the night Emily went missing; she needed to be prepared.

Briefly, she thought of her parents and how upset they'd be if they ever learned she'd left Emily unprotected that night—and then lied about it—before answering. "There you are," she said, keeping her voice strident. "I've been trying to reach you." It was important that she come off as strong as she had before and not change her manner or her approach. Detective Livingston was trained to detect falsehoods, and she had to convince him she was telling the truth.

"I've been out of town," he said.

"I know. Williams told me."

"Did he also tell you what Ben French had to say?"

"About Emily going to the beach? Of course."

There was a slight pause. Then he asked the big question, the one she'd been expecting and had been terrified she'd one day have to answer. "If you were at home that night, why would Emily need to go out looking for you?"

He acted as if he'd caught her in something. And since he had, she needed to be extremely careful. "I have no idea," she replied, resisting the urge to get too defensive and say more than she should. "That doesn't make any sense."

"You never left the house that night?"

She'd been the *smallish female* Delilah had seen with Cam at the beach, not Emily. But as far as Jewel knew, no one—besides Cam, who couldn't tell the truth without endangering himself—realized she'd been out of the house. She had to rely on that and hope no one came forward to contradict her. "Of course not. I was babysitting. I would never leave my little sister home alone."

"Are you saying you don't believe Ben talked to Emily?"

"I don't know that he did. But I don't know that he didn't, either."

Silence. She'd set Livingston back on his heels, but it didn't take long for him to rally. "Then what do you think happened? Why was she there?"

"You're asking me to guess?"

"I'd like to hear your thoughts."

"I have no idea," she said. "Maybe Emily snuck out of the house after I fell asleep. Or Ben found the key in the planter and kidnapped her."

"If he kidnapped her from the house, why would they walk all the way back to the beach, where it would be easy for someone else to see them?"

"Maybe he didn't think they'd be noticed," she replied. "It was late, which means it was dark, right? It's not like there are any streetlights on the beach. There probably weren't a lot of people around, either." Since she'd been there herself, she knew that was the case.

"Still, it seems an odd place to take Emily," the detective insisted. "Ben would've had to leave the beach, go to where you and your family were staying, kidnap Emily and bring her back there."

"That's not to say he didn't."

"How would he even know she was there? No, the simplest answer is usually the right one. It makes more sense that Ben was still at the beach when she arrived."

Jewel drew a steadying breath. "Detective Livingston, Emily had a mind of her own. We know she got mad and left me on the beach earlier. She probably didn't think it would be a big deal if she went back, as long as I didn't know about it."

He cleared his throat, started to say something and then seemed to change direction. "So now we have you asleep at home, Emily sneaking out and showing up at the beach with Cam. But later she's alone and very much alive when she speaks to Ben."

"Does that mean you no longer consider Cam a suspect?" she asked.

"It means our pool of suspects just got a heck of a lot wider. It doesn't even have to be Ben, right? It could be anyone who ran into her at the beach—or walking back from it."

"Cam lived just down the street from where we were staying," she pointed out. "He could easily have seen her again later, maybe while he was coming home, too."

"That might be true, but it's a very thin thread on which to hang a homicide investigation."

Closing her eyes, she dropped her head into her hand. She'd come here to bring her parents closure. What happened was Cam's fault. He was the reason she'd left the vacation rental in the first place. "I don't believe it was Ben. As you said, he would've had no idea where we were staying. It has to have been Cam."

"I need evidence before I can charge him or anyone else with murder, Ms. Hutchins."

"What about the autopsy? What have you learned from that?" There had to be something that would lead them to Cam.

"Nothing decisive."

"Is that true, or are you holding back?"

"I'm not at liberty to tell you everything," he clarified. "But I wouldn't set your expectations too high. It's been so long since Emily was killed. There simply isn't a lot left of a body after twenty years."

"Her clothes were found with her, weren't they? What about fibers or…or DNA evidence?"

"Trust me. We're checking for all of that."

"How much longer will it take?" she said, finally losing her patience. "My family and I…we can't tolerate much more."

"I understand, and I'm sorry," he said, gentling his voice. "I promise, I'm doing everything I can. And I know Warner Williams is, too."

"Can you at least tell me how she was killed?"

He seemed hesitant but finally gave her an answer instead of putting her off. "Her skull was fractured."

She caught her breath as she imagined what the coroner had seen—her baby sister's skull cracked, damaged. "What does that tell you?"

"She died by blunt force trauma," he replied. "Meaning she was struck with something heavy and solid."

"Like a hammer?"

"We don't know what it was."

Jewel attempted to thank him, but she'd started to tremble again. Her body was shaking so badly she could barely get any words out. "Can I…can I tell my parents about the manner of death?" she managed to ask. At least that would be something new she could show for her efforts in pushing the investigation.

"Yes. I plan to share that much with the media in hopes of dredging up more leads. It'll probably be on the news tonight."

So he hadn't really taken her into his confidence. Dimly, she realized that, but if she called him on it, she knew he'd tell her he was doing what was best for the investigation. Right now she was too upset about the images parading through her mind—created by the words *blunt force trauma*—to argue with him about anything, regardless.

Block it out. Block it out, she ordered herself and got off the phone as quickly as possible. Then she took two sleeping pills, even though it wasn't quite dinnertime. The past was once again becoming too much for her. She needed to stop all thought, the pain, the regret and the gruesome images—*blunt force trauma*—and check out for a little while.

nineteen

They were soaked to the skin by the time they reached Cam's house. Ariana had been expecting a downpour, but the wind had grown stronger and was worse than the rain. It kept pressing them back, making it hard to pedal. She was shivering from the cold but relieved when he put in the code to open the garage door, and they were finally able to get off their bikes and push them the last few feet.

"I'll put the bikes away later," he said. "Just lean it against the wall for now."

He set the example. Then he took her hand and pulled her into the house.

"How can it be so cold in the summer?" she complained.

"You must've forgotten what it's like here," he said, chuckling. "It can be sunny beach weather one day and feel like winter the next."

She allowed him to tug her up the stairs to the master bedroom.

"I'll get you a towel, or—" He frowned at her bedraggled appearance—she imagined she looked like a drowned rat—and seemed to reconsider. "Actually, why don't you get those clothes off and take a hot shower? That'll warm you up quicker than anything else. You can wear something of mine after you get out while I throw your clothes in the dryer."

"I can use the guest bath," she offered, but he gestured at the expansive bathroom off the master.

"Why? This one is bigger and nicer. Might as well enjoy it."

He went into the bathroom ahead of her and took a plush white towel from the linen closet. Everything in the bedroom was white and beige, a color scheme that looked fresh and perfectly clean. "Shampoo, conditioner and soap are in the shower already. Is there anything else you'll need?"

She wished she had a dry pair of panties, but she figured it wouldn't take long for her own stuff to dry. "No." Her teeth were chattering as she unzipped and peeled off the sweatshirt he'd lent her. "Just something to wear, I guess."

His gaze lowered and his lips parted as though he was transfixed by what he saw. When she glanced down, she understood why. The water had plastered the thin cotton of her tank top to her breasts. He could see the clear outline of her bra, which was as transparent as her shirt.

"Cam?"

"Sorry," he said, giving her a slightly sheepish look. "It's been a long time since… Never mind. Drop your wet clothes outside the door so I can grab them, and I'll leave you some sweats."

"Thanks."

After he went out, she stripped off the rest of her clothes, briefly cracked the door open so she could toss them out and stepped into the shower. She'd been raised in a home built at the turn of the century. Alice's was even older. So she couldn't help admiring the brand-new marble and gold fixtures in Cam's bathroom. The shower, the size of a steam room in a commercial gym, made it even more luxurious. His house was certainly a far cry from her tiny yet expensive apartment in New Jersey, from which she'd had to catch the train to Manhattan.

Dropping her head back, she let the hot water run through her hair and over her body. A shower had never felt quite so good. And she couldn't stop thinking about the rapt expression on Cam's face when she'd removed his sweatshirt.

He'd looked…hungry. She couldn't believe his sex life with Melanie had been very good. They couldn't get along in daily life. So she imagined he would've finished the sentence he'd started with something like, "It's been a long time since I've made love."

Or could he have been about to say something better? "It's been a long time since I've wanted to make love." Or maybe even, "It's been a long time since I've wanted a woman."

She reminded herself that he couldn't have been thinking about her like that, but after the way he'd looked at her when she removed his sweatshirt, it was easy to pretend he felt more than he did. When she closed her eyes, she imagined the water was his hands as it moved over her, cupping her breasts, sliding gently over her nipples, moving down her stomach to between her legs—

A knock at the door brought her out of her reverie. "Yes?"

"I just…I've got some dry clothes out here for you."

"Okay, thanks," she said and quickly lathered up her hair. She needed to have tighter control of her mind, or she was going to get herself in trouble.

Cam didn't know what he was doing, hovering at the bathroom door. Ariana was the last woman he should look to for what he wanted right now. But after holding himself to such a rigid standard for the past five years, he was starving for a physical outlet. He hadn't been attracted to Melanie in a long time. The sex they'd had was perfunctory at best. Rarely had he enjoyed it, because she'd complain about every little thing—he seemed preoccupied, he didn't make her feel attractive, he didn't act as though sex with her meant anything to him. It'd been easier to simply leave her alone until she approached him, and then it'd felt more like a duty.

But now that his marriage was over, all the emotions he'd been suppressing were welling up. He craved human contact—intimate contact—and the fact that Ariana was naked in his shower made the opportunity almost too tempting to resist.

How would she respond, he wondered as he paced outside the bathroom door, if he were to ask if he could join her?

She might say yes… That was a possibility.

But even if she did, he wasn't exactly in a position that lent itself to making wise decisions. The last thing he wanted was to create more regret—of any kind.

He told himself to walk away, use the other shower, get dressed and start dinner. But the memory of Ariana in that wet tank top kept him handcuffed to the spot.

"Damn it," he muttered. And then, he knocked again. "Ariana?"

"What?" came her response.

He ran his fingers through his hair, which was still damp from the rain. "Can I get in the shower with you?"

If she agreed, he was going to let go of all his inhibitions, he told himself. He'd fully embrace the next hour, enjoy the moment and forget everything else.

"What for?" she called back.

"What do you think?" he replied. "There's nothing stopping us."

After a long pause, she said, "No, thanks."

The disappointment that slammed into him took him by

surprise. He wanted to argue with her, talk her into it. What would it really matter? He was never going back to Melanie. Even Melanie knew that. And unless the police found out who'd really killed Emily Hutchins, he could still be in trouble with the law. He craved positive feelings and experiences in the midst of everything he'd been going through. A chance to forget. To live for the moment. To take what he wanted, the future be damned.

"I don't think that would be a good idea," she added.

He knew she was right, but he was too tired and frustrated to accept her answer that easily. "Because..."

"Because if you ever make love to me, I want to know it isn't just that I happened to be around when you needed a momentary escape."

He knew she understood how he'd used sex in the past to distract himself from loneliness. She wanted him to feel something more than a desperate need to avoid what was going on in his life. To understand the gravity of taking that step with her. To make a conscious choice he wouldn't shy away from later.

But he was so busy fighting the Dumpster fire that'd become his life, he wasn't anywhere near ready for that. He'd just barely called it quits on his marriage.

Leave the room, he ordered himself. But now that he'd let the thought cross his mind, he was somehow committed to it, probably because desire had such a tight grip on his body. "I don't see how it could hurt anything," he pressed.

"It could hurt *me*," she clarified, and then he felt guilty for being such a douchebag.

Wincing, he rubbed his forehead. "Right. Okay," he said. "I'm sorry."

The library brought Ivy peace. She found the shelves upon shelves of books, her great-great-grandfather gazing down on her from his somber portrait over the circulation desk, the gleaming woodwork and elegantly curved staircase, even the smell of the printed pages that surrounded her, reassuring. Maybe it was all the possibilities those things represented. She'd once read a quote about a bookstore being bigger than the universe, since the universe only contained what was, and she felt the same way about the library. There were so many facts and truths stored here. Those were important. But to her mind, it was the dreams and imagination a library contained that made it vital to humanity. She considered the ability to imagine and create the most beautiful part of the human mind. With it, one could convey an idea to thousands or even millions of others and change the world.

But did she want to live on Mariners for the rest of her life if it meant she'd always be alone? She'd have a much better chance of meeting someone if she moved to the mainland. There, she could make herself more accessible.

She'd never planned on leaving the island, not even as a little girl—*especially* as a little girl. But recently, she found herself thinking more and more about making a change. She wanted a husband, children. Would the library and the personal family history she was clinging to be worth the sacrifice of missing out on that?

Her parents had left. Tim had left, too. No one else in the family seemed to think twice about abandoning their roots. Was she crazy for caring so much about the island, the house, the library?

John Charles, an elderly man with a shaved head and thick white beard, who'd retired from managing one of the bigger hotels a few years ago, walked in with the stack of books he'd borrowed last week.

Ivy was glad to have a patron. She was tired of being alone with her thoughts, and late afternoons in the summer could get slow. Today even the tourists seemed to be holed up, avoiding the bad weather. Over an hour ago she'd tried to break up the monotony by calling Ariana, but she hadn't heard back. She'd tried calling Cam, too. She couldn't reach him, either.

"Don't tell me you're done with all of these," she said as John stacked the books on the counter.

"All but one. I realized after I started it that I've already read it."

"Wouldn't surprise me," she said. "You've gone through most of our collection."

Considering they had thousands of volumes, that was a bit of an overstatement, but she enjoyed teasing him. He probably did more reading than anyone else on Mariners, at least when it came to library books.

He smiled. "I've got a ways to go before that's true. But maybe I'll get there one day. Do you have anything new?"

"In physics? I ordered a book on Hawking radiation I thought you'd like. But it won't arrive until next week." She walked over to the science section with him, searched the shelves and pulled out a book. "Until then, you might like this. It's called *The Most Famous Paradox in Physics*."

"That's right up my alley, as long as it doesn't get too technical," he said. "The math in the books I like is way over my head, but I'm fascinated by the concepts."

"I think you missed your calling," she said jokingly. "You should've become a scientist."

"I wish I'd had the brainpower and the opportunity."

Leaving him to browse his favorite aisle, she returned to her desk, where she checked her phone. Still nothing from Ariana or Cam, which seemed odd. They were usually better at getting back to her. Surely, one of them must have checked their phone in the past hour.

Could it be that they were caught up in something else? Were they together without her? It was a weekday; Cam was supposed to be at his office. He didn't leave his work easily. So if he had, he must've felt sufficiently compelled…

She told herself it didn't matter. It shouldn't bother her either way. She didn't want to allow jealousy to get the best of her, like Melanie. But those feelings weren't easy to overcome. The entire world seemed to be moving on without her, leaving her behind to run the library as the last bastion of the Hawthorne family. She definitely didn't want to witness Cam and Ariana falling in love while she looked forward to a solo journey.

She remembered the conversation they'd had in her kitchen, where they'd explained that Melanie had been wrong when she accused them of sleeping together. Ivy hated to doubt their word. She told herself they'd never lie to her. But what were they both doing in Cam's bedroom when Melanie walked in? The timing was certainly suspect.

"Something wrong?" John Charles asked as he approached the desk with three books.

Ivy forced a smile. "No, why?"

"The look on your face a minute ago. You seem…troubled."

"I was just thinking. It's nothing."

He followed as she walked over to the circulation desk to scan the barcodes, and once she handed him the books, he turned to go.

"John?"

He looked back at her. "Yes?"

"Have you ever considered moving away from the island?" she asked.

He seemed startled by the question. "Occasionally. Why? Don't tell me *you're* thinking of leaving Mariners."

"Not seriously, no. Except…I'm wondering what might be out there that I'd miss if I spent the rest of my life here, you know?"

"It's a big world," he said. "Lots to see."

"Exactly. Do you ever regret not taking more advantage of it when you were younger?"

He tugged on his beard as he contemplated his response. "I don't know," he said. "You can drive yourself crazy with what-ifs."

That was true. She was more interested in knowing, specifically, if he regretted not marrying and having a family. Was he lonely? Did he now feel it was too late? Would her life turn out like his if she didn't make a change?

She wished she could ask all those questions. But they were too personal. He was always friendly and polite when he came in, but they'd never had a conversation that went deeper than a few comments on the books he was reading or the weather.

"True. Thanks," she said. "It's wet out. Be careful."

"I will. See you next time."

Silence fell like an anvil when the door shut behind him, making Ivy anxious to close up and go, too. What was the point of keeping the library open today if it wasn't being used? It was only twenty minutes away from closing time, anyway.

She'd leave early, she decided. Then she'd drive by Alice's house to see if Ariana was there. If she wasn't, and her grandmother was, chances were good she was with Cam.

The least they could've done was call her back.

By the time she got out of the shower, Ariana could smell bacon cooking. She wanted to go downstairs and help with dinner, but she took her time getting dressed because she was still thinking about Cam's voice coming through the door: *Can I get in the shower with you?*

That was the last thing she'd ever expected him to say. She was still surprised she'd managed to refuse. She had little doubt she'd made the right choice, but it hadn't been easy—and she wasn't feeling too certain about what she'd do if he approached her again tonight. Part of her was beginning to believe she should take what she'd always wanted. She'd certainly waited long enough for it, and she wasn't convinced she'd have another chance. She had no idea what might be coming.

The other part of her knew he wasn't in the right state of mind for something like that. Acting foolishly would only jeopardize their friendship.

While she was deliberating on what he might do or say and how she should respond, she received a text from Bruce.

Just wanted to check in. There was a news story online today about that girl who went missing from Mariners twenty years ago. You would've been in high school when that happened. Do you remember anything about it? As small as Mariners is, and as safe as it's perceived to be, I bet it was a big deal.

He had no idea. She'd never mentioned Emily's disappearance to him, because she'd been afraid something about her tone, expression or agitation would give away the fact that she remembered it far better than she probably would have if her friend hadn't been implicated.

Pausing while half-dressed, she sat on the bed to type her response.

I do remember it. It's such a sad story.

From what I read, the girl's older sister is on the island right now, pressing the police to do more. Are you hearing much about it?

Of course. Everyone's talking.

I wonder if they're going to be able to solve the crime.

I hope so, she wrote back. I feel terrible for her family.

So do I. How are you holding up?

And now the conversation was going to turn personal. She sighed as she stared at her phone.

I'm doing fine. Started work at a local coffee shop today.

You're way too talented to be serving coffee and croissants! Any teenager can do that. When you get bored there, let me know. I can get you your old job back. You're one heck of an editor.

She missed some of her coworkers and a number of authors on her list. Her favorite had a new book coming out in a few weeks. Hard as they'd both worked on the novel, she was eager to see how well it was received by readers.

I like publishing. But my grandmother needs me.

Do you think you'll stay longer than the summer?

It's a possibility.

New York's loss is Mariners' gain. ☺

He was always so supportive, even when it wasn't what he personally would want. He also kept his life simple—low-key, no stress. And he wasn't carrying any of the emotional baggage Cam hauled around. But it wasn't Cam's fault that he'd been born to parents who should never have had a child.

She sent a heart emoji—they were determined to remain friends; she knew he'd take it as such—and hurried to finish dressing. She could've told him she'd played a role in the investigation. He'd accuse her of walling him out again if he ever learned she was involved. But telling him would only create more questions, and she wasn't a good liar to begin with. She didn't want to have to lie to him, too.

After she finished blow-drying her hair, she took a final look at herself in the mirror. Cam's clothes hung on her—his T-shirt fell to midthigh, and to keep them up, she'd had to draw the string as taut as possible on his sweats. But the fabrics smelled so much like him she couldn't help lifting his T-shirt to her nose and breathing deeply. "God, I love you," she muttered and left the room.

Cam was still wearing his damp jeans, but he'd taken off his wet shirt. The sight of his bare chest didn't help her determination not to allow anything physical to occur between them tonight. She'd seen his body before. They'd even been skinny-dipping together as teenagers. But any degree of nudity was somehow more impactful after what'd happened in the bathroom a few minutes ago. "You didn't take a shower?" she said as she walked into the kitchen.

He looked back at her as he turned the bacon in a skillet on the stove. "I decided to start the dryer first. Then I figured I might as well make dinner now, too. I'm famished, aren't you?"

"I'm hungry. But you were right about the hot water warming me up." She pulled her gaze away from the smooth skin she longed to touch. "What are you making?"

"BLTs with avocado. Is that okay?"

"Sounds delicious." She sidled up next to him and took the tongs. "Here, let me finish while you go shower."

"Are you sure?" he said.

She grinned. "I think I can manage BLTs."

His gaze lowered. "You look good in my shirt."

He didn't say anything else, but he didn't turn and leave, either. For a second Ariana thought he was going to kiss her or slip his hands inside the clothes he'd loaned her. Her bra was in the laundry along with her underwear and all the rest.

Her heart started to pound, and her mouth started to water. But he didn't make a move. Although he seemed tempted, she could tell he was as torn as she was about taking their relationship to the next level when, abruptly, he turned to go.

Ariana glanced at the clock above the sink. It was after six. Ivy would be off work. If they called her and had her come over, they'd be safe. Neither one of them would dare do anything that would cross the "friend" boundary if she was around. And when Bruce had texted her, Ariana had noticed two missed calls and a text from Ivy. "The library's closed," she said before he was out of earshot. "Should I call Ivy?"

He stopped and faced her at the foot of the stairs. "Do you want her to join us?"

She had the chance to spend more time with him alone—just the two of them. After dreaming about Cam since she was a child, she couldn't allow this opportunity to slip through her fingers.

She told herself she'd be careful, that she wouldn't let things go too far. She'd have dinner with Cam and maybe watch another movie. That was all. Although she'd enjoyed being with him last night, too, tonight just looking at him was spellbinding, breathtaking. She couldn't bring herself to do anything to change the chemistry between them…

"It might be safer," she pointed out.

He seemed to consider that for a moment. Then he said, "I've always lived dangerously."

She started laughing. "And it's come back to bite you more than once."

"It's only one night," he said with an endearing yet devilish grin.

"What does that mean?" she asked tentatively.

"I'd rather just be with you."

twenty

After they cleaned up dinner, Ariana texted Ivy that she'd call her later and followed Cam into the living room section of the open kitchen/living room area in his house, where he turned on the Yankees game. Ariana had become a big fan while she was in New York. Bruce had followed them since he was a child and taken her to many of their games, and Cam had always liked baseball. She could've suggested a movie instead, but she wasn't in the mood for anything she had to pay close attention to. She was too focused on Cam and trying to walk the careful line she'd set for herself tonight.

Expecting him to take the recliner nearby, Ariana stretched out on the sofa, but he sat not too far away, and pulled her bare feet onto his lap. She knew that if the blinds were up, anyone who could see in would think they were a comfortably married couple. But his real wife had barely packed her bags and left, he was facing a divorce and, for Ariana, there was a great deal of emotion roiling underneath the surface.

"I know you took a DNA test. You told me that. But do you think you'll ever do anything more to find your father?" he asked as he began to rub her feet. "Or are you just going to sit back and wait?"

"I've sort of tried. Not too hard, but I know he doesn't have a Facebook profile," she replied. She didn't really want to talk about the Scottish tourist who'd left her mother pregnant, but she supposed it was at least a good distraction. "Last I checked there were only three profiles with his name. There's a Blair Gilchrist in Canada, one in Virginia and one in Stirling, Scotland."

"He's not the Stirling guy?"

"Surprisingly, no. That dude's only ten years older than we are."

"Have you ever considered hiring a private detective?"

The Yankee pitcher struck out a Cardinals player. "No."

"Because..."

"You know why—money. And fear."

His hand moved up her calf, using the perfect amount of pressure. "I get that," he said. "But your mother reacts negatively every time you mention trying to learn more about him. I could see her saying she told him when she didn't."

Ariana could see her mother doing that, too, which was why she felt as though she couldn't totally rely on Bridget's word. "She wants to pretend she never even met him."

"Of course. She has her life together, on an even keel. Introducing him back into the picture could disrupt everything."

"Yeah. She'd prefer me to be happy with the status quo."

"This isn't about how *she'd* feel. In my opinion you have a right to know who your father is."

Did she really want to head down that path? What if it didn't lead where she hoped? What if she regretted it later?

"If he wants me to find him, he'll make it easy by taking a DNA test," she said.

Cam frowned at her. "Even if he does, who knows if he'll use the same company you did."

"What else can I do but wait, Cam? Who would I hire to find him? I don't know any private investigators." She gave him a pointed look. "And don't say Williams."

He grabbed the remote and turned down the volume. "You could hire someone else."

She was weighing the possibility of finding the right kind of help when he suddenly changed direction.

"Or maybe you shouldn't," he said. "I'd hate to set you up for disappointment."

Ariana considered all the time she'd spent wondering about the man who'd contributed half of her DNA. She craved a connection with him, if only to satisfy—at long last—her curiosity. What was he like? Was he a good man? Where did he live these days? What did he do for work? Did he know about her? "Guess what I do when I'm sick at home or spending some time on my own."

His hands began to knead her feet again. "What?"

"I watch those reunion stories on YouTube, the ones where adopted children find their birth parents. Some of the situations are complicated—a man who never knew he even had a child, or a wife having to accept that her husband had a child with another woman after they were married—and yet, the parent and the child are so excited to be reunited. They're always glad they found each other."

"That could be you, Ari."

"What if it goes the other way? The rejection stories aren't the ones people post. No one wants to watch someone have his or her heart broken."

"You won't know unless you try," he said softly.

She sat up. "I'll make the effort one day. I think about him too much not to eventually do something about it."

"If you're going to take the risk anyway, why wait?" he asked. "You could waste years—and then be sorry you did."

He had a point. She was thirty-six. If her father was about twenty years older—and she imagined him being at least that old when he came to Mariners—he'd be in his mid-to-late fifties. What if he had a heart condition and wasn't going to live long? What if she missed meeting him because she put it off?

That was a terrifying thought, one that made her feel she could already be too late. "Where would I start?" she asked. "Even if I decide to hire a PI, I have to give him something to go on."

"You need to press your mom for more information. She must know *something* about your father. The names of his parents. Where he was living when he visited here. His exact age."

"She's always been vague about him."

"The less you know, the safer she feels. But she could still have the address where she supposedly sent that letter."

Ariana doubted it. Bridget preferred to wipe the slate clean and move on. But should Ariana allow her to take the possibility of having a relationship with her father away from her? What about *him*? Didn't he deserve to know, if he didn't already? Shouldn't she, at a minimum, make sure he was properly informed?

She'd quit her job in New York and was back on the island working in a coffee shop. She had the time and mental wherewithal to focus on this. It would be a good distraction from the Emily Hutchins case—and from how much she wanted to be with Cam.

"Time's running out," she said, finally acknowledging that. "If I'm ever going to do it, I need to get started."

He didn't comment, but she could feel his support.

"Problem is my mom and I can't talk about it. The minute I sense her resistance, I end up backing off."

He took her phone off the coffee table and handed it to her. "Then text her."

"Really?" she said in surprise.

"Why not? It gives you both a buffer. Might make it easier to deal with such a touchy subject."

Feeling fresh determination to battle her mother's resistance, Ariana typed Bridget a message:

Can you tell me anything more about my birth dad, Mom?

Cam slid close to her, so he could read whatever response came back.

Really? You're going to send me a text like this out of the blue?

"See what I mean?" Ariana muttered.

"You expected it," Cam said. "Keep pushing, but start slow, so she doesn't get mad. It won't help to make her even more stubborn than she already is."

"I don't know if anything will help, but I'll try."

It's not unreasonable that I'd like to know more about him. I've mentioned wanting to find him many times in the past. Why won't you help me?

Because I can't. I don't know that much about him myself.

You have to remember something.

Why does he matter so much? You have a father. Kevin has been good to you. He loves you.

"That's beside the point," Cam said.

"This is more about her," Ariana said. "She doesn't want any competition for my heart. If I have the opportunity to meet my father, there's nothing to say I won't like him better and go live in Scotland or something. I know that's at least part of what my mother fears. I've felt it in the past."

I understand that, she wrote. And I appreciate everything Kevin's done. But it's not the same.

You don't want to hurt him, do you?

"I can't believe it!" Cam exclaimed. "She's trying to manipulate you through guilt."

"It's not the first time. She's used that tactic before."

I hope he won't be hurt or offended. That isn't my intention. I'm asking him to understand. I'm asking the same of you.

"That's good," Cam said.

It was so long ago, honey. Who knows what your biological father is even like? You could be opening a can of worms.

Ariana shot Cam an exasperated look before texting back.

I've decided to take that risk. It's worth it to me.

When her mother didn't reply for more than fifteen minutes, Ariana assumed Bridget was going to ignore the conversation, hoping that if she made it too difficult to keep pushing, Ariana would let it go.

"Should I try calling her?" Ariana asked Cam. She hated the idea of getting her mom on the phone. It was always awkward to talk about her father. And she hated being on the receiving end of Bridget's disapproval.

But she refused to allow her mother to continue sabotaging her effort to at least meet her biological father.

"I would," Cam said.

Ariana tried, but Bridget didn't pick up. "This is ridiculous," she grumbled and sent another text.

Quit trying to get in the way, Mom! All these years I've been understanding of you and how you feel. You're the reason it's taken so long for me to come to this. I get that you don't want me to do it. You're afraid to introduce an unknown element into our lives. But it's time you realize how important this is to me. He's my father, for God's sake! Wouldn't you want to know your father?

I don't remember anything that will help, her mother finally replied.

"That's bullshit," she told Cam. I bet you could help if only you would.

Nothing.

Mom? Fine. Don't help me. I'll hire a private investigator, because I'm going to find him whether you're with me on this or not.

Bridget's answer came right away. I hope you don't regret it in the end.

Cam rolled his eyes. "Now she's trying to scare you."

"I'm not giving up," Ariana insisted.

If I do, I do, she texted back. That'll be on me. But if you make me do it on my own, the hard way, I'll never forgive you. You're the one who slept with him, the one who got pregnant. There are consequences, and it's time you faced the rest of them.

Ariana tapped her foot while waiting for her mother's response. She was just about to tell Cam that this was going to cause a fight between them when Bridget wrote back.

Fine. I don't know much, but I'll tell you what I can.

Ariana wasn't at home. And she still wasn't answering her phone. Neither was Cam. Ivy had received only one brief message from Ariana, saying she'd call later, which she hadn't done. Not yet, anyway.

Standing on the sidewalk outside Cam's house, she stared at the light glimmering around the blinds. From what she could tell, he was inside. There could be only one reason they'd *both* gone silent at the same time. They were together.

Why hadn't she been included?

She hated feeling like an outsider, especially when she'd risked so much to stand by them both.

She was about to start down the walkway to confirm her suspicions when a figure approached from somewhere across the street. She hadn't noticed anyone, so he had to have been standing back, out of sight—maybe in the trees or the shadow of the neighbor's house—but this was someone she easily recognized.

"I thought that was you," Williams said.

Unnerved that he was lurking about, Ivy rubbed her arms. "What are you doing here?"

"Same as you." He grinned. "I'm out takin' a walk."

She didn't find him funny; she was too upset. A lot of people walked on the island. It was a small place, and parking was tight. But he had a vehicle and she got the impression he used it—when he didn't mind announcing his presence.

"I spoke to Melanie," he said.

Even more tension began to creep into her already taut muscles. "Cam's wife?"

"Yep. Took me a while to track her down. I've been busy chasin' other leads with Delilah Jones and her brother. But I was surprised to find that Cam and Melanie aren't gettin' along. Sounds like she's gone to stay with her parents and won't be comin' back—at least not to him."

It was too bad Williams had managed to find Melanie before she left for Europe. Ivy knew that couldn't be a good thing for Cam—or for her and Ariana. "So?"

"She claims Cam admitted that he went back to the beach the night Emily was killed."

Ivy's skin began to prickle. Surely, he hadn't! Cam had always insisted he'd gone home and stayed put. "Of course she'd say that—or something like it. Anything to get Cam into more trouble, because you're right—they aren't getting along."

"You weren't with him after he walked you home that night..."

"No, and I've never said I was."

"Then how do you know he didn't go back?"

She swallowed hard, fighting her own panic and doubt. If he hadn't gone back, it was odd that Melanie would say he had *and* that Delilah would claim to have seen him there. Or had Williams told Melanie about Delilah, and she'd jumped on the bandwagon? "He's said as much."

"And now Melanie says the opposite."

"She wasn't there, either," Ivy pointed out. "She's out to get him. You can't trust a thing that woman says."

He clicked his tongue, obviously skeptical. "He's the father of her child. I can't imagine she'd want to see him go to prison."

"I've known her longer than you have," Ivy said. "If sending Cam to prison means she gets her revenge for the breakup of their marriage and she won't have to share Camilla, she'll say anything."

It seemed as though he was weighing her response, but it didn't take him long to come right back at her. "She was adamant that he told her he went back."

"It's her word against his," Ivy said with a forced shrug. "That's not evidence."

"Maybe not. But taken with what Delilah Jones said, it certainly helps build a stronger case."

"I don't know why you're telling me this."

"I like you," he said. "I just wanted you to know that your faith in your friend might be misplaced."

"It's not," she said and spun around to leave. She was no longer interested in confronting Cam and Ariana; she just wanted to get out of there. But Williams spoke up before she could take more than a step or two.

"There's somethin' else..."

She hated to bite the hook he'd thrown out, but she couldn't help it. Had he found evidence that directly implicated Cam in Emily's murder? The possibility made her blood run cold. "What is it?" she said, stopping.

"The coroner has established the cause of death."

How much worse was this situation going to get? "And? What was it? Or are you going to tell me you're not at liberty to say?"

"Blunt force trauma."

She felt her jaw drop. "Blunt force trauma?"

"She was hit over the head."

"I know what it means. I just... I can't imagine that. Not out on the beach. What was she struck with?"

"That, they haven't yet determined."

She winced as she imagined poor Emily's last moments. "Doesn't the cause of death seem strange to you?"

His eyes widened. "Why would it seem strange?"

"I guess...I've always assumed she was raped and strangled. Isn't that the most common scenario for a situation like this? There aren't many weapons at the beach—nothing much to hit someone with—which means her killer must've intended to murder her when he brought her to the lighthouse."

"Sounds like you've read your fair share of Sherlock Holmes."

He knew a lot about her, knew she worked at the library. But she didn't like the way he was trying to ingratiate himself. Ignoring the remark, she said, "What kind of weapon could've been used? A piece of driftwood?"

He shook his head. "The fracture doesn't look broad enough to be a piece of driftwood. If we knew the weapon the killer used, it could help solve the crime. So believe me, the family and I are as interested in that information as you are." He turned on the flashlight function on his phone, pulled a paper from his pocket and unfolded it. "Maybe you should take a look and tell me if you have any idea what could've caused this kind of damage."

Ivy didn't want to see the picture of a human skull from any murder victim, least of all Emily. But she was already staring at a photocopy of a picture most likely taken by the coroner. And Williams was right. The localized fracture suggested something more like a hammer than a large piece of driftwood. "The police don't know what kind of instrument could cause this particular type of damage?"

He gazed down at it, too. "Not yet. Do you?"

Now she understood why he'd approached her. He was wondering if this gruesome picture would jar loose a memory of something Cam had owned or carried with him that night. "A rock?" she said, guessing at the only other item that could be found at the beach that might be capable of doing so much damage.

"No. There'd be more crushin' around the edges than what you see here."

"Then I have no clue," she said.

He folded the paper and returned it to his pocket before turning off his flashlight. "You're a smart girl, well-read. Never hurts to check. If I've learned anythin' in my business, it's that you never know what offhand comment or observation might lead to the right answers."

Ivy glanced back at Cam's house. She was certain her two best friends were hanging out together. Why they wanted to be alone… Well, she could only imagine one reason for that, and she didn't think she could stand to watch a romantic relationship develop between them while she was also lying to protect Cam from whatever consequences he'd face if she told the truth. "I really don't want to be involved in the investigation," she said. "I had nothing to do with Emily's murder. Cam didn't, either."

Shoving his hands into his pockets, Williams jingled his change. "You never doubted him?"

Her stomach tensed. She hadn't been with Cam when she said she was. She had no idea what he'd done that night, where he'd gone. He'd snuck out of the house all the time back then, even when his parents were home. What was there to stop him from going back to the beach that night? He was always looking for people, company, distractions. She was terrified that she could be doing the wrong thing by standing by him simply because she loved him so much.

Was she playing the fool? Doing Emily's family a disservice?

"Of course not," she snapped and strode away.

When the movie ended Ariana got up and went to change into her own clothes. They'd been dry for a while, but she and Cam had been comfortable on the couch, talking about the letter she planned to send her father and then watching most of *Sleepless in Seattle*, which had been on another channel when they switched away from sports. Bridget had finally admitted that she still had the address Ariana's father had provided all those years ago, and she'd sent it to Ariana. That was something. Even if he was no longer living in the same place, and her letter was returned, at least she had *some* information she could take to a private investigator.

"Are you going to write your father tonight?" Cam asked when she came back down the stairs.

"I think I will—while I have the nerve," she replied. "It could take a while to hear back. I might as well get the ball rolling."

"Want to do it here? I'd be happy to help."

It was late. If she was heading home, she needed to get going. If she didn't leave now, she'd wind up staying over, and she was afraid of where that might lead. "It's okay. I can do it."

"Can I drive you home?"

"No. It's not far."

"It's not close, either. This late, I'd feel better if you'd let me."

But she'd rather not have anyone see her in his vehicle, not in the middle of the night. They'd been friends forever—the locals should be used to seeing them together—but now that they were adults, and she'd declared herself to Cam, it felt like everyone else would be able to see right through her and call bullshit on all the years she'd pretended she had no romantic interest in him.

She pulled her phone from her purse, noticed the many missed calls from Ivy and felt guilty—that she'd hidden so much from her best friend and for so long and that she hadn't gotten back to her tonight. She should have. She had no excuse. She'd purposely avoided checking her phone. She simply hadn't wanted anything, even a call from Ivy, to intrude on these precious few hours. "I'll be fine. I might stop by Ivy's on the way home. See if she's still awake."

"What are you going to tell her about tonight?"

"I'm not sure."

"Why don't we both call her right now? Ask her to come over?"

"And say what about the rest of the evening?"

"We could tell her we were busy searching for your father. That's at least partially true."

That wasn't something they had to leave Ivy out of, but it was a believable excuse for getting caught up and not paying attention to anything else. "That's a good suggestion." She hit Ivy's name on her list of favorites but wasn't surprised when their friend didn't pick up. "It's after eleven," she said as she slipped her phone back inside her purse. "She must be asleep."

"At least she'll see the missed call when she wakes up."

"That's better than nothing." She slipped the strap of her purse over her shoulder. "Thanks for dinner."

"Anytime." He followed her to the door, but when she went to open it, he put his hand on the panel, holding it shut, and he was close enough that when she turned, he was towering over her.

"What is it?" she asked.

His gaze lowered to her lips. "I don't want you to go."

"Because you're going through hell and you're lonely. Let's not get confused."

"That's not it," he argued.

She could smell the fabric softener on his clothes. She could also feel the heat of his body and the powerful magnetism that'd drawn her to him from the beginning. "Then what is it?"

"I can't quit thinking about what it might be like to kiss you."

She caught her breath. "It's probably best if we don't find out."

He didn't act as though he'd heard her. Instead, he seemed

completely focused on what he was doing when he ran a finger up her neck, around her jaw and across her bottom lip.

"Cam?" she said uncertainly. But she shouldn't have spoken. All that did was part her lips, and he took advantage of it by lowering his head until their mouths touched. His hand went around her neck, bracing it, as his tongue began to explore where his finger had left off.

It wasn't an overpowering kiss. Gentle and yet sensual at the same time, it set off a riot of butterflies in Ariana's stomach. Cam tasted even better than she'd thought he would. She'd been dreaming of this for so long she didn't fight it. She allowed her eyelids to slide closed as his mouth settled more firmly on hers.

She would've laughed if anyone else had told her a man's kiss could make her knees go weak. That was the stuff of romance novels and movies. But the feeling that swept through her could only be described that way. As his tongue met hers, she was grateful for the door at her back. It gave her the support she needed, because their only point of contact was the hand at the back of her neck and his warm, wet mouth.

The desire to slip her arms around him and bring their bodies into closer contact arose so quickly and acutely that it was all she could do not to act on it. She knew that would probably be the only incentive they'd need to start shedding their clothes and heading for the bedroom.

When he raised his head, he looked slightly troubled. Or confused… Ariana wished she knew why, but she didn't stay long enough to find out. After turning the knob behind her, she slipped around the door and out of the house without saying anything.

She could tell he'd followed her. His body blocked the light that would otherwise have spilled onto the walkway. But she had no idea what he was thinking or feeling. She only knew that if she didn't get away immediately, the need to touch and taste him again would draw her back inside.

When he called her name, his voice was huskier than usual. Even the sound of it appealed to her, so she didn't dare respond. Refusing to so much as look back at him, she fled.

twenty-one

The weather was much better today. There were quite a few people out, getting coffee or enjoying the dappled sunshine sifting through the broad leaves of the elm trees that lined the cobblestone streets while Ivy walked to the library.

Like yesterday, the morning was slow, but by noon several tourists had wandered in to browse the popular fiction section. Ivy kept an eye on them, in case someone needed help, while she sat at her desk with a pile of forensics books—all the library contained on weapons and the type of damage they might inflict on a human body. She was tired of waiting for the police to solve Emily's murder. If she could figure out the kind of weapon that might've caused the wound she'd seen in the picture Williams had shown her, maybe she could help the police find the real culprit. Then she'd no longer have to deal with the terrible conundrum she faced now, constantly wondering if she was going to be caught in her lies or should come forward because she was wrong for trying to cover for Cam in the first place.

She was poring over a chapter when a woman with dark brown hair and two young children approached the counter.

"Ready to check out?" Ivy asked.

"We are."

"Looks like you've found some of my favorites," she told the oldest, a girl of about nine.

Suddenly shy, the child stared down at her sandals. "You've read them?"

"All of them. I grew up on Harry Potter." She scanned two Potter books, plus *A Wrinkle in Time*, *Holes* and *Harriet the Spy*. "*Holes* is a very different read, far more realistic than the magic of Harry Potter, but I enjoyed it."

"I like the Boxcar Children!" the younger boy volunteered.

"I enjoyed those books, too, when I was your age," Ivy said, giving him a conspiratorial smile. "I'll never forget my first one."

"It's terrible about what's going on, isn't it?" the woman murmured while her children were distracted by a display Ivy had put up with a stuffed Paddington Bear and several different Paddington books.

"What do you mean?"

"About that girl. The one who was killed here."

Ivy felt her stomach tense. "Hopefully, the police will get to the bottom of it soon."

"I hope so, too." The woman accepted the books, put them into a canvas tote and called to her children.

With a sigh, Ivy watched as they left, then checked her phone. Ariana and Cam were both trying to reach her. But she had nothing to say to them. Not right now. She needed time to decide where she stood after so much had changed, with Emily's remains being found, Ariana coming back, Jewel being in town. She had to admit that she was no longer as eager to defend Cam.

Returning to her desk, she went back to the book she'd been reading. She'd never been particularly interested in criminology or forensics, but if she'd learned anything working in a library it was that knowledge was power—and she was tired of feeling powerless.

After several hours she learned that her library didn't have anything specific enough to facilitate the kind of research she needed to do, so she began downloading books from university libraries. And just before closing, she ran across something that sent a chill down her spine. It was pictures of skulls that'd been struck with various objects, and one in particular jumped out at her.

The hair stood on her arms as she noted the similarities between the picture she was looking at and the one Williams had shown her. This was a skull that had been struck by the corner of a square bottle, which was something she could easily believe was at the beach that night. They'd all been drinking.

"Hey, what's up?"

Ivy jumped. She'd been so shocked by what she'd found that she hadn't heard or seen Ariana come in. "Just...doing a little reading," she said, clicking away from the book so that Ariana couldn't see what she'd been studying. "What about you?"

"I left you a message last night, and several today, but you haven't called back. Cam tried to reach you, too. We've been worried that you're mad at us."

Not only had Ivy seen the missed calls, she'd also noted the time the first one had come in late last night. What had Ariana and Cam been doing all evening that they hadn't even thought of her until after eleven? "I've been busy."

Ariana looked around, seemed to take note that there were

a couple of other people in the library, and lowered her voice. "I'm sorry, Ivy."

"For..."

"For not telling you the truth from the beginning."

Probably because of what she'd been researching, a wave of foreboding swept through her. What was Ariana talking about? "This doesn't have anything to do with Emily, does it?"

Ariana seemed put off by the question, but Ivy couldn't help jumping to that conclusion, especially after what she'd learned from Williams last night. "No, of course not. Well, maybe a little. I guess...I guess everything's intertwined, isn't it?"

Ivy might've breathed easier at that point—at least Emily wasn't the focus—but she still had the image of the skull in her mind. "What do you mean?"

Ariana's chest lifted as she took a deep breath. "I've been in love with Cam almost since the day I met him."

Ivy had suspected something like this, but she'd never dreamed Ariana would offer such a frank confession. She blinked several times before trying to clarify. "Since you came back to the island and his marriage broke up?"

Ariana glanced away, seemingly reluctant to maintain eye contact. "Since we were teenagers."

Ivy gaped at her. "Why didn't you tell me?"

"Because I knew he wasn't interested in me, and once something like that is put into words... I don't know. I was terrified the truth would come out somehow. I didn't want him to know, was afraid you might eventually tell him—or tell me to tell him—and that would change so much between the three of us. The sleepovers, which were so innocent as friends, certainly wouldn't have been the same. And..."

"And?" Ivy repeated when her words trailed off.

"I didn't know if...if maybe you were hiding the same secret."

That was the thing. Neither did Ivy. Before Cam was married, there'd been plenty of times when she'd wished something more serious would happen between them. Even now that his marriage was over, she'd wondered if her love for him could move in a romantic direction. In many ways they'd be perfect for each other. But did she think so because she was afraid of being left behind, the only one of them to remain unmarried, childless and living on the island into her eighties?

She was afraid she'd wind up a lonely old lady, like her great-aunt, who'd died shortly after her grandmother. "Why are you telling me now?" she asked instead of commenting on her own mixed feelings.

"Because that's why neither of us called you last night. We were together."

"You're already sleeping with him," she guessed, unable to keep the disgust from her voice.

Ariana shook her head. "No."

"You *haven't* slept with him..."

"No!" she insisted, adamant. "With everything that's going on, that would be a mistake, and I know it. I can't tell whether he returns my feelings or is...just looking for some way to make himself feel better."

Ivy could understand why she might say that. Getting with Ariana could be a rebound kind of thing that would end up destroying the friendship they'd had almost since they first met.

And now there was even more to consider. Ivy might have discovered what was used to kill Emily...

"Ivy?" Ariana said when she didn't respond. "What's wrong? You look...shaken, upset. I was afraid you would be. I'm sorry. I know this must feel like a rug pull to you. I...I wish I could dictate my emotions. But I've fought my attraction to Cam from the beginning, and it hasn't done a damn bit of good."

Ivy could feel her pulse leaping in her throat. Should she tell Ariana what Williams had shared with her? Could Delilah Jones be right? *Had* Cam gone back to the beach and lied to them about it?

If so, what else was he hiding?

After swallowing against a dry throat, she said, "I understand. You—you can't simply decide not to love someone you love."

"I wish I had that kind of control, especially in this situation. But I don't."

Ivy took hold of her arm. "You need to be careful, Ariana. Don't get any more involved until…until this is all over."

"Why? What's going on?"

Ivy let go of her, checked to make sure the people who were still browsing weren't looking for help and lowered her voice even further. "I wasn't going to tell you, but…"

Ariana's eyes rounded. "What is it?"

"Williams found me and approached me last night." She didn't add where. She didn't want Ariana and Cam to know she'd been bothered enough to try to find them. "The coroner has established the cause of Emily's death."

"What was it?"

Once more she glanced around to make sure she could continue without being interrupted or overheard. "Blunt force trauma to the head."

"What?"

"She was hit with something. And I think it was a liquor bottle."

The color drained from Ariana's face. "What makes you think that?"

"Williams showed me a picture of the damage to her skull, and I've been looking for objects that make a similar fracture pattern."

"*You've* been looking…"

"Yes. In books by forensics experts. I have access to plenty of them. After spending almost all day researching it, I finally found a science journal that has a picture of a skull that looks almost exactly the same as Emily's. It's uncanny." Ivy waved her over, closer to the desk, and used her touchpad to navigate back to the book she'd been reading when Ariana walked in. "Look at this. This woman was murdered with a liquor bottle."

She leaned closer. "'Damage done by a square-shaped whiskey bottle,'" she read from the caption, then sank into the seat closest to Ivy's desk and added, as though shocked, "A bottle like...Jack Daniel's."

Alarmed by her reaction, Ivy squatted next to her. "Why'd you say that? Did Cam have a bottle of Jack Daniel's that night?"

She pressed a hand to her chest but didn't speak.

"Ariana?" Ivy prodded.

"Yes," she said at last. "Cam was drinking Jack Daniel's the night Emily was killed."

Ivy couldn't believe it. "Wait... Melanie is claiming Cam admitted to her that he went back to the beach that night. Delilah Jones is saying the same thing. Is it true?"

Looking miserable, Ariana nodded.

"No!" Ivy exclaimed. "He told us he didn't!"

"He—he admitted to me that he did—a couple of nights ago. I didn't want to tell you because I was afraid it would erode your trust, but Jewel brought a bottle of Jack Daniel's to his door after he got home, and they went to the lighthouse to drink it."

Ivy went around the desk and sat down, too. "Shit," she whispered. "That's how Jewel knows we've been lying about the timeline."

"Yes."

"Why hasn't she come forward to say she was with him?"

"Because she was supposed to be babysitting. She doesn't want to get blamed for letting someone get to her sister when she was supposed to be watching her."

"But why'd Cam tell us he went home and stayed there? Why would he need to say that if—"

"He was scared, Ivy," Ariana broke in. "Anyone would be terrified in his position."

The memory of the skull she'd seen in the book, and the picture she'd seen of Emily's injury, rose in Ivy's mind again. Ivy was certain the same type of weapon had been used on both victims. Knowing Cam had access to a bottle of Jack Daniel's at the beach certainly didn't help his case. "Are you sure that's all it was? Because… Oh, God," she mumbled, slumping into her own seat. Had she and Ariana been covering for a killer?

Cam couldn't get the kiss with Ariana out of his mind. That, coupled with the vision of her bare breasts when she'd taken off her shirt while changing in the seat of his Land Rover, made it impossible for him to focus on his work. He was almost afraid to see her again for fear too much had changed between them—shifted in a direction from which they could never move back.

He'd always had her in his corner. He didn't want to do anything that could cause her to leave the island again or move on without him. But he wasn't really himself; couldn't seem to get his legs underneath him. Although he'd been married, it felt as though he'd been in cold storage for three or four years. Now he was coming around to his old self, in some ways, and experiencing a strong craving for the wrong person.

Trying to distract himself, he made a few business calls. Then he tried to contact Melanie. He needed to reassure himself that his daughter was okay and let her know Daddy still loved her. But he doubted Melanie would even answer or allow him to speak to Camilla. She hadn't so far, so he was taken aback when, this time, she actually picked up.

"Why do you keep calling me?" she snapped. "What is it you want?"

She knew what he wanted. He'd left messages. But there was no point in allowing her to drag him into an argument. "I was hoping you'd let me say hello to Camilla."

"Oh, *now* you care about her?"

He'd thought he might eventually feel *some* regret for divorcing Melanie. That he'd discover a tiny amount of fondness for his wife or remember certain aspects of their years together with nostalgia. But he felt nothing, except the need to reconnect with his daughter. "I've always cared about her," he said as evenly as possible. "You know that. Why haven't you been answering my calls and texts?"

"We've been too busy having fun," she said flippantly.

Melanie was probably disappointed he hadn't called to beg her to come back to him. He understood that not pandering to her ego would have a detrimental effect on the situation with his daughter, and he felt bad about that, but he simply wasn't capable of kissing her ass any longer. "Can you put her on the phone?" he asked.

"She's not here."

Was that true? "Where is she?" he countered.

"With my mother."

He didn't believe it. If he had his bet, Camilla was standing right next to her.

Letting his head fall forward, he began to rub his left temple. "Melanie, please. I'll send you another thousand dollars for Europe if you'll just give me fifteen minutes on the phone with our daughter."

She was taking great pleasure in having the power to deny

him. But the way she liked to shop… She was tempted by the money. He could tell.

"How will you send it to me?" she asked, sounding suspicious.

"I'll Venmo you."

"Do that now. Then call back." She hung up as if she had the final word. But he didn't trust her enough to comply.

He texted her instead.

I'll send half now and half after I talk to Camilla. That's my final offer.

It took her fifteen minutes to respond.

Okay.

He sent five hundred dollars before calling again and was glad he'd done it when his little girl answered. Melanie had either lied about her not being there, or gone and picked her up in the interim.

"Hi, Daddy!"

The tension inside him immediately began to uncoil. "Hi, Camilla. How are you?"

"Good."

"Are you having fun with Grandma and Grandpa?"

"Yeah."

"What have you been doing?"

"Nothing."

"Playing?"

"Yeah. I have a new Barbie."

"That's nice." He was about to ask if her grandparents had bought it for her when she hit him with a question of her own. "When are you coming over, Daddy?"

He flinched at the stab of pain that question brought. "I won't be coming, baby. I can't."

"Because you have to work?"

"Yeah. You're going on a trip with Mommy and Grandma and Grandpa, and it's going to be so much fun. I'll see you when you get back."

"What if I don't want to go?" she asked. "What if I want to come home instead?"

"I would love to have you here," he admitted.

"Will you come get me?"

Relief and excitement rushed through him. Why couldn't he take her while Melanie was in Europe? He'd have to find day care while he worked, but a lot of single parents grappled with that. Courtney could even watch her in the office for short periods of time, or he could work at night, after she was in bed.

"Put your mom back on the phone for a minute, will you?"

As the phone transferred hands, he could hear Melanie in the background. "That's all he's got to say?"

"He wants to talk to you," Camilla explained.

A second later Melanie came on the line. "What is it?"

"It won't be easy to tour Europe with a four-year-old, Melanie. The plane ride alone will be incredibly long for Camilla. Why don't you leave her here with me while you go have fun with your parents?"

"No way," she said, but he wasn't willing to give up that easily.

"Take a minute to think about it before you refuse," he continued. "You're only saying no to hurt me, cutting off your nose to spite your face. Imagine going through all those museums and cathedrals trying to carry a four-year-old or find a bathroom or get her a nap or whatever."

"She'll be fine. My parents will help me."

"They weren't planning on having either one of you along. Not initially. Why make their trip any more difficult than it has to be?"

"I don't want her to be with you. I don't trust you anymore."

He cautioned himself to remain calm. "We lived together for four years. You know I'd never do anything to hurt her."

"Yeah, well, Emily probably thought you wouldn't hurt her, either."

The jab stung—so badly it took him a second to realize she'd disconnected.

He swore as he set his phone aside. He wasn't going to send her the rest of the money. She hadn't given him his fifteen minutes. He didn't even owe her the five hundred he'd sent. But it would be just like her to accuse him of not following through instead of blaming herself for not keeping her end of the bargain. "What am I going to do?" he muttered to the room at large but jerked to attention when he heard Ariana's voice only a second later.

"Hey, I hope you don't mind," she said. "I told Courtney you wouldn't care if I showed up."

"That's fine." Embarrassed that she'd caught him at such a vulnerable moment, he came to his feet. "What's going on?"

"I could ask you the same thing. You seemed pretty distraught when I walked in."

He waved a hand in the general direction of his phone. "Oh, it's nothing. Just…Melanie, you know? She's going to make the next few months as difficult as possible. But I already expected that."

"I'm sorry. I hate to make your day even worse, but…I just spoke to Ivy at the library."

Judging by the grave expression on her face, that talk hadn't gone well. "What's wrong? Is she mad at us?"

"She might be. But right now there's something even bigger to worry about. The fact that we didn't return her calls last night made her wonder how much she can trust us, which concerns me."

"You're referring to the case..."

"Yes. She told me that the coroner has finally determined Emily's cause of death."

He froze. He was definitely interested in this information, but he was also shocked that it would come through Ivy. "How'd she hear about that before we did? Has it been on the news?"

"Not yet. Williams approached her last night."

Cam rubbed the beard growth on his chin. "Where?"

"I didn't ask. I assumed it was at her house."

"Wherever it was, I can't imagine he was willing to share anything with her. The police are being very careful about what they release to the public. In cases like this, they often hold back pertinent details, hoping to find someone who knows more than what's been revealed so far."

"Maybe they've chosen to make the public aware, to show progress on the case and relieve some of the pressure on them. Or they could be hoping it'll garner more leads. They have to find the murder weapon if they can. It might help solve the case."

"Weapon?" he repeated. "I never pictured a weapon being used."

"I was surprised about that, too. But we're not talking about a knife or a gun. She died of blunt force trauma, was hit on the head with something heavy."

So not a weapon exactly—just something that could be used as one. "What'd the killer hit her with?"

"The police don't know yet. But...Ivy thinks she does."

"How?" he asked, stupefied.

"Last night Williams had a picture of Emily's skull that

showed the fracture, and the sight of it freaked Ivy out so much she spent the entire day reading forensics books."

"They have that kind of in-depth forensics book at our little library?"

"She was using some university library online, and eventually came across a picture of a skull with an injury that looks just like what Williams showed her last night."

"So…why would that be bad?" he asked. "If it helps solve the case—that's the best thing for everyone."

"Except…" Her forehead creased with worry.

He studied her. "What is it?"

"If Ivy's right, Emily was killed with a liquor bottle—the square kind with a neck."

He sank slowly into his seat. "You mean like a Jack Daniel's bottle."

She nodded.

Briefly, he closed his eyes while digesting this latest piece of bad news. "I didn't kill her, Ari," he said when he opened them again.

"I know."

To his relief she seemed as confident as ever.

"But if the police find out you were drinking a bottle of Jack Daniel's that night…"

"It won't look good," he finished.

"What'd you do with the bottle after you were done with it? Can you remember?"

She was all business, but he knew this had to shake her faith in him, if only a little. "No," he said. "But we must've left it at the lighthouse. Once it was gone, we had no reason to continue carrying it with us. We were young and nearly falling down drunk, so we weren't at our most environmentally conscious. And we were too busy doing—" he pinched the bridge of his nose as certain unwelcome memories began to parade before his mind's eye yet again "—other things."

"You probably just tossed it aside."

"Which means anyone could've come across it after we left," he pointed out. "That should open the pool of suspects."

"I'm sure the police will go out and attempt to search for it. If it's buried under the sand anywhere near where they discovered Emily's remains, they could possibly find it—and it might still have some DNA on it."

"After all this time?" he asked skeptically.

"There's probably only an outside chance. But if they find it and test it, and it *does* have your DNA…"

"Shit." He thought of the hope he'd had only a few minutes ago that he could care for Camilla while Melanie was in Europe. Now he didn't know what he'd been thinking. He couldn't take his daughter, even if Melanie would let him. Everything about his life was too precarious. "So what do we do?" he asked.

"I don't know." She walked over to close his office door before returning to his desk. This time she didn't sit down. "I'd like to go out there and look before the police do."

Surprised, he leaned back. "What does Ivy have to say about that?"

"She knows about the Jack Daniel's. I told her about you and Jewel that night, but I didn't say anything to her about this. She wouldn't approve."

"You think we should do it anyway?"

She began to pace. "I think *you* should stay away from the lighthouse entirely."

"You're saying *you'll* go? Alone? No way. Not after what happened to Emily there."

"We don't have any other choice. You didn't use the bottle you were drinking from to kill anyone. But if the police find it, I'm afraid they'll claim you did. They're under so much pressure to solve this case..."

"What if Ivy tells the police that the injury on Emily's skull is consistent with a Jack Daniel's bottle?"

"I've asked her not to say anything, at least for a few days."

"And she agreed to that?"

"She said she'd wait until Friday."

He stared at the carpet while trying to decide what to do. Technically, he shouldn't do anything. He could get into trouble simply for interfering in the investigation. But it felt as if Jewel and her family, Williams and the police were out to get him, whether he'd hurt Emily or not. He'd be stupid not to do what he could to protect himself from spending the rest of his life in prison. He knew that the moment Jewel learned Emily had been killed with a bottle like the one they'd been drinking from that night, she'd be even more convinced that he'd murdered her sister. It was a far greater stretch to believe that Ben French had bumped into Emily on the beach and they'd somehow wound up at the lighthouse together, where there just happened to be a square bottle he used to kill her.

"Cam?" Ariana said. "What are you thinking?"

He looked up. "The bottle we had that night couldn't be the one that was used to kill her. The chances of someone else coming across it while having Emily with him and using it to murder her... That's outlandish, right?"

"Sounds pretty outlandish," she agreed. "That's why we have to do something to make sure that bottle is never found."

"Okay. We'll go out late tonight, together, and see what we can find. Since the police haven't revealed the type of weapon that was used—since they don't even know yet—we aren't getting in the way of the investigation. The lighthouse is public property. We have every right to be there. And if we happen to find an empty Jack Daniel's bottle buried in the sand and throw it away, we're cleaning up the beach."

"Sounds good. But there's one more thing."

He held her gaze. "What is it?"

"Williams has been keeping a pretty close eye on the three of us."

"I'm sure he doesn't stay up all night. We'll wait until two. Then we'll sneak out and meet up at the beach before walking down to the lighthouse."

"Should I let Ivy know what we're doing?"

He wasn't sure whether to include her or not. He felt terrible for putting both his friends in such an untenable position. "No. Let's not get her involved. I feel bad enough that she's having to lie for me."

twenty-two

Should she come forward?

That evening Ivy sat at her kitchen table examining and reexamining the picture she'd asked Williams to send before leaving the library. She'd been comparing it to the screenshot she'd taken and printed out at the library from the forensics book. She'd even traced the damage pattern on each image with a marker to make the lines stand out. They were so similar that when she overlaid them, it appeared they were both from the same injury.

She kept telling herself that didn't necessarily mean anything. It wasn't as if she was using some special scientific method to arrive at her conclusions. This was just a visual inspection. Maybe there was another object that left the same pattern. Or...maybe she was missing something important.

But deep in her heart, she didn't think so. Was Cam guilty?

Had she been blinded by friendship, love and loyalty? Should she tell the police everything she knew and let the justice system take its course?

She thought most people would say that was the "right" thing to do…

Finally, too racked by guilt and uncertainty to relax or unwind, she called her brother.

"Hello?"

He sounded busy, distracted. She almost hung up and pretended it was a pocket dial. She had no idea how she was going to broach the subject she needed to talk about—or even if she should. But she had no one else to confide in and needed to share her misgivings with someone. "Tim?"

"Ivy? What's up?"

She pushed away from the table and wandered into the living room, where she'd left the TV on so that it wouldn't be so quiet while she was studying the skulls of two dead women. "I was just…wondering if you and the fam were still coming to the island this summer."

"I don't know. Mom called and was talking about coming at the same time, but I'm not excited about that. I want a vacation, and she's too hard to get along with."

For the most part, Ivy had always been able to get along with Priscilla. Her brother and her mother were just too much alike; they butted heads. "Why not stay here with me and let her take the house on Sandy Brook Lane? That should give you both some space. Then you can see her when you want and do other things on the island when you don't."

"That might work," he said.

"I would love to have you here." She desperately needed to find herself again and decide if she should put the house up for sale and leave Mariners.

"It'd be good to see you. What's been happening on the island?"

Seeing a potential opening in the change of subject, she drew a deep breath. "You mean other than trying to cope with all the fear and speculation caused by the discovery of Emily Hutchins's remains?"

"I saw something about that on TV," he said. "If someone gets a new car on Mariners, the locals consider that news. I can only imagine what it must be like in the wake of something sensational. Do the police know who did it?"

"Not yet."

"They aren't still looking at Cam, are they?"

"I think they are," she admitted.

"Damn. He must be pretty freaked out."

"He is. Especially because he and his wife are splitting up, so he's already having a rough time."

"Wow. I'm sorry for him. But the breakup doesn't have anything to do with the case…"

"I wouldn't say directly, but the added stress certainly hasn't helped their ability to get along. Did I tell you that Ariana's back for the summer?"

"No. The three of you are together again, huh?"

"Yeah."

"That's awesome. I know how much you've missed her. Sounds like you're set up for a great summer."

"I'd be enjoying it more, if only…"

When her voice wobbled and she didn't finish, and he fell silent, she knew he'd caught on that something was wrong. "Hang on a sec," he said. Then she heard him tell his wife, or maybe it was his kids, that he was going into the den.

Once he came back on the phone, Ivy could no longer hear the background noise that'd been there before, and she pictured him alone in his home office with the door closed.

"What's going on?" he asked.

She didn't know how to start the conversation she wanted to have—or if she'd regret having it...

"Ivy, I know you," he said when she didn't respond. "Something's wrong. What is it?"

She hadn't told a soul the truth about the night Emily was murdered. She'd maintained what she'd said for twenty years—lied boldly in the face of authority. She'd also promised Ariana they'd talk about it if she was ever tempted to break faith with her and Cam. But Cam and Ariana were growing so close, Ariana would only stick up for him. What good would such a conversation be? Given how Ariana felt about Cam, she could no longer be objective. That meant Ivy couldn't share the true level of her doubt. She'd tried earlier, in the library, only to hear even more fervent protestations of his innocence—innocence that was based on...what? The same things she'd always used to support covering for him?

Besides, she wasn't going to the authorities. Talking to her brother didn't count. She needed someone as levelheaded as Tim to help her figure out what her role in this thing should be.

"It's about Emily Hutchins," she said.

"Cam didn't murder her, did he?" he said, immediately putting the two pieces together.

She almost gave him an emphatic no, almost said what she'd said a million times before—Cam would never do anything to hurt anyone. But the truth was...she couldn't be a hundred percent certain of that. He'd been troubled, acted out, often drank too much. One time he vandalized the school. Another time he stole a bike just to piss off his parents. Besides all that, he'd lied to them about going back to the beach on the night in question and only admitted the truth in the past week—to Ariana alone. He'd known how to get inside Emily's home and that she was there alone with her sister. And it looked as though she'd been struck by the same type of bottle he'd been drinking from that night.

Everything seemed to be stacking up. How much evidence could she conscionably ignore before coming forward to remove the alibi she'd helped provide? "I don't know," she admitted.

"What does that mean?" her brother responded, obviously alarmed. "He was with you when Emily was kidnapped. I remember that much. So…it couldn't be him, right?"

"Except that—" She squeezed her eyes shut, trying to stem the tide of emotion that was welling up, but an errant tear rolled down her cheek. "He wasn't with us at ten-thirty like we said."

Dead silence. It felt as though all the air had been sucked out of the room—on his side, too. Another tear escaped as she waited for him to recover from the shock.

"You lied about that, Ivy? And you've kept quiet about it all these years?"

"Yes, but…I felt like I was doing the right thing until…"

"Until what?"

She told him about the cause of death and the picture Williams had shown her and what she'd found in her research.

"Holy shit," he said when she was done.

With a sniff, she used the back of her hand to wipe her nose. "I can't be sure that's the murder weapon. I mean, who am I to think I can make that determination? I'm not a specialist or anything."

"I don't know what to react to first," he said, his voice low and serious.

"What do you mean?"

"A twelve-year-old girl was murdered, for Christ's sake, and you lied to cover for the possible culprit?"

"You know Cam would never harm anyone!"

"I don't know that. What I do know is that most killers don't look like monsters. They're everyday people just like you or me—or Cam. So what if he's handsome and nice to you? That doesn't mean he isn't capable of doing what was done to Emily Hutchins. Plenty of people liked Ted Bundy. Everyone talked about his charisma. You must've seen the documentary on him."

Ivy already regretted having told Tim, knew immediately that it was a mistake. "There were warning signs with Bundy."

"That depends on who you ask."

"Well, I would know if Cam was capable of doing what was done to Emily," she argued.

"How?" he said, challenging her statement. "Could it be that he was in possession of the freaking *murder weapon*?"

"I told you—I don't know that…that a liquor bottle was the weapon. I'm not qualified to make that call. Besides, Cam isn't a psychopath! I would know it if he was."

"He doesn't have to be a psychopath to have killed that girl," he said, his voice rising. "That night could've been the product of the perfect storm—a night where every element came together to produce the worst possible outcome. It could even have been an accident, although I don't know how someone gets hit over the head with a liquor bottle by accident. Perhaps she did something to enrage him and that's how he can justify trying to cover it up—and having you and Ariana help him. But you can't *lie*. Especially now that you know about the murder weapon. It's not right."

"He's my friend, Tim!"

"I don't care. You have to go to the police. Tell them everything. Hold nothing back."

"You know Cam, too!" She was about to add, *Don't you care what happens to him?* but Tim spoke before she could.

"Yeah, and I always wondered why he had no guy friends and spent almost all his time with two girls. Maybe he's a pervert."

Anger charged through her, helping her fight back the tears. "I can't believe you just said that! Surely, you remember what it was like growing up on the island. There weren't a lot of kids. The guys my age were all douchebags or drug addicts or nerds who did nothing except play video games. I don't blame him for not wanting to hang out with them."

"Or was it that he got more sympathy and support from you?"

"Stop!" she cried. "He's never tried anything on me. I'm sorry I told you."

"Thank God you did. Now maybe I can talk some sense into you."

"I'm not going to the police. I can't do it."

"Then I will."

The panic that surged through her made her feel like one of the characters in *Alien* who had a monster rip its way out of his or her chest. "No!"

"Ivy, you have to let me do it," he said. "You don't want this on your conscience for the rest of your life, do you?"

It felt like the foundation was crumbling beneath her feet. She couldn't betray Cam. What if he didn't murder Emily but wound up going to prison for the rest of his life—because of her? "You don't understand—" she started, but he cut her off.

"I understand *completely*," he told her. "You're in a hard place. I feel for you. But you have to tell the truth. I don't want to see you get in trouble for lying about something this serious."

Was something wrong with her character because she wasn't marching down to the police station right now? Tim made it sound that way…

"You owe it to the Hutchins family," he continued. "They're seeking closure and justice, and rightfully so. Let the legal system run its course."

"You obviously have more confidence in the legal system than I do." Probably because it wasn't threatening one of *his* friends. "You know the Mariners Police Department has never dealt with a case like this, don't you? They only have one detective, and finding Emily's remains has drawn national attention. He's under so much pressure and scrutiny, he's got to be desperate to bring this case to a close."

"Then why are you making it harder?"

"Because I don't believe Cam did it!"

"You told me you couldn't be sure."

She returned to the kitchen and picked up the copy of the damaged skull she'd printed out from the book in the library. "I can't, but…that doesn't mean I want to do anything that could hurt him."

"Which is why I'm going to do it for you. We're not hurting anyone. We're just telling the truth."

"No! Give me a few days to think about it."

"You've had twenty years!"

"I need to decide if I'm ready."

"You're never going to be ready, Ivy. It's one of those things that isn't easy to do but has to be done."

"Tim, stop it! Please don't tell anyone, least of all the police."

"I can't know about this and do nothing."

"I shouldn't have called. I just—I needed to talk to someone. Are you telling me I can't confide in my own brother?"

"Not when it's information that could help solve a murder. God, Ivy. What'd you expect?"

"Please don't do anything," she said again and hung up because she could no longer speak around the lump in her throat.

Oh, my God. What have I done?

★★★

Ariana had spent the evening with her grandmother watching *Dances with Wolves* on Blu-ray. Then Alice had gone to bed, and to make her think she was turning in, too, Ariana had shut off the TV before retiring to her own room. But she was still fully dressed. She'd been on her phone since then, playing games, reading the news and scrolling through TikTok videos—anything to keep her mind occupied.

She checked the time: one-twenty. She didn't have much longer to wait. But she was growing bored, which made the minutes drag by. Since she planned to take her grandmother's old-model Lexus, which was parked behind the house in a detached one-car garage off the alley, she should be able to slip out without her hearing. And it wouldn't take long to reach the rendezvous point. That meant she still had half an hour to wait.

After navigating to Cam's cell number, she texted him.

You almost ready?

I am. You?

Cam had told her to meet him where they'd been partying with Ben and his sister the night Emily had been killed. It wasn't far from the lighthouse. And it was a place they both remembered well. Thanks to everything that'd happened after, the details of that night had been etched into their brains.

Been ready for hours, came his response.

Should we go now?

Might as well. I've been staring out through the crack in the blinds all evening. Coast looks clear to me. Any word from Ivy?

No. I'm worried about what she's thinking and feeling. But I didn't call her tonight for fear she might want to hang out. I know she wouldn't agree with what we're about to do.

Here's hoping she hasn't gone to the police with what she found in that forensics book—and that they haven't already figured it out for themselves.

If they *had* figured it out, she and Cam could be in for a surprise tonight. What if Detective Livingston was already out there, digging around?

Ariana had no texts or missed calls from Ivy. She wouldn't go to the police without warning them, would she?

Ariana hoped not, but she couldn't be sure. When she'd left the library, Ivy had definitely been upset. She'd put a voice to all the insidious doubts that'd made Ariana feel so conflicted while she was living in New York.

Even if the police have figured it out, they wouldn't go out to the lighthouse in the middle of the night. It'll be much easier to search during the day.

I'm counting on it.

So was she. Feeling a touch of foreboding, which she ignored—she was too in love with Cam not to take this risk for his sake—she wrote, See you there. Then she cracked open her bedroom door to make sure the house was as dark and quiet as it should be.

The wind coming in off the sea had a chilly edge to it, so Cam was glad Ariana had dressed appropriately. They were both wearing dark clothing with beanies and carrying the flashlights and shovels he'd brought from his garage as they walked down the beach to the lighthouse. They could've parked there instead of walking, but he didn't want his vehicle to be seen in that lot—not this late. It would look weird, and he knew it.

They were probably on a fool's errand, anyway. He couldn't believe the Jack Daniel's bottle he and Jewel had tossed aside so long ago would still be anywhere near the lighthouse. Chances were someone had picked it up and thrown it away—or it'd been broken and was currently turning into sea glass somewhere in the ocean.

He'd almost canceled their plans to come tonight, but the fact that Emily's remains had been discovered after *two decades* meant that anything could happen. He had to at least try. He hadn't seen the picture Ivy had shown Ariana, but he could tell by Ariana's reaction that finding that bottle, in case it still contained DNA evidence or word got out that he'd been drinking Jack Daniel's that night, could possibly save the rest of his life.

"Did you hear anything from Ivy after you got home from work?" Ariana asked, speaking over the sound of the surf as they trudged up the shoreline.

"No. You?"

"I haven't heard from her, either."

"What do you think it means?" he asked.

"She's having a hard time with…with what's going on. But it's not just that she believes a liquor bottle like the one you had was used to kill Emily."

The clouds parted overhead, and the moon came shining through, making it possible for him to turn off the flashlight he was using. This late he doubted anyone else was around, but just in case, he didn't want to draw outside attention if he could avoid it. "What else is bothering her?"

She didn't answer.

"Ariana?"

Stopping, she turned to face him, but when she seemed to struggle with what she wanted to say, he spoke.

"Is it that you told her I went back to the beach the night Emily was killed?"

She winced as she nodded. "I'm sorry. I wish I hadn't—not when I did, at any rate—but I feel a great deal of loyalty toward her, too. I mean, we're all in this together and have been since the beginning. I didn't want to lie to her, not when she was opening up and sharing what she'd found with me."

He felt his stomach knot. "She's going to go to the police. You know that, don't you?"

"No," she said, turning back around as they started moving again. "She would never do that. And if she was going to tell, she'd come to us first. We agreed to let each other know if...if we felt the need to change course."

Cam knew his marriage, and the demands Melanie had put on him, had taken a toll on his relationships with Ariana and Ivy. Maybe it was even worse with Ivy. They'd remained on the island together, could've been much closer. But he hadn't known how to fulfill both roles—husband and friend, not while keeping Melanie happy—and felt he'd had to choose. Now that his marriage was breaking up in spite of what he'd sacrificed, however, he understood that it made him appear to be a fickle friend.

"Even if—if she does go to the police, everything is circumstantial," Ariana added. "There's no hard forensic proof, because you didn't do anything wrong."

"If we can't find that bottle, there could be," he pointed out. "What if my DNA is still on it, and they establish that a bottle like that was indeed used as the murder weapon?"

"Someone could've found it and used it after you dumped it!" She was grasping at straws. What really happened wasn't always what mattered in a criminal trial. It was what the prosecutor could get twelve jurors to believe.

"That'd be hard to sell to a jury, especially when you combine it with all the other circumstantial stuff." She had to agree with him, or she wouldn't be out here, helping him look for that bottle.

"All we can do is search for the damn bottle," she muttered.

"What if we can't find it?"

"At least we can be reasonably sure it isn't here and they won't find it, either."

"And what do we do about Ivy?" he asked.

"I say we call her in the morning and meet for lunch after I get off work. We need to talk."

He nodded, but he wasn't convinced any amount of conversation could reach Ivy now that she believed he'd had the murder weapon in his hands the night Emily died.

The lighthouse came within view, and he sighed. He didn't want to be out here; didn't want to spend the next several hours digging frantically through the sand, hoping against hope they'd find something they were probably never going to find. But what else could he do? He had to try, even though, ever since Emily's remains had been found, it felt like he'd been hog-tied and dropped on a raft sailing down a river so powerful it would take him wherever it would—and there wasn't a damn thing he could do about it.

twenty-three

It took forever to do the digging. It was almost dawn before they'd managed to search even a portion of the area around where Emily had been found, and after being out all night, Cam was exhausted. He felt bad he'd kept Ariana out, too. She was still stubbornly trying to lift her shovel.

"We have to give up," he said, stopping her. "We're going to be seen if we don't get out of here. Joggers hit the beach early. Besides, you've got to work in less than three hours. I want you to be able to grab a nap, at least."

"I'll be fine." She stuck her shovel into the sand deep enough that it would stand upright, looking disheartened as she surveyed what they'd done and all the ground they had yet to cover. "We'll have to come back tonight. And probably the night after."

"I'm not sure we should," he told her. "This feels like a big waste of time and effort."

"It wouldn't feel that way if we found what we needed to find," she insisted.

They'd uncovered various trinkets dropped by people who'd visited the lighthouse over the years, as well as quite a bit of trash. Cam was tempted to leave it all in a pile for someone else to throw away. That was how tired he was. But he knew they had to haul it out, if only so it wouldn't look strange that someone had gathered all this junk so close to the site where Emily's remains had been discovered. Ariana stuffed everything into a plastic bag he'd found while he used his foot to level where they'd been working to make it less obvious that the sand had been disturbed. "We'll talk about it later," he said. "I don't have anything left in me tonight."

"What time is it?" she asked.

He checked his phone as he took the bag from her. "Five-fifteen." They'd talked through the night about what they were finding, where they should dig, what Ivy might do next and how to convince her that Cam hadn't used a bottle or anything else to harm Emily Hutchins. But as they started down the beach they remained silent.

After throwing away the sack in the first public garbage can they came across, he took Ariana's hand.

She looked up at him. They'd always been comfortable touching each other, but this was a different kind of contact. He couldn't even explain why he was doing it. He just needed to feel close to her, to gain strength and encouragement from the contact, and she seemed content to let him.

The pink streaks in the sky that'd started to appear when they were still at the lighthouse were growing more pronounced by the time they reached their cars. Ariana had just opened her door, and Cam was standing beside her, when they turned for a few seconds to take in the sunrise.

"That's incredible," Ariana whispered, and Cam couldn't help smiling down at her—right before he kissed her.

Her hands came up and went around his neck, and he could feel her whole body against his.

They were breathless by the time he lifted his head. He wanted to keep kissing, probably would have if they didn't need to get away from the area as soon as possible. "I can't believe what's happening," he murmured as he let go of her.

He knew she assumed he was talking about the investigation when she said, "We'll get through it." But he'd actually been referring to *them*. How could he suddenly be feeling so much desire for her? Especially in the middle of everything else that was going on in his life—not only with the Emily Hutchins case, but also with Melanie? His wife had left only a week ago.

But he'd never been in love with her. He'd tried to force it, but even though they'd been living together and raising a child together it was as if they'd been broken up for a long time. For the past three years, at least—once he realized that short of giving up his own identity and allowing her absolute control over his every thought, action and moment, which he couldn't do, nothing would significantly improve their situation.

Things were different with Ariana. They had so much more to build on—mutual trust, respect, loyalty, understanding. Even a shared history. Thanks to that strong foundation, the romantic side, now that it had flickered to life, was moving very fast. It felt like everything he'd ever wanted from a woman had been right in front of him all along, and he'd just missed it.

Until now.

He closed her door and watched her drive away before getting into his own vehicle. Of course he'd have to worry about being locked up for murder right when he might finally have a chance at building a much happier life.

★ ★ ★

Jewel was awakened by the ringing of her phone. She'd taken a clonazepam to be able to sleep, and it hadn't quite worn off. Drowsy and a bit disoriented, she fumbled around on the bedside table, trying to pick up her phone.

After dropping it once, she managed to get a firm grip on it and answer. "Hello?"

"Jewel?"

"Who is this?" she asked.

"You can't tell?"

That accent. Warner Williams. "It's eight-thirty, Warner. Why are you calling me so god-awful early?"

"I didn't realize it was early," he replied. "Most of the rest of the world is up."

"Yeah, well, most of the rest of the world can sleep without a pill. What's going on?"

"There's been a development in the case."

This helped bring her around. Yesterday he'd told her that the coroner had established the cause of death, but as far as she knew, the police hadn't figured out what weapon or other implement had been used.

Suddenly more alert, she slid into a sitting position with her back against the headboard. "What is it?"

"You were right."

"About what?"

"Ariana, Cam and Ivy have been lyin'."

A shot of adrenaline gave her the strength and energy to get out of bed. "How do you know?"

"Ivy's brother called the station this morning. Said she's been coverin' for Cam all along."

She squeezed her forehead, frustrated that the drug she'd taken made her brain so sluggish. "How does Ivy's brother know that?"

"She musta told him. Maybe Cam told her first. I don't

know. I don't have the specifics. I looked up the brother's contact info and tried callin' him, but he won't talk to me. Said he'd already told the police everything he knows. I'm goin' to pay Ivy a visit later. I don't want to do it at the library. I doubt she'll talk to me if there are people around."

Jewel blinked at the light glimmering at the edge of the shade covering the window. She could hear voices and traffic on the street below. Another ferry must've come in and everyone who'd been on board was walking or driving to their hotel or vacation home. "I can't believe she rolled over on Cam—after twenty years."

"She didn't. Like I said, her brother did. I'm eager to find out why."

"Me, too." She drew a deep breath as she sank slowly onto the edge of the bed. This was huge. They were one step closer to getting a conviction. But it meant Cam would probably tell the police he'd had sex with her at the lighthouse. The only thing that'd kept him silent was trying to avoid placing himself in the area that night—at least, not later than after he'd gone home with Ariana and Ivy. If Ivy changed her story and stripped away his alibi, he'd have no reason not to claim she—and not Emily—was what had drawn him back to the beach.

She was prepared for that, though. He had no proof she'd ever been there or that she'd ever had sex with him. All she had to do was act outraged. *I would never leave my little sister alone, especially to approach a boy I'd barely met!* Because there typically weren't a lot of girls who'd be bold enough to do what she'd done, and with her religious family behind her acting just as outraged, no one would believe him. In fact, such an accusation would only make him look worse. People would say, *As if killing Emily wasn't bad enough. Now he's trying to defame her sister in an attempt to get out of it.*

"Jewel? You there?"

Warner had said something she'd missed. Pulling herself out

of the deep well of her thoughts, she cleared her throat. "Yeah. I'm here. Just…stunned that we have some movement—that we might finally get justice."

"I'm startin' to feel a lot more optimistic myself."

"My parents won't believe it," she said.

But they'd be proud of her.

Ivy had several missed calls—all of them from Detective Livingston. The library had been quiet this morning, so she'd had nothing better to do than watch them come in. She could've answered; she'd chosen not to. She had no idea what she was going to say. She wanted to believe her brother hadn't come forward, but she couldn't think of any other reason the detective would be trying so hard to reach her.

She sat at her desk, all the books and other documents she'd studied to determine the kind of implement that might've been used to kill Emily Hutchins put away. Now she wished she'd never even done the research. If she hadn't bothered, she wouldn't have been freaked out by what she'd learned and probably wouldn't have felt the need to reach out to Tim. She'd had no idea he'd react the way he did. Her brother was so caught up in his own family and his dental practice—so far removed from the island these days—she'd believed she could confide in him, get some advice and make up her own mind.

On the verge of tears, she picked up her phone and texted him.

You called the police?

I told you I was going to.

Bastard. She'd never lashed out at him before. She'd always been the calm one. She and her father had a similar temperament, while Tim and Priscilla were far more excitable. So she was surprised when he actually exercised some restraint instead of lambasting her in return.

Someday you'll thank me.

She doubted it. What was she going to tell Ariana and Cam? Did this mean Cam would be arrested? Had they already taken him into custody?

If so, it would be her fault.

I won't thank you. I'll never forgive you, she wrote back. It was my problem. I was dealing with it.

It wasn't your problem. It affected other people—and could get a murderer off the streets.

His response only made her angrier. He was always in charge, always right, justified no matter what he did. And he thought he could complain about Priscilla? You're just like Mom.

Now you're starting to piss me off.

I don't care. If an innocent man goes to prison, it's going to be your fault. Cam has a four-year-old daughter. I hope you can sleep at night knowing that.

You're the one who shouldn't be able to sleep! The police can't make the right decisions if they don't have all the facts.

Because they always get it right when they do?

She was disappointed when he didn't respond. She was spoiling for a fight.

I don't have all the answers to give them. That's the problem. I only know a portion of what went on that night, and it just happens to be the portion that makes Cam look guilty, even though I know he would never hurt anyone.

With that, she put an end to the conversation.

The one patron who'd been browsing the popular fiction aisle left without borrowing anything, and Ivy felt a wave of relief at being alone. She shouldn't interact with the public today. She couldn't even muster a smile.

Maybe she should close the library early, take a sick day. Otherwise, the detective—or the investigator Jewel had hired—would probably show up. If they couldn't reach her by phone, one or both of them might well stop by...

Suddenly eager to keep that from happening, she hopped up, gathered her lunch, her purse and the keys so she could lock up. She was just walking over to flip the sign on the front door to Closed when the detective came in.

Oh, God. She should've left earlier.

"Ms. Hawthorne? Do you have a moment?" he asked.

Ivy wished she could tell him no. But she couldn't even pretend to be busy. There wasn't another soul around. "Do I *have* to talk to you?" she asked. "Legally?"

"Not if you don't want to. But if this goes to court, you'll be subpoenaed and have to give testimony under far less favorable circumstances."

Were there any *good* circumstances in which to rat out one of her best friends? "I don't believe Cam hurt Emily."

"That isn't my question."

She'd known it wouldn't be. "But I know he's not who you're looking for," she insisted.

"What matters is the truth, Ms. Hawthorne, and from what I

hear, you've been playing fast and loose with it for two decades. You understand that lying to the police is a crime, don't you?"

Ivy struggled to blink back tears. She did know. She'd looked it up on the internet more than once. She could be charged with obstruction of justice, a felony punishable by up to ten years in state prison. Or there was making a false report to a police officer, which was a misdemeanor and punishable with up to a year in jail. And because of her, Ariana could be charged with one or both of those crimes, too. "I didn't want to see Cam arrested for something he didn't do," she said stubbornly.

"It might help if you had a little faith in me. Please understand—I'm not out to get Cam. I'm not out to put just anyone in prison. I want to find the person who really committed this horrific crime."

That sounded good in theory. Any cop would say something similar. And yet, plenty of the wrongly accused went to prison. Livingston would go where the evidence led him, and so far the evidence led straight to Cam. Whoever had really killed Emily had somehow walked off without a trace. "It's nothing personal," she mumbled.

"Why don't you just tell me what really happened the night Emily was killed, and we'll go from there?"

"*Nothing* happened that night. We got in earlier than we said, that's all."

"Which means Cam wasn't with you when Emily was taken."

"Was she taken?" Ivy countered. "I mean…has that even been established? She was fully dressed. I saw it on the news. The clothes found with her remains suggest she could've left the house on her own."

He arched an eyebrow at her. "So now you're going to tell me how to do my job?"

The tears she'd been holding back finally began to stream down her face. Not only had she broken faith with her two best friends, she also hadn't taken the opportunity to warn them because she'd been hoping against hope that Tim wouldn't put her in this position.

But he had, and now the secret she'd sworn to keep for life was no longer a secret at all.

Ariana was working when Detective Livingston came into the coffee shop. She spotted him as soon as he walked through the door and immediately ducked down the hall to avoid him. Was he a regular here? she wondered. Or did he know that she and Cam had been out at the lighthouse, digging all night, and have questions about that?

Everything would be okay, she told herself. Even if he did know about the lighthouse, it wasn't illegal to hang out there. And digging in the sand caused no damage. They hadn't found anything, anyway. He probably just wanted a cup of coffee, like everyone else.

"Whoa! Careful."

Ariana was so caught up in her worries she wasn't paying enough attention and nearly collided with Kitty, who was coming out of the kitchen as she was going in. "Sorry," she said, barely managing to hang on to the dirty dishes she was carrying.

"No problem." Kitty continued for a few steps but then stopped. "Ariana?"

"Yes?" Ariana said, turning to face her.

"Are you okay?"

She blinked, hoping to look surprised. "What do you mean?"

"You look exhausted."

She *was* exhausted. She'd been up for thirty hours with only a two-hour nap before work and felt so dim-witted and clumsy she was afraid she wouldn't be able to make it through her shift. She was dying for it to be over already, and yet Kitty needed her for another two hours. The ferry had just come in; they were extra busy. "I couldn't sleep last night," she admitted. "But I'll be fine."

"If you're not feeling well, maybe you should clock out and go get some rest."

Her employer's concern made her feel guilty. "No. Really. We've got a line out the door."

"This time of year we always have a line out the door," Kitty said, sounding tired herself, and continued to the front to deliver two croissants.

Ariana had just taken her load of dishes to the sink and was about to relieve Joshua at the register so he could take his break when she noticed her boss looking at her from across the room. And Kitty wasn't alone. She was standing off to one side with Livingston.

That was when Ariana knew for sure. The detective hadn't come for a cup of coffee. He was looking for her.

Her heart began to pound as Kitty lifted a hand and beckoned her over.

Witnessing the exchange, Joshua stepped back up to the register. "I guess I've got this a while longer."

"I shouldn't be more than a few minutes," she murmured, then weaved her way through the busy kitchen to return to the front. Had someone seen her and Cam last night and reported it to Livingston? Why else would he want to talk to her again?

"Hello," she said, forcing a smile.

Kitty spoke first. "Ariana, Detective Livingston would like a second with you."

Ariana raised her eyebrows. "Now? But we're so busy..."

"We'll be okay," Kitty assured her. "You're free to take a few minutes. It's crowded in here, but there might be a seat out on the patio," she added for his sake.

Ariana didn't feel she had much choice as Kitty hurried off

and Livingston waited for her to precede him up the stairs to the sidewalk. Her feet felt like clumsy blocks of wood as she made her way up each step and over to the small side patio where several of their patrons lingered, drinking their lattes.

"What's this about?" she asked, choosing the table that was the farthest back, in the corner.

Livingston studied her closely as he took a seat across from her. "Ariana, some new information has come to light about the Emily Hutchins case that throws what you've told me in the past into question."

Her heart began to pound even harder. This wasn't about the lighthouse, but it sounded even worse. "What do you mean?"

"Ivy has come forward. She claims Cam wasn't with the two of you when you said he was—that he walked you both to your grandmother's place earlier than you told me before."

Ariana had known it was possible that Ivy might decide to tell the truth. But she'd never really believed Ivy would do it, especially not without coming to her first. After all, it was Ivy who'd made her promise they'd decide together.

Ariana could see Livingston's lips moving, but her ears were ringing so loudly she'd lost what he was saying.

"Ariana?" he said, leaning closer. "Did you hear me?"

She struggled to pull herself together, to focus and listen, but it wasn't easy. Physically and emotionally, she didn't have the reserves she needed today. "Um…sorry. I…I haven't been feeling my best. What was that again?"

"I asked if you were ready to tell me what really happened the night Emily was killed," he replied.

How should she respond? Did she dare claim that what Ivy had told him wasn't true? How could she essentially call Ivy a liar? That required an extra layer of nerve she didn't think she possessed. And yet… What choice did she really have?

"I've already given you my statement," she insisted. "I told you what happened exactly as I remember it."

Clearly displeased by her response, he frowned. "You're going to stick with that?"

Tears pricked her eyes. She was perched on an emotional precipice, but she couldn't allow herself to fall off. She knew how odd it would look if she suddenly burst into tears. "Ivy must be mistaken."

He lowered his voice. "I've spoken to Melanie Stafford, too. She claims that you and Cam are having an affair. She felt it was important I know. Is what she's saying true?"

Damn Melanie. "Cam and I are just friends. We've been friends since…since we were in middle school. I mean—" she couldn't help blinking faster and faster "—I admit I care for him a great deal. But we've never slept together."

"Melanie insists she found the two of you in her bed."

"It wasn't what it looked like! I stayed over, yes, but we… we didn't do anything. I don't see how that affects who killed Emily Hutchins, anyway."

"It might not affect who killed her, but it would provide you with a strong motivation to cover for Cam, right?"

Calm down. Think, before you blow this. "My story hasn't changed since I was in high school. Besides, I haven't slept with Cam."

"But are you covering for him?"

"No!"

"You can get into *a lot* of trouble lying to the police, Ariana. You know that, don't you? You could even go to prison for it."

The image of Jewel Hutchins confronting her and Ivy on the street, Jewel's parents pleading for help on TV, Ivy looking concerned as they discussed how to handle Warner Williams, her grandmother quietly deciding to help them give Cam an alibi—all these things passed before her mind's eye like a parade. The implications of what she was about to say were huge. They affected a lot of people. And that was even before she got to Cam.

It wasn't until she remembered him taking her hand as they left the lighthouse this morning that she knew, right or wrong, what she was going to do. "I understand that," she said.

"You're still going to stand by your man? Contradict Ivy?"

She loved Ivy, too. But Cam needed her more. She refused to abandon him. "She's the one who's contradicting me."

He laced his fingers together as he rested them on the small metal table. "Why would she do that?"

"I don't know," she replied. "Maybe she's upset with me, Cam or both of us. Or she doesn't remember that night as clearly as I do. It's even possible she's just…buckling under the pressure. Jewel had a few choice words for us in the street the other night. Maybe that confused Ivy, made her uncertain, and now she's rewriting the past to try to bring Jewel some peace."

He said nothing, which only tempted her to continue talking. Fortunately, the lump growing in her throat was threatening to choke her, so she stopped.

"You've heard that Emily was killed with a liquor bottle just like the one Cam was drinking from that night, haven't you?" he said when he finally spoke again.

He was trying a different approach. She needed to do all she could to fend off this attack, too. "Wasn't Ivy the one who determined that?" she asked. "Are you even sure she's right?"

Judging by his expression and the way he shifted in his chair, he hadn't expected her to call this information into question. "I'm having an expert double-check, of course. But it looks to me like she's right. The damage to Emily's skull could easily have been made with the bottle of a fifth of Jack Daniel's, and Ivy claims Cam was drinking Jack Daniel's that night."

"*Could* is the word I'd find concerning, if I were you. Besides, I never saw Cam with any Jack Daniel's."

"It was after he went back to the beach."

She feigned confusion. "*If* he went back, you mean. He claims he didn't and nothing I've heard is strong enough proof to make me believe otherwise. Anyway, if he did go back, I wasn't with him. So...who saw that? Delilah? Did she say he was drinking Jack Daniel's?"

He cleared his throat. "No, Ivy said he told *you* that, and you told her."

Ariana had never been more torn. She was being forced to choose between her two best friends. But if she sided with Cam, she couldn't see how Ivy would suffer any long-term consequences, not to the point that it might destroy her future. If she sided with Ivy, however... "She didn't get that from me," she said with conviction. "Besides, even if it was a Jack Daniel's bottle that killed Emily, a lot of people drink that kind of whiskey." She sat up taller to appear more self-assured. "Isn't this all circumstantial, anyway, Detective? Didn't the autopsy provide real evidence? *Forensic* evidence?"

His eyebrows shot up. "After being in the ground for twenty years?"

"I understand DNA would be unlikely to survive under those conditions, but isn't some kind of forensic evidence necessary—to be absolutely certain—before you make an arrest?"

Visibly angered by their encounter, he stood, his chair scraping the cement. "No," he said. "Actually, it's not. The district attorney has to convince twelve jurors—that's all. Convictions have been made on less than what I have here. And you'd better be careful. Because if I can prove you're lying to me, and I *know* you are—" he tilted his head to drive his point home "—I'm going to arrest you, too."

twenty-four

Ariana couldn't finish her shift, after all. She felt terrible for letting Kitty down—they still had an hour and a half till closing—but being shorthanded at the coffee shop suddenly seemed like a small problem compared to everything else that was going on. She *had* to talk to Cam, and he wasn't answering his phone.

Where was he? She'd ducked into the bathroom to call him. But his voice mail came on right away, a signal that his phone was turned off. She'd tried his office, too, but Courtney said he hadn't come in this morning. She was tempted to leave a message, telling him not to speak to the police or Williams before he spoke to her, but she didn't because she was afraid the police would get wind of it somehow. She didn't dare text him, either, in case those texts turned into evidence, especially since chances seemed to be growing greater and greater that Cam might actually see the inside of a courtroom.

After clocking out and removing her apron, she hurried up the stairs and charged down the street. Weaving in and out of the slower-moving tourists, who were strolling along in no particular hurry as they enjoyed the warmest day on Mariners since she'd been back, she grew breathless before she could even reach the corner. Cam's was a fifteen-minute walk from downtown. She preferred to save the time and drive. But if she returned home this early, her grandmother would ask why she was already off work, and she didn't have a good answer—not if she was only going to leave the house again. There was a chance Alice would be using the car, anyway. She'd said something about getting her hair done and maybe running a few errands.

Pulling her phone from her purse, she tried calling Cam again.

Hello, this is Cam Stafford. Please leave your name and a brief message, and I'll get back to you as soon as possible.

"Fuck!" she cursed, punching the end button with far more force than necessary.

The expletive caused a stranger she was passing to turn and glare at her, but she was too riddled with anxiety to apologize. What if Cam wasn't answering because someone else was already talking to him? What if they'd somehow planned a simultaneous visit so she and Cam would be confronted separately, denying them the opportunity to coordinate their stories?

That would be smart. It might even be the reason Livingston had come off so strong. If Cam admitted he'd walked them home much earlier on the night Emily went missing than they'd claimed, assuming she'd crumble and say the same thing now that Ivy had, she'd be arrested. Cam could be arrested, too. The evidence—and proof of deceit—was piling up.

She clung to her phone instead of sliding it back into her purse because she planned to continue calling him until she either got through or she was able to find him and tell him in person. So it was easy to feel the vibration when it went off.

With a rush of relief, she stopped to make sure it was Cam. But it wasn't; it was Ivy.

Her heart leaped into her throat. Should she answer? Tell Ivy how brokenhearted and betrayed she felt? That what Ivy had done might send Ariana to prison along with Cam?

It was hard not to be angry and let her know it. But—and this was of greater consideration at the moment—what if the police had somehow convinced Ivy to set a trap for her, or Cam, or both of them? She'd seen things like that on true crime shows, where one friend rolled over on another. Was Williams with Ivy, telling her to call while listening in?

Ariana shook her head. What was she thinking? Ivy would never purposely hurt her or Cam. And yet…Ivy had blindsided them both by going back on everything they'd discussed and decided. Why'd she do it? It wasn't easy to reconcile Ivy's actions with their lifelong friendship, not after Ivy had helped protect Cam for the past twenty years. What had gone wrong?

Ariana was eager to find out, but she ignored the call—in case it would be a mistake to answer. She was going on far too little sleep; couldn't think clearly enough to avoid the possible pitfalls. She could barely summon the energy she needed to look for Cam while trying to cope with her fatigue and the myriad emotions pouring through her.

As she broke away from the downtown area, Ivy tried to reach her again, but Ariana ignored that call, too. It wasn't until she'd arrived at Cam's house and spent ten minutes banging on the door, with no response, that she received a text from Ivy.

I'm so sorry. Please forgive me.

Why'd you do it? she wrote back.

It's not what you think. Will you answer your phone?

I can't, she wrote. I don't trust you anymore.

The tears she'd been holding back began to stream down her face when Ivy didn't text back. It felt as though she'd just lost both her best friends.

She sank down on the front steps, hoping against hope that Cam, wherever he was, would return or see his missed calls. But after another fifteen minutes or so when that didn't happen, Ariana finally stood up and, just in case, knocked on the door again. There was no movement or response from inside that she could detect, so she was about to give up and leave when the neighbor—a middle-aged man who'd been out mowing his yard—walked over. "You looking for Cam?" he asked.

She sniffed, nodding as she wiped her wet cheeks. "Do you know where he is?"

He shaded his eyes against the bright afternoon sun so he could see her. "A police cruiser drove up about forty minutes ago. The officer went to the door, and not too long after, Cam came out with him and got in the back of the car."

Her chest grew so tight she could barely breathe. *"He was arrested?"*

A sympathetic expression came over the man's face. "It appeared that way to me."

The room looked almost exactly like the interrogation rooms depicted on TV. It was small, had a desk in the middle with two plastic chairs, one on each side, and what Cam could only guess was a two-way mirror on the wall so other cops who weren't in the room could watch what was taking place. He'd been in here once before, twenty years ago, and it hadn't changed. His situation now was far more serious, however. He wasn't just being questioned; he'd been arrested. An officer wearing the name tag "J. Bishop" had shown up at his house an hour ago, roused him from a deep sleep and presented him with a warrant. Although Cam hadn't been cuffed, he'd been confined to this small room since Bishop had brought him in.

Cam assumed he was waiting for Detective Livingston but had no idea what was taking so long. No one had even checked on him—via the door, anyway—since Bishop had offered him a Coke when they first arrived.

Since he hadn't eaten yet today, Cam was glad he'd accepted the offer—not that eight ounces of soda had done much to curb his hunger.

Worried, tired and impatient, he crushed the empty can and shot it into the tiny wastebasket in one corner. What the hell was going on? Why was he here? Did he have Melanie to thank for this? Earlier, he'd encountered their friends from down the street—who'd been out walking their dog when he pulled into his driveway—and they'd both given him such dirty looks he knew Melanie had told them he'd been cheating on her. He suspected they were the neighbors who'd called Melanie to report Ariana coming to the house in the first place.

Finally, he heard voices, the door opened and Bishop thrust his head inside. "Detective Livingston just got back. He'll be right in to see you."

Growing nervous again, Cam straightened. He had no idea what would happen next, but he knew it was time to hire a good attorney. Problem was he didn't have much to spend on one. He lived well, was making good money, but it took a lot of resources to get a new business up and running and to buy a house like his—not to mention he'd just given Melanie twenty thousand dollars for her trip to Europe.

A few minutes later the door opened again, and Detective Livingston walked in. "Cam," he said with a polite nod.

Cam offered no greeting in return. He watched the detective warily as Livingston plopped a folder down on the desk and sat across from him. "What's this all about?"

"I take it Officer Bishop read you your Miranda rights."

"He did."

Livingston was wearing a drab brown tie, which looked as though it had seen better days. For that matter, his whole suit needed to be retired. "Are you still willing to talk to me?"

"That depends."

"On..."

"What's changed? Why am I here?"

"I wanted to give you one more chance to tell the truth."

"About..."

"Emily, of course."

"I didn't kill her! That's the truth."

"I want to believe you. I really do. But I'm having some trouble." He took a document out of the folder and slid it across the desk. "As you can see, Ivy Hawthorne has changed her statement."

Cam's heart sank as he began to read. Ivy was now admitting that he'd walked them home earlier than they'd claimed before. And here he'd thought it was Melanie who'd contacted Detective Livingston and said something to convince him to make the arrest. While Cam had known it was a possibility that Ivy could decide to go to the police, that she'd probably been wrestling with her conscience for years over lying for him, he'd never dreamed she'd catch him off guard like this.

When he remained silent, trying to absorb the blow, Livingston leaned forward. "Do you have anything to say about that?"

"No."

"So…the question is, who's lying? You and Ariana? Or Ivy and Delilah?"

"Like I just indicated, I have nothing to say."

"I think it's you and Ariana."

"I didn't kill Emily," he said again.

"You know, if Ariana *is* lying, that's a serious offense. I could charge her with obstruction of justice, which carries with it some hefty prison time, in case you're unaware."

The acid churning in Cam's stomach felt as though it might burn a hole right through him. He shouldn't have drunk that soda, after all. "Nothing is her fault," he said.

"Then why don't you tell me what really happened, and I'll leave her out of it?"

Cam stared at his feet. Ariana and Ivy had covered for him for twenty *years*. From this moment forward he was on his own. Somehow, as terrifying as that was, he felt better than he had in a long time, at least about that. He'd hated having to hide behind his friends, sincerely regretted putting them in such a difficult position, and now that Ivy had come forward, he wouldn't take an opposing stance. That would only force Ariana to choose a side, and he wouldn't make her do that, either. "Ariana, Ivy and I left the beach because the girls were cold. But Ivy's right. It was earlier, around ten o'clock."

"And? Did you go back to the beach that night?"

Cam was tempted to claim he hadn't, but Ben's sister had seen him. He wouldn't call her a liar, either. "Yes. It was close to eleven by then."

There was a brief moment of silence, of satisfaction on the investigator's part, Cam imagined. "*Why* did you go?" Livingston asked.

Cam thought about Jewel, how bitter and angry she was. In a way he felt she deserved to be called out for leaving Emily alone that night. Had she not appeared at his door, Emily would probably still be alive, and his future wouldn't be on the line right now. But telling Livingston about Jewel would only put him in possession of the murder weapon. "I've said all I'm going to say," he replied. "I want a lawyer."

"The police have arrested Cam."

It was Williams who broke the news to Jewel. He called while she was having dinner alone at a restaurant on the other side of the island that had tables coming right up to the beach and a gorgeous view of the ocean. The place was expensive, more than she should be spending, and she'd had to walk for nearly two hours to reach it, so she was planning to take an Uber back, which would cost even more. But she'd needed the solitude—a break from the crush of vacationers in town and the possibility of running into Cam, his friends, Williams, Livingston or anyone else associated with her sister's case. So it was ironic that she'd receive this call when she'd finally decided to back off for the evening and relax.

"I can't believe it," she said, holding her hair in one hand so it couldn't whip across her face as she talked.

"You did it," Williams said. "You pushed and pushed until the police got on the case and really did somethin' about what happened to Emily. You should be proud of yourself."

The praise made her feel validated, making the news he'd given her even better. "It wouldn't have happened if poor Emily's remains hadn't been found."

"True. But Livingston felt personally responsible to you, what with you bein' here and doin' what you've done with the media and all that."

"Thank you. I appreciate everything you've done, too. If

you hadn't tracked down Delilah Jones, we wouldn't have had a witness to place Cam at the beach again later that night. I feel like *that* was a turning point."

"Just glad I was able to do it."

"What's next?" she asked.

"For Cam, you mean? Trial. But don't expect that to happen fast. These things can take weeks, months. So it'll require a bit more patience."

"I've been waiting twenty years. I guess I can wait another few months. Does he have an attorney?"

"I haven't heard, but you can ask Detective Livingston yourself. He told me he'd like to speak to you."

She pulled the phone away from her ear to check for missed calls and texts. "I haven't heard anything from him."

"He's in no hurry. He said tomorrow morning would be fine. Or even the day after."

"Do you know what it's about?"

"He told me Cam said something after his arrest that raised a few questions. Livingston wouldn't elaborate on what they were. To be honest with you, I think he resents me getting involved and seems to think he's got it on his own."

"That's probably not unusual with law enforcement."

"No. I run into it all the time. The police can be fiercely territorial."

Jewel let go of her hair and finished the last of her wine. "How did Cam react when he was arrested?" she asked as she put down her glass. "Did Livingston tell you anything about that?"

"Said he didn't make a fuss, not after he learned that Ivy had come forward."

Jewel felt a flash of triumph. She'd won! She'd gone up against Ivy, Ariana and Cam—three of the most beautiful, privileged people she'd ever met—all of whom had been united against her, and she'd torn their friendship apart and forced the fact that he'd returned to the lighthouse to come out. Now that Ivy had cracked, Cam didn't have an alibi—at least not as solid as it was before. "What about Ariana? What's she saying?"

"Apparently, Ariana still maintains the story she told in high school is true."

"Livingston believes Ivy…or what?"

"He doesn't have to choose between them. When Livingston threatened to go after Ariana for obstruction of justice, Cam admitted that Ivy was the one telling the truth."

Despite how happy Jewel was at this moment, she couldn't help feeling a twinge of jealousy. She'd long told herself that not only was Cam responsible for Emily's death, he was also a selfish bastard. But this suggested otherwise. She also knew, deep down, that she'd never had a friend who'd make such a sacrifice for her. "I bet Cam's pissed at Ivy. Bet Ariana is, too."

"Probably."

"So…Livingston didn't say what he wants with me?" Although she could guess; more information was always better than less.

"I'm sure he's just going to bring you up to speed, ask you to verify the statements you've given him in the past, that sort of thing—so he can tie this up."

Her conversation with Livingston probably wouldn't be that innocuous. She had no doubt Cam had retaliated by telling the detective she'd left Emily alone and was with him that night. She'd have to put on the best show of her life to make Livingston believe he was simply trying to smear her reputation in a last-ditch effort to create the kind of questions and confusion that might save him.

But she'd been expecting this hurdle. She could clear it. And once she put those "accusations" to rest, and the press and the general public, including the residents on Mariners who'd been Cam's staunchest defenders, grew united in believing he wasn't the good guy he seemed to be, the worst would be behind her. She would've done her part; the attorneys could take over. "Will you be going with me?"

"Not unless you want me to. I figured, rather than stay any longer, I'd head home and stop the clock."

She thought that was probably best. He'd done all he could do, and she was eager to save the money. "Okay, I'll go myself," she said, anxious to get off the phone so she could call her parents.

But she'd just said goodbye and disconnected with Williams when her handsome young waiter approached.

"Can I get you any dessert?" he asked.

Jewel's smile came more easily than it had in years. She hadn't been planning to order anything else, but now… "I just got some *great* news. Why not celebrate? If you could bring me another glass of wine and some crème brûlée, that'd be perfect."

twenty-five

There was a soft knock on her door. Ariana was tempted to pretend she was asleep. She'd been sleeping for hours at a time, on and off between crying jags. She was awake again now, but she was too distraught to talk to anyone, especially her grandmother, who'd been checking on her ever since she got home. Because Ariana had gone straight up to her room, closed the door and hadn't come out, Alice had been concerned about her. She'd climbed the stairs to see if Ariana would like dinner. Ariana had said no. She'd climbed the stairs to see if Ariana would like a piece of the blackberry pie she'd baked for dessert—Ariana's favorite. She had said no. Alice had even climbed the stairs to see if she was ready to come out and possibly watch a movie or do something else to distract her from Cam's arrest. But Ariana had said no to that, too.

Now Alice was at her door again, probably to say good-night.

"Can I come in?" her grandmother asked after knocking.

Ariana was embarrassed to let anyone see her red, splotchy face—even Alice. She was in her thirties, for God's sake. She shouldn't be crying like a child. But this time she didn't say no. "Of course," she said and got up to unlock the door.

The compassion on her grandmother's face the minute she came in brought fresh tears, but Ariana was glad she'd opened the door when Alice scooped her into an embrace. It was her grandmother's hugs that'd soothed so many of her wounds in the past.

"I feel like a big crybaby," Ariana complained, chuckling as she pulled away.

Alice kept hold of her hands. "There's no shame in caring. If I've taught you anything, I hope I've taught you that."

"You have, of course. But I can't believe it's come to this," she said. "That one fateful night, when we were so young and just out having a good time, could overshadow so many years and possibly ruin Cam's future. I *know* he didn't kill Emily."

"I believe that, too," her grandmother said. "But all is not lost. An arrest isn't a conviction."

Ariana blinked back fresh tears. "This isn't just about Cam. It's also about Ivy."

"She must be upset, too."

"I'm not so sure about that," Ariana said with a grimace. "She should've expected something like this to happen when she told the police that Cam wasn't with us when we said he was."

Alice's eyes widened in surprise. "Oh, dear. I didn't know."

"I couldn't tell you. I was too upset when I got home."

Letting go of her, Alice sank onto the edge of the bed. "So Cam no longer has an alibi—" she sent Ariana a wry grin "—despite our best efforts to provide him with one."

Ariana couldn't avoid smiling, since her grandmother had

finally acknowledged the help she'd tried to give them simply by not contradicting what they'd said. "No."

"It takes more than the lack of an alibi to send someone to prison for murder, Ariana. It takes evidence, too."

Alice was an unfailing optimist. "With the witnesses Jewel's PI has dug up, placing Cam *and* Emily at the beach that night, and Jewel going on TV to spout off about how she's sure it was 'the suspect the police initially hit upon,' I'm not sure the DA won't be able to build a case. Especially because the police have determined that Emily was most likely killed with a liquor bottle like the one Cam was drinking from that night." She didn't add that Ivy probably had a hand in bringing that to light, too. "*All* signs seem to point to him. I don't get the impression they're even considering anyone else."

"I heard there was another boy who spoke to Emily that night."

"You're talking about Ben. But nothing seems to have come of that."

"Ariana, I've known Detective Livingston for years. Don't underestimate him. He's smarter than you think."

Ariana didn't believe Alice would like Detective Livingston so much after he'd threatened her at The Human Bean, but she was the one in the wrong, so she kept her mouth shut. She didn't want to ruin her grandmother's relationships with her friends and acquaintances in town. "He's inexperienced when it comes to this kind of murder—and under a great deal of pressure to solve the case," she said. "Without another viable suspect… I don't know, I guess I'm losing hope."

"It's a tragedy all the way around," her grandmother said.

Ariana's phone went off. She'd left the ringer on in case Cam was able to call her, or she heard from Williams or Livingston or anyone else who could tell her more about what was going on and what might happen next. She planned on visiting Cam tomorrow after she got off work, if they'd let her. From what she'd found on the county website visiting hours were listed as eight to eight on weekdays. But she didn't know if there was an initial waiting period before Cam could see anyone or something like that. She'd never been to the jail.

Unfortunately, the caller wasn't Cam. This late she'd pretty much given up hope of that, anyway. It wasn't even Ivy, who'd been trying to call her all night. It was a number she didn't recognize.

Assuming it had to be a spam call, she almost ignored it. But it was too late to be getting a spam call. That wasn't typical. And so much crazy stuff was going on right now it wasn't unreasonable to think she should take this call, regardless of the unknown number.

Putting up a hand to signal to Alice that she was going to answer it, she hit the talk button. "Hello?"

"Ariana?"

"Yes?"

"This is Giselle Stafford, Cam's mother. A friend of mine on Mariners just called to tell me she heard Cam's been arrested. Do you know if that's true?"

"I'm afraid it is," she said.

"I'll get the first flight I can out of Italy. Please tell him I'm coming."

Ariana knew how Cam felt about Giselle. But she also knew that if his mother was ever going to come through for him, now would be the time. Ariana planned to be there for him, of course, but with almost everyone else working against them, he could use all the help and support he could get. "I'll let him know."

Ivy didn't sleep a wink. She'd been up all night, tossing and turning and railing, in her mind, at her brother. She'd also been going over everything she wanted to say to Ariana and Cam—if they'd ever give her the chance.

When she got out of bed, it was still early, but she was eager to get over to the library and put up a sign saying it would be closed until further notice—until she could get a volunteer to cover for her, which she didn't add. There was no way she could sit placidly and work after being the reason Cam had been arrested. She was heading over to the jail to speak to him as soon as they'd allow it—if he didn't refuse to see her.

You could've been arrested, too. Be glad it wasn't you.

She didn't see that text until she got out of the shower. Apparently, Tim had quit ignoring her, like he'd been doing yesterday. She'd texted him once she'd learned—from Kitty, who'd heard it from her husband—that they'd arrested Cam. But he hadn't responded to that or the other angry messages she'd sent afterward.

She started to type an entire diatribe, once again explaining that it hadn't been his place to do what he did. But what good would it do to keep fighting with him? The damage had already been done.

I'll never forgive you.

She sent that to him instead. She'd said it before, but she was saying it again, just for good measure. Then she finished getting ready, was lucky enough to line up a volunteer to run the library for a few hours after lunch and adjusted the sign she'd printed to post on the door before driving it over there, taping it up and going to the county jail.

The weather was beautiful. She, Ariana and Cam should be out combing the beaches for sea glass today, not having to worry about Cam spending the rest of his life in prison. Emily's murder had loomed over them for years, but everything that'd happened in the past two days just seemed surreal. *Why* would Cam kill a twelve-year-old girl?

In her opinion, not enough people were concerned with the answer to that question. If he did it, he had to have had a reason.

As she put her Audi SUV in Park and climbed out, she wondered what Jewel was thinking now. She had to be relieved that Cam was in custody. She'd finally gotten what she wanted. But she was going to have some explaining to do, which wouldn't be pleasant. She'd hidden her involvement with Cam for a reason.

The sergeant stationed behind the counter, a heavyset woman who appeared to be in her thirties, looked up when she walked in. "Can I help you?"

"I'm hoping to visit Cam Stafford," Ivy said, fidgeting with her purse strap. She had some explaining of her own to do—to him—and it wasn't going to be easy for her, either. "He was arrested yesterday," she added.

"I'm well aware," the woman said drily. "What's your name?"

Ivy had seen the officer around town but had never met her. "Ivy Hawthorne."

"You run the library."

"Yes." She was also the one who'd figured out what had been used to murder Emily Hutchins—and the one to blame for Cam's arrest.

"You'll have to sign in." She handed Ivy a clipboard with a form to fill out.

Ivy took care of that quickly and handed it back. She was eager to see Cam—to apologize and tell him that she would help pay for his attorney. She might have caused this terrible turn of events, but she wouldn't abandon him.

The sergeant had her put her purse in a tray, which went through an X-ray machine while she walked through a metal detector. Then the woman pulled a ring of keys from her belt and asked Ivy to wait a moment while she unlocked a gray steel door and went inside.

Ivy didn't realize she'd been holding her breath, for fear Cam would refuse to see her, until the officer returned and beckoned her forward. "Right this way."

There were only six cells. They were all empty, except for one. Cam was standing at the front of the cage, unshaven and looking sleep-deprived. "Hey," he said dully.

She immediately burst into tears, making it hard to talk. She covered her mouth as the sergeant moved a short distance away and sat on a stool next to the door where they'd come in.

"It's okay. Come here." He put his hands through the bars, and she took them.

"I'm *so* sorry," she said between sniffs and gasps for breath. "I—I didn't mean for this to happen. I didn't go to the police. I was just…upset by what I found when I was researching the type of weapon that would cause a human skull to fracture like Emily's had, and—" she had to gulp for more breath before she could continue "—and I called my brother, you know, for some reassurance and support. I had no idea he'd take it upon himself to contact the police and tell them everything I told him. I swear it." She sniffed to stop her nose from running. "I'm never going to speak to him again."

Cam rested his forehead against the bars as he gazed down at their clasped hands. "Don't say that. He's your brother."

"I don't care!"

"I'm sort of relieved, to be honest with you," he said. "Now at least you and Ariana are off the hook."

"But at what cost? I know you didn't hurt Emily."

He attempted a shrug, which didn't look quite as careless as he probably intended. "The police have never really considered anyone else. I probably would've been arrested eventually."

"I'm going to find you the best attorney on the east coast," she said. "I've already started looking, and I'll help pay for it."

"I think my parents will do that," he said with a sigh. "I'm sure they won't be happy about it, but…I don't have enough on my own, not to fight a first-degree murder charge—unless I can sell the house, and that'll take time."

"I've got the money. You won't have to include your parents if you don't want to."

"We'll see how much money I'll need—and when I'll need it," he said, but it concerned her that he didn't seem terribly interested in his own defense. He seemed to think it didn't matter, that he'd wind up in prison, regardless.

She let go of him to dig through her pocket for a tissue. "Has Ariana been by?"

"Not yet. I think she's at work."

Ivy dried her cheeks. "She won't answer my calls or my texts."

"I'm sure she will once she realizes you didn't go to the police yourself. Don't worry. Everything's going to be okay."

Ivy couldn't believe *he* was the one telling *her* that, but he'd always tried to take care of them and make them happy. "Does Melanie know you've been arrested?" she asked.

"I doubt it. I haven't called her."

"Who have you called?"

He raked his fingers through his hair, which was already standing up. "No one. Yet."

"Not even your parents?" she demanded. "Why not?"

His shoulders lifted again. "I don't know. That one wasn't a call I wanted to make, I guess."

"We need to get hold of them, have them come back to the States. I'm sure they'd want to be here to support you through the next few months."

"I wouldn't be too convinced of that. It probably wouldn't do any good to have them here, anyway."

"Don't say that. This thing isn't over yet. I've already made a list of defense lawyers. According to the research I did last night, some attorneys will come meet with you for free if they think there's a chance they might get hired."

"Is there even a criminal defense attorney on the island?" he asked.

"No. But we're just a ferry ride from the mainland. I can get someone to come, someone who'll do a good job."

When he nodded and attempted to smile, she wanted to cry again. What had she done?

Jewel couldn't remember ever being so nervous. She also had a hangover, which wasn't good, considering she now had to face Livingston and try to convince him that Cam had been lying when he'd claimed she'd had sex with him at the lighthouse the night Emily died. The detective had told Williams that it didn't matter what time she came into the station, so she hadn't been concerned about drinking too much last night. She'd been taking a much-needed breather, just long enough to celebrate the end of what she'd suffered for the past twenty years, because she'd thought she could simply speak to him tomorrow, if necessary.

But when she crawled out of bed to go to the bathroom this morning and checked her phone, she saw she'd missed a call from him. His voice mail message said he had a few minutes at ten-thirty, if she wouldn't mind coming over, and she was afraid he'd find it strange if she put him off. After all, she'd come to Mariners to facilitate the investigation.

Since she couldn't risk any kind of blow to her credibility, not if she expected him to believe her, she'd called back to confirm the appointment, and now she was popping pain pills in an effort to get rid of a massive headache.

After she managed to apply her makeup, despite how terrible she was feeling, she smiled at herself in the mirror. *You can do it. You're almost there.*

When she grabbed her phone, which she'd silenced when she finally fell into bed last night, she saw a call coming in from her father's church. Her parents. She'd gotten them both on the phone at the same time when she delivered the news about Cam yesterday, and her mother had been so relieved she'd immediately burst into tears. Jewel suspected her father had, too, since they'd both gone silent. It'd been at least a minute before either one of them could speak.

Praise the Lord, her father had said at last, his words barely a whisper. No doubt they were checking back with her today to make sure that conversation hadn't been a dream—that what she'd told them was real and they'd soon see Cam stand trial.

She pressed the talk button before she could miss the call. "Hello?"

"Hi, honey."

Her father. It was usually her mother who contacted her and relayed everything they discussed, so this was a slight surprise. "Hi, Dad. How are you today?"

"Much better after the news you gave us."

"I'm glad. I feel better, too," she said with a grimace at the tequila bottle she'd brought back to her room.

"When will you be coming home?"

"Soon."

"Tomorrow?"

"Or the next day. I have to wrap up a few things first."

"Like what?"

She figured she might as well prepare him. Given how much interest there was in her sister's case, something as lascivious as Cam claiming she had sex with him at the lighthouse while she was supposed to be babysitting Emily would spread like wildfire. The media would probably pick it up. If she could gather the nerve, *she* should be the one to take it to them. That would be the most strategic way to handle it.

"Oh, it's nothing," she said. "Just…Cam. He told Detective Livingston some crazy stuff when he was arrested, and I have to go to police headquarters and address it this morning."

"What'd he say?"

Drawing a deep breath, she said, "It's too unbelievable to even tell you about. And it won't amount to anything. It's just a last-ditch effort to drag me down with him, since I've done so much to hold him accountable."

"He's slandering you?"

The outrage in her father's voice wasn't entirely unexpected. "Basically."

"Tell me what he's saying."

"I can't. It's too embarrassing."

"Tell me!" he insisted. "I want to hear."

"He's saying…" Terrified that she wouldn't sound as believable as she needed to, she cleared her throat. "He's saying I went to the lighthouse with him the night Emily died and…"

"And?" her father prompted.

"Well, you can probably guess."

"You've got to be kidding me!" he exploded. "As if that son of a bitch hasn't done enough to our family. Now he's trying to ruin your reputation?"

Jewel winced. She probably shouldn't have answered this call. She'd be late if she didn't hurry. But her father was going to hear about her leaving Emily and doing what she'd done sooner or later. "See? I knew better than to tell you. Now you're upset for no good reason. This won't amount to anything. He's desperate, that's all."

"He's a monster! I can't wait to face him in court."

"At least now our day will be coming. Let's focus on that."

"I should fly over there," he said. "I want to spit in the face of the man who murdered my daughter. I also want to know *why* he did what he did—and how he could accuse you of leaving Emily alone when you were babysitting, especially to… to…" Apparently, he couldn't bring himself to speak the words. "That he'd accuse you of being the kind of cheap, tawdry, worthless girl who'd do something like that!" he said instead.

His words hit Jewel like bullets. Her actions *had* been cheap and tawdry. Squeezing her eyes closed, she attempted to keep the tears that were welling up at bay, but it was no good. They streamed down her face, ruining her mascara. "Can you believe that?" she forced herself to say. "It's…unconscionable."

"I didn't think this could get any worse—"

"It won't," she broke in. "Just…ignore this part. No one will believe him."

"You don't know that. They could!"

"Dad, I have to go. Detective Livingston is waiting for me. I'll call you after, okay?"

"I'm going to call Livingston myself—right now," he said.

Jewel froze. She hadn't anticipated this. "No!" she cried. Livingston hadn't even told her what Cam had said. She only assumed it was about what they'd done that night because she could so easily guess what Williams was referring to when he'd said Livingston had a few questions for her about some things Cam said when he was arrested. What else could it be? "You can't do that," she told her father. "It'll only cause more problems. You *have* to let me handle it. I'm going to do that right away, and I'll call you after."

He didn't respond. She could tell he was still fuming. Could she talk him down? If she couldn't, everything she'd worked so hard to achieve would collapse around her, just when she thought she was going to be okay.

"Dad? Please?"

"We have to defend your honor. I won't let Cam Stafford get away with anything else."

"I've got it. You—you can jump in later. I'm only asking for an hour or two. I need to meet with the detective before you do anything."

"Okay," he said, grudgingly. "But call me as soon as you're finished."

"I will. I promise. Then you can do or say whatever you want." By the time she hung up, she was shaking so badly she could barely repair her makeup.

twenty-six

Jewel was in no frame of mind to meet with Detective Livingston. Her headache had improved, thanks to the painkiller, but she was still rattled from the close call she'd had with her father, and she was growing more nervous by the minute. She'd been shown into an interrogation room quite a while ago and given a cup of coffee, which was growing cold. Where was Livingston? She hadn't been *that* late.

Surely, her father hadn't contacted him in spite of telling her he wouldn't…

She kept looking at the two-way mirror, wishing she could see out. After silently rehearsing what she had to say in the Uber on the way over, she wanted to say it, then get the hell off Mariners. She was ready and eager to turn her back on the past and start over.

She was about to get up and poke her head out to ask

someone if she'd been forgotten when the door finally swung open. "I'm sorry," Livingston said as he came in. "I was dealing with a call."

Was it from her father? Her heart began to pound so loudly she was afraid he could hear it. She studied the detective's face as he held out his hand to shake hers before sitting on the other side of the desk. Did he know she *had* been with Cam on the night in question?

She couldn't tell what he was thinking or feeling. "What'd you want to talk to me about?"

"You've heard we arrested Cam Stafford."

"Williams told me." She clapped her hands together to show her enthusiasm. "I'm so relieved. What made you decide to do it?"

"He no longer had an alibi. Ivy told her brother that she'd been covering for him, and her brother called and told us. I had her come in and sign a new statement."

"What about Ariana?"

"She refuses to give him up. But when I threatened to go after her for obstruction of justice, Cam finally came clean and told me that Ivy was the one telling the truth."

"That's wonderful! He's admitted it! Does the DA think you have a case?" She craved as much information as possible, but she was also dreading the moment he asked her whether she'd gone to the lighthouse with Cam.

"I haven't talked to the DA yet. To be honest, I might've been a little premature in arresting Cam. But I wanted to shake him up a bit, see if he'd confess."

"And it worked. You just said he admitted he wasn't with Ivy and Ariana when he said he was. Isn't that enough?"

"A full confession would've been better."

"But you didn't get one."

"Not yet. And I don't think that'll change at this point. What I'm hoping for now is to find the murder weapon."

She looked up. "Murder weapon?"

"Yes. We're fairly certain it was a whiskey bottle."

"How can you tell?"

"We know she was struck on the head with something, and the square bottom of a Jack Daniel's bottle seems to match the fracture on her skull."

The image those words conjured up in Jewel's mind made her nauseated. "That's terrible," she said, covering her face in an attempt to block out what she was seeing in her mind's eye. "I don't even want to imagine it."

"I'm sorry," he said in a gentler tone. "I thought you'd want to know."

It took a moment, but she was finally able to lower her hands and look at him again. "Why didn't Williams tell me?"

"I doubt he's heard."

"He knew about the arrest. He told me just before he left to go back to Houston."

"I didn't mention the murder weapon to him. Ironically, Williams showed Ivy a picture of the fracture on Emily's skull, and she's the one who matched it to the damage done by a square whiskey bottle. Finding that upset her. Made her doubt Cam long enough that she went to her brother for support and advice, and he came forward. I haven't told anyone else."

"I see."

Livingston scooted his chair closer to the table. "You don't know if Cam was drinking Jack Daniel's that night, do you?"

This was it—her cue. She curled her fingernails into her palms. Giving herself another sensation to concentrate on helped her push through the nausea. "No. I mean…I can't really say. He didn't smell like alcohol when he was over at the house, helping Emily get in. But I didn't get too close to him."

Livingston frowned. "Ivy claims Cam told her you brought over a bottle of Jack Daniel's after he got home that night, and the two of you took it to the lighthouse. Is that true?"

She came to her feet, nearly knocking her chair over in the process. "*What?* Of course it's not true! I would never leave Emily alone."

He lifted a hand. "I'm sorry. I didn't mean to upset you. But…you understand why I had to ask."

"Of course, but…I was babysitting, for God's sake. This must be Cam's way of trying to drag me down with him. I'm sure he's angry that I've been so single-minded about seeing him arrested. That I hired a private investigator. That I've been on TV trying to propel the case forward. That I've been on social media raising money."

"I don't think that's what he's trying to do," Livingston said. "Ivy claims he said it before anyone even knew what the murder weapon was—and Ivy would know, since she's the one who figured it out."

That she couldn't claim Cam was trying to smear her name took most of the power out of her defense. All she could do now was deny it. "I don't know why he'd ever tell anyone that, because it's not true."

"I didn't think so. Considering how hard you've pushed to find your sister's killer, you would've said something if you knew more about that night."

A fresh avalanche of guilt threatened to crush her. "Of course I would have. It didn't happen. I was a good girl, Detective, a preacher's daughter. I would never sneak out to drink and have sex with a boy—especially one I'd barely met—while I was responsible for my little sister."

"I can't imagine you would." He stood and held out a hand to shake with her again. "Thanks for coming in."

With a sigh of relief, she picked up her Styrofoam coffee

cup, but he was standing between her and the wastebasket so he took it from her. "I'll take care of this," he said. "You're free to go."

"Thank you." She walked briskly out of the building, as if she felt fine, and used the app on her phone to get an Uber. But once she was in the back seat of her driver's car, she smacked herself in the forehead. *Shit. Shit, shit, shit.* She'd been so prepared for the accusation that she'd had sex with Cam that she'd mentioned it even though Livingston hadn't. He'd merely asked if she'd taken some Jack Daniel's over to Cam's and gone to the lighthouse with him.

Had he noticed? She didn't think so. He hadn't reacted to it. Fortunately, it was tough to accuse a grieving sister. She had that going for her.

"You okay?" her driver said.

She wanted to snap at him to mind his own business, but she also didn't want to make enough of an impression that he'd remember her reaction and possibly mention it to someone later. "I'm fine, thanks," she said and forced a smile. But she was dying inside.

How could she screw up just when everything had been going her way?

Ivy was waiting for her when she got off work. Ariana saw her on the sidewalk, put her head down and tried to circumvent her without speaking to her, but Ivy simply turned and fell in step beside her. "I'm sorry," she said.

"I don't want to hear it."

"I didn't go to the police. At least, it didn't happen the way you think."

Ariana stopped and gaped at her. "You expect me to believe that? How'd they find out, then?"

"It was Tim."

"Your brother? How'd *he* know?"

It was obvious she'd been crying. She looked close to tears now. "I told him. I was…upset, worried, thought he'd be able to give me some good advice. But I *never* dreamed he'd go to the police!"

Ariana had never particularly liked Ivy's brother. She found him egotistical, arrogant and aloof. Not a winning combo but, of course, she'd never said anything. "Did he tell you he was going to do it?"

"He said if I wouldn't do it he would, but I didn't take him seriously. Going to the police—or not—should've been up to me."

"Then why didn't he leave it up to you?"

"He didn't want me to get in trouble. He said I had to do what I could to help the investigation. Which sounded reasonable at the time. That's been the argument I've been having with myself almost from the beginning."

Begrudgingly, Ariana had to admit she could understand that. She'd had the same argument with herself—for years.

"And once he told the police, an officer came to get me and take me to the station and…and I couldn't lie any longer. Not with my brother telling them everything I'd said. There was no point in even trying."

"They got you to change your statement."

"Yes, but like I've been trying to tell you, I didn't set out to do that, especially without informing you both. The way it came about… Once I'd confided in Tim, there was nothing I could do. But seeing Cam get arrested, when I can't believe he hurt anyone, has been horrible, traumatic. I feel even worse because I'm responsible—in a roundabout way."

As upset as Ariana had been with Ivy, she felt her anger begin to dissipate. She could see Ivy needing to talk to someone, confiding in her brother and then having it go wrong because Tim took it upon himself to act on her behalf. Ariana could remember how badly she'd been tempted to talk to Bruce. What if she'd broken down and done it, and he'd responded in the same way? *She* could be the one responsible for Cam's arrest instead of Ivy, and if Bruce had been her brother, she would've been much more likely to trust him with such a secret.

"I'm sorry," Ivy repeated. "I hope…I hope you can forgive me. If I'd made the decision to come forward, I would definitely have let you know beforehand. But the way it went…I put you in a terrible position."

That was true. But she'd put Ivy in one, too, because of her feelings for Cam. That she'd changed from being Cam's friend to something more after so long had to feel weird, and probably even a little upsetting, from Ivy's viewpoint. And yet Ariana had been hoping Ivy would give *her* a little tolerance and understanding.

Maybe they needed to cut each other a break.

Drawing a deep breath, Ariana pulled the sea glass Cam had found at the beach from her pocket and put it in Ivy's hand.

"What's this?" Ivy asked.

"A symbol of our friendship, remember?"

"Of course I remember. But…where'd you find it?"

"Cam picked it up at the beach." That he'd given it to her made it difficult to part with, especially now, when she was so worried about him. She'd kept that piece of glass with her every second since he'd handed it to her. But she loved Ivy, too. She wanted Ivy to know that although there were bumps in every relationship, their friendship was far more durable than what had gone wrong this week.

"It's beautiful," Ivy said with a grateful smile. "Are you sure you want to give it to me?"

Ariana slipped her arm through her longtime friend's and smiled back. "Positive."

They walked the rest of that block in silence, and Ariana couldn't believe how much better she felt now that there was no longer a rift between them. They needed to see Cam through this difficult time so all three of them could be reunited.

"What are we going to do?" Ivy asked as they approached her house. "How can we help Cam?"

Ariana stopped at the wrought iron gate. "We dig."

Ivy blinked several times. "What?"

Ariana looked around to make sure no one was within earshot. "We need to go out to the lighthouse later and see if we can find that damn Jack Daniel's bottle Cam was drinking out of the night Emily was killed."

"What makes you think we'll be able to find it?" Ivy asked.

"Maybe we can't. But we have to try. If his DNA is on that bottle, it'll mean a conviction for sure, even though all he did was drink from it."

"Can DNA last twenty years?"

"Anything's possible these days. From what I found on the internet, DNA has a half-life of 521 years."

"You've got to be kidding me!"

"I'm not. A lot of factors come into play, of course, like whether the sample was in water or it remained dry, but—"

"The ocean never goes as high as the lighthouse."

"Exactly. And dry is better."

"But...couldn't we get into a lot of trouble for trying to steal what the police now believe is the murder weapon?" Ivy asked. "I mean...we'd be interfering in the investigation. *Again*."

"There's no law against digging in the sand, Ivy. It's not even fenced off anymore."

Ivy looked torn. "I feel terrible that I caused Cam to be

arrested. But when I asked how we could help, I was kind of hoping you'd suggest something that didn't come with the fear of getting arrested ourselves."

Ariana could tell Ivy was half joking, but she wanted to make it clear that each of them had to make her own choice. "You don't have to go with me."

"Well, I'm not going to let you go alone."

"Then meet me in the alleyway behind my grandma's house at midnight. We'll take her car, park at the beach and walk up to the lighthouse like Cam and I did the other night."

Her eyes widened. "You two have already been digging around up there?"

"For hours. We had no luck. But it's going to take several nights to cover the whole area."

"But even if we find a Jack Daniel's bottle, there's no guarantee, after twenty years, it'll be the right one," Ivy pointed out.

"Maybe he or Jewel threw it out. And that's okay. As a matter of fact, that's even better. We just have to make sure it's not there. As long as the police can't find it, either, Cam should be good."

"Got it." She held out her palm as she studied the piece of sea glass Ariana had given her.

"What?" Ariana said.

Ivy closed her fist tightly around it. "Thanks."

Because they didn't want to turn on the camping lanterns they were carrying and make a beacon of themselves, they only had the flashlight on Ariana's phone and a thin smile of moon overhead to light their way. As they trudged down the beach, Ivy wondered what her brother would think of what she was doing now. He definitely wouldn't approve. But she couldn't let Cam go to prison for a crime he didn't commit.

She believed in him, even if she'd waffled a bit when she figured out the murder weapon. That had to be a coincidence of some kind. Or she was wrong about what had killed Emily.

"You okay?" Ariana turned back since she was trailing behind.

"I'm okay."

"You're not having second thoughts, are you?"

"No."

They'd slept all afternoon so they'd have the strength and stamina necessary to get through the night. Ivy felt fresh and capable. But she'd never been out on the beach this late, not when it was completely deserted. She shivered as she gazed out to sea. The ocean looked inky and unfamiliar, like a sea monster coming out of the deep as it reached up the beach with long black fingers. "It's kind of scary out here," she said. "I hope it's safe."

"We've got our shovels," Ariana commented.

Ivy was beginning to grow winded. "You think we can protect ourselves with shovels?"

"Maybe we should've brought bats. But it's easier to dig with shovels."

Ivy chuckled. Humor helped keep her mind off darker imaginings. But she was apprehensive, and afraid she'd feel apprehensive the whole time she was out tonight. Knowing Emily had been killed and buried at the lighthouse didn't make it any easier to hang out there in the dark. "What if we find the bottle?" she asked.

"We take it home, smash it up and throw it away," Ariana replied.

"Yikes, Detective Livingston wouldn't like that."

"We're just being civic minded, cleaning up the island. Cam and I threw away a small bag of trash when we were here before."

By the time they reached the lighthouse, fog had begun to

roll in, making the area even less inviting. "Great," Ivy muttered. "That's all we need."

"What'd you say?"

"Nothing."

Fortunately, once they set to work, they were too busy to focus on anything except searching as large an area as possible before daybreak. They unearthed a Gatorade bottle, a plastic shopping bag, various pieces of small toys and a barrette, but no whiskey bottle.

"This feels futile," Ivy said, her back and arms aching after digging through the sand for hours.

"It's probably not here." Ariana sounded as exhausted and discouraged as she was.

"But like you said, we have to be sure." Ivy forced herself to lift another shovelful. As she sifted through the sand that poured off the end of it, something shiny caught her eye. But it wasn't large, and it wasn't glass.

She bent to examine what she'd found. It was a broken necklace.

With a sigh, she put it on top of the pile they were making to carry out—then, wondering if it was made of real gold, she put it in her pocket. She was about to continue working when the hair stood up on the back of her neck and she froze.

"What's wrong?" Ariana whispered.

"I thought I heard something."

"What?"

"I don't know. Voices?"

Ariana tilted her head, listening. "It's nothing, just the sea," she said at length.

Ivy gazed to the east. The barest glimmer of light was beginning to creep over the horizon. "If we don't want some jogger or dog walker to see us up here with shovels and lanterns, we'd better call it a night."

"I'm ready."

"Do you think we need to come back? I don't know how much ground you and Cam covered."

Ariana pushed her hair out of her face as she looked around. "I'd say we have another four or five hours."

"People will be on the beach much later tonight than they were last night. It's Friday."

"We might have to wait until Sunday night. I need a break, anyway."

"How are you going to get up and work in a few hours?"

"Fortunately, I don't have to go in today. I traded shifts with a coworker for tomorrow."

"That was smart."

They gathered the shovels and lamps they'd brought, threw away the trash as soon as they could and moved slowly down the beach. They were too exhausted to walk any faster.

With dawn coming on, Mariners felt more like the wonderful, safe island she'd always known. And they hadn't seen anyone out and about yet. Ivy assumed they were going to make it home without incident—until they reached the car and saw that a police cruiser had pulled alongside it.

twenty-seven

Ariana glanced at Ivy but didn't say anything as the officer stepped out of his vehicle and came toward them. It was still dark enough that he took his flashlight from his tool belt and snapped it on.

"Usually, the only shovels I see at the beach are small and made of plastic," he said as the beam passed over them from the neck down so he could see everything they were carrying. "You must've been building one hell of a sandcastle."

"We weren't doing anything wrong," Ariana said.

"I'll be the judge of that," he responded, "once you tell me what you *were* doing."

There were only thirty-seven or thirty-eight police officers on the island, but Ariana figured this guy had to be fairly new. Even Ivy didn't seem to recognize him. "I...I lost something," she piped up. "We were just trying to find it."

He raised the beam of his flashlight almost to her face, stopping just short of shining it directly into her eyes. "Where'd you lose it?"

Ariana caught her breath. Should they make something up? Because of their connection to Cam, and the fact that they'd tried to give him a false alibi, she hated to admit they were at the lighthouse, where Emily's remains had been found. He could've been waiting to make sure the people who'd left Alice's car parked in the tiny beach lot were safe. It was the only car there; she could see why he might wonder.

But it was also possible that he'd noticed the glimmer of their lamps when they were still digging and knew exactly where they'd been. Rather than get sand in his shoes by trekking down the beach, he'd simply waited for them to return to their car.

Fortunately, Ivy must've been aware of the risk, because she didn't attempt to lie. "At...at the lighthouse."

"That's a strange place to go in the middle of the night," he said. "Whatever you lost must've been pretty important."

Ivy cleared her throat. "To me, it was."

"What was it?"

Ariana could tell he didn't believe a word she'd said and was equally surprised when Ivy pulled a necklace from the pocket of her jeans and held it out. "This."

The beam of his flashlight landed directly on it, but even outside that halo in the half-dark, Ariana couldn't miss the shock on his face. *"Where'd you get this?"*

Ivy seemed startled by his reaction, too. She'd obviously thought she'd hit on the perfect excuse for their odd activities. It was as believable as anything they were going to come up with. While the necklace didn't look like anything special, there could be sentimental value attached. But it was easy to tell he recognized it. How? What was the significance of such a dainty birthstone pendant?

"Does it matter?" Ivy asked uncertainly.

"It could matter a lot," he replied. "This came from the lighthouse, right? I've seen it before, and it doesn't belong to you."

Had it been Emily's? Considering where they'd found it, and his odd reaction, Ariana guessed it must have been.

Ivy let him take it and stepped back. "Fine. Keep it."

"I will." He ran the beam of his flashlight over them again. "Did you dig up anything else?"

Fortunately, they hadn't found the whiskey bottle they'd been searching for, or he would, no doubt, have taken that away from them, too.

"No, that's it," Ariana said.

He gave them a skeptical look. "I feel like I should arrest you."

"For being out in the dark?" Ariana asked.

"With shovels and lanterns? Yes!"

"It's public property," she argued. "We haven't broken any laws!"

"You've been messing around a crime scene."

"There's no tape there anymore." Ariana gestured down the beach. "There's no fence around the lighthouse, either. And we didn't disturb anything. Go see for yourself."

Grudgingly, he snapped off the light. "I know where to find you if I need you. Go ahead and get out of here. But you might be hearing from me again."

Ariana and Ivy scrambled to fit the shovels and lanterns in Alice's trunk before climbing into the car themselves and pulling away. Ariana watched the officer in her rearview mirror stare down at the necklace for several seconds before reaching into his car to get his radio.

"What do you think that was all about?" Ivy asked, also trying to see what he was doing but using the side mirror.

"That had to be Emily's necklace," Ariana said. "Where'd you find it?"

"It was right there in the sand. The only reason I kept it was because it looked like it could be gold and the little stone might be a ruby. I didn't want it myself, but I hated to throw it away if it was real."

Eager to get out of the officer's sight, Ariana put on her blinker and made a left-hand turn much sooner than she needed to. "Do you think it'll help or hurt Cam's case?" They'd done everything they could to help him, so it would be ironic—not to mention terrible—if they'd only made things worse.

"I don't see how it'll do much of anything," Ivy said. "They already know Emily was probably killed at the lighthouse."

Ariana wasn't so sure the necklace was meaningless. The officer had been excited to recover it for a reason.

Cam had tried to distract himself from the meltdown of his life by doing some drawing instead of reading or watching TV, which were about his only other options in jail. With the small pencil they'd allowed him and some paper, he'd created a rough sketch of two different houses he was eager to transfer onto the computer. He had clients who were waiting for plans. But of course, he didn't have his computer—or any computer.

Courtney had come to see him yesterday. He'd instructed her to show up at the office every day to keep the business running and make it look as though his arrest was just a temporary thing—until the police could figure out who'd really killed Emily Hutchins. But he was beginning to think that charade was pointless. Without another suspect, he didn't believe they'd ever let him go. And he was conscious of the money he was spending to keep Courtney working and the office open. He needed as much as he could get to pay for an attorney. Although he hadn't yet spoken to his parents, someone must've told them what was going on because they'd sent a lawyer out to meet with him, a Gerald Fitzgibbons from New York, who'd come over on the first ferry this morning. Judging by the cut of his suit, he didn't work cheap, but he'd said he was willing to take Cam's case, and that was an important part of the equation. Not every good defense attorney would have the time and the inclination.

Cam had told Fitzgibbons he'd get back to him. He hadn't yet gone through the list Ivy was preparing. He had to get the right lawyer. His future could depend on it, which was crazy. That he was going to have to come up with a couple hundred thousand dollars to defend himself for something he didn't do was even crazier.

When he heard keys and the heavy outer door of the jail opened, he dropped his pencil on top of his latest drawing and got to his feet. It wasn't mealtime, and there was still no one else in the other cells, so he knew he might have another visitor.

Sure enough, Ariana followed the uniformed officer who worked the day shift into the jail.

"Hi," he said, immediately thrusting his hands through the bars to be able to touch her. He wished he could pull her into his arms, regretted he hadn't done more of that when it was possible. So what if it'd been too fast? He no longer cared about waiting until his divorce was final. Melanie had let him down so badly he didn't feel he owed her anything. All he wanted from her was access to his daughter.

Ariana watched as the corrections officer took up her usual post on the stool near the door before turning back to him. "How are you holding up?"

"I'm fine," he said, but he'd never felt less fine. Even if he was found innocent, by the time he spent a year or more in jail while the case wound its way through the legal system, most of his life would be rubble.

"Ivy said she was helping you find a good attorney. She even said she'd pay for some of your defense. I'd help, too, of course, if I had the money."

"My parents are planning on paying what I can't afford. At least, that's what they told the attorney who showed up here this morning."

"That's good."

He grimaced. He hated involving them.

"Did you like him?" Ariana asked.

"Seemed okay," he replied with a shrug.

"What'd he have to say about your case?"

"He could only judge from what I told him. He hasn't talked to the police yet, of course. But he said it sounds as though they've accumulated some decent circumstantial evidence."

"Is that a problem?"

"He doesn't think so, not without hard evidence. But it won't be my lawyer who decides. It'll be a jury, and a lot can sway those votes."

She glanced at the guard again, who was not only watching them but seemed to be unabashedly listening to their conversation. "Ivy and I were...out last night looking around like... you know...you and I did a couple of nights before..."

At the lighthouse? That had to be what she meant. "And? Did you find anything?"

"Just a broken necklace. Do you remember anything about a necklace?"

That was a disappointment. He'd been hoping they'd miraculously come up with the Jack Daniel's bottle and gotten rid of it for good. "What kind of necklace?" he asked.

"A gold choker with a little ruby birthstone."

Was she intimating that Emily had been wearing such a necklace? If so, he didn't remember it. But then…he hadn't been paying any attention to what Emily was wearing. "No."

"The police seem *very* excited about it."

He pulled his hands back to grip the bars. "How do they even know about it?"

"There was an officer waiting for us when we got back to our car."

"And you showed it to him?"

"It didn't happen quite that way, but…he has it now."

She obviously couldn't say much because they were being watched. "Are you trying to warn me about something?" he whispered.

She bit her lip. "Just wanted to make you aware—in case it comes up again."

"I don't remember seeing a necklace," he said.

"It's probably nothing," she said, but he could tell she was worried about it—so was he—as they went on to talk about other things.

It wasn't until several hours after she'd left, while he was drawing again, that a memory floated up from somewhere deep in his subconscious. He *had* seen a necklace like the one she'd described—and now he remembered where.

"Oh, my God!" Getting up, he began waving his arms at the closed-circuit television, trying to get the attention of the officer who monitored his behavior.

When she finally opened the door and asked what he needed, he said, "I want to talk to Detective Livingston—right away."

"You told me Jewel *didn't* come to your door with a bottle of Jack Daniel's and ask you to go to the lighthouse," Livingston said.

They were meeting in one of the rooms designated for attorney visits, and Cam's heart was racing, making him slightly short of breath, as if he'd been running for miles. "I know. I was afraid I'd just be putting the murder weapon in my own hand. But she was there with me that night."

Rocking back, Livingston folded his arms. "So why are you telling me now?"

"Because I think I've figured out what happened."

He looked mildly amused. "You have?"

Trying to ignore his facetious response, Cam lifted a hand. "Listen. Last night Ariana and Ivy found a necklace at the lighthouse. Have you seen it? Ariana told me a police officer took it from them when they got back to their car."

"I've seen it, but that's not what I want to talk about. I'd like to know what they were after in the first place," he said, still not showing much interest.

"They were looking for the Jack Daniel's bottle," Cam admitted. He had no more secrets, felt he had to put everything on the line, or he'd be spending the next several months in jail fighting murder charges—and possibly going to prison at the end of it. "They're afraid, and so am I, that if my DNA is still on it, that'll be enough to convict me, even though I drank out of the bottle but didn't kill Emily. They didn't find that, but they did find a necklace. And I'm almost positive it's the same one Jewel was wearing that night. If you'll give me a piece of paper, I'll draw a picture of it for you. I'm sure the two will match."

"So what if they match? How do I know Ariana or Ivy didn't just describe it to you?"

Cam's mind was racing. How could he prove it was hers? And that she was wearing it that night? "They were on vacation, weren't they?" he said. "They must've turned in photographs for you to use when you were searching for Emily—the latest photographs they had of her. Maybe in some of those pictures she was with Jewel, at the beach or whatever, and Jewel was wearing it."

"Why couldn't it have belonged to Emily?" he asked.

"Maybe it did. But I'm telling you it was Jewel who had it on that night. And that's important."

Seemingly more intrigued—enough to indulge him a bit longer, anyway—the detective went out and came back with a piece of paper and a pencil, which he set in front of Cam. "Go ahead and draw," he said.

Cam quickly sketched the choker-like necklace with the small ruby gemstone he remembered seeing on Jewel. It'd been fairly late at night, so it was dark, but the moon had been bright, and he remembered the necklace well. That necklace was what he'd been staring at while they were having sex. He hadn't wanted to look into Jewel's face. He knew she liked him way more than he liked her and was ashamed of what he was doing even while he was doing it.

When he finished drawing, he slid the paper across the table. "Does the necklace they found look anything like this?"

Lines of concentration appeared on the detective's forehead as he picked up the picture.

"The necklace was at the lighthouse because Jewel was there, too," Cam told him as he looked at it. "*She* was the girl Delilah saw me with at the beach, not her younger sister. Emily wasn't with us, because Jewel had left her at home."

Livingston rubbed his chin thoughtfully. "Even if you went to the beach with Jewel, it doesn't mean you didn't run into Emily later..."

Cam felt like screaming in frustration. Struggling to subdue the intensity of his emotions, he drew a deep, shaky breath. "Except...*why* would I kill her? What motivation would I have to murder a twelve-year-old girl? For sex? I'd just had sex with her sister!"

"Rape isn't about sex," he pointed out.

"But I don't have a history of rape! Of any violence! Please, listen to me. Ben encountered Emily at the beach. We know that. I think she came looking for her sister. I was worried that my parents would be getting home and wanted to get back, but she wouldn't leave. She wouldn't even get dressed. So I finally left her there. It's possible that Emily found her that way, drunk and only half-dressed, and threatened to tell their parents. And that angered Jewel so much she freaked out and hit her with the bottle we'd been drinking from. I left what little there was of the whiskey with her, because *she'd* brought it. It was hers. That means *she* had possession of the murder weapon, not me."

"You expect me to believe Jewel killed her own sister..."

Fortunately, he didn't sound quite as doubtful as those words could've indicated. "I know it sounds terrible and highly unlikely, especially with the way Jewel's become a big advocate for Emily and what the family has suffered. But it gives her someone else to point to so that everyone stops searching, and her parents are finally satisfied. If you were her, how would you like your parents to find out you'd murdered your own sister? Going after me would be the best way to cover for that."

"But why you?" he asked. "Why not Ben or someone else?"

"Because I was at the lighthouse that night, too. It could have been me, even though it wasn't. And she certainly has no affinity for me. I'm sure she feels I used her, even though she freely offered what I took."

Livingston didn't say anything, just kept rubbing his chin, so Cam dived in again, trying to convince him. "She and Emily were fighting earlier in the day, so badly that Emily came home from the beach on her own. They couldn't get along because Jewel resented having to babysit. She was on vacation. Wanted to have fun. She complained to me about it while we were walking to the beach, and she sure as hell didn't treat Emily very well when I was helping her get into the house, because they were mad at each other. Who knows how bad the fighting could get? Especially if Jewel felt threatened? She wouldn't want their strict, religious parents to know she'd been drinking and having sex with a boy she'd barely met!"

Livingston tapped the paper. "You're coming to all these conclusions from hearing that your friends found this necklace at the lighthouse last night?"

"Yes! And you want to know why? Because Jewel was still wearing that necklace when I left her. Since it was found at the lighthouse, and Ariana said it was broken, I'm thinking Emily must've grabbed it while they were fighting and yanked it off. It dropped into the sand and was forgotten or lost, with everything that happened afterward."

Cam paused, hoping and praying for a positive reaction. Surely, even Livingston could see how well the pieces fit together… "Do you believe me?" he asked.

"I'm not going to say," Livingston told him. "But I'm still listening, so you've got that."

"Think about it," Cam said. "If Jewel struck out in anger, hitting her sister with the whiskey bottle, and Emily fell and didn't get up, it would terrify her. Imagine her sobering quickly when she realizes what she's done. She knows the consequences if she tells the truth, so she panics, rushes to the rental to get a shovel or a big bowl or something else to dig with and buries Emily in the sand not far from where it happened. She certainly wouldn't be strong enough to drag her very far. Why would she try to move her, anyway? She was at the perfect spot to dig a grave."

"You bring up a good point. She's not a large person. How would she be strong enough to bury Emily that deep?"

"We're talking about sand!" Cam cried. "It doesn't take strength as much as time, right? And she had all night. Her parents didn't get home until the following morning around ten, and she had to have known they wouldn't. Once they missed the ferry, they would've called her. That was why she felt comfortable sneaking out and over to my house in the first place."

Livingston continued to study the drawing of the necklace.

"Do you believe me?" Cam asked again. "*Please* say you believe me..."

"It doesn't matter what I believe, Cam. I have to be able to build a case, and that takes opportunity, motive, evidence—"

"She had the same opportunity I did," he broke in. "She had equal access to the murder weapon. And if Emily found her the way I described, she had a much better motive."

The detective pressed his bottom lip between his teeth for several seconds before saying, "If you're right about the necklace, it also places her at what we believe was the scene of the crime."

"Yes!"

"And if any of the pictures I've collected from when they were at the beach earlier in the day show her wearing that necklace..."

"Just ask her if she was at the lighthouse that night," Cam said. "If she denies it, you'll know she's lying to you."

Livingston gave him a funny look. "I've already asked her."

"And?"

"She was appalled, claims she would never leave her sister."

"Her necklace says otherwise."

"If we can prove it *was* her necklace," he said.

"Her parents should know."

"We also have to prove she was wearing it earlier that day. Otherwise, she could claim she lost it there before the night Emily went missing."

With a defeated sigh, Cam slumped back in his chair. "Then it all comes down to the pictures." And what were the chances there'd be a picture of exactly what he needed?

"Maybe. Maybe not," Livingston said, surprising him. "I have one other avenue."

Cam was afraid to grasp the small bit of hope that statement offered him for fear he'd just be disappointed again. "What's that?"

"A confession."

"The last thing she'll do is confess. She's raised too big a fuss, drawn too much attention. She won't do it."

"You never know," he said, and with that he opened the door and instructed the corrections officer who stood outside to take Cam back to his cell.

twenty-eight

Livingston was back at his desk, sifting through the photographs in Emily's file, when the officer who'd brought him the necklace poked his head inside the room. Pete Gibbs was a good policeman who'd recently moved to the island from Nashville and hoped to make detective one day. He'd shown a great deal of interest in the Hutchins case. But that was true of most of the force. It was the greatest mystery Mariners PD had ever faced, and it involved a child, so everyone participated in the daily briefings he gave since Emily's remains had been found.

"You're working late again," Pete said.

"On the Emily Hutchins case, of course."

"How's it going?"

"There've been some interesting developments today."

Obviously intrigued, Pete came into the room and sat

down. "With that necklace I left on your desk before I headed home this morning?"

"Yes. Thanks for bringing that to me."

Pete had left a note with it, saying where he'd gotten it and that he thought it might be tied to the case. "I noticed it in the pictures you showed us—the ones her parents turned in when she went missing—so I knew it was Emily's the second I saw it."

"Actually, it didn't belong to Emily," Livingston said. "Emily had the same necklace but with a different birthstone." He'd known that when he was talking to Cam, even though he'd pretended otherwise. He'd held back a lot during that conversation. He'd learned that saying less was usually the more prudent approach.

"Damn," Pete said. "I thought I'd discovered something that might help. What a coincidence that Ariana Prince and Ivy Hawthorne would find such a similar necklace."

"It's actually not a coincidence at all," Livingston said. "It is, however, lucky."

"What do you mean?"

"I sent their mother a picture of the necklace when I left the jail a couple hours ago, and she called me right after she got it. Said that she and her husband bought Emily and Jewel matching birthstone necklaces, and this one had to be Jewel's. Emily's birthstone was emerald. Jewel's is ruby."

"So it's the older sister's? What was it doing at the lighthouse?"

"I think she was there the night Emily disappeared."

"No..." he said. "Why?"

"Cam told Ariana and Ivy that he had sex with Jewel at the lighthouse that night."

"And you believe him?"

"I didn't, at first. But when I asked her about it, I didn't say anything about sex. I said I'd been told she and Cam took a bottle of Jack Daniel's up to the lighthouse. That's it."

"And what'd she say?"

"She said—and I quote—'I would never sneak out to drink and have sex with a boy—especially one I'd barely met—while I was responsible for my little sister.'"

Pete whistled. "That was a major slipup."

"She was upset. People often say more than they mean to when they're flustered."

"Did you call her on it?"

"Not at the time. She's been through so much I didn't want to embarrass her. Even if she was up at the lighthouse, drinking and having sex, I didn't think it would *necessarily* impact the investigation. But now..."

"You've changed your mind."

He finally found the picture he'd been looking for. He didn't happen to have one of Jewel that showed the necklace. The only pictures he'd been given were of Emily alone. But he had one of Emily wearing hers. "More than that. I think it might make all the difference."

"So how do you place her there?"

He pulled the bottle of Jack Daniel's he'd bought from the liquor store—and emptied out before coming inside—on the desk.

"Oh, my God!" Pete exclaimed. "You found the murder weapon?"

Livingston began to tear off the label. "No. But once I make this bottle look as though it's been buried in sand for twenty years, Jewel won't know that."

Cam hadn't been able to sleep. The thin mattress on the hard concrete ledge that doubled as a cot wasn't comfortable to begin with. But last night his insomnia was due more to the thoughts racing around in his head. The longer he mulled over his own theory regarding how Emily died, the more convinced of it he became. It was Jewel. She was the one. It was just that no one had been able to see it. Who would suspect a sixteen-year-old girl, especially one who'd grieved her younger sister's loss as publicly as Jewel had, to be responsible?

He wanted to call Ariana and Ivy and his potential lawyers and anyone else he could speak to who might believe him—and help. But he had to be careful. If, somehow, word got back to Jewel, she might destroy any old pictures in which she was wearing that necklace. Or she could go on TV and make a big deal of how crazy and unfair it was that anyone would accuse *her.* It would be catastrophic for him if political pressure or public sentiment quashed any investigating Livingston was currently willing to do.

The door opened and one of the prison staff, a young dude, brought him his breakfast, but he waved it away. He was too agitated to eat. All he could do was pace back and forth in his narrow six-by-eight-foot cell and wait, hoping he'd hear some good news at last—that the seed of hope Livingston had offered him at the end of their meeting last night might actually grow to fruition.

"You sure you don't want this?" the guard asked.

"I'm sure," Cam said.

He shrugged and was just carrying it back out when the door opened again. This time it was the sergeant who worked days, and she had Cam's parents with her.

"Cam, we came as soon as we heard," his father said.

Cam had never dreamed he'd choke up when he saw his parents, but the lump that swelled in his throat made it impossible for him to speak. He'd known they were coming. The attorney they sent had told him as much. But the sight of them still hit him hard.

"We've been so worried," his mother said. "But you have nothing to fear. I talked to the attorney we sent over. He said the two of you got on well, and that he doesn't think much of the case they've built against you so far."

"It wasn't me," he managed to choke out.

His mother reached through the bars and took hold of his forearms. "We know that, son. We won't let them convict you of a crime you didn't commit. We're going to do everything in our power to help. Aren't we?" Giselle looked over at Jack.

"You're damn right," his father said. "I've lined up three other attorneys. They'll be coming out tomorrow. I want to vet them, too. We have to make sure you get the best defense money can buy."

"I can help pay," he said, but his mother waved his words away.

"We're your family," she said. "And we're going to be here for you, no matter how long this thing takes. I've already gone online and rented a house for the summer, and we'll extend as many months as we need to."

After feeling so terribly alone for most of his life, Cam didn't know what to say. They'd let him down so many times. But they were older now—and wiser, he supposed. His mother had been trying for years to right some of her past wrongs. He got the impression she saw this as her opportunity to finally bring them together and be the mother she should've been all along.

Despite his efforts to block the emotion that had been welling up, it was no use. A tear escaped and rolled slowly down his cheek to drip off his chin. "Thank you," he managed to say.

Jewel was packed and ready to go. She had to check out by noon, but her flight wasn't until three. She figured she'd ask the bellman to hold her bags and wander into some of Mariners many art galleries to help pass the time until she could take an Uber to the airport.

A call came in from Williams. She noticed it but decided not to answer. She guessed he was looking for an update on how things were developing since he'd left, but she didn't want to talk about the case. Every time she thought of it, she cringed—at jumping the gun when she told her father that Cam had accused her of drinking and having sex with him and making a similar blunder when she was speaking to Detective Livingston.

Yesterday had not been a good day.

How could she screw up so badly after navigating this nightmare so perfectly in most other ways?

It would be okay, she told herself. Those were small slips in the overall scheme of things and wouldn't come to anything, not now that Cam was in jail. Livingston had his murderer and was busy gathering more evidence against him.

After Williams's call disappeared from her screen, her phone alerted her that he'd left a voice mail. She was afraid to listen to it but felt she should make herself, just in case he had something important to say.

"This is Warner Williams. Just checkin' in with you, seein' how you're doin' now. I was thinkin' it might be smart to keep workin' with the media. The publicity might have an influence on the DA. Get him to proceed even without really hard evidence. Anyway, those are my thoughts. I hope you're home safe or soon will be."

She breathed a sigh of relief that he hadn't had anything upsetting to tell her. Now that Cam had been arrested, she was eager to stop the whole media circus, but Williams was right. It would probably help to keep the spotlight on Emily's case.

She was just gathering her purse and bags so she could take them to the lobby when she heard a soft knock on her door.

Assuming it was housekeeping, she said, "I'll be out in a minute." But when she opened the door, she saw the woman who worked at the front desk.

"Ms. Hutchins?"

"Yes?"

"There's a police officer downstairs who'd like to speak with you."

Jewel had to put a hand on the door frame to steady herself. "A-about what?" she stuttered.

The woman looked at her in surprise—of course she wouldn't have asked the officer his business—so Jewel forced a smile. "Right. I'm coming."

It wasn't easy to get her bags to the elevator. They rolled, which was why she rarely asked for a porter, but she'd lost all the strength in her limbs. She kept telling herself that she was overreacting, that this was nothing, but...was that really the case?

When she reached the lobby, she had the hotel hold her bags before turning to the officer—a man named P. Gibbs she noticed from his tag. "Hello," she said. "I was told you'd like to speak to me."

"Actually, it's Detective Livingston who would like a word, if you don't mind. I'm just here to give you a ride."

She'd never had an escort before. She'd always found her own way to the station. "Okay." She peered at him more closely. "Is...is something wrong?"

"Not that I know of," he said. "He's just got a couple questions on your sister's case."

"Right. Okay."

Jewel sat stiffly in the back of the cruiser for the ten minutes it took to arrive at the station. What was going on? What was this about? It couldn't be because of that statement she'd made when she included sex despite not being accused of it. Could it?

Instead of turning into the parking lot, the officer stopped right in front of the building. Then he came around and opened the door for her, and she stepped out—on rubbery legs. "Right this way," he said.

Jewel felt like she was being marched in front of a firing squad. *Quit assuming the worst. If you ever needed a clear head, it's now. You can't screw up again.*

This time when she was shown into the interrogation room, she didn't have to wait. Livingston was already there. And he had an old, scraped-up Jack Daniel's bottle sitting on the table.

Her eyes gravitated to it immediately. Did that mean…

"Hello," Livingston said, somewhat stiffly. He didn't seem as friendly as he had before. Or was that her imagination?

"Hi. What's going on?" She checked her watch. "I don't have much time. I have a flight this afternoon."

"This shouldn't take long."

Again, she felt her gaze being drawn to the Jack Daniel's bottle as if it were made of steel and her eyes were magnets. "Okay."

He slid a plastic bag across the table. "Do you recognize this?"

She hesitated, even though she recognized what was in that bag instantly. She smelled a trap, but she didn't see how she could deny having owned the necklace in question. Although Emily had been given one just like it, her parents could easily confirm that this was hers and not her sister's because of the birthstone. "That's mine," she said, infusing her voice with surprise. "Where did you find it?"

"At the lighthouse," he said.

She shoved her eyebrows up. "I wonder what it was doing there!"

"So do I."

She pressed a shaky hand to her chest. "I—I don't know.

Emily often wore my things. Maybe she had it on the night she was murdered."

"Emily was wearing her own necklace the day she went missing. I have pictures of it. Your mother told me you both wore them all the time. They were a Christmas present and the nicest jewelry you owned."

He'd spoken to her mother? "Then…I'm not sure what to say. I lost it somewhere, and it must've floated around the island a bit."

"Floated around the island to the lighthouse…"

Perspiration began to roll down her back. "I don't know how it got there," she said, more firmly.

He gave her a penetrating stare. "Did you kill your sister, Jewel?"

Jewel's eyes were once again attracted by that damn Jack Daniel's bottle. She'd had coffee here before, and Livingston had taken her cup. Had he swabbed it for DNA? Had he also found her DNA—*after twenty years*—under the lid of the Jack Daniel's bottle she and Cam had been drinking from that night?

Her mind raced through various responses. She had to admit being at the lighthouse and drinking with Cam. She no longer had any choice about that. It would be embarrassing, and it would upset and disappoint her parents, but that would cover for her DNA being on the bottle and her necklace being at the lighthouse. She could still deny hurting Emily. They wouldn't have any more evidence on her than they had on Cam, and if her sorrow came off as real—which in many respects it *was*—she could evoke enough sympathy to avoid being arrested.

But she was just opening her mouth when Livingston wagged a finger at her. "If you're about to lie to me again, don't do it."

Her throat had grown so dry she could scarcely swallow.

"So I went to the lighthouse with Cam," she said. "That isn't murder."

"But that isn't all you did. Emily saw you with him or saw you without your clothes after he left. She knew what you'd done, and she was going to tell your parents. You two had been fighting all day, and now she really had something that could get you in trouble."

She resisted the impulse to cover her ears. "That's not true!"

"What happened was your fault, not Cam's. Do you really want to see an innocent person pay the price *you* should be paying?"

"Cam's not innocent," she insisted.

He thrust his face forward so they were almost nose to nose. "He's innocent of murder."

She shook her head. "No."

"One of you used this bottle—" he gestured at it "—to kill Emily. And you're the one who was wearing a necklace that was ripped off when you were fighting with her."

Her chest was rising and falling fast as he smoothed the bag so she could see the break in the chain. As she stared down at it, the worst moment of her life flashed before her mind's eye. The yank around her neck she'd felt when Emily grabbed hold of that necklace, and her immediate response. After she'd swung the bottle, causing Emily to crumple to the ground, she hadn't even been worried. She'd stood over her with the bottle raised, ready to hit her again, still too angry to realize what she'd done.

And then she'd seen the blood…

She squeezed her eyes closed, attempting to block it out. But it haunted her dreams even if she refused to examine that image in the daylight. "I didn't do it," she insisted, but the words didn't come out with as much force as she'd wanted them to. She'd made a catastrophic mistake. If she'd thrown the bottle in the ocean or found a trash can, maybe the police would never have discovered it. But she'd been only sixteen and so filled with panic that her parents would beat her to the house. She'd wanted to simply bury everything—hide it as best she could—and run home to bed. So instead of taking it with her as she'd initially started to do, she'd stopped long enough to bury it in the sand on the other side of the lighthouse. She'd felt she had to do that. Dawn was breaking by that time, and she was afraid someone would see her with it.

"I think you did do it," Livingston said.

"No, I was a good girl—a preacher's daughter."

"If you were willing to approach a boy you'd barely met with alcohol and offer him sex at sixteen, I'm betting that wasn't the first example of wanton behavior. Are you telling me that if I go back and dig through your past, talk to your school friends and boyfriends and neighbors and teachers, I wouldn't find a history of that sort of thing?"

Could he find the people she'd known? What would they say?

She knew there were those who would substantiate the accusation. While pretending otherwise to her parents and the members of her father's congregation, she'd secretly committed every "sin" those churchgoing people could imagine.

"I hope you know I'm going to do that," he said. "Establish a history of your behavior, which, no doubt, will shock your parents. But I'm betting Emily knew about the things you did. Or at least some of them."

She said nothing. The room seemed to be spinning, making her feel faint.

"What if I asked your parents whether or not you could ever do what you did to Emily? What would they say?"

His words were now coming to her as if through a long tunnel. "They'll tell you I could never do such a thing."

"Not in your right mind. But you were drunk, maybe even

disappointed by the handsome guy you'd hoped to please and furious that your sister would threaten to tell your parents."

"My parents won't believe you," she said, still stuck on what he'd said a few seconds earlier because her mind couldn't seem to catch up. "No one will believe you."

"Jewel, twelve jurors are the only people who need to trust what I've found. When the prosecution presents your case, they'll start with the history of your behavior, how poorly you treated Emily, especially the day you killed her, and how embarrassed and upset you'd be to get caught with your pants down—literally—knowing your parents were going to find out about it. You'll see. The case will build slowly with the evidence piling higher and higher until—"

"There is no evidence," she broke in. She'd once believed that. She'd thought she'd taken care of all threats. But everything she'd done to keep herself safe—all the accusations she'd launched against Cam, all the pleading for help from the general public and all the sympathy mongering on social media designed to direct attention away from herself—had availed her nothing.

"What will I find when I search your apartment?" he asked.

"You're going to search my apartment?" she said in alarm.

"Of course. I'm going to examine every aspect of your life."

She hadn't kept one item of her sister's, because she couldn't bear to look at anything that reminded her of Emily. But he would find recreational drug paraphernalia and sex toys she'd be horrified to have her parents see. "You won't find anything!" she lied.

"Do you have any pictures of you and Emily that were taken that day?"

"No." That much was the truth.

"I bet your folks have some," he said. "It was a vacation. I'm guessing plenty were taken, and your parents would never part with them. So I'll search their house, too."

Her whole life was going to be exposed… All those media outlets that had taken such an interest in her sister's case would start circling around her like vultures—only they wouldn't be sympathizing with her any longer. They'd be swooping in to peck the skin off her bones.

"I'm going to get a conviction whether you tell me the truth or not," he said. "You realize that, don't you?"

She nodded wordlessly. He was so certain. And she believed him.

"So why don't you tell me what happened? If you do, things will go much easier on you, I promise."

Who could say if that was really true? But it no longer mattered. She was beaten down, exhausted and couldn't keep up the pretense any longer. "I didn't mean to kill her."

She'd spoken so softly, he leaned close again. "What'd you say?"

The truth came rising up again, almost involuntarily, like bile. "I didn't mean to kill her!" she shouted.

They both rocked back and gaped at each other as the sound of her voice seemed to echo in the room. What she'd hidden for so long was finally out. She'd said it. And it brought such tremendous relief, she couldn't even regret it.

"Tell me how it happened," he said evenly.

Her vision began to blur as tears filled her eyes. "It was just like you said. She found me at the lighthouse after Cam left. We started fighting. She grabbed my necklace, and I hit her with the bottle. I was *so* angry." She shook her head. "But I wasn't *trying* to kill her. You have to believe that, at least."

"I do." He reached out to touch her arm in an act of compassion—surprising considering everything she'd done to Emily and to Cam. "Your immediate future won't be easy. But I'll keep my promise and do what I can to help you. Your confession is what will make that possible."

twenty-nine

Ariana and Ivy were there to pick him up at three. As soon as Cam walked out of the building and stepped into the sunshine, he stopped and tilted his face up to the sky. The leaves of the elm boughs overhead turned a lighter shade of green—almost a lime green—where the light came through. He stared at that for a moment, thinking he'd never paid enough attention to the simple beauty of life. Nor had he ever valued his freedom quite so much.

"It's over. Can you believe it?" Ariana said, standing beside him and looking up at the trees, too. Ivy was watching them and smiling a broad, relieved smile.

"No," Cam said. "I thought for sure this was going to turn into a years-long nightmare. Maybe a lifelong nightmare."

"I can't believe Ivy found that necklace! What were the chances?"

"It feels like a miracle to me." Cam closed his eyes and drew in a deep breath. The air smelled like cookies, because there was a bakery close by. "I'm hungry," he said. "Let's go eat."

Ariana glanced at Ivy. "Actually..."

"What is it?" Cam said.

"Your mother's planned a party at her rental house. Everyone's there waiting for you. I hope that's okay. She was so excited that you were finally free of the Emily Hutchins case—I didn't want to disappoint her."

"After what I've been through, I'm not going to be upset about a party," he said. "I'm sure there'll be lots of food. Let's go."

Ivy drove. Ariana said Alice had already taken her car over.

"How many people are going to be there?" Cam asked when he heard that even Ariana's grandmother was going.

"Your parents invited everyone they could think of. We're all elated."

He was elated, too, until he arrived at the party and saw Melanie in the living room first thing. "You've got to be kidding me," he said to his friends. "What's she doing here?"

"Don't complain too loudly," Ivy said. "She brought Camilla."

His heart leaped. "Where's my girl?"

"She must be in the kitchen with your mother."

Melanie tried to approach him, but everyone else was excited to see him and to welcome him, so he was able to avoid her. All he wanted to do was find Camilla. Everyone was still congratulating him and saying how happy they were that he was free and asking if he'd like a drink when he said he needed to use the restroom first, so he'd have an excuse to slip away.

"Mom?" he called as he headed deeper into the house, looking for the kitchen.

Camilla was standing on a chair at the counter, wearing an apron while helping his mother frost a cake.

"Look who I've got here," Giselle said as soon as she saw him.

"Daddy!" Camilla cried and his mother helped her down so she could go to him.

Cam scooped her into his arms and held her close, breathing in the baby shampoo scent of her long, silky hair. "There's my girl," he said. "Daddy missed you so much."

"I missed you, too, Daddy," she said, locking her arms around his neck and hugging him back.

Afraid others, including Melanie, might drift down the hall toward the kitchen, removing the privacy he had now, he glanced over his shoulder to be sure they were still alone and lowered his voice. "How'd you arrange this?" he asked.

"I called Melanie and told her you were getting out, that Jewel had confessed to murdering Emily and this dark part of your life was behind you for good. I think being separated from you and facing life with her folks, at least until finances were such that she could get a place of her own, no longer seemed appealing. She told me she was eager to 'get her old life back.'"

"What if I don't want her back?" he asked.

"You don't have to take her back. But I thought it would be worth inviting her so you could see Camilla."

"That's worth anything. Isn't it, bug?" he said and kissed the top of her head.

"I'm making a cake with Grandma!" She was starting to squirm, and he could tell she wanted to get down.

He returned her to the stepstool as he jerked his chin toward the cake. "That for me?"

"Of course," his mother said.

"It's your favorite," Camilla announced.

"Any kind of cake is my favorite," he told her.

Giselle smiled up at him. "I'm so happy you're out. I was terrified for you."

"Thanks for coming right away," he said. "When you arrived, it felt like the cavalry had charged in."

She chuckled, then lowered her voice. "I know I haven't been the best mother to you, Cam, and I'm sorry about that. I'm trying harder. I hope you can tell."

He put an arm around her shoulders and gave her a squeeze. "I can tell. And I appreciate it."

"Where's the man of the hour?" someone called out, prodding him to get back to the living room and his guests.

While his father served drinks, Cam greeted Alice and Courtney and her parents, as well as several clients. Even his old college roommate, Eddie Schultz, had left his family to be on Mariners for the party.

"This dude took care of me when I was sicker than a dog," Eddie told everyone. "He pulled out of school and everything."

"I wasn't too happy about him dropping those classes," his father said. "It might've helped if he'd said why he did it."

Everyone laughed, but it wasn't entirely a joke. Cam had been too busy trying to make his parents miserable to give them the reason. He felt bad about that now, could see how he, too, could do more to bridge the gap.

He talked and laughed and played with Camilla for the next several hours. Had Melanie not been there, trying to sidle up to him at every opportunity, the afternoon would've been perfect. Compared to what he would've been doing today had Ivy not found that necklace, he certainly wasn't unhappy.

He'd just said goodbye to Eddie, who was hurrying to catch the ferry to get back to his family, and most other people were leaving, too, when Melanie finally caught his arm and asked if they could go into the other room and talk. He looked over her head, seeking out his mother, and asked Giselle to watch Camilla for a few minutes.

"I didn't expect to see you here," he said, once they were in a guest bedroom. "What happened to Europe?"

"My parents were driving me nuts!" she said. "I didn't want to spend a whole month in such close proximity to them. I swear, they act like I can't take care of my own kid. They're always nagging me to put a coat on her, wipe her nose, keep her out of the candy."

He leaned up against the closest wall. "That's why you came back? Because it's better than being with your parents?"

"Of course not." An earnest expression appeared on her face. "I came back because of you, Cam. I love you. I've always loved you. Now that we have our lives back, I think we should try again."

She'd wanted nothing to do with him when he was going through hell. As a matter of fact, she'd made it worse by trying to sabotage his situation so he'd go to prison. Did she think he could just forget about that?

Some of what he was feeling must've shown on his face because she said, "What?"

"I'm not interested in staying in our marriage, Melanie," he said. "I haven't been happy, and I don't think you've been happy, either."

"Don't you care about Camilla?"

"Of course I do. But don't bother threatening to keep her from me. I'll take you to court again and again, if I have to. I won't allow it."

"I think you're going to find out that single life isn't all it's cracked up to be."

"I'm not going to be single," he said.

Her jaw dropped. "What do you mean?"

"This is all new, so don't start accusing me of cheating again. I haven't ever slept with Ariana. But I'm in love with her, so I hope to change that soon."

She looked like she was about to slap him. But she didn't. She marched out of the room, grabbed Camilla and left. He assumed they were going to his house—the house they'd shared—so he decided he'd stay with his folks.

"What was that all about?" Ariana asked after Melanie had stormed out of the house, dragging Camilla along, and slammed the door behind them.

He took her hand. "I told her I'm not interested in reconciling. That my heart belongs to someone else."

Ariana looked slightly startled. "Were you talking about me?"

He chuckled as he pecked her on the lips. "I'm certainly not in love with anyone else."

After all the excitement on the island, Ivy was looking forward to a regular day spent working in the library. Of course, what'd happened in the Emily Hutchins case was playing on most news channels, and people were still talking about it. Ivy had seen various reporters explain the outcome of the investigation, but she couldn't bear to watch any more. They always cut away to Emily's parents, and she didn't want to witness their heartbreak over and over.

She was encouraged by the latest clip she'd caught, however, in which Emily's father said he would love Jewel, regardless, and he and her mother would forgive her and stand by her in spite of her tragic "mistake." That had been heartening. At least they wouldn't lose *both* daughters. Ivy had heard speculation that the district attorney would probably seek an involuntary manslaughter charge, which carried a much lighter sentence than first degree murder. If convicted, Jewel could get up to twenty years, but it was more likely she'd serve ten years, maybe less. She no longer had to hide from the truth, and she'd still have most of her life ahead of her when she got out. Maybe she could truly heal.

A girl of about sixteen approached the desk. "Do you have any historical romance?"

Ivy smiled and led her to the romance section before returning to her computer, where she'd been searching houses for rent in California.

When her phone went off, she glanced at the number. It was her brother. He'd been trying to reach her for the past two weeks, but she wouldn't answer. Fortunately, all had ended well for Cam, but it could easily have gone the other way. She was still grappling with what he'd done. His actions had put Cam at risk. If she and Ariana hadn't found that necklace, and Cam hadn't realized what it signified, he'd still be in jail, fighting a murder charge.

She clicked on yet another beach house in San Diego. If she moved to that part of the west coast she'd have temperate weather year-round and would still be near the ocean—albeit the Pacific instead of the Atlantic. Would California be the best place to meet someone?

There were certainly a lot of single men there…

When she didn't pick up, Tim sent her yet another text. Please talk to me. I was wrong. I'm so sorry.

She sighed. She'd never been someone who could refuse an outright apology, and especially now, since Cam was okay. Ignoring the lingering resentment she felt over what Tim had done, she called her brother back. "It's fine," she said when he answered. "We got lucky in the end."

"If it helps, I was only trying to look out for you," he told her. "*You* are what matters to me. Not Cam."

"Except that what you did hurt me, too. It nearly cost me my best friends!"

"I know. I've been kicking myself for going too far. We should've talked about it more, and I should've let you decide for yourself."

"Exactly! It's *my* life. You should never have betrayed my confidence. I'm your sister. I went to you for help and guidance—not because I wanted you to take over."

"I'm sorry," he said again.

Pursing her lips, she clicked on another house on the real estate app she was using. "I'll get over it, I guess."

"I hope so. Sounds like it's going to take a while."

"It might."

"You working?" he asked.

"Yeah. I'm at the library." Seeing an opportunity to finally share what she'd been considering, she added, "But right now I'm looking at real estate. I think I might move to California."

"*What?* I never dreamed you'd leave Mariners."

"Me, neither. I love it here. But…it's too hard to meet someone. I'm getting older, and I don't want to spend the rest of my life alone." Especially now that Ariana and Cam were a couple. Watching them hold hands or kiss—or seeing Cam smile into Ariana's eyes as if he'd never been so deliriously happy—was hard. Part of her was happy for them. She loved them. Of course she'd want them to have everything they wanted. But the other part was envious. She felt like she was suddenly on the outside looking in, that they'd rather be alone. Their threesome had become a twosome plus one, and she no longer fit.

"I wouldn't blame you," Tim said. "It might actually be a nice change."

He wasn't worried about everything she'd be leaving behind? The fact that she was protecting their heritage? "Is there any chance you'd consider moving here while I'm gone?" she asked. "You could live in my house—Grandma's house."

"You know I can't do that, Ive. My kids would freak out if I asked them to change schools. And I have a practice to consider."

She'd expected that answer, but couldn't help asking because she wanted to feel as though what she loved was being looked after in her absence. "Do you think Mom and Dad would come back? I can't leave the house empty, and I'd hate to sell it."

"I doubt it. You know them. They'll only come for a month or two in the summer. So maybe it's time you did sell it. We can't hang on to the past forever, Ivy. If you want to make a change, don't let anything hold you back."

Even the fear that she might regret it later?

She talked with him for a few more minutes about his trip to the island this summer, the things he and his family might like to do while they were here and whether he was really going to have a problem with their parents showing up for part of his family vacation.

"I guess not," he said. "It should be fine."

"It might be nice," she said encouragingly, then she told him she had to go. The girl she'd helped earlier was ready to check out.

"Did you find everything you need?" she asked her.

The girl stacked four books on the counter—*Of Noble Birth*, *Honor Bound*, *Through the Smoke* and *A Matter of Grave Concern*. "I think so."

After her only patron left, and Ivy was alone in the library, she tried to imagine her life in California—working somewhere so she'd have something to do during the days, maybe joining a gym, heading to the beach. It should've sounded like heaven. She'd be trading one beautiful place for another, and she'd have a much bigger group of potential mates to choose from.

But instead of sounding better than Mariners, it sounded lonely—like she'd be stuck thousands of miles away from home without all the people she cared about. So she went back to the computer to search for a house on the east coast. If she lived in Boston or New York, she could come back to the island whenever she wanted. That would be smarter, she decided. But trying to get a start in any new place didn't sound appealing. She loved Mariners; didn't want to leave. This was home, and the library and her grandmother's house—she wanted to continue to look after them.

What was she going to do?

After changing her search parameter to houses for rent in Boston, she was halfheartedly going through them when the door swung open and a man with dark, curly hair and a smile worthy of a movie star walked in. Instead of browsing the aisles, he approached her desk immediately.

"Hi, there," he said. "I'm Steve Branson. I'm new on Mariners and was hoping you could direct me to some good local history books. I'd like to become more familiar with my new home."

Branson looked to be about forty, maybe forty-two, and Ivy didn't see a wedding ring on his finger. "I'd be happy to help," she said. "What brings you to Mariners?"

"I'm a sculptor and I'm being featured in one of the galleries here. I recently went through a pretty brutal divorce, so...I decided to treat myself to a couple years of living on the island. Perfect way to recover, right?"

Ivy didn't answer. She was too stuck on the word *divorce*.

"Um...about those history books..." he said, filling the stretching silence.

"Oh, of course. We have quite a few, since that's a favorite topic of mine." She felt her face heat. "I think you'll like it here on Mariners. It's a great place for kids, too, if you have any..."

"No kids, I'm afraid."

He didn't seem to notice her interest. He was just...nice. Maybe he wasn't ready for another relationship. She guessed he probably wasn't. But having him move to Mariners and appear at such an opportune time gave her hope that she'd eventually meet someone—maybe someone like him.

Regardless, she wasn't going anywhere. She could never leave her little seaside library.

Closing the real estate app she'd been using, she stood. "You'll find what you're looking for over here," she said and smiled to herself. She had a feeling they'd *both* find what they were looking for on Mariners.

Ariana checked the clock as she slid the lasagna into the oven. She was cooking dinner at Cam's and wanted to time it to make sure the food would be hot when he got home from work. Melanie had taken Camilla and left the island the day after the party to catch up with her parents in Europe and was no longer using the house—thank goodness. Although his parents had stayed another three days, they'd left, too—a week ago. Since then, she and Cam had spent almost every minute together. He'd been working only until she got off at The Human Bean. Although he was terribly behind, he told her he couldn't bring himself to spend the kind of hours at the office he did before, not when he was so excited about being with her. But today had been an exception. He'd had a project he absolutely had to finish.

She smiled as she remembered the first time they'd made love. She'd never experienced anything like it—the closeness, the sense of fulfillment, the stronger commitment it brought. She knew Cam enjoyed their sex life, too, because he couldn't seem to make love to her often enough. And he didn't act like he cared that Melanie was trying to tell everyone she knew on the island that they'd been having an affair for the past several months. It was her way of saving face, of blaming Cam for the breakup of their marriage. Ariana guessed some people believed it—the neighbors down the street turned away instead of waving or speaking whenever she encountered them—but Cam shrugged it off, said he'd trade his reputation or almost anything else for what they had now.

She heard Cam's voice right before the door opened and he walked in.

"You're early," she commented in surprise.

He indicated he was on the phone but swept her up against him with his free arm and held the phone away while giving her a quick kiss.

"It's fine…" he said when he put the phone back to his ear. "I understand… Yes, of course… Thanks for calling. That was very kind of you." He disconnected and set his phone on the counter. "Something smells good."

"I made my grandmother's famous lasagna," Ariana told him.

"If I'd known you could cook, we probably would've gotten together right after high school," he teased.

She scowled at him. "You were too busy eyeing every other girl you met."

"I've learned my lesson," he said. "No one could make me happier than you."

Curious, she gestured at his phone. "Who were you talking to?"

"Warner Williams. He called to apologize."

"For investigating you?"

"For doing all he could to get me arrested. He said he never once doubted Jewel, and he should have. He's sorry that he let his sympathy blind him. Said he saw a young woman who had obviously suffered a great deal and jumped in to help her without being critical enough of what she told him."

"That *is* kind of him to admit," she said. "Do you think you'll ever hear from her parents?"

"I don't expect to. They're still going through a lot. But I don't hold anything against them."

"And that's kind of *you*," she said.

His hand slid up her shirt as he kissed her. "No one makes me feel like you do," he said, resting his forehead against hers. "When I'm with you, I know I've finally found what I've been looking for my whole life."

"Took you long enough to realize it," she teased and wiggled out of his grasp to finish her dinner preparations. "Did you get hold of the attorney you've been playing phone tag with?"

"The divorce attorney? I did. He finally got back to me. Said if the divorce is uncontested, it would take about ninety days."

She cast him a dubious glance before chopping the tomatoes for the salad. "Don't get your hopes up. You know Melanie will fight you on everything, if only just to be difficult. You need to prepare for that and dig in for the long haul."

"That's true, but he promised he'd get me visitation for Camilla as fast as humanly possible. That's what I'm most excited about."

"I'm excited about that, too."

He came up behind her and turned her in his arms, and she felt the same desire she'd always felt for him. "Maybe we could give Camilla a sister or brother one day," she murmured as she brushed her lips against his.

He tugged off her shirt, letting it fall to the floor as his mouth lowered to her breast. "I'm definitely planning on it."

epilogue

One year later…

Ariana shifted from foot to foot. Now that she'd entered her final trimester, the pregnancy was causing her feet to swell. She needed to get off them. But she was too anxious to sit down.

"You okay?" Cam asked.

She nodded. "Just…nervous. I've wondered for so long what my birth father's like."

"You're going to get to find out," he said, bending down to tie his daughter's shoe. Cam's divorce had finally come through, and it was summer, so Camilla was out of school and they had her for the next six weeks.

"How much longer do we have to stay here?" Camilla asked, growing impatient.

The plane had been delayed by three hours. That kind of

wait would be tedious even for an adult, so Ariana sympathized with her. But as hard as it had been for them, it had to be worse for her father. After all, he'd flown across the Atlantic, landed at JFK six hours ago, had to wait for his connection, which kept getting put off, and was only now coming to the island to meet her. "We're close, babe," Ariana told her soon-to-be stepdaughter. "Then we're going to get ice cream, remember?"

"I want strawberry!" she cried, clapping her hands in excitement.

"Strawberry is always good," Ariana responded, but it was difficult to muster a lot of enthusiasm. She couldn't concentrate on anything except what might happen in the next few minutes. The monitor had updated to show that her father's plane had finally landed.

Her phone signaled a text—from Ivy. So? What's he like?

Ivy would've come to the airport with them. They saw a lot of her, still hung out all the time, but she was spending the day with Steve, whom she'd been dating for nearly as long as Ariana had been with Cam. Ariana planned to host a dinner while her father was on the island and have Ivy and Steve join them—depending on how well things went before that.

None of the people on her father's plane had started to trickle in yet.

Don't know. Plane's late.

Of course that would happen. You must be dying.

I am.

Any word from your mother?

No. I think she prefers to ignore this is happening. She ended up helping when it came to tracking him down, but it'll take some time for her to get used to me having a relationship with him—if that really happens.

Of course you'll end up having a relationship. He wouldn't fly all the way from Scotland if he wasn't interested in that.

His visit was a surprise for her birthday this weekend. Cam had arranged it, with a little help from her mother, so Ariana didn't have much to go on. It wasn't as if she'd had a chance to get to know her father at all before this. We'll see.

"Who are you texting?" Cam asked.

She slipped her phone back into her purse. "Ivy. She's curious about how things are going."

He opened his mouth to say something else—probably more words of reassurance—but the new arrivals were beginning to walk into the airport and gather around the baggage terminal, so he didn't bother following up.

She wondered if she'd recognize her father, or if he'd recognize her. He probably would, she decided. He had a better idea of what she looked like; Cam had sent pictures. "I'm so scared," she whispered. "What if he decided not to come?"

"He would've let me know," Cam said. "And you have nothing to be scared of. He was very receptive when I reached out to him."

Cam had told her Bill Gilchrist had received her mother's letter so many years ago. He'd known she existed and always wondered about her but didn't know whether or not he'd be welcome in her life. Cam claimed he was excited to have this opportunity and to know she was open to getting to know him.

"Otherwise, he wouldn't have arranged to come," Cam added. "It's not cheap to fly all the way from the UK."

"But what if he doesn't end up liking me?" Ariana said. "What if—"

Cam took her hand. "Stop worrying. He'd have to be crazy not to love you. Right, Camilla?" he said to his daughter.

Camilla tilted her head back to give Ariana a sweet smile. Fortunately, she was nothing like her mother. "*I* love you," she said.

Ariana had just bent down to hug her when Cam cleared his throat. "There he is."

She straightened—and her eyes met those of a tall, rugged stranger with salt-and-pepper hair, hazel eyes and a friendly smile.

He didn't say anything as he approached, just pulled her into his arms and hugged her for a long time. When they finally separated, he had tears streaming down his cheeks, too.

★★★★★

THE SEASIDE LIBRARY

BRENDA NOVAK

Reader's Guide

QUESTIONS FOR DISCUSSION

1. Did you have a favorite character in *The Seaside Library*? If so, who, and why?

2. Ivy, Ariana and Cam all had very different home lives growing up. How do you think their families shaped their friendship with one another?

3. What did you think of Ivy and Ariana's choice to lie to protect Cam? Did you understand why they did it? How do you think you would have acted if you'd been in their situation?

4. Did you doubt Cam throughout the story, or did you feel sure he had nothing to do with Emily's disappearance?

5. What did you think of the dynamic among the three friends? How did you feel about Ivy's role within the threesome, given the charged relationship between Cam and Ariana?

6. What were your feelings about Jewel Hutchins? Could you empathize with her? How did your impression of her change over the course of the story?

7. Mariners Island is a fictional setting. How did it come to life for you on the page? Can you think of a real-life place that has the same feel to it?

8. How did you feel about the ending? Did you agree with how each character's story wrapped up?

9. Did you have a favorite scene? If so, why was it your favorite?

10. If there was a movie based on *The Seaside Library*, which actors would you cast as each of the characters?